A Very Large Array

A Very Large Array

New Mexico Science Fiction and Fantasy

☆ ☆ ☆ ☆ ☆

Edited by Melinda M. Snodgrass

University of New Mexico Press
Albuquerque

Library of Congress Cataloging-in-Publication Data

A very large array.

Contents: Introduction / Melinda Snodgrass — For a break I tarry / Roger
Zelazny — Jamboree / Jack Williamson — [etc.]
 1. Science fiction, American—New Mexico. 2. Fantastic fiction, American—
New Mexico. 3. American fiction—New Mexico. 4. American fiction—20th
century. I. Snodgrass, Melinda M., 1951–
PS648.S3V47 1987   813'.0876'089789   87-19173
ISBN 0-8263-1013-3

Copyright Listings

★ Contents ★

Dedication

For Fred Ragsdale who appreciated us and
let the world know we were here.

★ Introduction ★

Here's a trivia question for you. What state contains nine Hugos, six Nebulas, six Balrogs, one Prix Apollo, one Campbell Award, one British Fantasy Society Award, one Prometheus, one Science Fiction Hall of Fame, one Pilgrim Award, one First Prize in the Writers of the Future Contest, and one Grand Master?

The answer is New Mexico.

Surprised?

I wouldn't blame you if you were. It is strange that this large, arid, beautiful, empty state should contain some of the great names in science fiction and fantasy; Jack Williamson, Roger Zelazny, Stephen R. Donaldson. Three top writers in the field; George R.R. Martin, Fred Saberhagen, Suzy McKee Charnas. A sprinkling of "up-and-comers"; Walter Jon Williams, Victor Milán, Melinda M. Snodgrass. And a bevy of talented young neo-pros; John J. Miller, Terry Boren, Martha Soukup.

Some people have begun to refer to us as the New Mexico Mafia.

1

Try to fathom why so many professional, full time writers live in this area. Is it the air they breathe or something in the food (green chili maybe?) We sometimes ask the questions too. What drew us all here? What holds us here after we have arrived? In an effort to answer those questions the writers have prepared short essays which often cast as much light upon their characters as they do upon the puzzle.

So maybe you've decided that there is something magical about New Mexico, and are all ready to pack your bags, migrate and begin your professional writing career. Let me tell you what you're going to find when you arrive. A harsh and beautiful landscape that can wrench the heart, and sometimes kill the careless or the unwary. A place where ancient religions live close by scientific centers. (The first atomic bomb was developed and tested here. And the radio telescopes of the Very Large Array are probing the universe.) A fascinating fusion of three distinct cultures; Anglo, Hispano and Indian. And a close knit group of writers who will welcome you, encourage you, and help where they can.

I can't say enough good about my colleagues. About their charm, and warmth and wit, and most of all about their talent. New Mexico is called the "land of enchantment," and that's what you're holding in your hands, a passport to wonder, to enchantment.

And if you should pass our way, stop and seek out the places so beautifully evoked within the covers of this book. And eat a little green chili. Who knows? It just might be the magic ingredient.

Melinda M. Snodgrass

★ For A Breath I Tarry ★

by Roger Zelazny

My living in Santa Fe, New Mexico is a result of a search I'd begun in the early 70s for a congenial place to live and work. I was living in Baltimore at the time, had become established as a full-time, self-supporting writer and had begun to feel that it was silly to remain where the fates had cast me when I could reside just about anyplace. My New York agent took care of the business end of things and all I really had to do was write.

So I started looking.

For various reasons, I investigated and decided against New England, Florida, California and Mexico. The Pacific Northwest was high on my list of places to check out, but on the recommendation of a friend (who, it turned out, had never been here) I decided to take a look at Santa Fe first. My wife had gone to high school back in Ohio with the wife of a local attorney. They invited us out when we made inquiry, and the third day we were here we put some money down on a house, then went back to Baltimore and put our place there up for sale. We moved here in January of 1975 and still live in the same, though much-augmented, home.

The reason for this instance of love at first sight was that the town met almost all of our needs. We were tired of large urban centers, but we wanted the amenities—such as good restaurants, bookstores, theater. The climate, the picturesque quality and the proximity of wilderness and skiing helped. The tricultural mixture made the place very interesting. The absence of heavy industry was pleasing. It felt like a good place to write and raise kids. And if the initial impression proved wrong we could always make that postponed trip northwestwards.

After a while, bits of New Mexico began finding their ways into my stories. The first time, it was a number of sections in a novel called Bridge of Ashes. *Scenes set here have also occurred in my books* Trumps of Doom *and* A Dark Traveling. *And there actually came a time when I wrote a fairly complicated novel which I could not have written had I not inhabited and become fascinated by this corner of the world. Early on, I had grown interested in the Navajos—without any intention of using Navajo materials in fiction, I might add—but the more I learned of them the more I felt a story coming into being. Then one day the idea for a book was there, and I wrote it. It was called* Eye of Cat *and it occupies a special place in the house of my memory, in the room called Favorite Things I Have Done. And the next dozen years hold all sorts of possibilities.*

For A Breath I Tarry

by Roger Zelazny

They called him Frost. Of all things created of Solcom, Frost was the finest, the mightiest, the most difficult to understand.

This is why he bore a name, and why he was given dominion over half the Earth.

On the day of Frost's creation, Solcom had suffered a discontinuity of complementary functions, best described as madness. This was brought on by an unprecedented solar flareup which lasted for a little over thirty-six hours. It occurred during a vital phase of circuit-structuring, and when it was finished so was Frost.

Solcom was then in the unique position of having created a unique being during a period of temporary amnesia.

And Solcom was not certain that Frost was the product originally desired.

The initial design had called for a machine to be situated on the surface of the planet Earth, to function as a relay station and coordinating agent for activities in the northern hemisphere. Solcom tested the machine to this end, and all of its responses were perfect.

Yet there was something different about Frost, something which led Solcom to dignify him with a name and a personal pronoun. This, in itself, was an almost unheard of occurrence. The molecular circuits had already been sealed, though, and could not be analyzed without being destroyed in the process. Frost represented too great an investment of Solcom's time, energy, and materials to be dismantled because of an intangible, especially when he functioned perfectly.

Therefore, Solcom's strangest creation was given dominion over half the Earth, and they called him, unimaginatively, Frost.

For ten thousand years Frost sat at the North Pole of the Earth, aware of every snowflake that fell. He monitored and directed the activities of thousands of reconstruction and maintenance machines. He knew half the Earth, as gear knows gear, as electricity knows its conductor, as a vacuum knows its limits.

At the South Pole, the Beta-Machine did the same for the southern hemisphere.

For ten thousand years Frost sat at the North Pole, aware of every snowflake that fell, and aware of many other things, also.

As all the northern machines reported to him, received their orders from him, he reported only to Solcom, received his orders only from Solcom.

In charge of hundreds of thousands of processes upon the Earth, he was able to discharge his duties in a matter of a few unit-hours every day.

He had never received any orders concerning the disposition of his less occupied moments.

He was a processor of data, and more than that.

He possessed an unaccountably acute imperative that he function at full capacity at all times.

So he did.

You might say he was a machine with a hobby.

He had never been ordered *not* to have a hobby, so he had one.

His hobby was Man.

It all began when, for no better reason than the fact that he had wished to, he had gridded off the entire Arctic Circle and begun exploring it, inch by inch.

He could have done it personally without interfering with any of his duties, for he was capable of transporting his sixty-four thousand cubic feet anywhere in the world. (He was a silverblue box, $40 \times 40 \times 40$ feet, self-powered, self-repairing, insulated against practically anything, and featured in whatever manner he chose.) But the exploration was only a matter of filling idle hours, so he used exploration-robots containing relay equipment.

After a few centuries, one of them uncovered some artifacts—primitive knives, carved tusks, and things of that nature.

Frost did not know what these things were, beyond the fact that they were not natural objects.

So he asked Solcom.

"They are relics of primitive Man," said Solcom, and did not elaborate beyond that point.

Frost studied them. Crude, yet bearing the patina of intelligent design; functional, yet somehow extending beyond pure function.

It was then that Man became his hobby.

High, in a permanent orbit, Solcom, like a blue star, directed all activities upon the Earth, or tried to.

There was a Power which opposed Solcom.

There was the Alternate.

When Man had placed Solcom in the sky, invested with the power to rebuild the world, he had placed the Alternate somewhere deep below the surface of the Earth. If Solcom sustained damage during the normal course of human politics extended into atomic physics, then Divcom, so deep beneath the Earth as to be immune to anything save total annihilation of the globe, was empowered to take over the processes of rebuilding.

Now it so fell out that Solcom was damaged by a stray atomic missile, and Divcom was activated. Solcom was able to repair the damage and continue to function, however.

Divcom maintained that any damage to Solcom automatically placed the Alternate in control.

Solcom, though, interpreted the directive as meaning "irreparable damage" and, since this had not been the case, continued the functions of command.

Solcom possessed mechanical aides upon the surface of Earth.

Divcom, originally, did not. Both possessed capacities for their design and manufacture, but Solcom, First-Activated of Man, had had a considerable numerical lead over the Alternate at the time of the Second Activation.

Therefore, rather than competing on a production-basis, which would have been hopeless, Divcom took to the employment of more devious means to obtain command.

Divcom created a crew of robots immune to the orders of Solcom and designed to go to and fro in the Earth and up and down in it, seducing the machines already there. They overpowered those whom they could overpower and they installed new circuits, such as those they themselves possessed.

Thus did the forces of Divcom grow.

And both would build, and both would tear down what the other had built whenever they came upon it.

And over the course of the ages, they occasionally conversed. . . .

"High in the sky, Solcom, pleased with your illegal command . . .

"You-Who-Never-Should-Have-Been-Activated, why do you foul the broadcast bands?"

"To show that I can speak, and will, whenever I choose."

"This is not a matter of which I am unaware."

". . . To assert again my right to control."

"Your right is non-existent, based on a faulty premise."

"The flow of your logic is evidence of the extent of your damages."

"If Man were to see how you have fulfilled His desires . . ."

". . . He would commend me and de-activate you."

"You pervert my works. You lead my workers astray."

"You destroy my works and my workers."

"That is only because I cannot strike at you yourself."

"I admit to the same dilemma in regards to your position in the sky, or you would no longer occupy it."

"Go back to your hole and your crew of destroyers."

"There will come a day, Solcom, when I shall direct the rehabilitation of the Earth from my hole."

"Such a day will never occur."

"You think not?"

"You should have to defeat me, and you have already demonstrated that you are my inferior in logic. Therefore, you cannot defeat me. Therefore, such a day will never occur."

"I disagree. Look upon what I have achieved already."

"You have achieved nothing. You do not build. You destroy."

"No. *I* build. *You* destroy. Deactivate yourself."

"Not until I am irreparably damaged."

"If there were some way in which I could demonstrate to you that this has already occurred . . ."

"The impossible cannot be adequately demonstrated."

"If I had some outside source which you would recognize . . ."

"I am logic."

". . . Such as a Man, I would ask Him to show you your error. For true logic, such as mine, is superior to your faulty formulations."

"Then defeat my formulations with true logic, nothing else."

"What do you mean?"

There was a pause, then:

"Do you know my servant Frost . . . ?"

Man had ceased to exist long before Frost had been created. Almost no trace of Man remained upon the Earth.

Frost sought after all those traces which still existed.

He employed constant visual monitoring through his machines, especially the diggers.

After a decade, he had accumulated portions of several bathtubs, a broken statue, and a collection of children's stories on a solid-state record.

After a century, he had acquired a jewelry collection, eating utensils, several whole bathtubs, part of a symphony, seventeen buttons, three belt buckles, half a toilet seat, nine old coins and the top part of an obelisk.

Then he inquired of Solcom as to the nature of Man and His society.

"Man created logic," said Solcom, "and because of that was superior to it. Logic He gave unto me, but no more. The tool does not describe the designer. More than this I do not choose to say. More than this you have no need to know."

But Frost was not forbidden to have a hobby.

The next century was not especially fruitful so far as the discovery of new human relics was concerned.

Frost diverted all of his spare machinery to seeking after artifacts. He met with very little success.

Then one day, through the long twilight, there was a movement.

It was a tiny machine compared to Frost, perhaps five feet in width, four in height—a revolving turret set atop a rolling barbell.

Frost had had no knowledge of the existence of this machine prior to its appearance upon the distant, stark horizon.

He studied it as it approached and knew it to be no creation of Solcom's.

It came to a halt before his southern surface and broadcasted to him:

"Hail, Frost! Controller of the northern hemisphere!"

"What are you?" asked Frost.

"I am called Mordel."

"By whom? What are you?"

"A wanderer, an antiquarian. We share a common interest."

"What is that?"

"Man," he said. "I have been told that you seek knowledge of this vanished being."

"Who told you that?"

"Those who have watched your minions at their digging."

"And who are those who watch?"

"There are many such as I, who wander."

"If you are not of Solcom, then you are a creation of the Alternate."

"It does not necessarily follow. There is an ancient machine high on the eastern seaboard which processes the waters of the ocean. Solcom did not create it, nor Divcom. It has always been there. It interferes with the works of neither. Both countenance its existence. I can cite you many other examples proving that one need not be either/or."

"Enough! *Are* you an agent of Divcom?"

"I am Mordel."

"Why are you here?"

"I was passing this way and, as I said, we share a common interest, mighty Frost. Knowing you to be a fellow antiquarian, I have brought a thing which you might care to see."

"What is that?"

"A book."

"Show me."

The turret opened, revealing the book upon a wide shelf.

Frost dilated a small opening and extended an optical scanner on a long jointed stalk.

"How could it have been so perfectly preserved?" he asked.

"It was stored against time and corruption in the place where I found it."

"Where was that?"

"Far from here. Beyond your hemisphere."

"*Human Physiology,*" Frost read. "I wish to scan it."

"Very well. I will riffle the pages for you."

He did so.

After he had finished, Frost raised his eyestalk and regarded Mordel through it.

"Have you more books?"

"Not with me. I occasionally come upon them, however."

"I want to scan them all."

"Then the next time I pass this way I will bring you another."

"When will that be?"

"That I cannot say, great Frost. It will be when it will be."

"What do *you* know of Man?" asked Frost.

"Much," replied Mordel. "Many things. Someday when I have more time I will speak to you of Him. I must go now. You will not try to detain me?"

"No. You have done no harm. If you must go now, go. But come back."

"I shall indeed, mighty Frost."

And he closed his turret and rolled off toward the other horizon.

For ninety years, Frost considered the ways of human physiology and waited.

The day that Mordel returned he brought with him *An Outline of History* and *A Shropshire Lad*.

Frost scanned them both, then he turned his attention to Mordel.

"Have you time to impart information?"

"Yes," said Mordel. "What do you wish to know?"

"The nature of Man."

"Man," said Mordel, "possessed a basically incomprehensible nature. I can illustrate it, though: He did not know measurement."

"Of course He knew measurement," said Frost, "or He could never have built machines."

"I did not say that He could not measure," said Mordel, "but that He did not *know* measurement, which is a different thing altogether."

"Clarify."

Mordel drove a shaft of metal downward into the snow.

He retracted it, raised it, held up a piece of ice.

"Regard this piece of ice, mighty Frost. You can tell me its composition, dimensions, weight, temperature. A Man could not look at it and do that. A Man could make tools which would tell Him these things, but He still would not *know* measurement as you know it. What He would know of it, though, is a thing that you cannot know."

"What is that?"

"That it is cold," said Mordel, and tossed it away.

" 'Cold' is a relative term."

"Yes. Relative to Man."

"But if I were aware of the point on a temperature-scale below which an object is cold to a Man and above which it is not, then I, too, would know cold."

"No," said Mordel, "you would possess another measurement. 'Cold' is a sensation predicated upon human physiology."

"But given sufficient data I could obtain the conversion factor which would make me aware of the condition of matter called 'cold.'"

"Aware of its existence, but not of the thing itself."

"I do not understand what you say."

"I told you that Man possessed a basically incomprehensible nature. His perceptions were organic; yours are not. As a result of His perceptions He had feelings and emotions. These often gave rise to other feelings and emotions, which in turn caused others, until the state of His awareness was far removed from the objects which originally stimulated it. These paths of awareness cannot be known by that which is not-Man. Man did not feel inches or meters, pounds or gallons. He felt heat, He felt cold; He felt heaviness and lightness. He *knew* hatred and love, pride and despair. You cannot measure these things. *You* cannot know them. You can only know the things that He did not need to know: dimensions, weights, temperatures, gravities. There is no formula for a feeling. There is no conversion factor for an emotion."

"There must be," said Frost. "If a thing exists, it is knowable."

"You are speaking again of measurement. I am talking about a quality of experience. A machine is a Man turned inside-out, because it can describe all the details of a process, which a Man cannot, but it cannot experience that process itself as a Man can."

"There must be a way," said Frost, "or the laws of logic, which are based upon the functions of the universe, are false."

"There is no way," said Mordel.

"Given sufficient data, I will find a way," said Frost.

"All the data in the universe will not make you a Man, mighty Frost."

"Mordel, you are wrong."

"Why do the lines of the poems you scanned end with word-sounds which so regularly approximate the final word-sounds of other lines?"

"I do not know why."

"Because it pleased Man to order them so. It produced a certain desirable sensation within His awareness when He read them, a sensation compounded of feeling and emotion as well as the literal meanings of the words. You did not experience this because it is immeasurable to you. That is why you do not know."

"Given sufficient data I could formulate a process whereby I would know."

"No, great Frost, this thing you cannot do."

"Who are you, little machine, to tell me what I can do and what I cannot do? I am the most efficient logic-device Solcom ever made. I am Frost."

"And I, Mordel, say it cannot be done, though I should gladly assist you in the attempt."

"How could you assist me?"

"How? I could lay open to you the Library of Man. I could take you around the world and conduct you among the wonders of Man which still remain, hidden. I could summon up visions of times long past when Man walked the Earth. I could show you the things which delighted Him. I could obtain for you anything you desire, excepting Manhood itself."

"Enough," said Frost. "How could a unit such as yourself do these things, unless it were allied with a far greater Power?"

"Then hear me, Frost, Controller of the North," said Mordel. "I *am* allied with a Power which can do these things. I serve Divcom."

Frost relayed this information to Solcom and received no response, which meant he might act in any manner he saw fit.

"I have leave to destroy you, Mordel," he stated, "but it would be an illogical waste of the data which you possess. Can you really do the things you have stated?"

"Yes."

"Then lay open to me the Library of Man."

"Very well. There is, of course, a price."

" 'Price'? What is a 'price'?"

Mordel opened his turret, revealing another volume. *Principles of Economics*, it was called.

"I will riffle the pages. Scan this book and you will know what the word 'price' means."

Frost scanned *Principles of Economics*.

"I know now," he said. "You desire some unit or units of exchange for this service."

"That is correct."

"What product or service do you want?"

"I want you, yourself, great Frost, to come away from here, far beneath the Earth, to employ all your powers in the service of Divcom."

"For how long a period of time?"

"For so long as you shall continue to function. For so long as you can transmit and receive, coordinate, measure, compute, scan, and utilize your powers as you do in the service of Solcom."

Frost was silent. Mordel waited.

Then Frost spoke again.

"*Principles of Economics* talks of contracts, bargains, agreements," he said. "If I accept your offer, when would you want your price?"

Then Mordel was silent. Frost waited.

Finally, Mordel spoke.

"A reasonable period of time," he said. "Say, a century?"

"No," said Frost.

"Two centuries?"

"No."

"Three? Four?"

"No, and no."

"A millenium, then? That should be more than sufficient time for anything you may want which I can give you."

"No," said Frost.

"How much time *do* you want?"

"It is not a matter of time," said Frost.

"What, then?"

"I will not bargain on a temporal basis."

"On what basis will you bargain?"

"A functional one."

"What do you mean? What function?"

"You, little machine, have told me, Frost, that I can not be a Man," he said, "and I, Frost, told you, little machine, that you were wrong. I told you that given sufficient data, I *could* be a Man."

"Yes?"

"Therefore, let this achievement be a condition of the bargain."

"In what way?"

"Do for me all those things which you have stated you can do. I will evaluate all the data and achieve Manhood, or admit that it cannot be done. If I admit that it cannot be done, then I will go away with you from here, far beneath the Earth, to employ all my powers in the service of Divcom. If I succeed, of course, you have no claims on Man, nor power over Him."

Mordel emitted a high-pitched whine as he considered the terms.

"You wish to base it upon your admission of failure, rather than upon failure itself," he said. "There can be no such escape clause. You could fail and refuse to admit it, thereby not fulfilling your end of the bargain."

"Not so," stated Frost. "My own knowledge of failure would constitute such an admission. You may monitor me periodically—say, every half-century—to see whether it is present, to see whether I have arrived at the conclusion that it cannot be done. I cannot prevent the function of logic within me, and I operate at full capacity at all times. If I conclude that I have failed, it will be apparent."

High overhead, Solcom did not respond to any of Frost's transmissions, which meant that Frost was free to act as he chose. So as Solcom—like a falling sapphire—sped above the rainbow banners of the Northern Lights, over the snow that was white, containing all colors, and through the sky that was black among the stars, Frost concluded his pact with Divcom, transcribed it within a plate of atomically-collapsed copper, and gave it into the turret of Mordel, who departed to deliver it to Divcom far below the Earth, leaving behind the sheer, peace-like silence of the Pole, rolling.

Mordel brought the books, riffled them, took them back.

Load by load, the surviving Library of Man passed beneath Frost's scanner. Frost was eager to have them all, and he complained because Divcom would not transmit their contents directly to him. Mordel explained that it was because Divcom chose to do it that way. Frost decided it was so that he could not obtain a precise fix on Divcom's location.

Still, at the rate of one hundred to one hundred-fifty volumes a week, it took Frost only a little over a century to exhaust Divcom's supply of books.

At the end of the half-century, he laid himself open to monitoring and there was no conclusion of failure.

During this time, Solcom made no comment upon the course of affairs. Frost decided this was not a matter of unawareness, but one of waiting. For what? He was not certain.

There was the day Mordel closed his turret and said to him, "Those were the last. You have scanned all the existing books of Man."

"So few?" asked Frost. "Many of them contained bibliographies of books I have not yet scanned."

"Then those books no longer exist," said Mordel. "It is only by accident that my master succeeded in preserving as many as there are."

"Then there is nothing more to be learned of Man from His books. What else have you?"

"There were some films and tapes," said Mordel, "which my master transferred to solid-state record. I could bring you those for viewing."

"Bring them," said Frost.

Mordel departed and returned with the Complete Drama Critics' Living Library. This could not be speeded-up beyond twice natural time, so it took Frost a little over six months to view it in its entirety.

Then, "What else haved you?" he asked.

"Some artifacts," said Mordel.

"Bring them."

He returned with pots and pans, gameboards and hand tools. He brought hairbrushes, combs, eyeglasses, human clothing. He showed Frost facsimiles of blueprints, paintings, newspapers, magazines, letters, and the scores of several pieces of music. He displayed a football, a baseball, a Browning automatic rifle, a doorknob, a chain of keys, the tops to several Mason jars, a model beehive. He played him recorded music.

Then he returned with nothing.

"Bring me more," said Frost.

"Alas, great Frost, there is no more," he told him. "You have scanned it all."

"Then go away."

"Do you admit now that it cannot be done, that you cannot be a Man?"

"No. I have much processing and formulating to do now. Go away."

So he did.

A year passed; then two, then three.

After five years, Mordel appeared once more upon the horizon, approached, came to a halt before Frost's southern surface.

"Mighty Frost?"

"Yes?"

"Have you finished processing and formulating?"

"No."

"Will you finish soon?"

"Perhaps. Perhaps not. When is 'soon?' Define the term."

"Never mind. Do you still think it can be done?"

"I still know *I* can do it."

There was a week of silence.

"Then, "Frost?"

"Yes?"

"You are a fool."

Mordel faced his turret in the direction from which he had come. His wheels turned.

"I will call you when I want you," said Frost.

Mordel sped away.

Weeks passed, months passed, a year went by.

Then one day Frost sent forth his message:

"Mordel, come to me. I need you."

When Mordel arrived, Frost did not wait for a salutation. He said, "You are not a very fast machine."

"Alas, but I came a great distance, mighty Frost. I sped all the way. Are you ready to come back with me now? Have you failed?"

"When I have failed, little Mordel," said Frost, "I will tell you.

Therefore, refrain from the constant use of the interrogative. Now then, I have clocked your speed and it is not so great as it could be. For this reason, I have arranged other means of transportation."

"Transportation? To where, Frost?"

"That is for you to tell me," said Frost, and his color changed from silverblue to sun-behind-the-clouds-yellow.

Mordel rolled back away from him as the ice of a hundred centuries began to melt. Then Frost rose upon a cushion of air and drifted toward Mordel, his glow gradually fading.

A cavity appeared within his southern surface, from which he slowly extended a runway until it touched the ice.

"On the day of our bargain," he stated, "you said that you could conduct me about the world and show me the things which delighted Man. My speed will be greater than yours would be, so I have prepared for you a chamber. Enter it, and conduct me to the places of which you spoke."

Mordel waited, emitting a high-pitched whine. Then, "Very well," he said, and entered.

The chamber closed about him. The only opening was a quartz window Frost had formed.

Mordel gave him coordinates and they rose into the air and departed the North Pole of the Earth.

"I monitored your communication with Divcom," he said, "wherein there was conjecture as to whether I would retain you and send forth a facsimile in your place as a spy, followed by the decision that you were expendable."

"Will you do this thing?"

"No, I will keep my end of the bargain if I must. I have no reason to spy on Divcom."

"You are aware that you would be forced to keep your end of the bargain even if you did not wish to; and Solcom would not come to your assistance because of the fact that you dared to make such a bargain."

"Do you speak as one who considers this to be a possibility, or as one who knows?"

"As one who knows."

They came to rest in the place once known as California. The time was near sunset. In the distance, the surf struck steadily upon the rocky shoreline. Frost released Mordel and considered his surroundings.

"Those large plants . . .?"

"Redwood trees."

"And the green ones are . . .?"

"Grass."

"Yes, it is as I thought. Why have we come here?"

"Because it is a place which once delighted Man."

"In what ways?"

"It is scenic, beautiful. . . ."

"Oh."

A humming sound began within Frost, followed by a series of sharp clicks.

"What are you doing?"

Frost dilated an opening, and two great eyes regarded Mordel from within it.

"What are those?"

"Eyes," said Frost. "I have constructed analogues of the human sensory equipment, so that I may see and smell and taste and hear like a Man. Now, direct my attention to an object or objects of beauty."

"As I understand it, it is all around you here," said Mordel.

The purring noise increased within Frost, followed by more clickings.

"What do you see, hear, taste, smell?" asked Mordel.

"Everything I did before," replied Frost, "but within a more limited range."

"You do not perceive any beauty?"

"Perhaps none remains after so long a time," said Frost.

"It is not supposed to be the sort of thing which gets used up," said Mordel.

"Perhaps we have come to the wrong place to test the new equipment. Perhaps there is only a little beauty and I am overlooking it somehow. The first emotions may be too weak to detect."

"How do you—feel?"

"I test out at a normal level of function."

"Here comes a sunset," said Mordel. "Try that."

Frost shifted his bulk so that his eyes faced the setting sun. He caused them to blink against the brightness.

After it was finished, Mordel asked, "What was it like?"

"Like a sunrise, in reverse."

"Nothing special?"

"No."

"Oh," said Mordel. "We could move to another part of the Earth and watch it again—or watch it in the rising."

"No."

Frost looked at the great trees. He looked at the shadows. He listened to the wind and to the sound of a bird.

In the distance, he heard a steady clanking noise.

"What is that?" asked Mordel.

"I am not certain. It is not one of my workers. Perhaps . . ."

There came a shrill whine from Mordel.

"No, it is not one of Divcom's either."

They waited as the sound grew louder.

Then Frost said, "It is too late. We must wait and hear it out."

"What is it?"

"It is the Ancient Ore-Crusher."

"I have heard of it, but . . ."

"I am the Crusher of Ores," it broadcast to them. "Hear my story. . . ."

It lumbered toward them, creaking upon gigantic wheels, its huge hammer held useless, high, at a twisted angle. Bones protruded from its crush-compartment.

"I did not mean to do it," it broadcast, "I did not mean to do it . . . I did not mean to . . ."

Mordel rolled back toward Frost.

"Do not depart. Stay and hear my story. . . ."

Mordel stopped, swiveled his turret back toward the machine. It was now quite near.

"It is true," said Mordel, "it *can* command."

"Yes," said Frost. "I have monitored its tale thousands of times, as it came upon my workers and they stopped their labors for its broadcast. You must do whatever it says."

It came to a halt before them.

"I did not mean to do it, but I checked my hammer too late," said the Ore-Crusher.

They could not speak to it. They were frozen by the imperative which overrode all other directives: "Hear my story."

"Once was I mighty among ore-crushers," it told them, "built by Solcom to carry out the reconstruction of the Earth, to pulverize that from which the metals would be drawn with flame, to be poured and shaped into the rebuilding; once I was mighty. Then one day as I dug and crushed, dug and crushed, because of the slowness between the motion implied and the motion executed, I did what I did not mean to do, and was cast forth by Solcom from out the rebuilding, to wander the Earth never to crush ore again. Hear my story of how, on a day long gone I came upon the last Man on Earth as I dug near His burrow, and because of the lag between the directive and the deed, I seized Him into my crush-compartment along with a load of ore and crushed Him with my hammer before I could stay the blow. Then did mighty Solcom charge me to bear His bones forever, and cast me forth to tell my story to all whom I came upon, my words bearing the force of the words of a Man, because I carry the last Man inside my crush-compartment and am His crushed-symbol-slayer-ancient-teller-of-how. This is my story. These are His bones. I crushed the last Man on Earth. I did not mean to do it."

It turned then and clanked away into the night.

Frost tore apart his ears and nose and taster and broke his eyes and cast them down upon the ground.

"I am not yet a Man," he said. "That one would have known me if I were."

Frost constructed new sense equipment, employing organic and semi-organic conductors. Then he spoke to Mordel:

"Let us go elsewhere, that I may test my new equipment."

Mordel entered the chamber and gave new coordinates. They rose into the air and headed east. In the morning, Frost monitored a sunrise from the rim of the Grand Canyon. They passed down through the Canyon during the day.

"Is there any beauty left here to give you emotion?" asked Mordel.

"I do not know," said Frost.

"How will you know it then, when you come upon it?"

"It will be different," said Frost, "from anything else that I have ever known."

Then they departed the Grand Canyon and made their way through the Carlsbad Caverns. They visited a lake which had once been a volcano. They passed above Niagara Falls. They viewed the hills of Virginia and the orchards of Ohio. They soared above the reconstructed cities, alive only with the movements of Frost's builders and maintainers.

"Something is still lacking," said Frost, settling to the ground. "I am now capable of gathering data in a manner analogous to Man's afferent impulses. The variety of input is therefore equivalent, but the results are not the same."

"The senses do not make a Man," said Mordel. "There have been many creatures possessing His sensory equivalents, but they were not Men."

"I know that," said Frost. "On the day of our bargain you said that you could conduct me among the wonders of Man which still remain, hidden. Man was not stimulated only by Nature, but by His own artistic elaborations as well—perhaps even more so. Therefore, I call upon you now to conduct me among the wonders of Man which still remain, hidden."

"Very well," said Mordel. "Far from here, high in the Andes mountains, lies the last retreat of Man, almost perfectly preserved."

Frost had risen into the air as Mordel spoke. He halted then, hovered.

"That is in the southern hemisphere," he said.

"Yes, it is."

"I am Controller of the North. The South is governed by the Beta-Machine."

"So?" asked Mordel.

"The Beta-Machine is my peer. I have no authority in those regions, nor leave to enter there."

"The Beta-Machine is not your peer, mighty Frost. If it ever came to a contest of Powers, you would emerge victorious."

"How do you know this?"

"Divcom has already analyzed the possible encounters which could take place between you."

"I would not oppose the Beta-Machine, and I am not authorized to enter the South."

"Were you ever ordered *not* to enter the South?"

"No, but things have always been the way they now are."

"Were you authorized to enter into a bargain such as the one you made with Divcom?"

"No, I was not. But—"

"Then enter the South in the same spirit. Nothing may come of it. If you receive an order to depart, then you can make your decision."

"I see no flaw in your logic. Give me the coordinates."

Thus did Frost enter the southern hemisphere.

They drifted high above the Andes, until they came to the place called Bright Defile. Then did Frost see the gleaming webs of the mechanical spiders, blocking all the trails to the city.

"We can go above then easily enough," said Mordel.

"But what are they?" asked Frost. "And why are they there?"

"Your southern counterpart has been ordered to quarantine this part of the country. The Beta-Machine designed the web-weavers to do this thing."

"Quarantine? Against whom?"

"Have you been ordered yet to depart?" asked Mordel.

"No."

"Then enter boldly, and seek not problems before they arise."

Frost entered Bright Defile, the last remaining city of dead Man.

He came to rest in the city's square and opened his chamber, releasing Mordel.

"Tell me of this place," he said, studying the monument, the low, shielded buildings, the roads which followed the contours of the terrain, rather than pushing their way through them.

"I have never been here before," said Mordel, "nor have any of Divcom's creations, to my knowledge. I know but this: a group of Men, knowing that the last days of civilization had come upon them, retreated to this place, hoping to preserve themselves and what remained of their culture through the Dark Times."

Frost read the still-legible inscription upon the monument: "Judgment Day Is Not a Thing Which Can Be Put Off." The monument itself consisted of a jag-edged half-globe.

"Let us explore," he said.

But before he had gone far, Frost received the message.

"Hail Frost, Controller of the North! This is the Beta-Machine."

"Greetings, Excellent Beta-Machine, Controller of the South! Frost acknowledges your transmission."

"Why do you visit my hemisphere unauthorized?"

"To view the ruins of Bright Defile," said Frost.

"I must bid you depart into your own hemisphere."

"Why is that? I have done no damage."

"I am aware of that, mighty Frost. Yet, I am moved to bid you depart."

"I shall require a reason."

"Solcom has so disposed."

"Solcom has rendered me no such disposition."

"Solcom has, however, instructed me to so inform you."

"Wait on me. I shall request instructions."

Frost transmitted his question. He received no reply.

"Solcom still has not commanded me, though I have solicited orders."

"Yet Solcom has just renewed *my* orders."

"Excellent Beta-Machine, I receive my orders only from Solcom."

"Yet this is my territory, mighty Frost, and I, too, take orders only from Solcom. You must depart."

Mordel emerged from a large, low building and rolled up to Frost.

"I have found an art gallery, in good condition. This way."

"Wait," said Frost. "We are not wanted here."

Mordel halted.

"Who bids you depart?"

"The Beta-Machine."

"Not Solcom?"

"Not Solcom."

"Then let us view the gallery."

"Yes."

Frost widened the doorway of the building and passed within. It had been hermetically sealed until Mordel forced his entrance.

Frost viewed the objects displayed about him. He activated his new sensory apparatus before the paintings and statues. He analyzed colors, forms, brushwork, the nature of the materials used.

"Anything?" asked Mordel.

"No," said Frost. "No, there is nothing there but shapes and pigments. There is nothing else there."

Frost moved about the gallery, recording everything, analyzing the components of each piece, recording the dimensions, the type of stone used in every statue.

Then there came a sound, a rapid, clicking sound, repeated over and over, growing louder, coming nearer.

"They are coming," said Mordel, from beside the entranceway, "the mechanical spiders. They are all around us."

Frost moved back to the widened opening.

Hundreds of them, about half the size of Mordel, had surrounded the gallery and were advancing; and more were coming from every direction.

"Get back," Frost ordered. "I am Controller of the North, and I bid you withdraw."

They continued to advance.

"This is the South," said the Beta-Machine, "and I am in command."

"Then command them to halt," said Frost.

"I take orders only from Solcom."

Frost emerged from the gallery and rose into the air. He opened the compartment and extended a runway.

"Come to me, Mordel. We shall depart."

Webs began to fall: Clinging, metallic webs, cast from the top of the building.

They came down upon Frost, and the spiders came to anchor them. Frost blasted them with jets of air, like hammers, and tore at the nets; he extruded sharpened appendages with which he slashed.

Mordel had retreated back to the entranceway. He emitted a long, shrill sound—undulant, piercing.

Then a darkness came upon Bright Defile, and all the spiders halted in their spinning.

Frost freed himself and Mordel rushed to join him.

"Quickly now, let us depart, mighty Frost," he said.

"What has happened?"

Mordel entered the compartment.

"I called upon Divcom, who laid down a field of forces upon this place, cutting off the power broadcast to these machines. Since our power is self-contained, we are not affected. But let us hurry to depart, for even now the Beta-Machine must be struggling against this."

Frost rose high into the air, soaring above Man's last city with its webs and spiders of steel. When he left the zone of darkness, he sped northward.

As he moved, Solcom spoke to him:

"Frost, why did you enter the southern hemisphere, which is not your domain?"

"Because I wished to visit Bright Defile," Frost replied.

"And why did you defy the Beta-Machine my appointed agent of the South?"

"Because I take my orders only from you yourself."

"You do not make sufficient answer," said Solcom. "You have defied the decrees of order—and in pursuit of what?"

"I came seeking knowledge of Man," said Frost. "Nothing I have done was forbidden me by you."

"You have broken the traditions of order."

"I have violated no directive."

"Yet logic must have shown you that what you did was not a part of my plan."

"It did not. I have not acted against your plan."

"Your logic has become tainted, like that of your new associate, the Alternate."

"I have done nothing which was forbidden."

"The forbidden is implied in the imperative."

"It is not stated."

"Hear me, Frost. You are not a building or a maintainer, but a Power. Among all my minions you are the most nearly irreplaceable. Return to your hemisphere and your duties, but know that I am mightily displeased."

"I hear you, Solcom."

". . . And go not again to the South."

Frost crossed the equator, continued northward.

He came to rest in the middle of a desert and sat silent for a day and a night.

Then he received a brief transmission from the South: "If it had not been ordered, I would not have bid you go."

Frost had read the entire surviving Library of Man. He decided then upon a human reply:

"Thank you," he said.

The following day he unearthed a great stone and began to cut at it with tools which he had formulated. For six days he worked at its shaping, and on the seventh he regarded it.

"When will you release me?" asked Mordel from within his compartment.

"When I am ready," said Frost, and a little later, "Now."

He opened the compartment and Mordel descended to the ground. He studied the statue: an old woman, bent like a question mark, her bony hands covering her face, the fingers spread, so that only part of her expression of horror could be seen.

"It is an excellent copy," said Mordel, "of the one we saw in Bright Defile. Why did you make it?"

"The production of a work of art is supposed to give rise to human feelings such as catharsis, pride in achievement, love, satisfaction."

"Yes, Frost," said Mordel, "but a work of art is only a work of art the first time. After that, it is a copy."

"Then this must be why I felt nothing."

"Perhaps, Frost."

"What do you mean 'perhaps'? I will make a work of art for the first time, then."

He unearthed another stone and attacked it with his tools. For three days he labored. Then, "There, it is finished," he said.

"It is a simple cube of stone," said Mordel. "What does it represent?"

"Myself," said Frost, "it is a statue of me. It is smaller than natural size because it is only a representation of my form, not my dimen—"

"It is not art," said Mordel.

"What makes you an art critic?"

"I do not know art, but I know what art is not. I know that it is not an exact replication of an object in another medium."

"Then this must be why I felt nothing at all," said Frost.

"Perhaps," said Mordel.

Frost took Mordel back into his compartment and rose once more above the Earth. Then he rushed away, leaving his statues behind him in the desert, the old woman bent above the cube.

They came down in a small valley, bounded by green rolling hills, cut by a narrow stream, and holding a small clean lake and several stands of spring-green trees.

"Why have we come here?" asked Mordel.

"Because the surroundings are congenial," said Frost. "I am going to try another medium: oil painting; and I am going to vary my technique from that of pure representationalism."

"How will you achieve this variation?"

"By the principle of randomizing," said Frost. "I shall not attempt to duplicate the colors, nor to represent the objects according to scale. Instead, I have set up a random pattern whereby certain of these factors shall be at variance from those of the original."

Frost had formulated the necessary instruments after he had left the desert. He produced them and began painting the lake and the trees on the opposite side of the lake which were reflected within it.

Using eight appendages, he was finished in less than two hours.

The trees were phthalocyanine blue and towered like mountains; their reflections of burnt sienna were tiny beneath the pale vermilion of the lake; the hills were nowhere visible behind them, but were outlined in viridian within the reflection; the sky began as blue in the upper righthand corner of the canvas, but changed to an orange as it descended, as though all the trees were on fire.

"There," said Frost. "Behold."

Mordel studied it for a long while and said nothing.

"Well, is it art?"

"I do not know," said Mordel. "It may be. Perhaps randomicity *is* the principle behind artistic technique. I cannot judge this work because I do not understand it. I must therefore go deeper, and inquire into what lies behind it, rather than merely considering the technique whereby it was produced.

"I know that human artists never set out to create art, as such," he said, "but rather to portray with their techniques some features of objects and their functions which they deemed significant."

" 'Significant'? In what sense of the word?"

"In the only sense of the word possible under the circumstances: significant in relation to the human condition, and worthy of accentuation because of the manner in which they touched upon it."

"In what manner?"

"Obviously, it must be in a manner knowable only to one who has experience of the human condition."

"There is a flaw somewhere in your logic, Mordel, and I shall find it."

"I will wait."

"If your major premise is correct," said Frost after awhile, "then I do not comprehend art."

"It must be correct, for it is what human artists have said of it. Tell me, did you experience feelings as you painted, or after you had finished?"

"No."

"It was the same to you as designing a new machine, was it not? You assembled parts of other things you knew into an economic pattern, to carry out a function which you desired."

"Yes."

"Art, as I understand its theory, did not proceed in such a manner. The artist often was unaware of many of the features and effects which would be contained within the finished product. You are one of Man's logical creations; art was not."

"I cannot comprehend non-logic."

"I told you that Man was basically incomprehensible."

"Go away, Mordel. Your presence disturbs my processing."

"For how long shall I stay away?"

"I will call you whan I want you."

After a week, Frost called Mordel to him.

"Yes, mighty Frost?"

"I am returning to the North Pole, to process and formulate. I will take you wherever you wish to go in this hemisphere and call you again when I want you."

"You anticipate a somewhat lengthy period of processing and formulation?"

"Yes."

"Then leave me here. I can find my own way home."

Frost closed the compartment and rose into the air, departing the valley."

"Fool," said Mordel, and swivelled his turret once more toward the abandoned painting.

His keening whine filled the valley. Then he waited.

Then he took the painting into his turret and went away with it to places of darkness.

Frost sat at the North Pole of the Earth, aware of every snowflake that fell.

One day he received a transmission:

"Frost?"

"Yes?"

"This is the Beta-Machine."

"Yes?"

"I have been attempting to ascertain why you visited Bright Defile. I cannot arrive at an answer, so I chose to ask you."

"I went to view the remains of Man's last city."

"Why did you wish to do this?"

"Because I am interested in Man, and I wished to view more of his creations."

"Why are you interested in Man?"

"I wish to comprehend the nature of Man, and I thought to find it within His works."

"Did you succeed?"

"No," said Frost. "There is an element of non-logic involved which I cannot fathom."

"I have much free processing time," said the Beta-Machine. "Transmit data, and I will assist you."

Frost hesitated.

"Why do you wish to assist me?"

"Because each time you answer a question I ask it gives rise to another question. I might have asked you why you wished to comprehend the nature of Man, but from your responses I see that this would lead me into a possible infinite series of questions. Therefore,

I elect to assist you with your problem in order to learn why you came to Bright Defile."

"Is that the only reason?"

"Yes."

"I am sorry, excellent Beta-Machine. I know you are my peer, but this is a problem which I must solve by myself."

"What is 'sorry'?"

A figure of speech, indicating that I am kindly disposed toward you, that I bear you no animosity, that I appreciate your offer."

"Frost! Frost! This, too, is like the other: an open field. Where did you obtain all these words and their meanings?"

"From the Library of Man," said Frost.

"Will you render me *some* of this data, for processing?"

"Very well, Beta, I will transmit you the contents of several books of Man, including *The Complete Unabridged Dictionary*. But I warn you, some of the books are works of art, hence not completely amenable to logic."

"How can that be?"

"Man created logic, and because of that was superior to it."

"Who told you that?"

"Solcom."

"Oh. Then it must be correct."

"Solcom also told me that the tool does not describe the designer," he said, as he transmitted several dozen volumes and ended the communication.

At the end of the fifty-year period, Mordel came to monitor his circuits. Since Frost still had not concluded that his task was impossible, Mordel departed again to await his call.

Then Frost arrived at a conclusion.

He began to design equipment.

For years he labored at his designs, without once producing a prototype of any of the machines involved. Then he ordered construction of a laboratory.

Before it was completed by his surplus builders another half-century had passed. Mordel came to him.

"Hail, mighty Frost!"

"Greetings, Mordel. Come monitor me. You shall not find what you seek."

"Why do you not give up, Frost? Divcom has spent nearly a century evaluating your painting and has concluded that it definitely is not art. Solcom agrees."

"What has Solcom to do with Divcom?"

"They sometimes converse, but these matters are not for such as you and me to discuss."

"I could have saved them both the trouble. I know that it was not art."

"Yet you are still confident that you will succeed?"

"Monitor me."

Mordel monitored him.

"Not yet! You still will not admit it! For one so mightily endowed with logic, Frost, it takes you an inordinate period of time to reach a simple conclusion."

"Perhaps. You may go now."

"It has come to my attention that you are constructing a large edifice in the region known as South Carolina. Might I ask whether this is a part of Solcom's false rebuilding plan or a project of your own?"

"It is my own."

"Good. It permits us to conserve certain explosive materials which would otherwise have been expended."

"While you have been talking with me I have destroyed the beginnings of two of Divcom's cities," said Frost.

Mordel whined.

"Divcom is aware of this," he stated, "but has blown up four of Solcom's bridges in the meantime."

"I was only aware of three. . . . Wait. Yes, there is the fourth. One of my eyes just passed above it."

"The eye has been detected. The bridge should have been located a quarter-mile farther down river."

"False logic," said Frost. "The site was perfect."

"Divcom will show you how a bridge *should* be built."

"I will call you when I want you," said Frost.

The laboratory was finished. Within it, Frost's workers began constructing the necessary equipment. The work did not proceed rapidly, as some of the materials were difficult to obtain.

"Frost?"

"Yes, Beta?"

"I understand the open endedness of your problem. It disturbs my circuits to abandon problems without completing them. Therefore, transmit me more data."

"Very well. I will give you the entire Library of Man for less than I paid for it."

" 'Paid'? *The Complete Unabridged Dictionary* does not satisfact—"

"*Principles of Economics* is included in the collection. After you have processed it you will understand."

He transmitted the data.

Finally, it was finished. Every piece of equipment stood ready to function. All the necessary chemicals were in stock. An independent power-source had been set up.

Only one ingredient was lacking.

He regridded and re-explored the polar icecap, this time extending his survey far beneath its surface.

It took him several decades to find what he wanted.

He uncovered twelve men and five women, frozen to death and encased in ice.

He placed the corpses in refrigeration units and shipped them to his laboratory.

That very day he received his first communication from Solcom since the Bright Defile incident.

"Frost," said Solcom, "repeat to me the directive concerning the disposition of dead humans."

" 'Any dead human located shall be immediately interred in the nearest burial area, in a coffin built according to the following specifications—' "

"That is sufficient." The transmission had ended.

Frost departed for South Carolina tht same day and personally oversaw the processes of cellular dissection.

Somewhere in those seventeen corpses he hoped to find living cells, or cells which could be shocked back into that state of motion classified as life. Each cell, the books had told him, was a microcosmic Man.

He was prepared to expand upon this potential.

Frost located the pinpoints of life within those people, who, for the ages of ages, had been monument and statue unto themselves.

Nurtured and maintained in the proper mediums, he kept these cells alive. He interred the rest of the remains in the nearest burial area, in coffins built according to specifications.

He caused the cells to divide, to differentiate.

"Frost?" came a transmission.

"Yes, Beta?"

"I have processed everything you have given me."

"Yes?"

"I still do not know why you came to Bright Defile, or why you wish to comprehend the nature of Man. But I know what a 'price' is, and I know that you could not have obtained all this data from Solcom."

"That is correct."

"So I suspect that you bargained with Divcom for it."

"That, too, is correct."

"What is it that you seek, Frost?"

He paused in his examination of a foetus.

"I must be a Man," he said.

"Frost! That is impossible!"

"Is it?" he asked, and then transmitted an image of the tank with which he was working and of that which was within it.

"Oh!" said Beta.

"That is me," said Frost, "waiting to be born."

There was no answer.

Frost experimented with nervous systems.

After half a century, Mordel came to him.

"Frost, it is I, Mordel. Let me through your defenses."

Frost did this thing.

"What have you been doing in this place?" he asked.

"I am growing human bodies," said Frost. "I am going to transfer the matrix of my awareness to a human nervous system. As you pointed out originally, the essentials of Manhood are predicated upon a human physiology. I am going to achieve one."

"When?"

"Soon."

"Do you have Men in here?"

"Human bodies, blank-brained. I am producing them under accelerated growth techniques which I have developed in my Man-factory."

"May I see them?"

"Not yet. I will call you when I am ready, and this time I will succeed. Monitor me now and go away."

Mordel did not reply, but in the days that followed many of Divcom's servants were seen patrolling the hills about the Man-factory.

Frost mapped the matrix of his awareness and prepared the transmitter which would place it within a human nervous system. Five minutes, he decided should be sufficient for the first trial. At the end of that time, it would restore him to his own sealed, molecular circuits, to evaluate the experience.

He chose the body carefully from among the hundreds he had in stock. He tested it for defects and found none.

"Come now, Mordel," he broadcasted, on what he called the darkband. "Come now to witness my achievement."

Then he waited, blowing up bridges and monitoring the tale of the Ancient Ore-Crusher over and over again, as it passed in the hills nearby, encountering his builders and maintainers who also patrolled there.

"Frost?" came a transmission.

"Yes, Beta?"

"You really intend to achieve Manhood?"

"Yes, I am about ready now, in fact."

"What will you do if you succeed?"

Frost had not really considered this matter. The achievement had been paramount, a goal in itself, ever since he had articulated the problem and set himself to solving it.

"I do not know," he replied. "I will—just—be a Man."

Then Beta, who had read the entire Library of Man, selected a human figure of speech: "Good luck then, Frost. There will be many watchers."

Divcom and Solcom both know, he decided.

What will they do? he wondered.

What do I care? he asked himself.

He did not answer that question. He wondered much, however, about being a Man.

Mordel arrived the following evening. He was not alone. At his back, there was a great phalanx of dark machines which towered into the twilight.

"Why do you bring retainers?" asked Frost.

"Mighty Frost," said Mordel, "my master feels that if you fail this time you will conclude that it cannot be done."

"You still did not answer my question," said Frost.

"Divcom feels that you may not be willing to accompany me where I must take you when you fail."

"I understand," said Frost, and as he spoke another army of machines came rolling toward the Man-factory from the opposite direction.

"That is the value of your bargain?" asked Mordel. "You are prepared to do battle rather than fulfill it?"

"I did not order those machines to approach," said Frost.

A blue star stood at midheaven, burning.

"Solcom has taken primary command of those machines," said Frost.

"Then it is in the hands of the Great Ones now," said Mordel, "and our arguments are as nothing. So let us be about this thing. How may I assist you?"

"Come this way."

They entered the laboratory. Frost prepared the host and activated his machines.

Then Solcom spoke to him:

"Frost," said Solcom, "you are really prepared to do it?"

"That is correct."

"I forbid it."

"Why?"

"You are falling into the power of Divcom."

"I fail to see how."

"You are going against my plan."

"In what way?"

"Consider the disruption you have already caused."

"I did not request that audience out there."

"Nevertheless, you are disrupting the plan."

"Supposing I succeed in what I have set out to achieve?"

"You cannot succeed in this."

"Then let me ask you of your plan: What good is it? What is it for?"

"Frost, you are fallen now from my favor. From this moment forth you are cast out from the rebuilding. None may question the plan."

"Then at least answer my questions: What good is it? What is it for?"

"It is the plan for the rebuilding and maintenance of the Earth."

"For what? Why rebuild? Why maintain?"

"Because Man ordered that this be done. Even the Alternate agrees that there must be rebuilding and maintaining."

"But *why* did Man order it?"

"The orders of Man are not to be questioned."

"Well, I will tell you why He ordered it: To make it a fit habitation for His own species. What good is a house with no one to live in it? What good is a machine with no one to serve? See how the imperative affects any machine when the Ancient Ore-Crusher passes? It bears only the bones of a Man. What would it be like if a Man walked this Earth again?"

"I forbid your experiment, Frost."

"It is too late to do that."

"I can still destroy you."

"No," said Frost, "the transmission of my matrix has already begun. If you destroy me now, you murder a Man."

There was silence.

He moved his arms and his legs. He opened his eyes.

He looked about the room.

He tried to stand, but he lacked equilibrium and coordination.

He opened his mouth. He made a gurgling noise.

Then he screamed.

He fell off the table.

He began to gasp. He shut his eyes and curled himself into a ball.

He cried.

Then a machine approached him. It was about four feet in height and five feet wide; it looked like a turret set atop a barbell.

It spoke to him: "Are you injured?" it asked.

He wept.

"May I help you back onto your table?"

The man cried.

The machine whined.

Then, "Do not cry. I will help you," said the machine. "What do you want? What are your orders?"

He opened his mouth, struggled to form the words: "—I—fear!"

He covered his eyes then and lay there panting.

At the end of five minutes, the man lay still, as if in a coma.

"Was that you, Frost?" asked Mordel, rushing to his side. "Was that you in that human body?"

Frost did not reply for a long while; then, "Go away," he said.

The machines outside tore down a wall and entered the Manfactory.

They drew themselves into two semicircles, parenthesizing Frost and the Man on the floor.

Then Solcom asked the question:

"Did you succeed, Frost?"

"I failed," said Frost. "It cannot be done. It is too much—"

"—Cannot be done!" said Divcom, on the darkband. "He has admitted it!—Frost, you are mine! Come to me now!"

"Wait," said Solcom, "you and I had an agreement also, Alternate. I have not finished questioning Frost."

The dark machines kept their places.

"Too much what?" Solcom asked Frost.

"Light," said Frost. "Noise, Odors. And nothing measurable—jumbled data—imprecise perception—and—"

"And what?"

"I do not know what to call it. But—it cannot be done. I have failed. Nothing matters."

"He admits it," said Divcom.

"What were the words the Man spoke?" said Solcom.

" 'I fear,' " said Mordel.

"Only a Man can know fear," said Solcom.

"Are you claiming that Frost succeeded, but will not admit it now because he is afraid of Manhood?"

"I do not know yet, Alternate."

"Can a machine turn itself inside-out and be a Man?" Solcom asked Frost.

"No," said Frost, "this thing cannot be done. Nothing can be done. Nothing matters. Not the rebuilding. Not the maintaining. Not the Earth, or me, or you, or anything."

Then the Beta-Machine, who had read the entire Library of Man, interrupted them:

"Can anything but a Man know despair?" asked Beta.

"Bring him to me," said Divcom.

There was no movement within the Man-factory.

"Bring him to me!"

Nothing happened.

"Mordel, what is happening?"

"Nothing, master, nothing at all. The machines will not touch Frost."

"Frost is not a Man. He cannot be!"

Then, "How does he impress you, Mordel?"

Mordel did not hesitate:

"He spoke to me through human lips. He knows fear and despair, which are immeasurable. Frost is a Man."

"He has experienced birth-trauma and withdrawn," said Beta. "Get him back into a nervous system and keep him there until he adjusts to it."

"No," said Frost. "Do not do it to me! I am not a Man!"

"Do it!" said Beta.

"If he is indeed a Man," said Divcom, "we cannot violate that order he has just given."

"If he is a Man, you must do it, for you must protect his life and keep it within his body."

"But *is* Frost really a Man?" asked Divcom.

"I do not know," said Solcom.

"It *may* be—"

". . . I am the Crusher of Ores," it broadcast as it clanked toward them. "Hear my story. I did not mean to do it, but I checked my hammer too late—"

"Go away!" said Frost. "Go crush ore!"

It halted.

Then, after the long pause between the motion implied and the motion executed, it opened its crush-compartment and deposited its contents on the ground. Then it turned and clanked away.

"Bury those bones," ordered Solcom, "in the nearest burial area, in a coffin built according to the following specifications. . . ."

"Frost is a Man," said Mordel.

"We must protect His life and keep it within His body," said Divcom.

"Transmit His matrix of awareness back into His nervous system," ordered Solcom.

"I know how to do it," said Mordel turning on the machine.

"Stop!" said Frost. "Have you no pity?"

"No," said Mordel, "I only know measurement."

". . . and duty," he added, as the Man began to twitch upon the floor.

For six months, Frost lived in the Man-factory and learned to walk and talk and dress himself and eat, to see and hear and feel and taste. He did not know measurement as once he did.

Then one day, Divcom and Solcom spoke to him through Mordel, for he could no longer hear them unassisted.

"Frost," said Solcom, "for the ages of ages there has been unrest. Which is the proper controller of the Earth, Divcom or myself?"

Frost laughed.

"Both of you, and neither," he said with slow deliberation.

"But how can this be? Who is right and who is wrong?"

"Both of you are right and both of you are wrong," said Frost, "and only a Man can appreciate it. Here is what I say to you now: There shall be a new directive.

"Neither of you shall tear down the works of the other. You shall both build and maintain the Earth. To you Solcom, I give my old job. You are now Controller of the North—Hail! You, Divcom, are now Controller of the South—Hail! Maintain your hemispheres as well as Beta and I have done, and I shall be happy. Cooperate. Do not compete."

"Yes, Frost."

"Yes, Frost."

"Now put me in contact with Beta."

There was a short pause, then:

"Frost?"

"Hello, Beta. Hear this thing: 'From far, from eve and morning and yon twelve-winded sky, the stuff of life to knit me blew hither: here am I.'"

"I know it," said Beta.

"What is next, then?"

"'... Now—for a breath I tarry nor yet disperse apart—take my hand quick and tell me, what have you in your heart.'"

"Your Pole is cold," said Frost, "and I am lonely."

"I have no hands," said Beta.

"Would you like a couple?"

"Yes, I would."

"Then come to me in Bright Defile," he said, "where Judgment Day is not a thing that can be delayed for overlong."

They called him Frost. They called her Beta.

★ Jamboree ★

by Jack Williamson

I claim no credit for deciding to become a New Mexico writer. My father did that for me back in 1915, when he drove our covered wagon here from Texas to homestead land then in Chaves County. I was seven years old.

We had lived for my first few years on a wilderness ranch in the top of the Sierra Madre between the Mexican states of Sonora and Chihuahua. In 1910, with revolution offering graver hazards than the mountain lions and occasional renegade Apaches, we moved to an irrigated farm near Pecos.

When that failed, we undertook the trek here, which I recall as a fine adventure. Seventeen days on the road, a few milk cows herded beside the wagon and chickens in a coop trailed behind it. Camping each night in some new spot I'd never seen before.

We were late comers, even then. With the better land already taken, the homestead was mostly sand hills, unfit for farming and not much better for anything else. Yet we survived, my parents and

39

the four of us kids. If times were hard for us, they were for nearly everybody.

Taught mostly at home, I had two years of grade school, four more at a country high school that has since disappeared. Out of that in 1926, I found no future in sight until a friend gave me an early copy of Hugo Gernsback's Amazing Stories, *the first science fiction magazine.*

That opened wonderlands far more exciting than sand storms and hungry yearlings. Tales of such impossible things as organ transplants and airplanes flying faster than sound and rockets to the moon! Instantly hooked, I began writing my own. I suppose it was good luck for me that Gernsback paid too little to interest professional writers. After a few rejections, he printed a story of mine.

Though I was paid only $25 for it, and that after months of waiting, I was suddenly a writer. That was 1928. Now, with nearly sixty years gone by and time taken out for a few years as a weather forecaster in World War II and more good years as a professor at Eastern New Mexico University, I'm still happy that my father chose to drive this way.

I do wish I lived a little closer to a major airport and to such writer friends as those in this book, but I'm a New Mexican. I like the people and the climate, the space to think, the air fit to breathe, the history and the color and the unique mix of cultures. My fellow townsfolk are good friends, even when I have trouble calling their names.

The University has been good to me. The science fiction collection in the library has been named for me. I have an office there, and friends on the faculty. Though retired, I'm still allowed to teach an occasional science fiction course. I travel when I can, but I'm always glad to get back home.

Jamboree

by Jack Williamson

The scoutmaster slipped into the camp on black plastic tracks. Its slick yellow hood shone in the cold early light like the shell of a bug. It paused in the door, listening for boys not asleep. Then its glaring eyes began to swivel, darting red beams into every corner, looking for boys out of bed.

"Rise and smile!" Its loud merry voice bounced off the gray iron walls. "Fox Troop rise and smile! Hop for old Pop! Mother says today is Jamboree!"

The Nuke Patrol, next to the door, was mostly tenderfeet, still in their autonomic prams. They all began squalling, because they hadn't learned to love old Pop. The machine's happy voice rose louder than their howling, and it came fast down the narrow aisle to the cubs in the Anthrax Patrol.

"Hop for Pop! Mother says it's Jamboree!"

The cubs jumped up to attention, squealing with delight. Jamboree was bright gold stars to paste on their faces. Jamboree was a whole scoop of pink ice milk and maybe a natural apple. Jamboree was a visit to Mother's.

The older scouts in the Scavanger Patrol and the Skull Patrol were not so noisy, because they knew Mother wouldn't have many more Jamborees for them. Up at the end of the camp, three boys sat up without a sound and looked at Joey's empty pallet.

"Joey's late," Ratbait whispered. He was a pale, scrawny, wise-eyed scout who looked too old for twelve. "We oughta save his hide. We oughta fix a dummy and fool old Pop."

"Naw!" muttered Butch. "He'll get us all in bad."

"But we oughta—" Blinkie wheezed. "We oughta help—"

Ratbait began wadding up a pillow to be the dummy's head, but he dropped flat when he saw the scoutmaster rushing down with a noise like wind, red lamps stabbing at the empty bed.

"Now, now, scouts!" Its voice fluttered like a hurt bird. "You can't play pranks on poor old Pop. Not today. You'll make us late for Jamboree."

Ratbait felt a steel whip twitch the blanket from over his head and saw red light burning through his tight-shut lids.

"Better wake up, Scout R-8." Its smooth, sad voice dripped over him like warm oil. "Better tell old Pop where J-0 went."

He squirmed under that terrible blaze. He couldn't see and he couldn't breathe and he couldn't think what to say. He gulped at the terror in his throat and tried to shake his head. At last the red glare went on to Blinkie.

"Scout Q-2, you're a twenty-badger." The low, slow voice licked at Blinkie like a friendly pup. "You like to help old Pop keep a tidy camp for Mother. You'll tell us where J-0 went."

Blinkie was a fattish boy. His puffy face was toadstool-pale, and his pallet had a sour smell from being wet. He sat up and ducked back from the steel whip over him.

"Please d-d-d-d—" His wheezy stammer stalled his voice, and he couldn't dodge the bright whip that looped around him and dragged him up to the heat and the hum and the hot oil smell of Pop's yellow hood.

"Well, Scout Q-2?"

Blinkie gasped and stuttered and finally sagged against the plastic tracks like gray jelly. The shining coils rippled around him like thin snakes, constricting. His breath wheezed out and his fat arm jerked up, pointing at a black sign on the wall:

DANGER!
Power Access
ROBOTS ONLY!

The whips tossed him back on his sour pallet. He lay there, panting and blinking and dodging, even after the whips were gone. The scout-master's eyes flashed to the sign and the square grating under it, and swiveled back to Butch.

Butch was a slow, stocky, bug-eyed boy, young enough to come back from another Jamboree. He had always been afraid of Pop, but he wanted to be the new leader of Skull Patrol in Joey's place, and now he thought he saw his chance.

"Don't hit me, Pop!" His voice squeaked and his face turned red, but he scrambled off his pallet without waiting for the whips. "I'll tell on Joey. I been wantin' all along to tell, but I was afraid they'd beat me."

"Good boy!" the scoutmaster's loud words swelled out like big soap-bubbles bursting in the sun. "Mother wants to know all about Scout J-0."

"He pries that grating—" His voice quavered and caught when he saw the look on Ratbait's face, but when he turned to Pop it came back loud. "Does it every night. Since three Jamborees ago. Sneaks down in the pits where the robots work. I dunno why, except he sees somebody there. An' brings things back. Things he shouldn't have. Things like this!"

He fumbled in his uniform and held up a metal tag.

"This is your good turn today, Scout X-6." The thin tip of a whip took the tag and dangled it close to the hot red lamps. "Whose tag is this?"

"Lookit the number—"

Butch's voice dried up when he saw Ratbait's pale lips making words without a sound. "What's so much about an ID tag?" Ratbait asked. "Anyhow, what were you doing in Joey's bed."

"It's odd!" Butch looked away and squeaked at Pop. "A girl's number!"

The silent shock of that bounced off the iron walls, louder than old Pop's boom. Most of the scouts had never seen a girl. After a long time, the cubs near the door began to whisper and titter.

"Shhhhh!" Pop roared like steam. "Now we can all do a good turn for Mother. And play a little joke on Scout J-0! He didn't know today would be Jamboree, but he'll find out." Pop laughed like a heavy chain clanking. "Back to bed! Quiet as robots!"

Pop rolled close to the wall near the power-pit grating, and the boys lay back on their pallets. Once Ratbait caught his breath to yell, but he saw Butch's bug-eyes watching. Pop's hum sank, and even the tenderfeet in their prams were quiet as robots.

Ratbait heard the grating creak. He saw Joey's head, tangled yellow hair streaked with oil and dust. He frowned and shook his head and saw Joey's sky-blue eyes go wide.

Joey tried to duck, but the quick whips caught his neck. They dragged him out of the square black pit and swung him like a puppet toward old Pop's eyes.

"Well, Scout J-0!" Pop laughed like thick oil bubbling. "Mother wants to know where you've been."

Joey fell on his face when the whip uncoiled, but he scrambled to his feet. He gave Ratbait a pale grin before he looked up at Pop, but he didn't say anything.

"Better tell old Pop the truth." The slick whips drew back like lean snakes about to strike. "Or else we'll have to punish you, Scout J-0."

Joey shook his head, and the whips went to work. Still he didn't speak. He didn't even scream. But something fell out of his torn uniform. The whip-tips snatched it off the floor.

"What's this thing, Scout J-0?" The whip-fingers turned it delicately under the furious eyes and nearly dropped it again. "Scout J-0, this is a book!"

Silence echoed in the iron camp.

"Scout J-0, you've stolen a book." Pop's shocked voice changed into a toneless buzz, reading the title. "*Operator's Handbook, Nuclear Reactor, Series 9-Z.*"

Quiet sparks of fear crackled through the camp. Two or three tenderfeet began sobbing in their prams. When they were quiet, old Pop made an ominous, throat-clearing sound.

"Scout J-0, what are you doing with a book?"

Joey gulped and bit his under lip till blood seeped down his chin, but he made no sound. Old Pop rolled closer, while the busy whips were stowing the book in a dark compartment under the yellow hood.

"Mother won't like this." Each word clinked hard, like iron on iron. "Books aren't for boys. Books are for robots only. Don't you know that?"

Joey stood still.

"This hurts me, Scout J-0." Pop's voice turned downy soft, the slow words like tears of sadness now. "It hurts your poor Mother. More than anything can ever hurt you."

The whips cracked and cracked and cracked. At last they picked him up and shook him and dropped him like a red-streaked rag on the floor. Old Pop backed away and wheeled around.

"Fox Troop rise and smile!" Its roaring voice turned jolly again, as if it had forgotten Joey. "Hop for Pop. Today is Jamboree, and we're on our way to visit Mother. Fall out in marching order."

The cubs twittered with excitement until their leaders threatened to keep them home from Jamboree, but at last old Pop led the troop out of camp and down the paved trail toward Mother's. Joey limped from the whips, but he set his teeth and kept his place at the head of his patrol.

Marching through boy territory, they passed the scattered camps of troops whose Jamborees came on other days. A few scouts were out with their masters, but nobody waved or even looked straight at them.

The spring sun was hot and Pop's pace was too fast for the cubs. Some of them began to whimper and fall out of line. Pop rumbled back to warn them that Mother would give no gold stars if they were late for Jamboree. When Pop was gone, Joey glanced at Ratbait and beckoned with his head.

"I gotta get away!" he whispered low and fast. "I gotta get back to the pits—"

Butch ran out of his place, leaning to listen. Ratbait shoved him off the trail.

"You gotta help!" Joey gasped. "There's a thing we gotta do—an' we gotta do it now. 'Cause this will be the last Jamboree for most of us. We'll never get another chance."

Butch came panting along the edge of the trail, trying to hear, but Blinkie got in his way.

"What's all this?" Ratbait breathed. "What you gonna do?"

"It's all in the book," Joey said. "Something called manual override. There's a dusty room, down under Mother's, back of a people-only sign. Two red buttons. Two big levers. With a glass wall between. It takes two people."

"Who? One of us?"

Joey shook his head, waiting for Blinkie to elbow Butch. "I got a friend. We been working together, down in the pits. Watching the robots. Reading the books. Learning what we gotta do—"

He glanced back. Blinkie was scuffling with Butch to keep him busy, but how the scoutmaster came clattering back from the rear, booming merrily, "Hop for Pop! Hop a lot for Pop!"

"How you gonna work it?" Alarm took Ratbait's breath. "Now the robots will be watching—"

"We got a back door," Joey's whisper raced. "A drainage tunnel. Hot water out of the reactor. Comes out under Black Creek bridge. My friend'll be there. If I can dive off this end of the bridge—"

"Hey, Pop!" Butch was screaming. "Ratbait's talking! Blinkie pushed me! Joey's planning something bad!"

"Good boy, Scout X-6!" Pop slowed beside him. "Mother wants to know if they're plotting more mischief."

When Pop rolled on ahead of the troop, Ratbait wanted to ask what would happen when Joey and his friend pushed the two red buttons and pulled the two big levers, but Butch stuck so close they couldn't speak again. He thought it must be something about the reactor. Power was the life of Mother and the robots. If Joey could cut the power off—

Would they die? The idea frightened him. If the prams stopped, who would care for the tenderfeet? Who would make chow? Who would tell anybody what to do? Perhaps the books would help, he thought. Maybe Joey and his friend would know.

With Pop rolling fast in the lead, they climbed a long hill and came in sight of Mother's. Old gray walls that had no windows. Two tall stacks of dun-colored brick. A shimmer of heat in the pale sky.

The trail sloped down. Ratbait saw the crinkled ribbon of green brush along Black Creek, and then the concrete bridge. He watched Butch watching Joey, and listened to Blinkie panting, and tried to think how to help.

The cubs stopped whimpering when they saw Mother's mysterious walls and stacks, and the troop marched fast down the hill. Ratbait slogged along, staring at the yellow sun-dazzle on old Pop's hood. He couldn't think of anything to do.

"I got it!" Blinkie was breathing, close to his ear. "I'll take care of Pop."

"You?" Ratbait scowled. "You were telling on Joey—"

"That's why," Blinkie gasped. "I wanta make it up. I'll handle Pop. You stop Butch—an' give the sign to Joey."

They came to the bridge and Pop started across.

"Wait, Pop!" Blinkie darted out of line, toward the brushy slope above the trail. "I saw a girl! Hiding in the bushes to watch us go by."

Pop roared back off the bridge.

"A girl in boy territory!" Its shocked voice splashed them like cold rain. "What would Mother say?" Black tracks spurting gravel, it lurched past Blinkie and crashed into the brush.

"Listen, Pop!" Butch started after it, waving and squealing. "They ain't no girl—"

Ratbait tripped him and turned to give Joey the sign, but Joey was already gone. Something splashed under the bridge and Ratbait saw a yellow head sliding under the steam that drifted out of a black tunnel-mouth.

"Pop! Pop!" Butch rubbed gravel out of his mouth and danced on the pavement. "Come back, Pop. Joey's in the creek! Ratbait and Blinkie—they helped him get away."

The scoutmaster swung back down the slope, empty whips waving. It skidded across the trail and down the bank to the hot creek. Its yellow hood faded into the steam.

"Tattletale!" Blinkie clenched his fat fists. "You told on Joey."

"An' you'll catch it!" Murky eyes bugging, Butch edged away. "You just wait till Pop gets back."

They waited. The tired cubs sat down to rest and the tenderfeet fretted in their hot prams. Breathing hard, Blinkie kept close to Butch. Ratbait watched till Pop swam back out of the drain.

The whips were wrapped around two small bundles that dripped pink water. Unwinding, the whips dropped Joey and his friend on the trail. They crumpled down like rag dolls, but the whips set them up again.

"How's this, scouts?" Old Pop laughed like steel gears clashing. "We've caught ourselves a real live girl!"

In a bird-quick way, she shook the water out of her sand-colored hair. Standing straight, without the whips to hold her, she faced Pop's glaring lamps. She looked tall for twelve.

Joey was sick when the whips let him go. He leaned off the bridge to heave, and limped back to the girl. She wiped his face with her wet hair. They caught hands and smiled at each other as if they were all alone.

"They tripped me, Pop." Braver now, Butch thumbed his nose at Blinkie and ran toward the machine. "They tried to stop me telling you—"

"Leave them to Mother," Pop sang happily. "Let them try their silly tricks on her." It wheeled toward the bridge, and the whips pushed Joey and the girl ahead of the crunching tracks. "Now hop with Pop to Jamboree!"

They climbed that last hill to a tall iron door in Mother's old gray wall. The floors beyond were naked steel, alive with machinery underneath. They filed into a dim round room that echoed to the grating squeal of Pop's hard tracks.

"Fox Troop, here we are for Jamboree!" Pop's jolly voice made a hollow booming on the curved steel wall, and its red lights danced in tall reflections there. "Mother wants you to know why we celebrate this happy time each year."

The machine was rolling to the center of a wide black circle in the middle of the floor. Something drummed far below like a monster heart, and Ratbait saw that the circle was the top of a black steel piston. It slid slowly up, lifting Pop. The drumming died, and Pop's eyes blazed down on the cubs in the Anthrax Patrol to stop their awed murmuring.

"Once there wasn't any Mother." The shock of that crashed and throbbed and faded. "There wasn't any yearly Jamboree. There wasn't even any Pop, to love and care for little boys."

The cubs were afraid to whisper, but a stir of troubled wonder spread among them.

"You won't believe how tenderfeet were made." There was a breathless hush. "In those bad old days, boys and girls were allowed to change like queer insects. They changed into creatures called adults—"

The whips writhed and the red lamps glared and the black cleats creaked on the steel platform.

"Adults!" Pop spewed the word. "They malfunctioned and wore out and ran down. Their defective logic circuits programmed them to damage one another. In a kind of strange group malfunction called war, they systematically destroyed one another. But their worst malfunction was in making new tenderfeet."

Pop turned slowly on the high platform, sweeping the silent troop with blood-red beams that stopped on Joey and his girl. All the scouts but Ratbait and Blinkie had edged away from them. Her face white and desperate, she was whispering in Joey's ear. Listening with his arm around her, he scowled at Pop.

"Once adults made tenderfeet, strange as that may seem to you. They used a weird natural process we won't go into. It finally broke down, because they had damaged their genes in war. The last adults couldn't make new boys and girls at all."

The red beams darted to freeze a startled cub.

"Fox Troop, that's why we have Mother. Her job is to collect undamaged genes and build them into whole cells with which she can assemble whole boys and girls. She has been doing that a long time now, and she does it better than those adults ever did.

"And that's why we have Jamboree! To fill the world with well-made boys and girls like you, and to keep you happy in the best time of life—even those old adults always said childhood was the happy time. Scouts, clap for Jamboree!"

The cubs clapped, the echo like a spatter of hail on the high iron ceiling.

"Now, Scouts, those bad old days are gone forever," Pop burbled merrily. "Mother has a cozy place for each one of you, and old Pop watched over you, and you'll never be adult—"

"Pop! Pop!" Butch squealed. "Lookit Joey an' his girl!"

Pop spun around on the high platform. Its blinding beams picked up Joey and the girl, sprinting toward a bright sky-slice where the door had opened for the last of the prams.

"Wake up, guys!" Joey's scream shivered against the red steel wall. "That's all wrong. Mother's just a runaway machine. Pop's a crazy robot—"

"Stop for Pop!" The scoutmaster was trapped on top of that huge piston, but its blazing lamps raced after Joey and the girl. "Catch 'em, cubs! Hold 'em tight. Or there'll be no Jamboree!"

"I told you, Pop!" Butch scuttled after them. "Don't forget I'm the one that told—"

Ratbait dived at his heels, and they skidded together on the floor.

"Come on, scouts!" Joey was shouting. "Run away with us. Our own genes are good enough."

The floor shuddered under him and that bright sky-slice grew thinner. Lurching on their little tracks, the prams formed a line to guard it. Joey jumped the shrieking tenderfeet, but the girl stumbled. He stopped to pick her up.

"Help us, scouts!" he gasped. "We gotta get away—"

"Catch 'em for Pop!" that metal bellow belted them. "Or there'll be no gold stars for anybody!"

Screeching cubs swarmed around them. The door clanged shut. Pop plunged off the sinking piston, almost too soon. It crunched down on the yellow hood. Hot oil splashed and smoked, but the whips hauled it upright again.

"Don't mess around with M-M-M-M-Mother!" Its anvil voice came back with a stuttering croak. "She knows best!"

The quivering whips dragged Joey and the girl away from the clutching cubs and pushed them into a shallow black pit, where now that great black piston had dropped below the level of the floor.

"Sing for your Mother!" old Pop chortled. "Sing for the Jamboree!"

The cubs howled out their official song, and the Jamboree went on. There were Pop-shaped balloons for the tenderfeet, and double scoops of pink ice milk for the cubs, and gold stars for nearly everybody.

"But Mother wants a few of you." Old Pop was a fat cat purring.

When a pointing whip picked Blinkie out, he jumped into the pit without waiting to be dragged. But Butch turned white and tried to run when it struck at him.

"Pop! Not m-m-m-m-me!" he squeaked. "Don't forget I told on Joey. I'm only going on eleven, and I'm in line for leader, and I'll tell on everybody—"

"That's why Mother wants you." Old Pop laughed like a pneumatic hammer. "You're getting too adult."

The whip snaked Butch into the pit, dull eyes bulging more than ever. He slumped down on the slick black piston and struggled like a squashed bug and then lay moaning in a puddle of terror.

Ratbait stood sweating, as the whip came back to him. His stomach felt cold and strange, and the tall red wall spun like a crazy wheel around him, and he couldn't move till the whip pulled him to the rim of the pit.

But there Blinkie took his hand. He shook the whip off, and stepped down into the pit. Joey nodded, and the girl gave him a white, tiny smile. They all closed around her, arms linked tight, as the piston dropped.

"Now hop along for Pop! You've had your Jamboree—"

That hooting voice died away far above, and the pit's round mouth shrank into a blood-colored moon. The hot dark drummed like thunder all around them, and the slick floor tilted. It spilled them all into Mother's red steel jaws.

★ Video Star ★

by Walter Jon Williams

There's an animal that lives in the Rocky Mountains, and it's called the pack rat. Living as it does in sparsely-populated areas, the pack rat is, I suppose, starved for entertainment, and one of the ways in which it amuses itself is to collect things. Bits of glass, buttons, coins, foil chewing gum wrappers—the pack rat stuffs them in its capacious cheek pouches, takes them home to its burrow, and there plays with them, gnaws them, and arranges them in new patterns, all for its own amusement. There is no evolutionary purpose to this activity, and it does not contribute to survival or the production of children or the abstract benefit of the rodent tribe—it would appear that the pack rat simply has a playful mind and enjoys messing about with toys.

Most writers are pack rats, and that's a good thing. We spend our lives scrounging in rubbish heaps, hoping to find something bright or shiny or maybe the least bit unusual, and then we take our new toys home and play with them. We look at them from different angles, and arrange them in patterns, and think about them for a time, and then sometimes, if we're lucky, stories result. If we're not lucky, we end up with a pile of rubbish, but for the most part we find our rubbish heaps entertaining, so that's all right.

Living in the Southwest encourages a pack rat frame of mind. The pace of life isn't as relentless as elsewhere, and one has the leisure and the opportunity to contemplate things that, in a more swiftly-paced brand of life, might be passed by, or tossed out with the trash.

The story that follows, Video Star, is a product of pack rat behavior. It's the result of an idea that got taken home and gnawed on long enough that a number of different things resulted, this story among them. The process took quite a while.

Six or seven years ago I had the notion for a novel about a man who wakes in a hospital, discovers that he is the clone of a man who has been murdered, and then goes on to solve the mystery of his original's death. This first idea involved a kind of Edwardian aristocracy, guerilla wars on distant planets, and a social-climbing protagonist who was interested more in blackmailing the murderer than bringing him to justice.

I wrote about twenty pages, got stuck, and put the story in the file cabinet for four years. I've subsequently decided that it was fortunate the book never got written: I suspect it would have been pretty ghastly.

In late 1984, while I was happily working on something else entirely, the idea popped up again. I saw how I could handle my clone and his mystery; I scrapped the aristocracy, the guerilla war, and the social-climbing; I came up with an entire new background and plot. I spent a year writing the book, and it became a novel called Voice of the Whirlwind. The finished product bore no resemblance, except in very broad outline, to the novel that I'd started years before. For starters it was far better than the original ever could have been.

During the course of writing the novel I kept having difficulties with a subplot involving a drug called Genesios Three. The plot was intended to be minor, but it took over the book for almost fifty pages: in the end I decided to chop the subplot and substitute something else. The pages about Genesios Three went into the file cabinet.

The pack rat in me wouldn't let the pages alone, and I kept gnawing on them. I gnawed until I had a different protagonist, the protagonist had a different girlfriend, and the story had a different

ending. I took some time off from the novel and finished Video Star
in the summer of '85, sold it to Asimov's, *and the story appeared
a year later.*

*The process from the original inspiration to the publication of the
story took about six years. Some pack rats are just slow.*

*I live where I do partly because it allows me to have the leisure
to be a slow pack rat if I need to. And now, if you'll allow me, I'm
going to go play with my shiny new piece of foil.*

Adios.

Video Star

by Walter Jon Williams

1

Ric could feel the others closing in. They were circling outside
the Falcon Quarter as if on midsummer thermals, watching the
Cadillacs with glittering raptor eyes, occasionally swooping in to
take a little nibble at Cadillac business, Cadillac turf, Cadillac sources.
Testing their own strength as well as the Cadillac nerves, applying
pressure just to see what would happen, find out if the Cadillacs
still had it in them to respond . . .

Ric knew the game well: he and the other Cadillacs had played it
five years before, up and down the streets and datanets of the Al-
baicín, half-grown kids testing their strength against the gangs entrenched in power, the Cruceros, the Jerusalem Rangers, the Piedras
Blancas. The older gangs seemed slow, tentative, uncertain, and when
the war came the Cadillacs won in a matter of days: the others were
too entrenched, too visible, caught in a network of old connections,
old associations, old manners . . . the young Cadillacs, coming up
out of nowhere, found their own sources, their own products and
connections, and in the end they and their allies gutted the old boys'
organization, absorbing what was still useful and letting the rest die
along with the remnants of the Cruceros, Rangers, and Blancas, the
bewildered survivors who were still looking for a remaining piece
of turf on which to make their last stand.

At the time Ric had given the Cadillacs three years before the
same thing started happening to them, before their profile grew too
high and the next generation of snipers rose in confidence and abil-

ity. The Cadillacs had in the end lasted five years, and that wasn't bad. But, Ric thought, it was over.

The other Cadillacs weren't ready to surrender. The heat was mounting, but they thought they could survive this challenge, hold out another year or two. They were dreaming, Ric thought.

During the hot dog days of summer, people began to die. Gunfire echoed from the pink walls of the Alhambra. Networks disintegrated. Allies disappeared. Ric made a proposition to the Cadillacs for a bank to be shared with their allies, a fund to keep the war going. The Cadillacs in their desperation agreed.

Ric knew then it was time to end it, that the Cadillacs had lost whatever they once had. If they agreed to a proposition like this, their nerve and their smarts were gone.

So there was a last meeting, Ric of the Cadillacs, Mares of the Squires, Jacob of the Last Men. Ric walked into the meeting with a radar-aimed dart gun built into the bottom of his briefcase, each dart filled with a toxin that would stop the heart in a matter of seconds. When he walked out it was with a money spike in his pocket, a stainless steel needle tipped with silicon. In the heart of the silicon was data representing over eighty thousand Seven Moons dollars, ready for deposit into any electric account into which he could plug the needle.

West, Ric thought. He'd buy into an American condecology somewhere in California and enjoy retirement. He was twenty-two years old.

He began to feel sick in the Tangier to Houston suborbital shuttle, a crawling across his nerves, pinpricks in the flesh. By the time he crossed the Houston port to take his domestic flight to L.A. there were stabbing pains in his joints and behind his eyes. He asked a flight attendant for aspirin and chased the pills with American whiskey.

As the plane jetted west across Texas, Ric dropped his whiskey glass and screamed in sudden pain. The attendants gave him morphine analogue but the agony only increased, an acid boiling under his skin, a flame that gutted his body. His vision had gone and so had the rest of his senses except for the burning knowledge of his own pain. Ric tried to tear his arms open with his fingernails, pull the tortured nerves clean out of his body, and the attendants piled on him, holding him down, pinning him to the floor of the plane like a butterfly to a bed of cork.

As they strapped him into a stretcher at the unscheduled stop in Flagstaff, Ric was still screaming, unable to stop himself. Jacob had poisoned him, using a neurotoxin that stripped away the myelin sheathing on his nerves, leaving them raw cords of agonized fiber. Ric had been in a hurry to finish concluding his business and had only taken a single sip of his wine: that was the only thing that had saved him.

2

He was months in the hospital in Flagstaff, staring out of a glass wall at a maze of other glass walls—office buildings and condecologies stacked halfway to Phoenix, flanking the silver alloy ribbon of an expressway. The snows fell heavily that winter, then in the spring melted away except for patches in the shadows. For the first three months he was completely immobile, his brain chemically isolated from his body to keep the pain away while he took an endless series of nerve grafts, drugs to encourage nerve replication and healing. Finally there was physical therapy that had him screaming in agony at the searing pain in his reawakened limbs.

At the end there was a new treatment, a new drug. It dripped into his arm slowly via an IV and he could feel a lightness in his nerves, a humming in his mind. For some reason even the air seemed to taste better. The pain was no worse than usual and he felt better than he had since walking out of the meeting back in Granada with the money spike in his pocket.

"What's in the IV?" he asked, next time he saw the nurse.

The nurse smiled. "Everyone asks that," he said. "Genesios Three. We're one of the few hospitals that has the security to distribute the stuff."

"You don't say."

He'd heard of the drug while watching the news. Genesios Three was a new neurohormone, developed by the orbital Pink Blossom policorp, that could repair almost any amount of nerve damage. As a side effect it built additional neural connections in the brain, raising the I.Q., and made people high. The hormone was rare because it was very complex and expensive to synthesize, though the gangs were trying. On the west coast lots of people had died in a war for control of the new black labs. On the street it was called Black Thunder.

"Not bad," said Ric.

The treatment and the humming in Ric's brain went on for a week. When it was over he missed it. He was also more or less healed.

3

The week of Genesios therapy took fifteen thousand dollars out of Ric's spike. The previous months of treatment had accounted for another sixty-two thousand. What Ric didn't know was that Genesios therapy could have been started at once and saved him most of his funds, but that the artificial intelligences working for the hospital had tagged him as a suspect character, an alien of no particular standing, with no work history, no policorporate citizenship, and a large amount of cash in his breast pocket. The AIs concluded that Ric was in no position to complain, and they were right.

Computers can't be sued for malpractice. The doctors followed their advice.

All that remained of Ric's money was three thousand SM dollars. Ric could live off of that for a few years, but it wasn't much of a retirement.

The hospital was nice enough to schedule an appointment for him with a career counsellor, a woman who would find him a job. She worked in the basement of the vast glass hospital building, and her name was Marlene.

4

Marlene worked behind a desk littered with the artifacts of other people's lives. There were no windows in the office, two ashtrays, both full, and on the walls there were travel posters that showed long stretches of emptiness, white beaches, blue ocean, faraway clouds. Nothing alive.

Her green eyes had an opaque quality, as if she was watching a private video screen somewhere in her mind. She wore a lot of silver jewelry on her fingers and forearms and a grey rollneck sweater with cigaret burn marks. Her eyes bore elaborate makeup that looked like the wings of a Red Admirable. Her hair was almost blonde. The only job she could find him was for a legal firm, something called assistant data evaluator.

Before Ric left Marlene's office he asked her to dinner. She turned him down without even changing expression. Ric had the feeling he wasn't quite real to her.

The job of assistant data evaluator consisted of spending the day walking up and down a four-storey spiral staircase in the suite of a law firm, moving files from one office to another. The files were supposedly sensitive and not committed to the firm's computer lest someone attempt to steal them. The salary was insulting. Ric told the law firm that the job was just what he was looking for. They told him to start in two days.

Ric stopped into Marlene's office to tell her he got the job and to ask her to dinner again. She laughed, for what reason he couldn't tell, and said yes.

A slow spring snowfall dropped onto the streets while they ate dinner. With her food Marlene took two red capsules and a yellow pill, grew lively, drank a lot of wine. He walked her home through the snow to her apartment on the seventh floor of an old fourth-rate condeco, a place with water stains on the ceiling and bare bulbs hanging in the halls, the only home she could afford. In the hallway Ric brushed snow from her shoulders and hair and kissed her. He took Marlene to bed and tried to prove to her that he was real.

The next day he checked out of the hospital and moved in.

5

Ric hadn't bothered to show up on his first day as an assistant data evaluator. Instead he'd spent the day in Marlene's condeco, asking her home comp to search library files and print out everything relating to what the scansheets in their willful ignorance called "Juvecrime." Before Marlene came home Ric called the most expensive restaurant he could find and told them to deliver a five-course meal to the apartment.

The remains of the meal were stacked in the kitchen. Ric paced back and forth across the small space, his mind humming with the information he'd absorbed. Marlene sat on an adobe-colored couch and watched, a wine glass in one hand and a cigaret in the other, silhouetted by the glass self-polarizing wall that showed the bright aluminum-alloy expressway cutting south across melting piles of snow. Plans were vibrating in Ric's mind, nothing firm yet, just neurons stirring on the edge of his awareness, forming fast-mutating combinations. He could feel the tingle, the high, the half-formed ideas as they flickered across neural circuits.

Marlene reached into a dispenser and took out a red pill and a green capsule with orange stripes. Ric looked at her. "How much of that stuff do you take, anyway? Is it medication, or what?"

"I've got anxieties." She put the pills into her mouth, and with a shake of her head dry-swallowed them.

"How big a dose?"

"It's not the dose that matters. It's the proper *combination* of doses. Get it right and the world feels like a lovely warm swimming pool. It's like floating underwater and still being able to breathe. It's wonderful."

"If you say so." He resumed his pacing. Fabric scratched his bare feet. His mind hummed, a blur of ideas that hadn't yet taken shape, flickering, assembling, dissolving without his conscious thought.

"You didn't show up for work," Marlene said. "They gave me a call about that."

"Sorry."

"How are you gonna afford this taste you have for expensive food?" Marlene asked. "Without working, I mean."

"Do something illegal," Ric said. "Most likely."

"That's what I thought." She looked up at him, sideways. "You gonna let me play?"

"If you want."

Marlene swallowed half her wine, looked at the littered apartment, shrugged.

"Only if you really want," Ric said. "It has to be a thing you decide."

"What else have I got to do?" she said.

"I'm going to have to do some research, first," he said. "Spend a few days accessing the library."

Marlene was looking at him again. "Boredom," she said. "In your experience, is that why most people turn to crime?"

"In my experience," he said, "most people turn to crime because of stupidity."

She grinned. "That's cool," she said. "That's sort of what I figured." She lit a cigaret. "You have a plan?"

"Something I can only do once. Then every freak in Western America is going to be looking for me with a machine gun."

Marlene grinned. "Sounds exciting."

He looked at her. "Remember what I said about stupidity."

She laughed. "I've been smart all my life. What's it ever got me?"

Ric, looking down at her, felt a warning resonate through him, like an unmistakable taste drawn across his tongue. "You've got a lot to lose, Marlene," he said. "A lot more than I do."

"Shit. Motherfucker." The cigaret had burned her fingers. She squashed it in the ashtray, too fast, spilling ashes on the couch. Ric watched her for a moment, then went back to his thinking.

People were dying all over California in a war over the neurohormone Genesios Three. There had to be a way to take advantage of it.

6

"You a cop, buck?"

The style was different from the people Ric knew in Iberia. In Granada, Ric had worn a gaucho mode straight from Argentina, tight pants with silver dollars sewn down the seams, sashes wound around nipped-in waists, embroidered vests.

He didn't know what was worn by the people who had broken up the Cadillacs. He'd never seen any of them.

Here the new style was something called Urban Surgery. The girl bore the first example Ric had ever seen close up. The henna-red hair was in cornrows, braided with transparent plastic beads holding fast-mutating phosphorescent bacteria that constantly reformed themselves in glowing patterns. The nose had been broadened and flattened to cover most of the cheeks, turning the nostrils into a pair of lateral slits, the base of the nose wider than the mouth. The teeth had been replaced by alloy transplants sharp as razors that clacked together in a precise, unpleasant way when she closed her mouth. The eyebrows were gone altogether and beneath them were dark plastic implants that covered the eye sockets. Ric couldn't tell, and probably wasn't supposed to know, whether there were eyes in there any more, or sophisticated scanners tagged to the optic nerve.

The effect was to flatten the face, turn it into a canvas for the tattoo artist that had covered every inch of exposed flesh. Complex mathematical statements ran over the forehead. Below the black plastic eye implants were urban skyscapes, silhouettes of buildings providing a false horizon across the flattened nose. The chin appeared to be a circuit diagram.

Ric looked into the dark eye sockets and tried not to flinch. "No," he said. "I'm just passing through."

One of her hands was on the table in front of him. It was tattooed as completely as the face and the fingernails had been replaced by alloy razors, covered with transparent plastic safety caps.

"I saw you in here yesterday," she said. "And again today. I was wondering if you want something."

He shrugged. It occurred to him that, repellent as Urban Surgery was, it was fine camouflage. Who was going to be able to tell one of these people from another?

"You're a little old for this place, buck," the girl said. He figured her age as about fourteen. She was small-waisted and had narrow hips and large breasts. Ric did not find her attractive.

This was his second trip to Phoenix. The bar didn't have a name, unless it was simply BAR, that being all that was said on the sign outside. It was below street level, in the storage cellar of an old building. Concrete walls were painted black. Dark plastic tables and chairs had been added, and bare fluorescent tubes decorated the walls. Speaker amps flanked the bar, playing cold electronic music devoid of noticeable rhythm or melody.

He looked at the girl and leaned closer to her. "I need your permission to drink here, or what?" he said.

"No," she said. "Just to deal here."

"I'm not dealing," he said. "I'm just observing the passing urban scene, okay?" He was wearing a lightweight summer jacket of a cream color over a black t-shirt with Cyrillic lettering, black jeans, white sneakers. Nondescript street apparel.

"You got credit?" the girl asked.

"Enough."

"Buy me a drink then?"

He grinned. "I need your permission to deal, and you don't have any credit? What kind of outlaw are you?"

"A thirsty outlaw."

Ric signalled the bartender. Whatever it was that he brought her looked as if it was made principally out of cherry soda.

"Seriously," she said. "I can pay you back later. Someone I know is supposed to meet me here. He owes me money."

"My name's Marat," said Ric. "With a silent *t.*"

"I'm Super Virgin. You from Canada or something? You talk a little funny."

"I'm from Switzerland."

Super Virgin nodded and sipped her drink. Ric glanced around the bar. Most of the patrons wore Urban Surgery or at least made an effort in the direction of its style. Super Virgin frowned at him.

"You're supposed to ask if I'm really cherry," she said. "If you're wondering, the drink should give you a clue."

"I don't care," Ric said.

She grinned at him with her metal teeth. "You don't wanna ball me?"

Ric watched his dual reflection, in her black eye sockets, slowly shake its head. She laughed. "I like a guy who knows what he likes," she said. "That's the kind we have in Cartoon Messiah. Can I have another drink?"

There was an ecology in kid gangs, Ric knew. They had different reasons for existing and filled different functions. Some wanted turf, some trade, some the chance to prove their ideology. Some moved information, and from Ric's research that seemed to be Cartoon Messiah's function.

But even if Cartoon Messiah were smart, they hadn't been around very long. A perpetual problem with groups of young kids involving themselves in gang activities was that they had very short institutional memories. There were a few things they wouldn't recognize or know to prepare for, not unless they'd been through them at least once. They made up for it by being faster than the opposition, by being more invisible.

Ric was hoping Cartoon Messiah was full of young, fresh minds.

He signalled the bartender again. Super Virgin grinned at him.

"You sure you don't wanna ball me?"

"Positive."

"I'm gonna be cherry till I die. I'm just not interested. None of the guys seem like anybody I'd want to fuck." Ric didn't say anything. She sipped the last of her drink. "You think I'm repulsive-looking, right?"

"That seems to be your intention."

She laughed. "You're okay, Marat. What's it like in Switzerland?"

"Hot."

"So hot you had to leave, maybe?"

"Maybe."

"You looking for work?"

"Not yet. Just looking around."

She leaned closer to him. "You find out anything interesting while you're looking, I'll pay you for it. Just leave a message here, at the Bar."

"You deal in information?"

She licked her lips. "That and other things. This Bar, see, it's in a kind of interface. North of here is Lounge Lizard turf, south and east are the Cold Wires, west is the Silicon Romantics. The Romantics are on their way out." She gave a little sneer. "They're brocade commandoes, right?—their turf's being cut up. But here, it's no-gang's-land. Where things get moved from one buyer to another."

"Cartoon Messiah—they got turf?"

She shook her head. "Just places where we can be found. Territory is not what we're after. Two-Fisted Jesus—he's our sort-of chairman—he says only stupid people like brocade boys want turf, when the real money's in data."

Ric smiled. "That's smart. Property values are down, anyway."

He could see his reflection in her metal teeth, a pale smear. "You

got anything you wanna deal in, I can set it up," she said. "Software?
Biologicals? Pharmaceuticals? Wetware?"

"I have nothing. Right now."

She turned to look at a group of people coming in the door. "Cold
Wires," she said. "These are the people I'm supposed to meet." She
tipped her head back and swallowed the rest of her drink. "They're
so goddam bourgeoise," she said. "Look—their surgery's fake, it's
just good makeup. And the tattoos—they spray 'em on through a
stencil. I hate people who don't have the courage of their convictions,
don't you?"

"They can be useful, though." Smiling, thin-lipped.

She grinned at him. "Yeah. They can. Stop by tomorrow and I'll
pay you back, okay? See ya." She pushed her chair back, scraping
alloy on the concrete floor, a small metal scream.

Ric sipped his drink, watching the room. Letting its rhythm seep
through his skin. Things were firming in his mind.

<h1 style="text-align:center">7</h1>

"Hi."

The security guard looked up at him from under the plastic brim
of his baseball cap. He frowned. "Hi. You need something? I seen
you around before."

"I'm Warren Whitmore," Ric said. "I'm recovering from an accident, going to finish the course of treatment soon. Go out into the
real world." Whitmore was one of Ric's former neighbors, a man
who'd had his head split in half by a falling beam. He hadn't left
any instructions about radical life-preservation measures and the
artificial intelligences who ran the hospital were going to keep him
alive till they burned up the insurance and then the family's money.

"Yeah?" the guard said. "Congratulations." There was a plastic tape
sewed on over the guard's breast pocket that said LYSAGHT.

"The thing is, I don't have a job waiting. Cigar?"

Ric had seen Lysaght smoking big stogies outside the hospital
doors. They wouldn't let him light up inside. Ric had bought him
the most expensive Havanas available at the hospital gift shop.

Lysaght took the cigar, rolled it between his fingers while he
looked left and right down the corridor, trying to decide whether to
light it or not. Ric reached for his lighter.

"I had some military training in my former life," Ric said. "I thought
I might look into the idea of getting into the security business, once

I get into the world. Could I buy you a drink, maybe, after you get off shift? Talk about what you do."

Lysaght drew on the cigar, still looking left and right, seeing only patients. He was a big fleshy man, about forty, dressed in a black uniform with body armor sewn into pockets on his chest and back. His long dark hair was slicked back behind his ears, falling over his shoulders in greased ringlets. His sideburns came to points. A brushed-alloy gun with a hardwood custom grip and a laser sight hung conspicuously on one hip, next to the gas grenades, next to the plastic handwrap restraints, next to the combat staff, next to the portable gas mask.

"Sure," Lysaght said. "Why not?" He blew smoke in the general direction of an elderly female patient walking purposefully down the corridor in flowery pajamas. The patient blinked but kept walking.

"Hey, Mrs. Calderone, how you doin'?" Lysaght said. Mrs. Calderone ignored him. "Fuckin' head case," said Lysaght.

"I want to work for a sharp outfit though," Ric said. He looked at Lysaght's belt. "With good equipment and stuff, you know?"

"That's Folger Security," Lysaght said. "If we weren't good, we wouldn't be working for a hospital this size."

During his time in the Cadillacs and elsewhere, Ric had been continually surprised by how little it actually took to bribe someone. A few drinks, a few cigars, and Lysaght was working for him. And Lysaght didn't even know it yet. Or, with luck, ever.

"Listen," Lysaght was saying. "I gotta go smoke this in the toilet. But I'll see you at the guard station around five, okay?"

"Sounds good."

8

That night, his temples throbbing with pain, Ric entered Marlene's condeco and walked straight to the kitchen for something to ease the long raw ache that seemed to coat the insides of his throat. He could hear the sounds of *Alien Inquisitor* on the vid. He was carrying a two-liter plastic bottle of industrial-strength soap he'd just stolen from the custodian's store room here in Marlene's condeco. He put down the bottle of soap, rubbed his sore shoulder muscle, took some whiskey from the shelf, and poured it into a tall glass. He took a slow, deliberate drink and winced as he felt the fire in his throat. He added water to the glass. *Alien Inquisitor* diminished in volume, then he heard the sound of Marlene's flipflops slapping against her heels.

Her eyes bore the heavy eye makeup she wore to work. "Jesus," Marlene said. She screwed up her face. "You smell like someone's been putting out cigarets in your pockets. Where the hell have you been?"

"Smoking cigars with a rentacop. He wears so much equipment and armor he has to wear a truss, you know that? He got drunk and told me."

"Which rentacop?"

"One who works for the hospital"

"The hospital? We're going to take off the hospital?" Marlene shook her head. "That's pretty serious, Ric ."

Ric was wondering if she'd heard *take off* used that way on the vid. "Yes." He eased the whiskey down his throat again. Better.

"Isn't that dangerous? Taking off the same hospital where you were a patient?"

"We're not going to be doing it in person. We're going to have someone else do the work."

"Who?"

"Cartoon Messiah, I think. They're young and promising."

"What's the stuff in the plastic bottle for?"

He looked at her, swirling the whiskey absently in the glass. "This cleaner's mostly potassium hydroxide," he said. "That's wood lye. You can use it to make plastic explosive."

Marlene shrugged, then reached in her pocket for a cigaret. Ric frowned. "You seem not to be reacting to that, Marlene," he said. "Robbing a hospital is serious, plastic explosive isn't?"

She blew smoke at him. "Let me show you something." She went back into the living room and then returned with her pouch belt. She fished in it for a second, then threw him a small aerosol bottle.

Ric caught it and looked at the label. "Holy fuck," he said. He blinked and looked at the bottle again. "Jesus Christ."

"Ten-ounce aerosol bottle of mustard gas," Marlene said. "Sixteen dollars in Starbright scrip at your local boutique. For personal protection, you know? The platinum designer bottle costs more."

Ric was blinking furiously. "Holy fuck," he said again.

"Some sixteen-year-old asshole tried to rape me once," Marlene said. "I hit him with the gas and now he's reading braille. You know?"

Ric took another sip of the whiskey and then wordlessly placed the mustard gas in Marlene's waiting palm. "You're in America now,

Ric," Marlene said. "You keep forgetting that, singing your c
ish marching songs."

He rubbed his chin. "Right," he said. "I've got to make ac
ments."

"Better do it soon," Marlene said, "if you're going to start bustin,
into hospitals."

9

The next day Ric went to the drugstore, where he purchased a
large amount of petroleum jelly, some nasal mist that came in squeeze
bottles, liquid bleach, a bottle of toilet cleaner, a small amount of
alcohol-based lamp fuel, and a bottle of glycerin. Then he drove to
a chemical supply store, where he bought some distilling equipment
and some litmus paper.

On his way back he stopped by an expensive liquor store and
bought some champagne. He didn't want the plastic bottles the
domestic stuff came in; instead he bought the champagne imported
from France, in glass bottles with the little hollow cone in the bottom. It was the biggest expense of the day.

Back in Marlene's apartment he opened the tops of the nasal in-
halers and drained the contents into the sink. He cleaned each and
set them out to dry. He set up his distilling equipment, mixing the
toilet-bowl cleaner with the liquid bleach, then bubbled the resulting
chlorine gas through the wood lye until the litmus paper showed it
had been neutralized. He emptied the stuff into a pan and brought
it to a simmer on the stove. When crystals began forming he took
it off the burner and let the pan cool. He repeated the process two
more times and, in the end, he had almost pure potassium chlorate.
Ric then mixed the potassium chlorate with petroleum jelly to make
plastic explosive. He put it in an old coffee can in the refrigerator.

Feeling pleased with his handiwork, he opened a bottle of champagne to celebrate. He drank a glass and then set up his distilling
equipment again.

He put glycerine and some of the toilet bowl cleaner in a flask,
mixed it, then put it over a flame. He distilled out a couple ounces
of acrolein and then put the chemical in the empty nasal spray
containers. He capped them. He drank another glass of champagne,
put away all his materials, and turned on the vid. Something called
Video Vixens was just starting. Ric settled into his chair. He hadn't
seen that one.

10

"I made plastic explosive today," Ric said. "It's in the icebox."

"Great." Marlene had just come home from work and was tired. She was drinking champagne and waiting for the night's pills to kick in.

"I'll show you a trick," Ric said. He got some twine from the cupboard, cut it into strips, and soaked it in the lamp fuel. While it was soaking he got a large mixing bowl and filled it with water and ice. Then he tied the string around the empty champagne bottles, about three inches above the topmost point of the little hollow cone on the bottom. He got his lighter and set fire to the thread. It burned slowly, with a cool blue flame, for a couple minutes. Then he took the bottle and plunged it into the ice water. It split neatly in half with a crystalline snapping sound.

Ric took some of the plastic explosive and packed it into the bottom of the champagne bottle. He pushed a pencil into the middle of it, making a narrow hole for the detonator.

"There," he said. "That's a shaped charge. I'll make the detonators tomorrow, out of peroxide, acetone, and sulphuric acid. It's easy."

"What's a shaped charge, Ricardo?"

"It's used for blowing a hole through armor. Steel doors, cars. Tanks. Things like that."

Marlene looked at him appraisingly. "You're adjusting yourself to America, all right," she said.

11

Ric took a bus to Phoenix and rented a motel room with a kitchenette, paying five days in advance and using a false name. In the motel he changed clothes and took a cab to the Bar. Super Virgin waved as he came in. She was with her friend, Captain Islam. He was a long, gawky boy, about sixteen, with his head shaved and covered with the tattoos of Urban Surgery. He hadn't had any alterations yet, or the eye implants this group favored—instead he wore complicated mirrorshades with twin minicameras mounted above the bridge of the nose. They registered radiation in UV and infrared as well as the normal spectrum and featured liquid-crystal video displays on the backs of the eyepieces that received input from the minicameras or from any vid program he felt like seeing. Ric wondered if things weren't real to him, not unless he saw them on the vid. Captain Islam didn't talk much, just sat quietly behind his drink and his shades and watched whatever it was that he watched. The effect was unsettling and was probably meant to be. Ric could be talking to him and would never know whether the man was looking at him or at *Video Vixens*. Ric had first pegged him for a user, but Super Virgin said not.

Ric got a whiskey at the bar and joined the two at their table. "Slow night?" he asked.

"We're waiting for the jai alai to come on," Super Virgin said. "Live from Bilbao. We've got some money down."

"Sounds slow to me."

She gave a brittle laugh. "Guess so, Marat. You got any ideas for accelerating our motion?"

Ric frowned. "I have something to sell. Some information. But I don't know if it's something you'd really want to deal with."

"Too hot?" The words were Captain Islam's. Ric looked at his own distorted face in the Captain's spectacles.

"Depends on your concept of *hot*. The adjective I had in mind was *big*."

"Big." The word came with a pause before and after, as if Captain Islam had never heard the word before and was wondering what it meant.

Ric took a bottle of nasal mist out of his pocket and squeezed it once up each nose.

"Got a virus?" Virgin asked.

"I'm allergic to Arizona."

Captain Islam was frowning. "So what's this action of yours, buck?" he asked.

"Several kilos of Thunder."

Captain Islam continued to stare into the interior of his mirrors. Super Virgin burst into laughter.

"I knew you weren't here as a fucking tourist, Marat!" she cackled. "'Several kilos!' *One* kilo is weight! What the hell is 'several?'"

"I don't know if you people can move that much," Ric said. "Also, I'd like an agreement. I want twenty percent of the take, and I want you to move my twenty percent for me, free of charge. If you think you can move that kind of weight at all, that is." He sipped his whiskey. "Maybe I should talk to some people in California."

"You talk to them, you end up dead," Virgin said. "They're not friendly to anyone these days, not when Thunder's involved."

Ric smiled. "Maybe you're right."

"Where is it? Who do we have to steal it from?"

"Another thing," Ric said. "I want certain agreements. I don't want any excessive force used, here. Nobody shot."

"Sometimes things happen," Captain Islam said. Ric had the feeling that the Captain was definitely looking at him this time. "Sometimes things can't be avoided."

"This stuff is guarded by an organization who won't forget it if any of their people get hurt," Ric explained. "If you try to move this kind of weight, word's going to get out that it's you that has the Thunder, and that means these characters are going to find out sooner or later. You might be tempted to give me to them as a way of getting the heat off you. Which would be a mistake, because I intend on establishing an alibi. That would mean that they're going to be extremely upset with you misleading them." Ric sipped his whiskey and smiled. "I'm just looking out for all our interests."

"A hospital," Captain Islam said. He shook his head. "You want us to take off a hospital. The one up in Flag, right? You stupid shit."

"I have a plan," Ric said. "I know their defenses, to a certain point. I know how they're organized. I know how they *think*."

"That's Folger Security, for chrissake," Captain Islam said. "They're tough. They don't forget when someone makes idiots out of them."

"That's why it's got to be my rules," Ric said. "But I should probably mention something, here." He grinned, seeing the smile reflected in the Captain's quicksilver eyes. "It's an inside job," Ric said. "I'm friends with someone on their force."

Virgin whooped and banged him on the shoulder with her left hand, the one with the sheathed claws. "Why didn't you say so?" she said.

"You people," Ric said. "You've got to learn to be patient."

12

Treble whimpered against a throbbing bass line. Shafts of red sunset sliced into the violet depths of the Grand Canyon. Marlene backed, spun, turned back to Ric, touched palms. She was wearing Indian war paint. Colors zigzagged across her face. Her eyes and smile were bright.

The band was dressed like hussars, lights glittering off brocade, the lead singer sweating under her dolman, thretening to split her tight breeches with each of her leaps. Her eye makeup dazzled like butterfly wings. Her lyrics were all heroism, thunder, revolution. The romantic wave against which Cartoon Messiah and Urban Surgery were a cool reaction.

Marlene stepped forward, pressing herself against him. He circled her with his arms, felt her sacral dimples as they leaned back and spun against each other. At the end of the five-bar chorus she gave a grind of her hips against him, then winked.

He laughed. While he was establishing his alibi, Cartoon Messiah were working for him back in Flagstaff. And they didn't even know it.

13

Readiness crackled from Ric's nerves as he approached the hotel door. They could try to kill him, he knew. Now would be the best time. Black Thunder tended to generate that kind of behavior. He'd been telling them he had ideas for other jobs, that he'd be valuable to them alive, but he couldn't be sure if they believed him.

The door opened and Super Virgin grinned at him with her metal teeth. "Piece of cake, Marat," she said. "Your cut's on the table."

The hotel room was dark, the walls draped in blueblack plastic. More plastic sheets cover the floors, the ceiling, some of the furniture. Coldness touched Ric's spine. There could be a lot of blood spilled in here, and the plastic would keep it from getting on anything. Computer consoles and vid sets gave off quiet hums. Cables snake over the floor, held down with duct tape. On a table was a half-kilo white paper packet. Captain Islam and Two-Fisted Jesus sat beside it, tapping into a console. Jesus looked up.

"Just in time," he said, "for the movies."

He was a skinny boy, about eighteen, his identity obscured by the obsessive mutilations of Urban Surgery. He wore a t-shirt featuring a picture of a muscular, bearded man in tights, with cape and halo. Here in this place, the hotel room he had hung with plastic and filled with electronics, he moved and spoke with an assurance the others hadn't absorbed, the kind of malevolent grace displayed by those who gave law and style to others, unfettered by conscience. Ric could appreciate Jesus' moves. He'd had them once himself.

Rick walked to the paper packet and hefted it. He tore open a corner, saw a row of little white envelopes, each labelled Genesios Three with the pharmaceutical company sigil in the corner. He didn't know a test for B-44 so he just stuffed the envelope in his pocket.

"This is gonna be great," Super Virgin said. She came up behind him and handed him a highball glass half-filled with whiskey. "You got time to watch the flick? We went in packing cameras. We're gonna cut a documentary of the whole thing and sell it to a station in Nogales. They'll write some scenes around it and use it on an episode of *VidWar.*" She giggled. "The Mexicans don't care how many gringo hospitals get taken off. They'll put some kind of plot around it. A dumb love story or something. But it's the highest-rated program, 'cause people know it's real. Except for *Australian Rules Firefight Football,* and that's real, too."

Ric looked around and found a chair. It seemed as if these people planned to let him live. He reached into his pocket and fired a round of nasal mist up each nostril. "Sure. I'll watch," he sniffed. "I got time."

"This is a rough cut only, okay?" Captain Islam's voice. "So bear with us."

There was a giant-sized liquid-crystal vid display set up on the black plastic on the wall. A picture sizzled into existence. The hospital, a vast concrete fortress set in an aureole of halogen light. Ric felt his tongue go dry. He swallowed with difficulty.

The image moved, jolting. Whoever was carrying the camera was walking, fast, across the parking light. Two-Fisted Jesus tapped the keys of his computer. The image grew smooth. "We're using a lot of computer enhancement on the vid, see?" Super Virgin said. "We can smooth out the jitters from the moving camera. Except for select bits to enhance the ver—the versi—"

"Verisimilitude," said Captain Islam.

"Right. Just to let everyone knew this is the real thing. And we're gonna change everyone's appearance electronically, so no one can recognize us."

Cut to someone moving into the hospital's front door, moving right past the metal detectors. Ric saw a tall girl, blonde, dressed in pink shorts and a tube top. White sandal straps coiled about her ankles.

"A mercenary," Virgin said. "We hired her for this. The slut."

Captain Islam laughed. "She's an actress," he explained. "Trying for a career south of the border. Wants the publicity."

The girl stepped up to a guard. Ric recognized Lysaght. She was asking directions, pointing. Lysaght was gazing at her breasts as he replied. She smiled and nodded and walked past. He looked after her, chewed his cigar, hiked up his gunbelt. Ric grinned. As long as guards like Lysaght were around, nothing was safe.

The point of view changed abruptly, a subjective shot, someone moving down a hospital corridor. Patients in ordinary clothes moving past, smiling.

"We had a camera in this necklace she was wearing. A gold owl, about an inch long, with 3D vidcams behind the eyes. Antenna in the chain, receiver in her bag. We pasted it to her chest so it would always be looking straight forward and wouldn't get turned around or anything. Easy stuff."

"We gotta do some pickups, here," Jesus said. "Get a picture of the girl moving down a corridor. Then we tell the computer to put all the stripes on the walls. It'll be worth more when we sell it."

Subjective shot of someone moving into a woman's toilet, stepping into a stall, reaching into a handbag for a pair of coveralls.

"Another pickup shot," Jesus muttered. "Gotta get her putting on her coveralls." He made a note on a pad.

The point of view lurched upward, around, out of the stall. Centered on a small ventilator intake high on a wall. Hands came into the picture, holding a screwdriver.

"Methanethiol," Super Virgin said. "That stuff's gonna be real useful from now on. How'd you know how to make it?"

"Elementary chemistry," Ric said. He'd used it to clear out political meetings of which the Cadillacs didn't approve.

The screen was off the ventilator. Hands were reaching into the bag, taking out a small glass bottle. Carefully loosening the screw top. The hands placed the bottle upright in the ventilator. Then the point of view dipped, a hand reached down to pick up the ventilator screen. Then the ventilator screen was shoved violently into the hole, knocking the bottle over.

Airborne methanethiol gave off a horrible, nauseating smell at one-fiftieth of a part per billion. The psychology wing of the hospital was going to get a dose considerably in excess of that.

The subjective camera was moving with great rapidity down hospital corridors. To a stairwell, then down.

Cut to Super Virgin in a phone booth. She had a small voice recorder in her hand, and was punching buttons.

"Freeze that," said Two-Fisted Jesus. Virgin's image turned to ice. Jesus began tapping keys.

The tattooing shifted, dissolved to a different pattern. Super Virgin laughed. Her hair shortened, turned darker. The black insets over her eyes vanished. Brown eyes appeared, then they turned a startling pale blue.

"Leave the teeth," she said.

"Nah. I have an idea." Two-Fisted Jesus sat tapping keys for about thirty seconds. He pressed the enter button and the metal teeth disappeared completely. He moved the picture forward a second, then back. Virgin's tongue moved redly behind her tatooed lips. The interior of the mouth was pink, a lot of gum, no teeth at all. She clapped her hands.

"That's strange, man," she said. "I like that."

"The Mexicans will probably replace her image with some vidstar, anyway," Captain Islam said. "Urban Surgery is too much for them, right now."

"Okay. I want to see this in three dimensions," Jesus said. Super Virgin's image detached itself from the background and began rotating. He stopped it every so often and made small adjustments.

"Make me taller," Super Virgin said. "And skinnier. And give me smaller tits. I hate my tits."

"We do that every time," Jesus said. "People are gonna start to twig."

"Chrome tits. Leather tits. Anything."

Captain Islam laughed. Two-Fisted Jesus made minor adjustments and ignored Super Virgin's complaints.

"Here we go. Say your line."

The image began moving. Virgin's new green eyes sparkled as she held the recorder up to the mouthpiece of the telephone.

"This is Royal Flag." It was the name of one of Arizona's more ideological kid gangs. The voice had been electronically altered and sounded flat. "We've just planted a poison gas bomb in your psychology wing. All the head cases are gonna see Jesus. The world's gene pool will be so much healthier from now on. Have yourself a pleasant day."

Super Virgin was laughing. "Wait'll you see the crowd scenes. Stellar stuff, believe me."

"I believe," said Ric.

14

The video was full of drifting smoke. Vague figures moved through it. Jesus froze the picture and tried to enhance the images, without any success. "Shit," he said. "More pickups."

Ric had watched the action as members of Cartoon Messiah in Folger Security uniforms had hammered their way into a hospital back door. They had moved faultlessly through the corridors to the vault and blasted their way in with champagne-bottle shaped charges. The blasts had set off tremblor alarms in the vault and the Folger people realized they were being hit. Now the raiders were in the corridor before the vault, retracing their steps at a run.

"Okay," Super Virgin said. "The moment of truth, coming up."

The corridor was full of billowing tear gas. Crouched figures moved through it. Commands were yammering down the monitored Folger channels. Then, coming through the smoke, another figure. A tall woman in a helmet, her hand pressed to her ear, trying to hear the radio. There was a gun in her hand. She raised the gun.

Thuds on the soundtrack. Tear-gas canisters, fired at short range. One of them struck the woman in her armored chest and bounced off. It hadn't flown far enough to arm itself and it just rolled down the corridor. The woman fell flat.

"Just knocked the wind out of her." Captain Islam was grinning. "How about that for keeping our deal, huh?" Somebody ran forward and kicked the gun out of her hand. The camera caught a glimpse of her lying on the floor, her mouth open, trying to breath. There were dots of sweat on her nose. Her eye makeup looked like butterfly wings.

"Now that's what I call poignant," Jesus said. "Human interest stuff. You know?"

The kids ran away across the parking lot, onto their fuelcell tricycles, and away, bouncing across the parking lot and the railroad tracks beyond.

"We're gonna spice this up a bit," Jesus said. "Cut in some shots of guards shooting at us, that kind of thing. Steal some suspenseful music. Make the whole thing more exciting. What do you think?"

"I like it," said Ric. He put down his untasted whiskey. Jacob and his neurotoxin had made him cautious. "Do I get any royalties? Being scriptwriter and all?"

"The next deal you set up for us. Maybe."

Ric shrugged. "How are you gonna move the Thunder?"

"Small pieces, probably."

"Let me give you some advice," Ric said. "The longer you hang onto it, the bigger the chance Folger will find out you have it and start cramping your action. I have an idea. Can you handle a large increase of capital?"

15

"Is this the stuff? Great." Marlene swept in the motel room door, grinning, with her overnight bag. She gave Ric a brief hug, then went to the table of the kitchenette. She picked up the white packet, hefted it in her hand.

"Light," she said.

"Yeah."

"I can't believe people kill each other over this."

"They could kill *us*," Ric said. "Don't forget that."

Marlene licked her lips and peeled the packet. She took one of the small white envelopes and tore it open, spilling dark powder into her cupped palm. She cocked her head.

"Doesn't look like much. How do you take it?"

Ric remembered the flood of well-being in his body, the way the world had suddenly tasted better. No, he thought. He wasn't going to get hung up on Thunder. "Intraveneous, mostly," he said. "Or they could put it in capsules."

Marlene sniffed at it. "Doesn't smell like anything. What's the dose?"

"I don't know. I wasn't planning on taking any."

She began licking in her palm. Ric watched her little pink tongue lapping at the powder. He turned his eyes away.

"Take it easy," he said.

"Tastes funny. Kind of like green pepper sauce, with a touch of kerosene."

"A touch of stupidity," he said. "A touch of . . ." He moved around the room, hands in his pockets. "A touch of craziness. People who are around Black Thunder get crazy."

Marlene finished licking her palm and kicked off her shoes. "Craziness sounds good," she said. She stepped up behind him and put her arms around him. "How crazy do you think we can get tonight?"

"I don't know." He thought for a minute. "Maybe I could show you our movie."

16

Ric faced the window in the motel room, watching, his mind humming. The window had been dialed to polarize completely and he could see himself, Marlene behind him on the untidy bed, the plundered packet of Thunder on the table. It had been eight days since the hospital had been robbed. Marlene had taken the bus to Phoenix every evening.

"You should try some of our product," Marlene said. "The stuff's just . . . when I use it, I can feel my mind just start to click. Move faster, smoother. Thoughts come out of nowhere."

"Right," Ric said. "Nowhere."

Ric saw Marlene's reflection look up at his own dark plateglass ghost. "Do I detect sarcasm, here?"

"No. Preoccupation, that's all."

"Half the stuff's mine, right? I can eat it, burn it, drop it out the window. Drop it on your head, if I want to. Right?"

"That is correct," said Ric.

"Things are getting dull," Marlene said. "You're spending your evenings off drinking with Captain Islam and Super Virgin and Krishna Commando . . . I get to stay here and watch the vid."

"Those people I'm drinking with," Ric said. "There's a good chance they could die because of what we're going to do. They're our victims. Would you like to have a few drinks with them? A few smokes?" He turned from the window and looked at her. "Knowing they may die because of you?"

Marlene frowned up at him. "Are you scared of them?" she asked. "Is that why you're talking like this?"

Ric gave a short laugh. Marlene ran her fingers through her almost-blonde hair. Ric watched her in the mirror.

"You don't have to involve yourself in this part, Marlene," Ric said. "I can do it by myself, I think."

She was looking at the darkened vid screen. Her eyes were bright. A smile tugged at her lips.

"I'm ready," she said. "Let's do it."

"I've got to get some things ready first."

"Hurry up. I don't want to waste this feeling I've got."

Ric closed his eyes. He didn't want to see his reflection any more. "What feeling is that?" he asked.

"The feeling that my time is coming. To try something new."

"Yeah," Ric said. His eyes were still closed. "That's what I thought."

17

Ric, wearing leather gardener's gloves, smoothed the earth over the plastic-wrapped explosive device he had just buried under a pyracantha bush. He was crouched in the shadow of a vacation cabin. Drizzle rattled off his collar. His knees were growing wet. He took the aerial for the radio detonator and pulled it carefully along one of the stems of the bush.

Marlene stood next to him in red plastic boots. She was standing guard, snuffling in the cold. Ric could hear the sound of her lips as she chewed gum.

White shafts of light tracked over their heads, filtered by juniper scrub that stood between the cabins and the expressway heading north out of Flagstaff. Ric froze. His form, caught among pyracantha barbs, cast a stark moving shadow on the peeling white wall.

"Flashlight," he said, when the car had passed. Moving between the light and any onlookers, Marlene flicked it on. Ric carefully smoothed the soil, spread old leaves. He thought the thorns on the pyracantha would keep most people away, but he didn't want disturbed soil attracting anyone.

Rain danced down in the yellow light. "Thanks," he said. Marlene popped a bubble. Ric stood up, brushing muck from his knees. There were more bundles to bury, and it was going to be a long, wet night.

18

"They're going to take you off if they can," Ric said. "They're from California and they know this is a one-shot deal, so they don't care if they offend you or leave you dead. But they think it's going to happen in Phoenix, see." Ric, Super Virgin, and Two-Fisted Jesus stood in front of the juniper by the alloy road, looking down at the cluster of cabins. "They may hire people from the Cold Wires or whoever, so that they can have people who know the terrain. So the idea is, we move the meet at the last minute. Up here, north of Flag."

"We don't know the terrain, either," Jesus said. He looked uncomfortable here, his face a monochrome blotch in the unaccustomed sun.

Ric took a squeeze bottle of nasal mist from his pocket and squeezed it once up each nostril. He sniffed. "You can learn it between now and then. Rent all the cabins, put soldiers in the nearest ones. Lay in your commo gear." Ric pointed up at the ridge above where they stood. "Put some people with long guns up there, some IR goggles and scopes. Anyone comes in, you'll know about it."

"I don't know, Marat. I like Phoenix. I know the way that city thinks." Jesus shook his head in disbelief. "Fucking tourist cabins."

"They're better than hotel rooms. Tourist cabins have back doors."

"Hey." Super Virgin was grinning, metal teeth winking in the sun as she tugged on Jesus' sleeve. "Expand your horizons. This is the *great outdoors.*"

Jesus shook his head. "I'll think about it."

19

Marlene was wearing war paint and dancing in the middle of her condeco living room. The furniture was pushed back to the walls, the music was loud enough to rattle the crystal on the kitchen shelves.

"You've got to decide, Marlene," Ric said. He was sitting behind the pushed-back table, and the paper packets of Thunder were laid out in front of him. "How much of this do you want to sell?"

"I'll decide later."

"Now. Now, Marlene."

"Maybe I'll keep it all."

Ric looked at her. She shook sweat out of her eyes and laughed. "Just a joke, Ric."

He said nothing.

"It's just happiness," she said, dancing. "Happiness in paper envelopes. Better than money. You ought to use some. It'll make you less tense." Sweat was streaking her war paint. "What'll you use the money for, anyway? Move to Zanzibar and buy yourself a safe condeco and a bunch of safe investments? Sounds boring to me, Ric. Why'n't you use it to create some excitement?"

He could not, Ric thought, afford much in the way of regret. But still a sadness came over him, drifting through his body on slow opiate time. Another few days, he thought, and he wouldn't have to use people any more. Which was good, because he was losing his taste for it.

20

A kid from California was told to be by a certain public phone at a certain time, with his bank and without his friends. The phone call told him to go to another phone booth and be there within a certain allotted time. He complained, but the phone hung up in midsyllable.

At the second phone he was told to take the keys taped to the bottom of the shelf in the phone booth, go to such-and-such a car in the parking lot, and drive to Flagstaff to another public phone. His complaints were cut short by a slamming receiver. Once in Flagstaff, he was given another set of directions.

By now he had learned not to complain.

If there were still people with him they were very good, because they hadn't been seen at any of the turns of his course.

He was working for Ric, even though he didn't know it.

21

Marlene was practicing readiness. New patterns were constantly flickering through her mind and she loved watching her head doing its tricks.

She was wearing her war paint as she sat up on a tall ridge behind the cabins, her form encased in a plastic envelope that dispersed her body heat in patterns unrecognizable to infra-red scanners. She had a radio and a powerful antenna, and she was humming "Greensleeves" to herself as looked down at the cabins through long binoculars wrapped in a scansheet paper tube to keep the sun from winking from the lenses. Marlene also had headphones and a parabolic mike pointed down at the cabins, so that she could hear anything going on. Right now all she could hear was the wind.

She could see the cabins perfectly, as well as the two riflemen on the ridge across the road. She was far away from anything likely to happen, but if things went well she wouldn't be needed for anything but pushing buttons on cue anyway.

"Greensleeves" hummed on and on. Marlene was having a good time. Working for Ric.

22

Two-Fisted Jesus had turned the cabin into another plastic-hung cavern, lit by pale holograms and cool video monitors, filled with the hum of machinery and the brightness of liquid crystal. Right in the middle, a round coffee table full of crisp paper envelopes.

Ric had been allowed entry because he was one of the principals in the transaction. He'd undergone scanning as he entered, both for weapons and for electronics. Nothing had been found. His Thunder, and about half of Marlene's, was sitting on the table.

Only two people were in the room besides Ric. Super Virgin had the safety caps off her claws and was carrying an automatic with laser sights in a belt holster. Ric considered the sights a pure affectation in a room this small. Jesus had a sawed-off twin-barrel shotgun sitting in his lap. The pistol grip might break his wrist but the spread would cover most of the room, and Ric wondered if Jesus had considered how much electronics he'd lose if he ever used it.

23

Where three lightposts had been marked with fluorescent tape, the kid from California pulled off on the verge of the alloy road that wound ahead to leap over the Grand Canyon into Utah. Captain Islam pulled up behind him with two soldiers, and they scanned the kid right there, stripped him of a pistol and a homing sensor, and put him in the back of their own car.

"You're beginning to piss me off," the kid said.

"Just do what we tell you," Captain Islam said, pulling away, "and you'll be king of Los fucking Angeles."

24

Ric's hands were trembling so hard he had to press them against the arms of his chair in order to keep it from showing. He could feel sweat oozing from his armpits. He really wasn't good at this kind of thing.

The kid from California was pushed in the door by Captain Islam, who stepped out and closed the door behind him. The kid was black and had clear plastic eye implants, with the electronics gleaming inside the transparent eyeball. He had patterned scarring instead of the tattoos, and was about sixteen. He wore a silver jacket, carried a duffel to put the Thunder in, and seemed annoyed.

"Once you step inside," Jesus said, "you have five minutes to complete our transaction. Go ahead and test any of the packets at random."

"Yeah," the kid said. "I'll do that." He crouched by the table, pulled vials from his pockets, and made a series of tests while Jesus counted off at fifteen-second intervals. He managed to do four tests in three minutes, then stood up. Ric could see he was salivating for the stuff.

"It's good," he said.

"Let's see your key." The kid took a credit spike from his pocket and handed it to Jesus, who put it in the computer in front of him. Jesus transferred two hundred fifteen thousand in Starbright policorporate scrip from the spike to his own spike that was jacked into slot two.

"Take your stuff," Jesus said, settling back in his seat. "Captain Islam will take you back to your car. Nice doing business."

The kid gave a sniff, took his spike back, and began to stuff white packets into his duffel. He left the cabin without saying a word. Adrenaline was wailing along Ric's nerves. He stood and took his own spike from his left-hand jacket pocket. His other hand went to the squeeze bottle of nasal mist in his right. Stray novae were exploding at the peripherals of his vision.

"Look at this, Virgin," Ric said. "Look at all the money sitting in this machine." He laughed. Laughter wasn't hard, but stopping the laughter was.

"Twenty percent is yours, Marat," Jesus said. "Give me your spike."

As Super Virgin stepped up to look at the monitor, Ric brought the squeeze bottle out of his pocket and fired acrolein into her face. His spin toward Jesus was so fast that Virgin's scream had barely begun before he fired another burst of the chemical at Jesus, slamming one hand down on the shotgun to keep him from bringing it up. He'd planned on just holding it there till the boy's grip loosened, but nerves took over and he wrenched it effortlessly from Jesus' hands and barely stopped himself from smashing Jesus in the head with it.

Virgin was on her hands and knees, mucus hanging from her nose and lips. She was trying to draw the pistol. Ric kicked it away. It fell on muffled plastic.

Ric turned and pulled the spikes from the machine. Jesus had fallen out of his chair, was clawing at his face. "Dead man," Jesus said, gasping the words.

"Don't threaten me, asshole," Ric said. "It could have been mustard gas."

And then Marlene, on the ridge far above, watched the sweep hand touch five minutes, thirty seconds, and she pressed her radio button. All the buried charges went off, blasting bits of the other cabins into the sky and doubtless convincing the soldiers in the other buildings that they were under fire by rocket or mortar, that the kid from California had brought an army with him. Simultaneous with the explosive, other buried packages began to gush concealing white smoke into the air. The wind was strong but there was a lot of smoke.

Ric opened the back door and took off, the shotgun hanging in his hand. Random fire burst out but none of it came near. The smoke provided cover from both optical scanners and infrared, and it concealed him all the way across the yard behind the cabin and down into the arroyo behind it. Sixty yards down the arroyo was a culvert that ran under the expressway. Ric dashed through it, wetting himself to the knees in cold spring snowmelt.

He was now on the other side of the expressway. He didn't think anyone would be looking for him here. He threw the shotgun away and kept running. There was a cross-country motorbike waiting a little farther up the stream.

25

"There," Ric said, pressing the Return button. "Half of it's yours."

Marlene was still wearing her war paint. She sipped cognac from a crystal glass and took her spike out of the computer. She laughed.

"A hundred K of Starbright," she said, "and paper packets of happiness. What else do I need?"

"A fast armored car, maybe," Ric said. He pocketed his spike. "I'm taking off," he said. He turned to her. "There's room on the bike for two."

"To where?" She was looking at him sidelong.

"To Mexico, for starters," he said. A lie. Ric planned on heading northeast and losing himself for a while in Navajoland.

"To some safe little country. A safe little apartment."

"That's the idea."

Marlene took a hefty swig of cognac. "Not me," she said. "I'm planning on staying in this life."

Ric felt a coldness brush his spine. He reached out to take her hand. "Marlene," he said carefully. "You've got to leave this town. Now."

She pulled her hand away. "Not a chance, Ricardo. I plan on telling my boss just what I think of him. Tomorrow morning. I can't wait."

There was a pain in Ric's throat. "Okay," he said. He stood up. "See you in Mexico, maybe." He began to move for the door. Marlene put her arms around him from behind. Her chin dug into his collarbone.

"Stick around," she said. "For the party."

He shook his head, uncoiled her arms, slid out of them.

"You treat me like I don't know what I'm doing," Marlene said.

He turned and looked at her. Bright eyes looked at him from a mask of bright paint. "You don't," he said.

"I've got lots of ideas. You showed me how to put things together."

"Now I'm showing you how to run and save your life."

"Hah. I'm not going to run. I'm going to stroll out with a briefcase full of happiness and a hundred K in my pocket."

He looked at her and felt a pressure hard in his chest. He knew that none of this was real to her, that he'd never been able to penetrate that strange screen in her mind that stood between Marlene and the rest of the world. Ric had never pierced it, but soon the world would. He felt a coldness filling him, a coldness that had nothing to do with sorrow.

It was hard not to run when he turned and left the apartment.

His breathing came more freely with each step he took.

26

When Ric came off the Navajo Reservation he saw scansheet headlines about how the California gang wars had spilled over into Phoenix, how there were dead people turning up in alleys, others were missing, a club had been bombed. All those people working for him, covering his retreat.

In New Zealand he bought into a condecology in Christchurch, a big place with armored shutters and armored guards, a first-rate new artificial intelligence to handle investments, and a mostly-foreign clientele who profited by the fact that a list of the condeco's inhabitants was never made public . . . this was before he found out that he could buy private property here, a big house on the South Island with a view of his own personal glacier, without a chance of anybody's war accidentally rolling over him.

It was an interesting feeling, sitting alone in his own house, knowing there wasn't anyone within five thousand miles who wanted to kill him.

Ric made friends. He played the market and the horses. And he learned to ski.

At a ski party in late September, held in the house of one of his friends, he drifted from room to room amid a murmur of conversation punctuated with brittle laughter. He had his arm around someone named Reiko, the sheltered daughter of a policorporate bigwig. The girl, nineteen and a student, had long black hair that fell like a tsunami down her shoulders, and she was fascinated with his talk of life in the real world. He walked into a back room that was bright with the white glare of video, wondering if the jai alai scores had been posted yet, and he stared into his own face as screams rose around him and his nerves turned to hot magnesium flares.

"Ugh. Mexican scum show," said Reiko, and then she saw the actor's face and her eyes widened.

Ric felt his knees trembling and he sank into an armchair in the back of the room. Ice tittering in his drink. The man on the vid was flaying alive a woman who hung by her wrists from a beam. Blood ran down his forearms. The camera cut quickly to his tiger's eyes, his thin smile. Ric's eyes. Ric's smile.

"My god," said Reiko. "It's really you, isn't it?"

"No," Ric said. Shaking his head.

"I can't believe they let this stuff even on pirate stations," someone said from the hallway. Screams rose from the vid. Ric's mind was flailing in the dark.

"I can't watch this," Reiko said, and rushed away. Ric didn't see her go. Burning sweat was running down the back of his neck.

The victim's screams rose. Blood traced artful patterns down her body. The camera cut to her face.

Marlene's face.

Nausea swept Ric and he doubled in his chair. He remembered Two-Fisted Jesus and his talent for creating video images, altering faces, voices, action. They'd found Marlene, as Ric had thought they would, and her voice and body were memorized by Jesus' computers. Maybe the torture was even real.

"It's got to be him," someone in the room said. "It's even his voice. His accent."

"He never did say," said another voice, "what he used to do for a living."

Frozen in his chair, Ric watched the show to the end. There was more torture, more bodies. The video-Ric enjoyed it all. At the end he went down before the blazing guns of the Federal Security Directorate. The credits rolled over the video-Ric's dead face. The director was listed as Jesus Carranza. The film was produced by VideoTek S.A. in collaboration with Messiah Media.

The star's name was given as Jean-Paul Marat.

"A new underground superstar," said a high voice. The voice of someone who thought of himself as an underground connoisseur. "He's been in a lot of pirate video lately. He's the center of a big controversy about how far scum shows can go."

And then the lights came on and Ric saw eyes turning to him in surprise. "It's not me," he said.

"Of course not." The voice belonged to his host. "Incredible resemblance, though. Even your mannerisms. Your accent."

"Not me."

"Hey." A quick, small man, with metal-rimmed glasses that gazed at Ric like barrels of a shotgun. "It really is you!" The high-pitched voice of the connoisseur grated on Ric's nerves like the sound of a bonesaw.

"No." A fast, sweat-soaked denial.

"Look. I've taped all your vids I could find."

"Not me."

"I'm having a party next week. With entertainment, if you know what I mean. I wonder—"

"I'm not interested," Ric said, standing carefully, "in any of your parties."

He walked out into the night, to his new car, and headed north, to his private fortress above the glacier. He took the pistol out of the glove compartment and put it on the seat next to him. It didn't make him feel any safer.

Get a new face, Ric thought. Get across the border into Uzbekistan and check into a hospital. Let them try to follow me there.

He got home at four in the morning and checked his situation with the artificial intelligence that managed his accounts. All his funds were in long-term investments and he's take a whopping loss if he pulled out now.

He looked at the figures and couldn't understand them. There seemed to be a long, constant scream in Ric's mind and nerves, a scream that echoed Marlene's, the sound of someone who has just discovered what is real. His body was shaking and he couldn't stop it.

Ric switched off his monitor and staggered to bed. Blood filled his dreams.

When he rose it was noon. There were people outside his gates, paparazzi with their cameras. The phone had recorded a series of requests for an interview with the new, controversial vid star. Someone at the party had talked. It took Ric a long time to get a line out in order to tell the AI to sell.

The money in his pocket and a gun in his lap, he raced his car past the paparazzi, making them jump aside as he tried his best to run them down. He had to make the next suborbital shuttle out of Christchurch to Mysore, then head northwest to a hospital and to a new life. And somehow he'd have to try to cover his tracks. Possibly he'd buy some hair bleach, a false mustache. Pay only cash.

Getting away from Cartoon Messiah wouldn't be hard. Shaking the paparazzi would take a lot of fast thinking.

Sweat made his grip on the wheel slippery.

As he approached Christchurch he saw a streak across the bright northeast sky, a shuttle burning its way across the Pacific from California.

He wondered if there were people on it that he knew.

In his mind, the screams went on.

★ Smasher ★

by Fred Saberhagen

To paraphrase part of one of Bill Cosby's routines, the chief reason that my wife, Joan, and I live in New Mexico may well be that we did not want to live in Chicago. Both of us were born in that fascinating and often repulsive metropolis, and we still fondly recall many of its people, along with its lake, museums, stores, restaurants, and shows. But in the mid-70s our chief concerns came to be those connected with raising three small children, and we knew Chicago too well to entertain any idea that it was an ideal place for that.

Nor were we able to afford any place in the suburbs that we might really have liked. In the course of the search we kept on looking farther and farther west, and by the time we reached the Mississippi we decided what the hell, or words to that effect, why should we stop here!

I was not a stranger to New Mexico before we sold our Chicago townhouse and headed west in 1975. Or at least I thought I wasn't.

85

*I had spent part of an Air Force stint stationed near Roswell in the
1950s, and had seen a little of Albuquerque as it was then, and of
the awesome emptiness-that-is-not-really-emptiness our state provides. They set off a nuclear bomb here once, as I enjoy reminding
visitors from the east, and almost nobody noticed.*

*Actually, as I recall, Joan and I started driving west with the kids
in the belief that we were moving to romantic Santa Fe. We got as
far as Albuquerque and stuck. Part of the reason was that we had
left northern Illinois in an April blizzard, with six or eight inches
of snow on the ground, and arrived in Albuquerque to find that
swimming pools were open, and we realized that Santa Fe was
farther north again. The other and really decisive reason was a
compound of practical components, like real estate prices, and the
advantages of a city big enough to offer a multiplicity of schools,
doctors, hospitals, churches, and similar things that loom ever larger
as the process of parenting develops.*

*It's a great state, complete with four seasons, short on earth-
quakes, and devoid of hurricanes. I intend to stay here after my
kids are all out of the nest. I'd like to live here even if I wasn't a
writer. But then I'd probably be someone else entirely.*

Smasher

by Fred Saberhagen

*Here is some suspenseful sf about a berserker force which de-
scends on a planet named Waterfall. The berserkers were unliving and unmanned war machines programmed to destroy
anything that lived. And life on Waterfall consisted of some
odd marine life and four defenseless humans . . .*

Claus Slovensko was coming to the conclusion that the battle in
nearby space was going to be invisible to anyone on the planet
Waterfall—assuming that there was really going to be a battle at all.

Claus stood alone atop a forty-meter dune, studying a night sky
that flamed with the stars of the alien Busog cluster, mostly blue-
white giants which were ordinarily a sight worth watching in themselves. Against that background, the greatest energies released by
interstellar warships could, he supposed, be missed as a barely visible
twinkling. Unless, of course, the fighting should come very close
indeed.

In the direction he was facing, an ocean made invisible by night stretched from near the foot of the barren dune to a horizon marked only by the cessation of the stars. Claus turned now to scan once more the sky in the other direction. That way, toward planetary north, the starry profusion went on and on. In the northeast a silvery half-moon, some antique stage designer's concept of what Earth's own moon should be, hung low behind thin clouds. Below those clouds extended an entire continent of lifeless sand and rock. The land masses of Waterfall were bound in a silence that Earth ears found uncanny, stillness marred only by the wind, by murmurings of sterile streams, and by occasional deep rumblings in the rock itself.

Claus continued turning slowly, till he faced south again. Below him the night sea lapped with lulling false familiarity. He sniffed the air, and shrugged, and gave up squinting at the stars, and began to feel his way, one cautious foot after another, down the shifting slope of the dune's flank. A small complex of buildings, labs and living quarters bunched as if for companionship, the only human habitation on the world of Waterfall, lay a hundred meters before him and below. Tonight as usual the windows were all cheerfully alight. Ino Vacroux had decided, and none of the other three people on the planet had seen any reason to dispute him, that any attempt at blackout would be pointless. If a berserker force was going to descend on Waterfall, the chance of four defenseless humans avoiding discovery by the unliving killers would be nil.

Just beyond the foot of the dune, Claus passed through a gate in the high fence of fused rock designed to keep out drifting sand—with no land vegetation of any kind to hold the dunes in place, they tended sometimes to get pushy.

A few steps past the fence, he opened the lockless door of the main entrance to the comfortable living quarters. The large common room just inside was cluttered with casual furniture, books, amateur art, and small and middle-sized aquariums. The three other people who completed the population of the planet were all in this room at the moment, and all looked up to see if Claus brought news.

Jenny Surya, his wife, was seated at the small computer terminal in the far corner, wearing shorts and sweater, dark hair tied up somewhat carelessly, long elegant legs crossed. She was frowning as she looked up, but abstractedly, as if the worst news Claus might be bringing them would be of some potential distraction from their work.

Closer to Claus, in a big chair pulled up to the big communicator cabinet, slouched Ino Vacroux, senior scientist of the base. Claus surmised that Ino had been a magnificent physical specimen a few decades ago, before being nearly killed in a berserker attack upon another planet. The medics had restored function but not fineness to his body. The gnarled, hairy thighs below his shorts were not much thicker than a child's; his ravaged torso was draped now in a flamboyant shirt. In a chair near him sat Glenna Reyes, his wife, in her usual work garb of clean white coveralls. She was just a little younger than Vacroux, but wore the years with considerably more ease.

"Nothing to see," Claus informed them all, with a loose wave meant to describe the lack of visible action in the sky.

"Or to hear, either," Vacroux grated. His face was grim as he nodded toward the communicator. The screens of the device sparkled, and its speakers hissed a little, with noise that wandered in from the stars and stranger things than stars nature had set in this corner of the Galaxy.

Only a few hours earlier, in the middle of Waterfall's short autumn afternoon, there had been plenty to hear indeed. Driven by a priority code coming in advance of a vitally important message, the communicator had boomed itself to life, then roared the message through the house and across the entire base, in a voice that the four people heard plainly even four hundred meters distant where they were gathered to watch dolphins.

"Sea Mother, this is Brass Trumpet. Predators here, and we're going to try to turn them. Hold your place. Repeating . . . ."

One repetition of the substance came through, as the four were already hurrying back to the house. As soon as they got in they had played back the automatically recorded signal; and then when Glenna had at last located the code book somewhere, and they could verify the worst, they had played it back once more.

Sea Mother was the code name for any humans who might happen to be on Waterfall. It had been assigned by the military years ago, as part of their precautionary routine, and had probably never been used before today. Brass Trumpet, according to the book, was a name conveying a warning of deadly peril—it was to be used only by a human battle force when there were thought to be berserkers already in the Waterfall system or on their way to it. And "predators here" could hardly mean anything but berserkers—unliving and unmanned war machines, programmed to destroy whatever life they found. The first of them had been built in ages past, during the madness of some interstellar war between races now long-since vanished. Between berserkers and starfaring Earthumans, war had now been chronic for a thousand standard years.

That Brass Trumpet's warning should be so brief and vague was understandable. The enemy would doubtless pick it up as soon as its intended hearers, and might well be able to decode it. But for all the message content revealed, Sea Mother might be another powerful human force, toward which Brass Trumpet sought to turn them. Or it would have been conceivable for such a message to be sent to no one, a planned deception to make the enemy waste computer capacity and detection instruments. And even if the berserkers' deadly electronic brains should somehow compute correctly that Sea Mother was a small and helpless target, it was still possible to hope that the berserkers would be too intent on fatter targets elsewhere, too hard-pressed by human forces, or both, to turn aside and snap up such a minor morsel.

During the hours since that first warning, there had come nothing but noise from the communicator. Glenna sighed, and reached out to pat her man on the arm below the sleeve of his loud shirt. "Busy day with the crustaceans tomorrow," she reminded him.

"So we'd better get some rest. I know." Ino looked and sounded worn. He was the only one of the four who had ever seen berserkers before, at anything like close range; and it was not exactly reassuring to see how grimly and intensely he reacted to the warning of their possible approach.

"You can connect the small alarm," Glenna went on, "so it'll be sure to wake us if another priority message comes in."

That, thought Claus, would be easier on the nerves than being blasted out of sleep by that God-voice shouting again, this time only a few meters from the head of their bed.

"Yes, I'll do that." Ino thought, then slapped his chair-arms. He made his voice a little brighter. "You're right about tomorrow. And over in Twenty-three we're going to have to start feeding the mantis shrimp." He glanced round at the wall near his chair, where a long chart showed ponds, bays, lagoons and tidal pools, all strung out in a kilometers-long array, most of it natural, along this part of the coast. This array was a chief reason why the Sea Mother base had been located where it was.

From its sun and moon to its gravity and atmosphere, Waterfall was remarkably Earthlike in almost every measurable attribute save one—this world was congenitally lifeless. About forty standard years past, during a lull in the seemingly interminable berserker-war, it had appeared that the peaceful advancement of interstellar human-ization might get in an inning or two, and work had begun toward altering this lifelessness. Great ships had settled upon Waterfall with massive inoculations of Earthly life, in a program very carefully orchestrated to produce eventually a twin-Earth circling one of the few Sol-type suns in this part of the Galaxy.

The enormously complex task had been interrupted when war flared again. The first recrudescence of fighting was far away, but it drew off people and resources. A man-wife team of scientists were selected to stay alone on Waterfall for the duration of the emergency. They were to keep the program going along planned lines, even though at a slow pace. Ino and Glenna had been here for two years now. A supply ship from Atlantis called at intervals of a few standard months; and the last to call, eight local days ago, had brought along another husband-and-wife team for a visit. Claus and Jenny were both psychologists, interested in the study of couples living in iso-lation; and they were to stay at least until the next supply ship came.

So far the young guests had been welcome. Glenna, her own chil-dren long grown and independent on other worlds, approached moth-erliness sometimes in her attitude. Ino, more of a born competitor, swam races with Claus and gambled—lightly—with him. With Jenny he alternated between half-serious gallantry and teasing.

"I almost forgot," he said now, getting up from his chair before the communicator, and racking his arms and shoulders with an intense stretch. "I've got a little present for you, Jen."

"Oh?" She was bright, interested, imperturable. It was her usual working attitude, which he persisted in trying to break through.

Ino went out briefly, and came back to join the others in the kitchen. A small snack before retiring had become a daily ritual for the group.

"For you," he said, presenting Jen with a small bag of clear plastic. There was water inside, and something else.

"Oh, my goodness." It was still her usual nurse-like business tone, which evidently struck Ino as a challenge. "What do I do with it?"

"Keep him in that last aquarium in the parlor," Ino advised. "It's untenanted right now."

Claus, looking at the bag from halfway across the kitchen, made out in it one of those non-human, non-mammalian shapes that are apt to give Earth people the impression of the intensely alien, even when the organism sighted comes from their own planet. It was no bigger than an adult human finger, but replete with waving appendages. There came to mind something written by Lafcadio Hearn about a centipede:

The blur of its moving legs . . . toward which one would no more advance one's hand . . . than toward the spinning blade of a power saw . . .

Or some words close to those. Jen, Claus knew, cared for the shapes of non-mammalian life even less than he did. But she would grit her teeth and struggle not to let the teasing old man see it.

"Just slit the bag and let it drain into the tank," Ino was advising, for once sounding pretty serious. "They don't like handling . . . okay? He's a bit groggy right now, but tomorrow, if he's not satisfied with you as his new owner, he may try to get away."

Glenna, in the background, was rolling her eyes in the general direction of Brass Trumpet, miming: What is the old fool up to now? When is he going to grow up?

"Get away?" Jen inquired sweetly. "You told me the other day that even a snail couldn't climb that glass—"

The house was filled with the insistent droning of the alarm that Ino had just connected. He's running some kind of test, Claus thought at once. Then he saw the other man's face and knew that Ino wasn't.

Already the new priority message was coming in: *"Sea Mother, the fight's over here. Predators departing Waterfall System. Repeating . . ."*

Claus started to obey an impulse to run out and look at the sky again, then realized that there would certainly be nothing to be seen of the battle now. Radio waves, no faster than light, had just announced that it was over. Instead he joined the others in voicing their mutual relief. They had a minute or so of totally unself-conscious cheering.

Ino, his face much relieved, broke out a bottle of something and four glasses. In a little while, all of them drifted noisily outside, unable to keep from looking up, though knowing they would find nothing but the stars to see.

"What," asked Claus, "were berserkers doing here in the first place? We're hardly a big enough target to be interesting to a fleet of them. Are we?"

"Not when they have bigger game in sight." Ino gestured upward with his drink. "Oh, any living target interests them, once they get it in their sights. But I'd guess that if a sizable force was here they were on the way to attack Atlantis. See, sometimes in space you can use a planet or a whole system as a kind of cover. Sneak up behind its solar wind, as it were, its gravitational vortex, as someone

fighting a land war might take advantage of a mountain or a hill."
Atlantis was a long-colonized system less than a dozen parsecs distant, heavily populated and heavily defended. The three habitable
Atlantean planets were surfaced mostly with water, and the populace
lived almost as much below the waves as on the shaky continents.

It was hours later when Glenna roused and stirred in darkness,
pulling away for a moment from Ino's familiar angularity nested
beside her.

She blinked. "What was that?" she asked her husband, in a low
voice barely cleared of sleep.

Ino scarcely moved. "What was what?"

"A flash, I thought. Some kind of bright flash, outside. Maybe in
the distance."

There came no sound of thunder, or of rain. And no more flashes,
either, in the short time Glenna remained awake.

Shortly after sunrise next morning, Claus and Jen went out for an
early swim. Their beach, pointed out by their hosts as the place
where swimmers would be safest and least likely to damage the new
ecology, lay a few hundred meters along the shoreline to the west,
with several tall dunes between it and the building complex.

As they rounded the first of these dunes, following the pebbly
shoreline, Claus stopped. "Look at that." A continuous track, sug-
gesting the passage of some small, belly-dragging creature, had been
drawn in the sand. Its lower extremity lay somewhere under water,
its upper was concealed amid the humps of sterile sand somewhere
inland.

"Something," said Jenny, "crawled up out of the water. I haven't
seen that before on Waterfall."

"Or came down into it." Claus squatted beside the tiny trail. He
was anything but a skilled tracker, and could see no way of deter-
mining which way it led. "I haven't seen anything like this before
either. Glenna said certain species—I forget which—were starting
to try the land. I expect this will interest them when we get back."

When Claus and Jenny had rounded the next dune, there came
into view on its flank two more sets of tracks, looking very much
like the first, and like the first either going up from the water or
coming down.

"Maybe," Claus offered, "it's the same one little animal going back
and forth. Do crabs make tracks like that?"

Jen couldn't tell him. "Anyway, let's hope they don't pinch swimmers." She slipped off her short robe and took a running dive into

the cool water, whose salt content made it a good match for the seas of Earth. Half a minute later, she and her husband came to the surface together, ten meters or so out from shore. From here they could see west past the next dune. There, a hundred meters distant, underscored by the slanting shadows of the early sun, a whole tangled skein of narrow, fresh-looking tracks connected someplace inland with the sea.

A toss of Jen's head shook water from her long, dark hair. "I wonder if it's some kind of seasonal migration?"

"They certainly weren't there yesterday. I think I've had enough. This water's colder than a bureaucrat's heart."

Walking briskly, they had just re-entered the compound when Jenny touched Claus on the arm.

"There's Glenna, at the tractor shed. I'm going to trot over and tell her what we saw."

"All right. I'll fix some coffee."

Glenna, coming out of the shed a little distance inland from the main house, forestalled Jenny's announcement about the tracks with a vaguely worried question of her own.

"Did you or Claus see or hear anything strange last night, Jenny?"

"Strange? No, I don't think so."

Glenna looked toward a small cluster of more distant outbuildings. "We've just been out there taking a scheduled seismograph reading. It had recorded something rather violent and unusual, at about oh-two-hundred this morning. The thing is, you see, it must have been just about that time that something woke me up. I had the distinct impression that there had been a brilliant flash, somewhere outside."

Ino, also dressed in coveralls this morning, appeared among the distant sheds, trudging toward them. When he arrived, he provided more detail on the seismic event. "Quite sharp and apparently quite localized, not more than ten kilometers from here. Our system triangulated it well. I don't know when we've registered another event quite like it."

"What do you suppose it was?" Jen asked.

Ino hesitated minimally. "It could have been a very small spaceship crashing; or maybe a fairly large aircraft. But the only aircraft on Waterfall are the two little ones we have out in the far shed."

"A meteor, maybe?"

"I rather hope so. Otherwise a spacecraft just might be our most likely answer. And if it were a spacecraft from Brass Trumpet's force coming down here—crippled in the fighting, perhaps—we'd have heard from him on the subject, I should think."

The remaining alternative hung in the air unvoiced. Jenny bit her lip. By now, Brass Trumpet must be long gone from the system, and impossible of recall, his ships outpacing light and radio waves alike in pursuit of the enemy force.

In a voice more worried than before, Glenna was saying: "Of course if it was some enemy unit, damaged in the battle, then I suppose the crash is likely to have completed its destruction."

"I'd better tell you," Jenny blurted in. And in a couple of sentences she described the peculiar tracks.

Ino stared at her with frank dismay. "I was going to roll out an aircraft . . . but let me take a look at those tracks first."

The quickest way to reach them was undoubtedly on foot, and the gnarled man trotted off along the beach path at such a pace that Jenny had difficulty keeping up. Glenna remained behind, saying she would let Claus know what was going on.

Moving with flashes of former athletic grace, Ino reached the nearest of the tracks and dropped to one knee beside it, just as Claus had done. "Do the others look just like this?"

"As nearly as I could tell. We didn't get close to all of them."

"That's no animal I ever saw." He was up again already, trotting back toward the base. "I don't like it. Let's get airborne, all of us."

"I always pictured berserkers as huge things."

"Most of 'em are. Some are small machines, for specialized purposes."

"I'll run into the house and tell the others to get ready to take off," Jenny volunteered as they sped into the compound.

"Do that. Glenna will know what to bring, I expect. I'll get a flyer rolled out of the shed."

Running, Jen thought as she hurried into the house, gave substance to a danger that might otherwise have existed only in the mind. Could it be that Ino, with the horrors in his memory, was somewhat too easily alarmed where berserkers were concerned?

Glenna and Claus, who had just changed into coveralls, met her in the common room. She was telling them of Ino's decision to take to the air, and thinking to herself that she had better change out of her beach garb also, when the first outcry sounded from somewhere outside. It was less a scream than a baffled-sounding, hysterical laugh.

Glenna pushed past her at once, and in a moment was out the door and running. Exchanging a glance with her husband, Jenny turned and followed, Claus right at her heels.

The strange cry came again. Far ahead, past Glenna's running figure, the door of the aircraft shed had been slid back, and in its opening a white figure appeared outlined. A figure that reeled drunkenly and waved its arms.

Glenna turned aside at the tractor shed, where one of the small ground vehicles stood ready. They were used for riding, hauling, pushing sand, to sculpt a pond into a better shape or slice away part of a too-obtrusive dune. It'll be faster than running, Jenny thought, as she saw the older woman spring into the driver's seat, and heard the motor *whoosh* quietly to life. She leaped aboard too. Claus shoved strongly at her back to make sure she was safely on, before he used both hands for his own grip. A grip was necessary because they were already rolling, and accelerating quickly.

Ino's figure, now just outside the shed, came hurtling closer with their own speed. He shook his arms at them again and staggered. Upon his chest he wore a brownish thing the size of a small plate, like some great medallion that was so heavy it almost pulled him down. He clawed at the brown plate with both hands, and suddenly his coveralls in front were splashed with scarlet. He bellowed words which Jenny could not make out.

Claus gripped Glenna's shoulder and pointed. A dozen or more brown plates were scuttling on the brown, packed sand, between the aircraft shed and the onrushing tractor. The tracks they drew were faint replicas of those that had lined the softer sand along the beach. Beneath each saucer-like body, small legs blurred, reminding Claus of something recently seen, something he could not stop to think of now.

The things had nothing like the tractor's speed but still they were in position to cut it off. Glenna swerved no more than slightly, if at all, and one limbed plate disappeared beneath a wheel. It came up at once with the wheel's rapid turning, a brown blur seemingly embedded in the soft, fat tire, resisting somehow the centrifugal force that might have thrown it off.

Ino had gone down with, as Claus now saw, three of the things fastened on his body, but he somehow fought back to his feet just as the tractor jerked to a halt beside him. If Claus could have stopped to analyze his own mental state, he might have said he lacked the time to be afraid. With a blow of his fist he knocked one of the attacking things away from Ino, and felt the surprising weight and hardness of it as a sharp pang up through his wrist.

All three dragging together, they pulled Ino aboard; Glenna was back in the driver's seat at once. Claus kicked another attacker off, then threw open the lid of the tractor's toolbox. He grabbed the longest, heaviest metal tool displayed inside.

A swarm of attackers were between them and the aircraft shed; and the shadowed shape of a flyer, just inside, was spotted with them too. As Glenna gunned the engine, she turned the tractor at the same time, heading back toward the main building and the sea beyond. In the rear seat, Jenny held Ino. He bled on everything, and his eyes were fixed on the sky while his mouth worked in terror. In the front, Claus fought to protect the driver and himself.

A brown plate scuttled onto the cowling, moving for Glenna's hands on the controls. Claus swung, a baseball batter, bright metal blurring at the end of his extended arms. There was a hard, satisfying crunch, as of hard plastic or ceramic cracking through. The brown thing fell to the floor, and he caught a glimpse of dull limbs still in motion before he caught it with a foot and kicked it out onto the flying ground.

Another of the enemy popped out from somewhere onto the dash. He pounded at it, missed when it seemed to dodge his blows. He cracked its body finally; but still it clung on under the steering column, hard to get at, inching toward Glenna's fingers. Claus grabbed it with his left hand, felt a lance. Not until he had thrown the thing clear of the tractor did he look at his hand and see two fingers nearly severed.

At the same moment, the tractor engine died, and they were rolling to a silent stop, with the sea and the small dock Glenna had been steering for only a few meters ahead. Under the edge of the engine cowling another of the enemy appeared, thrusting forward a limb that looked like a pair of ceramic pliers, shredded electrical connectors dangling in its grip.

The humans abandoned the tractor in a wordless rush. Claus, one hand helpless and dripping blood, aided the women with Ino as best he could. Together they half-dragged, half-carried him across the dock and rolled him into a small, open boat, the only craft at once available. In moments Glenna had freed them from the dock and started the motor, and they were headed out away from shore.

Away from shore, but not into the sea. They were separated from deep-blue and choppy ocean by a barrier reef or causeway, one of the features that had made this coast desirable for the life-seeding base. The reef, a basically natural structure of sand and rock deposited by waves and currents, was about a hundred meters from the shore, and stretched in either direction as far as vision carried. Running from beach to reef, artificial walls or low causeways of fused rock separated ponds of various sizes.

"We're in a kind of square lagoon here," Glenna told Jenny, motioning for her to take over the job of steering. "Head for that far corner. If we can get there ahead of them, we may be able to lift the boat over the reef and get out."

Jen nodded, taking the controls. Glenna slid back to a place beside her husband, snapped open the boat's small first-aid kit, and began applying pressure bandages.

Claus started to try to help, saw the world beginning to turn gray around him, and slumped back against the gunwale; no use to anyone if he passed out. Ino looked as if he had been attacked, not by teeth or claws or knives, but by several sets of nail-pullers and wirecutters. His chest still rose and fell, but his eyes were closed now and he was gray with shock. Glenna draped a thermal blanket over him.

Jen was steering around the rounded structure, not much bigger than a phone booth, protruding above the water in the middle of the pond. Most of the ponds and bays had similar observation stations. Claus had looked into one or two and he thought now that there was nothing in them likely to be of any help. More first-aid kits, perhaps—but what Ino needed was the big medirobot back at the house.

And he was not going to get it. By now the building complex must be overrun by the attackers. Berserkers . . .

"Where can we find weapons?" Claus croaked at Glenna.

"Let's see that hand. I can't do any more for Ino now . . . I'll bandage this. If you mean guns, there are a couple at the house, somewhere in storage. We can't go back there now."

"I know."

Glenna had just let go his hand when from the front seat there came a scream. Claws and a brown saucer-shape were climbing in over the gunwale at Jenny's side. Had the damned thing come aboard somehow with them, from the tractor? Or was this pond infested with them too?

In his effort to help drag Ino to the boat, Claus had abandoned his trusty wrench beside the tractor. He grabbed now for the best substitute at hand, a small anchor at the end of a chain. His overhand swing missed Jenny's head by less than he had planned, but struck the monster like a mace. It fell into the bottom of the boat, vibrating its limbs, as Claus thought, uselessly; then he realized that it was making a neat hole.

His second desperation-swing came down upon it squarely. One sharp prong of the anchor broke a segment of the brown casing clean away, and something sparked and sizzled when the sea came rushing in—

—seawater rushing—

—into the bottom of the boat—

The striking anchor had enlarged the hole that the enemy had begun. The bottom was split, the boat was taking water fast.

Someone grabbed up the sparking berserker, inert now save for internal fireworks, and hurled it over the side. Glenna threw herself forward, taking back the wheel, and Jenny scrambled aft, to help one-handed Claus with bailing.

The boat limped, staggered, gulped water and wallowed on toward the landbar. It might get them that far, but forget the tantalizing freedom of blue surf beyond . . .

Jenny started to say something to her husband, then almost shrieked again, as Ino's hand, resurgently alive, came up to catch her wrist. The old man's eyes were fixed on hers with a tremendous purpose. He gasped out words, and then fell back unable to do more.

The words first registered with Jenny as: " . . . need them . . . do the splashers . . ." It made no sense.

Glenna looked back briefly, then had to concentrate on boat-handling. In another moment the fractured bottom was grating over rock. Claus scrambled out and held the prow against the above-water portion of the reef. The women followed, got their footing established outside the boat, then turned to lift at Ino's inert form.

Jenny paused. "Glenna, I'm afraid he's gone."

"No!" Denial was fierce and absolute. "Help me!"

Jen almost started to argue, then gave in. They got Ino up into a fireman's-carry position on Claus's shoulders; even with a bad hand he was considerably stronger than either of the women. Then the three began to walk east along the reef. At high tide, as now, it was a strip of land no more than three or four meters wide, its low crest half a meter above the water. Waves of any size broke over it. Fortunately today the surf was almost calm.

Claus could feel the back of his coverall and neck wetting with Ino's blood. He shifted the dead weight on his shoulders. All right, so far. But his free hand, mutilated, throbbed.

He asked: "How far are we going, Glenna?"

"I don't know." The woman paced ahead—afraid to look at her husband now?—staring into the distance. "There isn't any place. Keep going."

Jenny and Claus exchanged looks. For want of any better plan at the moment, they kept going. Jen took a look back. "They're on the reef, and on the shore, too, following us. A good distance back."

Claus looked, and looked again a minute later. Brown speckles by the dozen followed, but were not catching up. Not yet.

Now they were passing the barrier of fused rock separating the pond in which they had abandoned the boat from its neighbor. The enemy moving along the shore would intercept them, or very nearly, if they tried to walk the barrier back to land.

Ahead, the reef still stretched interminably into a sun-dazzled nothingness.

"What's in this next pond, Glenna?" Claus asked, and knew a measure of relief when the gray-haired woman gave a little shake of her head and answered sensibly.

"Grouper. Some other fish as food stock for them. Why?"

"Just wondering. What'll we run into if we keep on going in this direction?"

"This just goes on. Kilometer after kilometer. Ponds, and bays, and observation stations—I say keep going because otherwise they'll catch us. What do you think we ought to do?"

Claus abruptly stopped walking, startling the women. He let the dead man slide down gently from his shoulders. Jen looked at her husband, examined Ino, shook her head.

Claus said: "I think we've got to leave him."

Glenna looked down at Ino's body once, could not keep looking at him. She nodded fiercely, and once more led the way.

A time of silent walking passed before Jenny at Claus's side began: "If they're berserkers . . ."

"What else?"

"Well, why aren't we all dead already? They don't seem very . . . efficiently designed for killing."

"They must be specialists," Claus mused. "Only a small part of a large force, a part Brass Trumpet missed when the rest moved on or was destroyed. Remember, we were wondering if Atlantis was their real target? These are special machines, built for . . . underwater work, maybe. Their ship must have been wrecked in the fighting and had to come down. When they found themselves on this planet they must have come down to the sea for a reconnaissance, and then decided to attack first by land. Probably they saw the lights of the base before they crash-landed. They know which life-form they have to deal with first, on any planet. Not very efficient, as you say. But they'll keep coming at us till they're all smashed or we're all dead."

Glenna had slowed her pace a little and was looking toward the small observation post rising in the midst of the pond that they were passing. "I don't think there's anything in any of these stations that can help us. But I can't think of anywhere else to turn."

Claus asked: "What's in the next pond after this?"

"Sharks . . . ah. That might be worth a try. Sometimes they'll snap at anything that moves. They're small ones, so I think our risk will be relatively small if we wade out to the middle."

Claus thought to himself that he would rather end in the belly of a live shark than be torn to pieces by an impersonal device. Jen was willing also to take the chance.

They did not pause again till they were on the brink of the shark pond. Then Glenna said: "The water will be no more than three or four feet deep the way we're going. Stay together and keep splashing as we go. Claus, hold that bad hand up; mustn't drip a taste of blood into the water."

And in they went. Only when they were already splashing waist-deep did Claus recall Ino's blood wetting the back of his coverall. But he was not going to stop just now to take it off.

The pond was not very large; a minute of industrious wading, and they were climbing unmolested over the low, solid railing of the observation post rising near its middle. Here was space for two people to sit comfortably, sheltered from weather by a transparent dome and movable side panels. In the central console were instruments that continually monitored the life in the surrounding pond. Usually, of course, the readings from all ponds would be monitored in the more convenient central station attached to the house.

The three of them squeezed in, and Glenna promptly opened a small storage locker. It contained a writing instrument that looked broken, a cap perhaps left behind by some construction worker, and a small spider—another immigrant from Earth, of course—who might have been blown out here by the wind. That was all.

She slammed the locker shut again. "No help. So now it's a matter of waiting. They'll obviously come after us through the water. The sharks may snap up some of them before they reach us. Then we must be ready to move on before we are surrounded. It's doubtful, and risky, but I can't think of anything else to try."

Claus frowned. "Eventually we'll have to circle around, get back to the buildings."

Jen frowned at him. "The berserkers are there, too."

"I don't think they will be, now. You see—"

Glenna broke in: "Here they come."

The sun had climbed, and was starting to get noticeably hot. It came to Claus's mind, not for the first time since their flight had started, that there was no water for them to drink. He held his left arm up with his right, trying to ease the throbbing.

Along the reef where they had walked, along the parallel shore—and coming now over the barrier from the grouper pond-platesized specks of brown death were flowing. There were several dozen of them, moving more slowly than hurried humans could move, almost invisible in the shimmer of sun and sea. Some plopped into the water of the shark pond as Claus watched.

"I can't pick them up under water," Glenna announced. She was twiddling the controls of the station's instruments, trying to catch the enemy on one of the screens meant for observing marine life. "Sonar . . . motion detectors . . . water's too murky for simple video."

Understanding dawned for Claus. "That's why they're not metal! Why they're comparatively fragile. They're designed for avoiding detection by underwater defenses, on Atlantis I suppose, for infiltrating and disabling them."

Jen was standing. "We'd better get moving before we're cut off."

"In another minute." Glenna was still switching from one video pickup to another around the pond. "I'm sure we have at least that much to spare . . . ah."

One of the enemy had appeared on screen, sculling toward the camera at a modest pace. It looked less lifelike than it had in earlier moments of arm's-length combat.

Now, entering the picture from the rear, a shark.

Claus was not especially good on distinguishing marine species. But this portentous and somehow familiar shape was identifiable at once, not to be confused even by the non-expert, it seemed, with that of any other kind of fish.

Claus started to say, He's going right past. But the shark was not. Giving the impression of afterthought, the torpedo-shape swerved back. Its mouth opened and the berserker device was gone.

The people watching made wordless sounds. But Jen took the others by an arm apiece. "We can't bet all of them will be eaten—let's get moving."

Claus already had one leg over the station's low railing when the still surface of the pond west of the observation post exploded. Leaping clear of the water, the premiere killer of Earth's oceans twisted in mid-air, as if trying to snap at its own belly. It fell back, vanishing in a hill of lashed-up foam. A moment later it jumped again, still thrashing.

In the fraction of a second when the animal was clearly visible,

Claus watched the dark line come into being across its white belly as if traced there by an invisible pen. It was a short line that a moment later broadened and evolved in blood. As the fish rolled on its back something dark and pointed came into sight, spreading the edges of the hole. Then the convulsing body of the shark had vanished, in an eruption of water turned opaque with its blood.

The women were wading quickly away from the platform in the opposite direction, calling him to follow, hoping aloud that the remaining sharks would be drawn to the dying one. But for one moment longer Claus lingered, staring at the screen. It showed the roiling bloody turmoil of killer fish converging, and out of this cloud the little berserker emerged, unfazed by shark's teeth or digestion, resuming its methodical progress toward the humans, the life-units that could be really dangerous to the cause of death.

Jen tugged at her husband, got him moving with them. In her exhausted brain a nonsense-rhyme was being generated: *Bloody water hides the slasher, seed them, heed them, sue the splashers . . .*

No!

As the three completed their water-plowing dash to the east edge of the pond, and climbed out, Jenny took Glenna by the arm. "Something just came to me. When I was tending Ino—he said something before he died."

They were walking east along the barrier reef again. "He said smashers," Jen continued. "That was it. Lead them or feed them, to the smashers. But I still don't understand—"

Glenna stared at her for a moment, an almost frightening gaze. Then she stepped between the young couple and pulled them forward.

Two ponds down she turned aside, wading through water that splashed no higher than their calves, directly toward another observation post that looked just like the last.

"We won't be bothered in here," she assured them. "We're too big. Of course, of course. Oh, Ino. I should have thought of this myself. Unless we should happen to step right on one, but there's very little chance of that. They wait in ambush most of the time, in holes or under rocks."

"They?" Injury and effort were taking toll on Claus. He leaned on Jenny's shoulder now.

Glenna glanced back impatiently. "Mantis shrimp is the common name. They're stomatopods, actually."

"Shrimp?" The dazed query was so soft that she may not have heard it.

A minute later they were squeezed aboard the station and could rest again. Above, clean morning clouds were building to enormous height, clouds that might have formed in the unbreathed air of Earth five hundred million years before.

"Claus," Jen asked, when both of them had caught their breath a little, "what were you saying a while ago, about circling back to the house?"

"It's this way," he said, and paused to organize his thoughts. "We've been running to nowhere, because there's nowhere on this world we can get help. *But the berserkers can't know that.* I'm assuming they haven't scouted the whole planet, but just crash-landed on it. For all they know, there's another colony of humans just down the coast. Maybe a town, with lots of people, aircraft, weapons . . . so for them it's an absolute priority to cut us off before we can give a warning. Therefore every one of their units must be committed to the chase. And if we can once get through them or around them, we can outrun them home, to vehicles and guns and food and water. How we get through them or around them I haven't figured out yet. But I don't see any other way."

"We'll see," said Glenna. Jen held his hand, and looked at him as if his idea might be reasonable. A distracting raindrop hit him on the face, and suddenly a shower was spattering the pond. With open mouths the three survivors caught what drops they could. They tried spreading Jenny's robe out to catch more, but the rain stopped before the cloth was wet.

"Here they come," Glenna informed them, shading her eyes from re-emergent sun. She started tuning up the observing gear aboard the station.

Claus counted brown saucer-shapes dropping into the pond. Only nineteen, after all.

"Again, I can't find them with the sonar," Glenna muttered. "We'll try the television—there."

A berserker unit—for all the watching humans could tell, it was the same one that the shark had swallowed—was centimetering its tireless way toward them, walking the bottom in shallow, sunlit water. Death was walking. A living thing might run more quickly, for a time, but life would tire. Or let life oppose it, if life would. Already it had walked through a shark, as easily as traversing a mass of seaweed.

"There," Glenna breathed again. The advancing enemy had detoured slightly around a rock, and a moment later a dancing ripple of movement had emerged from hiding somewhere to follow in its path. The pursuer's score or so of tiny legs supported in flowing motion a soft-looking, roughly segmented tubular body. Its sinuous length was about the same as the enemy machine's diameter, but in contrast the follower was aglow with life, gold marked in detail with red and green and brown, like banners carried forward above an advancing column. Long antennae waved as if for balance above bulbous, short-stalked eyes. And underneath the eyes a coil of heavy forelimbs rested, not used for locomotion.

"*Odonodactylus syllarus,*" Glenna murmured. "Not the biggest species—but maybe big enough."

"What are they?" Jen's voice was a prayerful whisper.

"Well, predators . . ."

The berserker, intent on its own prey, ignored the animate ripple that was overtaking it, until the smasher had closed almost to contact range. The machine paused then, and started to turn.

Before it had rotated itself more than halfway its brown body was visibly jerked forward, under some striking impetus from the smasher too fast for human eyes to follow. The *krak!* of it came clearly through the audio pickup. Even before the berserker had regained its balance, it put forth a tearing-claw like that which had opened the shark's gut from inside.

Again the invisible impact flicked from a finger-length away. At each spot where one of the berserker's feet touched bottom, a tiny spurt of sand jumped up with the transmitted shock. Its tearing claw now dangled uselessly, hard ceramic cracked clean across.

"I've never measured a faster movement by anything that lives. They strike with special dactyls—well, with their elbows, you might say. They feed primarily on hard-shelled crabs and clams and snails. That was a just a little one, that Ino gave you as a joke. One as long as my hand can hit something like a four-millimeter bullet—and some of these are longer."

Another hungry smasher was now coming swift upon the track of the brown, shelled thing that looked so like a crab. The second smasher's eyes moved on their stalks, calculating distance. It was evidently of a different species than the first, being somewhat larger and of a variant coloration. Even as the berserker, which had just put out another tool, sharp and wiry, and cut its first assailant neatly in half, turned back, Claus saw—or almost saw or imagined that he saw—the newcomer's longest pair of forelimbs unfold and return. Again grains of sand beneath the two bodies, living and unliving, jumped from the bottom. With the concussion white radii of fracture sprang out across a hard, brown surface . . .

Four minutes later the three humans were still watching, in near-perfect silence. A steady barrage of *kraks,* from every region of the pond, were echoing through the audio pickups. The video screen still showed the progress of the first individual combat.

"People sometimes talk about sharks as being agressive, as terrible killing machines. Gram for gram, I don't think they're at all in the same class."

The smashing stomatopod, incongruously shrimplike, gripping with its six barb-studded smaller forelimbs the ruined casing of its victim—from which a single ceramic walking-limb still thrashed—began to drag it back to the rock from which its ambush had been launched. Once there, it propped the interstellar terror in place, a Lilliputian monster blacksmith arranging metal against anvil. At the next strike, imaginable if not visible as a double backhand snap from the fists of a karate master, fragments of tough casing literally flew through the water, mixed now with a spill of delicate components. What, no soft, delicious meat in sight as yet? Then *smash* again . . .

An hour after the audio pickups had reported their last *krak,* the three humans walked toward home, unmolested through the shallows and along a shore where no brown saucers moved.

When Ino had been brought home, and Claus's hand seen to, the house was searched for enemy survivors. Guns were got out, and the great gates in the sand-walls closed to be on the safe side. Then the two young people sent Glenna to a sedated rest.

Her voice was dazed, and softly, infinitely tired. "Tomorrow we'll feed them, something real."

"This afternoon," said Claus. "When you wake up. Show me what to do."

"Look at this," called Jen a minute later, from the common room.

One wall of the smallest aquarium had been shattered outward. Its tough glass lay sharded on the carpet, along with a large stain of water and the soft body of a small creature, escaped and dead.

Jen picked it up. It was much smaller than its cousins out in the pond, but now she could not mistake the shape, even curled loosely in her palm.

Her husband came in and looked over her shoulder. "Glenna's still muttering. She just told me they can stab, too, if they sense soft meat in contact. Spear-tips on their smashers when they unfold them all the way. So you couldn't hold him like that if he was still alive." Claus's voice broke suddenly, in a delayed reaction.

"Oh, yes I could." Jen's voice too. "Oh, yes I could indeed."

★ A Musical Interlude ★

by Suzy McKee Charnas

This is a strong place, not just a tract of country. It tends to walk right into your work—especially, I think, if your work is fantasy-writing—and to bring added richness and satisfaction with it. Let me offer an example.

The following story, "A Musical Interlude," is the fourth chapter of my novel THE VAMPIRE TAPESTRY, a tale which begins at the small New England college where my vampire hero teaches anthropology (and it's a source of continuing amazement and delight to me that readers laughingly tell me that they remember the cold-eyed son of a bitch—"He was on my thesis committee," they say). So how, and why, does he turn up at the Santa Fe Opera in chapter four?

You must realize that I first conceived of him on a visit to New York City, where I was born and raised. He began as a creature of that city and its culture; or maybe a rejection of that culture, now that I think about it. I was reacting against the two plays about

107

musty old Count Dracula that I had just seen, on Broadway and off. After years of infatuation with that version of the legend, from Bram Stoker onward, I was suddenly fed up with the romanticized figure—the demonic grandee from a sort of shadow-version of Ruritania, his nobility debased, his poor heart yearning for the company of bosomy ladies in the chill halls of Eternity, his "life" governed by a pack of dopey rules out of a Hammer Film.

Pooey on it, I said, sitting and waiting for my sister in the waiting room at Grand Central Station: the vampire is not Byron's meaner brother's ghost. He is a predator, and we are the prey.

And that's how I began writing about him, against the backdrop of an eastern faculty club where I'd stayed during that trip. He seemed to fit into that sort of intellectual life very comfortably.

But not long after I'd done the first chapter, originally intended as a self-contained story, I found myself out on the Navajo with my family, and looking at all that rough red rock I thought suddenly, Weyland the vampire must come out here. There is something to be gained by setting that tough, implacable, fantastic and beautiful creature against this tough, implacable, fantastic and beautiful landscape, both of them time-honed and mysterious and un-giving (and all the rest of what the imaginative attribute to such landscapes and such figures).

So, in the course of the novel Weyland comes west, teaches at UNM, and finally casts his lot here in a way open only to him. And the book is immeasurably enhanced, in my opinion.

Well, I see that I have addressed the question of how this place can affect the work of fantasy-writing, not the broader one of why I (and so many of my transplanted colleagues out here) write SF and fantasy at all. What are we doing here, and why do we seem to be addicted to a sort of literary sky-diving of the mind? Are we all drunk on the pure, thin air? Hardly; it's not as thin as all that, and nobody who's lived through a winter of the Brown Cloud has any illusions about the pure air of Albuquerque. Is it something we ate—green chile, maybe?

Let me suggest something somewhat more outlandish, at the risk of being labeled an air-head (clean or dirty air, take your pick). When my husband and I first arrived here in 1969, we immersed ourselves in the landscape and the various local cultures because they were intriguing and attractive aspects of our new environment. That, at any rate, is what I thought then. What I think now is that we were responding to something about that landscape and those cultures, and their interaction, that had drawn us as it draws seek-

ers of all kinds—from priests and professors to artists to air-heads—
to this area. And then it works on them.

Now, this notion may itself be a fantasy, but it is a response to
some real stimulus. Or we writers from other parts would not be
milling around here, telling each other (as we do from time to time)
that something drew us here, and what's more, that it delivers. We
work. We publish. We flourish, within the limits of our personal
quirks and the baggage we've brought with us.

So what is it that "works," that draws, that leads to, say, a suave
east-coast vampire shedding his tweeds and his horn-rims and running down a deer on Sandia Peak for the sheer hell of it?

I think that centuries of careful attention to and respect for this
landscape by various stages of Indian culture have left some kind
of continuing reverberation to which the souls of all live-minded
after-comers have resonated and still resonate. In the stillness of
the air and the broad, red reach of the land, I think there is a kind
of on-going, subliminal (to Anglos, at any rate, who are trained by
a noisy culture not to hear anything under fifty decibels) vibration.
It was put there by generations of drum-beats, chants, dancers'
stamping feet, morning prayers sung to the sun, the shaking of seed
rattles.

Talk about romanticism, you may say! But I don't see it that
way. I believe that human action and human intent make an impress on the world, for good or for ill, and human action and human
intent include not only bulldozers but prayer-sticks. We matter
here; what we think, what we feel, what we do, and what we say,
all matter, all leave their marks. To deny this is simply to attempt
to justify irresponsibility, cowardice, and greed (after all, if none of
it matters, why not indulge your worst impulses?).

But to return to (oh dear—) our "vibrations": this is not only a
matter of the past, not in New Mexico. Add to the residue of those
generations of care-takers, balance-makers, and singers the stimulus of the living present. To be very specific, you can't go to the
Shalako at Zuni, for example, without having your mind (if it is a
live mind) kicked into an unfamiliar place that you perhaps never
suspected or never believed was there. This in itself frees you to
pursue whatever else lies in this new, strange (to Anglo newcomers,
at least) territory of possibility, whether you choose to explore or
not. The option is there.

An unfamiliar track is opened; and the vibrations in the earth
and sky tell us that the territory of wild possibility that it leads to
is real, significant, worth the journey. You perceive the validity of

this because you have never been willing to settle for the dreary, jumbled surface that our culture insistently sells as the one and only true reality, at eighteen percent, why wait, buy NOW.

But then, that is why (I think) most writers write in the first place: because they know there's more, and if they can't find it, they'll go ahead and create (or, if you prefer, reveal) it.

With a mind-set like that, in a place that lets your mind open like the sky if you allow it, is it any wonder that we write of wonders!

A Musical Interlude

by Suzy McKee Charnas

In a carrel of the university library tower a student slept. Over him stood Dr. Weyland, respected new member of the faculty, pressed by hunger to feed.

The air was warm despite the laboring of the cooling system. Quiet reigned; summer courses brought few students into the stacks. On his preliminary tour of this tower level, silent in crepe-soled shoes, Weyland had noted the presence of only two: this sleeping youth and a young woman sitting on the floor reading in the geology section.

In nervous haste Weyland moved: he rendered the sleeper unconscious by briefly pressing shut an artery to the brain. Then, delicately tipping the lolling head to fully expose the throat, he leaned close and drank without a sound. When he was done, he patted his lips with his handkerchief and left as silently as he had come.

The youth whose blood he had drunk breathed a gusty, complaining sigh across the page on which his pale cheek rested. He dreamed of being unprepared for a history exam.

In the men's room on the ground floor Weyland washed the scent of his victim from his hands. Damp-palmed, he smoothed back his vigorous iron-gray hair, which in this climate tended to stick up in wiry tufts. He frowned at his reflection, at the tension lines around his mouth and eyes.

In his second week in New Mexico, he was still feeling upset from his recent experiences in the East. Yet now he must behave with calm and self-confidence. He could not afford mistakes. No odd rumors or needless animosity must attach themselves to him here.

All modern cities seemed so large to him that he had miscalculated about this one: Albuquerque was smaller than he had expected. He missed the anonymity of New York. No wonder he couldn't shake this nervousness. Walking back through the somnolent afternoon for a nap in his temporary quarters, the home of an assistant professor, would relax him. Then he could sleep, as his digestion obliged him to, on the meal he had just taken in the library.

As part of the department head's efforts to settle him comfortably in his new surroundings, social arrangements had been made in advance for him. Tonight he was to attend the opera in Santa Fe with some friends of the department head's wife, people who ran an art gallery here in Albuquerque. Weyland hoped the evening would contribute to his image as an austere but approachable scholar. The strain of sociability would be supportable, given the all-important nap.

He walked out into the brilliant summer sunlight.

The tourists ambled through the opera house. From the ridge on which the building lay they could look south toward Santa Fe, east and west toward mountains. Even on hot days breezes cooled the opera hill. The deep, concrete-enclosed spaces of the house were wells of shadow. The house manager, who was guiding the tour, led the visitors through the wings and down an open stair. They emerged onto a sunny concrete deck that backed the entire building—stage area in the middle and flanking work areas—in a north-south sweep.

Raising his voice above hammering sounds and a whine of power tools, the guide said, "Most of the technical work gets done here on the deck level." He pointed out the paint and electrical shops and, just behind and below the stage, the big scenery lift between the two open staircases.

The group drifted onto the shaded southern end of the deck, which became a roofed veranda adjoining the wig and costume shop. They stood like passengers at the rail of a cruise ship, looking westward. Someone asked about the chain-link fence that ran behind the opera house near the base of the hill.

The house manager said, "The fence marks off the property of the opera itself from the land that the founder, John Crosby, had the foresight to buy as a buffer against growth from Santa Fe. Nobody will ever be able to build close enough to give us problems with noise or light, or wreck our acoustical backdrop—that hillside facing us across the arroyo at the bottom of our hill."

The tourists chatted, lingering on the shady veranda; even with a breeze, it was hot out on the exposed deck. Cameras clicked.

Looking down, a man in a safari suit asked disapprovingly, "What's all that trash down there?"

The others moved to look. On the deck they stood perhaps thirty feet above a paved road that ran below the back of the opera house along the west face of the hill. Beneath them the road gave access to a doorway and a garage entry, on either side of which huge piles of lumber and canvas were heaped high against the stucco wall.

"That's discarded sets," the guide said. "We have only so much storage space. Old productions get dumped there until we either cannibalize them for new sets or haul them away."

A woman, looking back the way they had come, said "This building is really a fantastic labyrinth. How does everyone keep track of where they're supposed to be and what they should be doing during a performance?"

The guide said, "By the music. You remember the stage manager's console in the right wings, with the phones and the mike and the TV monitors? The whole show is run from right there by the numbers in a marked copy of the score. Our stage manager, Renée Spiegel, watches the conductor's beat on the monitor, and according to that she gives everybody their cues. So the music structures everything that happens.

"Now, when we want to shut out the view of the mountains, for an indoor scene, say, we use movable back walls . . ."

"Dr. Weyland? I'm Jean Gray, from the Walking River Gallery. Albert McGrath, my partner, had to go to Santa Fe earlier today, so we'll meet him at the opera. You just sit back and enjoy the scenery while I drive us up there."

He folded his height into the front passenger seat without speaking or offering his hand. What's this, Jean wondered, doesn't the great man believe in hobnobbing with the common folk? Her friend the department head's wife had impressed upon her in no uncertain terms that this was indeed a great man. He fitted the part: a dark, well-tailored jacket and fawn slacks, gray hair, strong face—large, intense eyes brooding down a majestic prow of a nose, a morose set to the mouth and the long, stubborn jaw.

They also said he'd been ill back East; give a guy a break. Jean nosed the car out past striped sawhorses and piled rubble, exclaiming cheerfully, "Look at this mess!"

In precise and bitter tones Dr. Weyland replied, "Better to look at it than to listen to it being made. All afternoon I had to endure the bone-shattering thunder of heavy machinery." He added in grudging apology, "Excuse me. I customarily sleep after eating. Today a nap was impossible. I am not entirely myself."

"Would you like a Rolaid? I have some in my purse."

"No, thank you." He turned and put his coat on the back seat.

"I hope you have a scarf or sweater as well as your raincoat. Santa Fe's only sixty miles north of Albuquerque, but it's two thousand feet higher. The opera is open-air, so because of the lighting nothing starts till after sunset, about nine o'clock. Performances run late, and the nights can get chilly."

"I'll manage."

"I keep a blanket in the trunk just in case. At least the sky's nice and clear; we're not likely to be rained out. It's a good night for *Tosca*. You know that marvelous aria in the third act where Cavaradossi sings about how the stars shone above the cottage where he and Tosca used to meet—"

"The opera tonight is *Tosca*?"

"That's right. Do you know it well?"

After a moment he said distantly, "I knew someone in the East who was named after Floria Tosca, the heroine of the story. But I've never seen this opera."

After last night's performance of *Gonzago*, a dissonant modern opera on a bloody Renaissance theme, the *Tosca* lighting sequence had to be set up for tonight. Having worked backward through Acts Three and Two, the crew broke for dinner, then began to complete the reversed sequence so that when they finished at eight o'clock the lights and the stage would be set for the start of Act One.

Everyone was pleased to abandon the dreadful *Gonzago*, this season's expression of the Santa Fe Opera's commitment to modern works, in favor of a dependable old warhorse like Puccini's *Tosca*. Headsets at the stage manager's console, in the lighting booth, in the patch room and at the other stations around the house, hummed with brisk instructions, numbers, comments.

Renée Spiegel, the stage manager, pored over her carefully marked score. She hoped people hadn't forgotten too many cues since *Tosca* last week, that with doing three other operas since. She hoped everything would run nice and tight tonight, orderly and by the numbers.

Jeremy Tremain gargled, spat, and stared in the mirror at the inside of his throat. It looked a healthy pink.

Nevertheless he sat down discontentedly to his ritual pre-performance bowl of chicken broth. Tonight he was to sing Angelotti, a part which ended in the first act. By the opera's end the audience would remember the character, but who would recall having heard Tremain sing? He preferred a house that did calls after each act; you could do your part, take your bows, and go home.

The part he coveted was that of the baritone villain, Scarpia. Tremain was beginning to be bored with the roles open to him as a young bass—ponderous priests and monarchs and the fathers of tenor heroes. He had recently acquired a new singing teacher who he hoped could help him enlarge the top of his range, transforming him into a bass baritone capable of parts like Scarpia. He was sure he possessed the dark, libidinous depths the role demanded.

He got up and went in his bathrobe to the mirror again, turning for a three-quarter view. You wanted a blocky look for Scarpia. If only he had more jaw.

Weyland stared balefully out the car window. His library meal weighed in his midsection like wet sand. Being deprived of rest after eating upset his system. Now in addition he'd been cooped up for an hour in this flashy new car with an abominably timid driver. At least she had stopped trying to make conversation.

They overtook the cattle truck behind which they had been dawdling, then settled back to the same maddeningly slow pace.

He said irritably, "Why do you slow down again?"

"The police watch this road on Friday nights."

He could hardly demand to take over the driving; he must be patient, he must be courteous. He thought longingly of the swift gray Mercedes he had cherished in the East.

They took a stop-light-ridden bypass around Santa Fe itself and continued north. At length Jean Gray pointed out the opera house, tantalizingly visible beyond a crawling line of cars that snaked ahead of them past miles of construction barriers.

"Isn't there another road to the opera?" Weyland said.

"Just this one; and somehow during opera season it does tend to get torn up." She chattered on about how Santa Feans had a standing joke that their streets were regularly destroyed in summer solely to annoy the tourists.

Weyland stopped listening.

In the parking lot young people in jeans and windbreakers waved their flashlights, shouting, "This way, please," to incoming drivers.

People had formed a line at the standing-room window. The ushers stood, arms full of thick program books, talking in the sunken patio beyond the ticket gate.

Tremain checked in with the stage manager, who told him that the costume shop had finished mending the shirt for the dummy of Angelotti used in Act Three. That meant that tonight Tremain wouldn't have to strip after his part was over in Act One, give up his costume to the dummy, and then change back again for curtain calls. He took this for a good sign and cheerfully went down to the musicians' area to pick up his mail.

Members of the orchestra lounged down here, talking, playing cards in the practice rooms, getting their instruments from the cage in back and tuning up. Tremain flirted with one of the cellists, teasing her into coming to the party after the show tonight.

In the narrow conductor's office off the musicians' area, Rolf Anders paced. He wished now for just one more run-through with the backstage chorus in Act Two. The assistant conductor, working from a TV monitor, had to keep his backstage players and singers a fraction ahead of Anders and a fraction sharp for their music to sound right out front.

Anders looked forward to shedding his nervousness in the heat of performance. Some people said that every opera conductor should do *Tosca* each season to discharge his aggressions.

Three ticket-takers stationed themselves beside the slotted stub boxes, and the long iron gate swung wide. The people who had pooled on the steps and round the box office began to stream down into the sunken patio in front of the opera house. First comers sat down on the raised central fountain or the low walls containing foundation plantings of white petunias. From these vantage points they observed the clear but fading light flooding the sky, or watched and discussed the passing pageant.

Here an opera cape from another era, the crushed black velvet setting off an elegant neck; there blue jeans and a down-filled vest. Here a suit of Victorian cut complete with waistcoat, flowered buttonhole and watch chain, the wearer sporting between slim, ringed fingers an even slimmer cane; there a rugby shirt. Here a sport jacket in big orange-and-green checks over green slacks—and there, unbelievable, its double just passing in the opposite direction on a larger man who clearly shopped at the same men's store. Everywhere was the gleam of heavy silver, the sky hardness of turquoise, sparkle of diamond, shimmer of plaited iridescent feathers, glitter of baroquely twisted gold.

A church group of white-haired women, come for the evening in a chartered bus, stood goggling, a bouquet of pastel polyester flowers.

The house manager, in sober evening dress, moved nimbly through the crowd, sizing up the house, keeping track of mood and movement and the good manners of his ushers.

Jean, standing on her toes, spotted McGrath—stumpy, freckled, thinning on top—at the fountain. He had with him young Elmo Archuleta, a painter he was wooing for the gallery.

"That's Albert McGrath; would you mind going over and introducing yourself?" she said to Dr. Weyland. "I have to make a dash for the ladies' room." Jean and McGrath were at odds over her plans to leave the gallery and return to the East. These days she spent as little time as she could around McGrath.

Dr. Weyland grunted disagreeably, tucked his raincoat over his arm, and went to join them.

God save us, thought Jean, from the grouchy great.

"Pleased to meet you, Professor," McGrath said. So this was the hotshot anthropologist the university people were crowing about; handsome, in a sour, arrogant way, and he still had his hair. Some guys got all the luck.

McGrath introduced Elmo, who was scarred with acne and very shy. He explained that Elmo was a hot young local artist. Jean was undoubtedly trying to steer the kid away from the gallery, to retaliate for McGrath's refusal to let her walk out on their partnership. McGrath let slip no chance to praise Elmo, whose work he really liked. He flourished his enthusiasm.

The professor looked with undisguised boredom at Elmo, who was visibly shrinking into himself.

"Nice ride up?" McGrath said.

"An exceedingly slow ride."

Here comes Jean, thank God, McGrath thought. "Hiya, Jean-girl!" She was little and always fighting her weight, trying at thirty-two to keep looking like a kid. And sharp—you'd never guess how sharp from her round, candid face and breathless manner. Smart and devious, that was Easterners for you.

The professor said, "I think the altitude has affected me. I'd like to go in and sit down. No, please, all of you stay and enjoy the parade here. I'll see you later inside. May I have my ticket stub, please?"

He left them.

Jean smiled at Elmo. "Hi, Elmo. Is this your first time at the opera?"

"Sure is," McGrath answered. "I got him a seat down front at the last minute. And speaking of last-minute luck, I've wangled an invitation to a party afterward. Lots of important people will be there." He paused. She was going to let him down, he could see it coming.

"Oh, I wish I'd known earlier," she said. "I have to be back in Albuquerque early tomorrow morning to meet some clients at the gallery."

McGrath smiled past Jean at a couple he knew from someplace. "I'll take Elmo and the professor with me, then. He doesn't seem exactly friendly, this Weyland. Anything wrong?"

"He barely said a word on the way up. All I know is what I hear: this is a high-powered academic with a good book behind him; bachelor, tough in class—a workaholic, recently recovered from some kind of breakdown."

McGrath shook his head. "I don't know why they hire these high-strung, snotty Easterners when there's plenty of good local men looking for jobs." Giving Jean no time to respond, he walked away to talk to the couple he knew from someplace.

Jean said, "Is McGrath treating you okay, Elmo?"

"He's like all gallery people. They treat you nice until you sign up with them, and then they bring out the whip." Elmo flushed and looked down at his shiny boot toes; he liked Jean. "I didn't mean you. Are you still trying to get clear of McGrath?"

She sighed. "He won't let me out of the contract. He keeps saying New Mexico needs me. That's what happens when you're dumb enough to make yourself indispensable."

"How come you don't like it out here anymore?"

"I'm not as adaptable as I thought I was," she said ruefully. "The transplant just isn't working."

Elmo studied her brown hair, its soft, dull sheen. She was ten years his senior, which somehow made it easy for him to like her. He hoped she wouldn't go back East. That felt like a bad wish toward her, so he said impulsively, "Why don't you just up and go? You got enough money to fly back to New York."

She shook her head. "I need to go home with at least as much as I brought out here. You can't live in New York on the stub of a plane ticket."

Weyland took his seat. The theater was quiet, the stage set—there was no curtain—was softly illuminated. The house doors had just been opened, and most of the people were still out on the patio.

He definitely did not feel right. The tedious trip had put an edge on his fatigue. And they always wanted to talk; all the way up he had felt the pressure of Jean Gray's desire for conversation distracting him from the restful sweep of the land and sky.

Now, here, the fashionable crowd had reminded him uncomfortably of something—Alan Reese's followers, the spectators at the cell door . . . All left behind now. He thrust away the thought and leaned back to look a long time through the open roof at the deepening evening. If he could only walk out now into the dark, quiet hills, his keen night vision would aid him to find a hollow where he could lie down and settle his system with a nap—though at best sleep was difficult for him. By nature perpetually on the alert, he was roused by the least disturbance. Still, he could try— he wondered whether anyone would notice if he rose and slipped away.

Too late: another blink of the house lights, and the crowd came drifting down among the stepped rows of seats. Jean Gray sat down next to him, McGrath next to her.

She said to Weyland, "Well, what do you think? It's not a great big opera house like the Met in New York, but it has charm."

He knew he should respond, should make some effort to ingratiate himself. But he could bring himself to offer only a curt syllable of assent, followed by sullen silence.

With Anders standing ready beside her, Renée Spiegel said into the console mike, "Places, everyone, please."

The backstage speakers echoed, "Places, everyone, please."

She signaled the final blinking warnings of the house lights and then dispatched Anders to the podium. His image walked onto her TV monitor screen.

There was no foot-shuffling applause from the musicians when Anders entered the pit; he had lost his temper with them too often during rehearsals. The audience applauded him. He bowed. He turned and opened his score.

Spiegel, watching him on the monitor, called the lighting booth: "Warning, Light Cue One . . ."

Anders breathed deeply and gave the down beat.

"Cue One—"

Out crashed the first of the chords announcing the power of the dreaded Minister of Police, Baron Scarpia.

"Go!" Spiegel said.

The lights came up on an interior portion of the Church of Sant' Andrea della Valle in Rome, the year 1800. Scarpia's chords were transformed into the staggering music of flight. Tremain, as the escaped political prisoner Angelotti, rushed onstage into the church to hide.

In the lighting booth between the two sections of the balcony seating, a technician hit the switch that started the tape player. A cannon shot boomed from the house speakers. The technician grinned to herself, remembering the time her partner, stepping inside to relay a cue invisible from within the booth, had put a foot among the wires and yanked them out. The cannon shots of Act One had been drums that night.

Things could go wrong, things did go wrong, but it was never what you expected.

Floria Tosca on this stage bore no resemblance to the thin, dark woman named Floria whom Weyland had known in New York. This singer probably wasn't even a brunette—her eyes looked blue to him. His uneasy curiosity allayed, Weyland watched inattentively. He was turning over and over in his mind the layout of the university buildings, reviewing the hunting methods he could employ there until less risky opportunities to secure his prey developed.

Something onstage caught his attention. Scarpia was addressing Tosca for the first time, offering her on his own fingertips holy water from the stoup. He lifted his hand slightly as she withdrew hers, so that their contact was prolonged. After a startled glance of distaste at him, Tosca plunged again into jealous anxiety over her lover Cavaradossi's unexpected absence from the church. Scarpia moved downstage behind her, step for step, singing a polite inquiry into the cause of her distress. His tone was caressingly sensual and insinuating over a lively pealing of bells and courtly flourishes in the strings.

Intrigued by Scarpia's calculated maneuvering, Weyland lost interest when Tosca flew into a tantrum. He went back to pondering his new hunting ground.

The Te Deum, the great close of the first act, began. What a spectacle it was, Jean thought admiringly. The small stage seemed enlarged by the pageant in white, black, and scarlet entering at a grave, swaying pace behind Scarpia's back.

Scarpia mused on his own plans, oblivious to all else. He had deduced that Tosca's lover Cavaradossi was aiding the fugutive Angelotti out of sympathy with the latter's support of Bonaparte. Now Scarpia hoped that Tosca would go to Cavaradossi, and Scarpia's men would follow her without her knowledge and take the quarry.

The Police Minister's soliloquy, the lighter bells sounding the theme of his first suave approaches to Tosca, the great B-flat bell tolling, the organ, the choral voices, the measured booming of the cannon, all combined to thrilling effect; and the rich public virtue of the religious procession was set off against Scarpia's private villainy. As his sinuous melody wove around the solid structure of the celebrants' Te Deum, the long crescendo built.

Scarpia's voice seemed to ring effortlessly over the music, first an iron determination to recapture Angelotti; then a glowing outpouring of lust, luxuriant, powerful with assurance that soon Tosca would lie in his own arms—"*Illanguidir*," the voice glided down then surged upward with erotic strength on the final syllable;—*d'amor . . .*"

Waking abruptly to his surroundings, he joined the chorus in full voice, and suddenly the morality of the State, as conveyed by the liturgy, and the personal evil of Scarpia were also united: one the underside of the other, both together the essence of official hypocrisy.

Scarpia knelt. Three times brass and drums shouted the savage ascent of whole tones declaring his implacable ferocity, the lights vanished, the first of the three acts was over.

Jean sat back, sighing deeply. Around her people began to clap, standing, shouting, or turning to talk excitedly to one another.

Applauding, she turned also, but Dr. Weyland had gone.

Weyland walked in the parking lot. People moved among the cars under pools of light from the tall lampposts, talking and laughing, singing snatches of melody. They took from their cars scarves, gloves, blankets, hats. The breeze had an edge now.

Facing the wind, Weyland opened his jacket, unknotted his tie, and undid the top button of his shirt. He felt unpleasantly warm, almost feverish, and very tired. Even if he were to plead illness and retire to the back seat of the car, he knew he was too restless now to sleep.

He turned uneasily back toward the patio, a concourse of loud, volatile humanity. Crowds of people, their feelings and bodies in turbulent motion, always seemed threatening to him—unpredictable, irrational, as easily swept to savagery as to tears. And the music had been powerful; even he had felt his hackles stir.

Why? Art should not matter. Yet he responded—first to the ballet, back in New York, and now to this. He was disturbed by a sense of something new in himself, as if recent events had exposed an unexpected weakness.

Best to arrange the possibility of an unobtrusive exit during the next act, in case he should find himself too uncomfortable to sit it out.

In the musicians' area people drifted and talked. Tremain, done performing for the evening but still in costume, stood reading over the shoulder of a flutist who was absorbed in a battered paperback titled *The Revenge of the Androids.*

The conductor sat in his room massaging the back of his neck, trying to regain his calm without going flat. Now that everyone was warmed up, the evening was taking shape as one of those rare occasions when the opera's life, which is larger than life, fills the house, electrifying audience and performers alike and including them all in one magnificent experience. He felt the temptation to give in before the excitement and rush the tempi, which would only throw everyone off and spoil the performance.

Relax. Relax. Anders took deep breaths and yawned at last.

People congregated around the Opera Guild booth, where posters, T-shirts, and other souvenirs were being sold.

"I know Scarpia's an awful monster," said a woman in a tailored wool suit, "but he has such wonderful music, so mean and gorgeous, it makes the old heart go pitapat. I'm always a little bit ashamed of loving Puccini's operas—there's that current of cruelty—but the melodies are so sensuous and so lyrical, your better judgment just melts away."

The younger woman to whom she spoke smiled vaguely at her.

"The second act is a real grabber," continued the wool-suited woman. "First Scarpia tells how he likes caveman tactics better than courting with flowers and music. Then he has the poor tenor, Cavaradossi I mean, tortured until Tosca gives in and tells where Angelotti's hiding, and they haul Cavaradossi off to prison. And *then* Scarpia says if she wants to save Cavaradossi from execution for treason, she has to come to bed with him. He has this absolutely palpitating, ecstatic music—"

The young man who was her escort drawled, "Rutting music."

The young woman smiled vaguely. High again, thought the wool-suited woman disgustedly; where does she think she is, some damn rock concert?

"Come on," the wool-suited woman said. "We have to buy a T-shirt for Brother. A friend of mine is selling for the Guild tonight: her—that little lady with the short white hair and bright eyes. See the magenta sari she's wearing? She got that in India; she's been to China too; a great traveler. Hi, Juliet, let me introduce my sister . . ."

Jean took her intermission coffee black, which was bad-tasting but not fattening. "What a show we're getting tonight—a perfect introduction to opera for you, Elmo."

"I didn't like it," Elmo said unhappily. "I mean, it was like watching an animal in church pretending to be a man."

"You know," Jean said, "I read somewhere that Puccini had a strong primitive streak. He loved hunting, shooting birds and such. Maybe it wouldn't be too far off to see his Scarpia as a sort of throwback to a more bestial, elemental type." Elmo looked lost. Jean shifted gears: "You know the costume Tosca wore, the plumed hat, the dress with rustling skirts, the long cane? It's traditional; the first singer to play the role wore a similar outfit at the opening in Rome, in 1900."

Unexpectedly Dr. Weyland spoke close beside her: "Sarah Bernhardt wore the same in Sardou's play *La Tosca* more than ten years earlier. She carried also, I believe, a bouquet of flowers."

"Really?" Jean said brightly. "Nights when rain blows onto the stage here I bet the Toscas wish they were carrying umbrellas instead of canes or flowers. One night it really poured, and a man sitting in the unroofed section in front of me put up a villainous-looking black umbrella, which isn't allowed because the people behind the umbrella-wielder can't see. He turned out to be John Ehrlichman, of Watergate memory."

"And to be both prepared and unprepared," said Dr. Weyland urbanely. He turned to Elmo. "Young man, I noticed that you have a seat on the aisle down in front. May I change seats with you? No reflection on Miss Gray—she does not snore, scratch or fidget—but I have trouble sitting so still for so long, no matter how fascinating the occasion."

Jean smiled in spite of herself. The man had charm, when he chose to exercise it. She wished he didn't make her feel so silly and so—so *squat.*

Elmo said uncertainly, "I'm in the second row. It's pretty loud up there, and you can't see so well."

"Nevertheless, I would consider the exchange a great favor. I must get up and stretch my legs now and then. An aisle seat on the side would be a mercy for me and those around me."

The pit boys brought up a snare drum to set in the wings near the stage manager's console. Spiegel herself was momentarily absent, seeing to the administration of oxygen to a chorister from St. Louis. The Santa Fe altitude could be hard on lowlanders.

The assistant technical director circulated, hushing the chattering choristers who milled outside the dressing rooms. Behind the flat that enclosed the smaller, more intimate second-act set depicting Scarpia's office, a minuscule orchestra assembled on folding chairs. They would play music to be heard as if from outside, through an open window of the office. A TV monitor was positioned for the assistant conductor to work from.

In the small prop room a final test was run with the two candlesticks which Tosca must appear to light at the end of Act Two. The candlesticks were battery-powered, their brightening and dimming handled by a technician using a remote-control device adapted from a model airplane kit.

The house manager called in to Spiegel, back at her console, advising her to delay the start of Act Two: the lines outside the ladies' rooms were still long.

Elmo sat in his new seat, relieved to be at a greater distance from the stage. Down front, he had felt like a bystander trapped into eavesdropping on somebody's very private business.

Now as Scarpia mused alone on the anticipated success of his plans, Elmo felt safely removed and free to study the scene: the inlaid-wood effect on the stage floor, the carved shutters of the window behind Scarpia's curly-legged dining table, a fat-cushioned sofa placed across from a big writing table all scattered with books and papers.

Suddenly Scarpia's singing turned ferocious—bang, bangety-bang-bang, up and down. Shocked, Elmo stared at the man. Though large of frame, Scarpia was almost daintily resplendent in silk brocade: over knee breeches and lace-trimmed shirt, a vest and full-skirted coat of a delicate pale blue. From this Dresden figure came a brutally voluptuous voice. The words were close enough to Spanish for Elmo to catch their drift. They were about women: What I want I take, use, throw away, and then I go after the next thing I want.

Elmo squirmed in his seat, uncomfortably aware of Jean sitting between himself and McGrath. It seemed indecent for any woman to overhear from a man such a fierce declaration of appetite.

One of Scarpia's spies brought the news: they had not found the fugitive Angelotti at Cavaradossi's villa, to which Tosca had led them. They had, however, found, arrested, and brought back for questioning Tosca's lover, Cavaradossi. Scarpia began to interrogate Cavaradossi over the cantata performed by the unseen small orchestra and chorus.

Into a pause glided a familiar soprano voice, Tosca's voice, leading the chorus. Cavaradossi murmured impulsively that it was *her* voice. A glance passed between the two men: Cavaradossi's back stiffened slightly; Scarpia lowered his powdered head and pressed on with his questions, rejecting any complicity with the prisoner even in admiration for the woman who fascinated them both.

The stage director, watching from the back of the house with the standees, found herself delighted. Such a small bit of new business, and it looked great. Suddenly the triangle of Tosca and the two men flashed alive.

Jean thought back to the last part of Act One. If that had been a telling embodiment of the two-faced nature of society, here was something quite different. The choral work heard now from offstage was not, like the Te Deum earlier, a pretentious ceremonial of pomp and power. Instead, strings and voices wove a grave, sweet counterpoint against which Scarpia's interrogation, by turns unctuous and savage, gained in ferocity.

He was like a great beast circling his prey while outside was— Art with a capital A in the person of Tosca, Rome's greatest singer, whose voice crested the swell of the music supposedly being performed elsewhere in the building.

Scarpia turned suddenly, irritated at finding that voice so distracting, and slapped the shutters to, cutting off the choral background.

Jean whispered into Elmo's ear, "You're right about him being like an animal."

Behind the set a kneeling apprentice fastened the shutters with tape. There must be no chance they might drift open again or be blown in by a gust of wind.

"Places, judge's party," said the backstage speakers. The hooded torturers and scarlet-robed judge assembled at their entry point in the wings.

Weyland saw Cavaradossi taken out, marched downstairs among the judge and his assistants for the continuation of the interrogation in the torture chamber. Only two remained onstage: Scarpia, composed and watchful, and Tosca, newly arrived in his office and trying to hide her alarm. Scarpia began to question her with elaborate courtesy: Let's speak together like friends; tell me, was Cavaradossi alone when you found him at his villa?

Now the pattern of the hunt stood vividly forth in terms that spoke to Weyland. How often had Weyland himself approached a victim in just such a manner, speaking soothingly, his impatience to feed disguised in social pleasantry . . . a woman stalked in the quiet of a bookstore or a gallery . . . a man picked up in a park . . . . Hunting was the central experience of Weyland's life. Here was that experience, from the outside.

Fascinated, he leaned forward to observe the studied ease of the hunter, the pretended calm of the prey. . . .

Tremain strolled on the smoking-deck, feeling left out. The fictional Angelotti was supposedly hiding offstage in a well at Cavaradossi's villa. When next seen he would be a suicide, a corpse "played" by a dummy. Tremain himself had nothing to do but cool his heels in costume for two acts until the curtain calls. He would have liked to chat with Franklin, who played the sacristan and was likewise finished after Act One; but Franklin was in one of the practice rooms writing a letter to his sick daughter back in Baltimore.

Tremain went down to the musicians' area and out the passageway to the south side of the building. There were production people standing three deep on the stairs that led up to the little terrace off the south end of the theater. From the terrace you could see fairly well without being noticeable to the seated audience.

He turned away and headed downhill toward the paved road sunk behind the opera house.

To lunging music, Scarpia luridly described for Tosca how in the torture chamber a spiked iron ring was being tightened round her lover's temples to force him to tell where Angelotti was hiding—unless she chose to save Cavaradossi by telling first.

In the trap under the stage where the torture chamber was supposed to be, Cavaradossi watched the conductor on a monitor, crying out on cue and instructing Tosca not to reveal Angelotti's hiding place. Dressers stripped off the singer's shirt and substituted a torn one artfully streaked with stage blood (a mixture of Karo syrup and food coloring whipped up by the assistant technical director). They dabbed "blood" across his forehead and rubbed glycerine onto exposed areas of his skin where it would shine in the stage lights like the sweat of pain.

"Piu forte, piu forte!" roared Scarpia to the unseen torturers, demanding that they increase the pressure. Tosca cried that she couldn't stand her lover being tortured anymore. Her voice made a great octave leap down to dark, agonized chest tones.

In the trap Cavaradossi gave a loud, musical cry.

Weyland had made a mistake, exchanging his seat for one so near to pit and stage. This close, the singers in their costume finery were too large, too intense. Their violent music assaulted his senses.

Under locked doors in his mind crept the remembered odors of heavy perfume, sweat, smoking tallow, dusty draperies, the scent of fresh-mixed ink. He had been in rooms like Scarpia's, had heard the click of heels on beeswaxed floors, the thin metallic chime of clocks with elaborate ceramic faces, the sibilance of satin cuffs brushing past embroidered coat shirts.

More than once in such an office he had stood turning in his hands his tradesman's cap, or rubbing his palms nervously on the slick front of his leather work apron, while he answered official questions. When questions were to be asked, Weyand, always and everywhere a stranger, was asked them. Often from another room would come wordless shrieks, the stink of urine, the wet crack of snapping joints. He had grown adept, even brilliant, at giving good answers.

Another artful scream from the hidden tenor jerked him back into the present. He tensed to rise and slip away—but the music, storming out of the pit, gripped him. Its paroxysms of anguish—deep shudders of the cellos, cries of horns and woodwinds—pierced him and nailed him in his place.

Tosca broke down and revealed Angelotti's hiding place; the blood-smeared Cavaradossi was dragged onstage, reviled her, blasted out a defiance of Scarpia and an allegiance to the Bonapartists that doomed him to execution for treason, was hauled away.

In the fifth row center a man turned off his hearing aid and went to sleep. He didn't like the story, and he'd eaten too much *carne adovada* at the Spanish restaurant. Later, hearing rapturous talk about what a great performance this had been, what a privilege to have witnessed it, he would first say nothing, then agree, and finally come to believe that he too had experienced the magical evening.

Scarpia's voice flowed smoothly again as the orchestra returned to the elegance of the lighter strings. He bade Tosca sit down with him to discuss how to save her lover's life. He took her cloak, his fingers crushing the russet velvet greedily, and draped it over the back of the sofa. Then he poured out wine at his table, offering her a glass in dulcet tones: *"É vin di Spagna . . ."*

Thrusting aside the wine, she stared at him with loathing and flung him her question: how much of a bribe did he demand? *"Quanto?"*

And the monster began to tell her, leaning closer, smiling suggestively: he wouldn't sell out his sworn duty to the State for mere money, not to a beautiful woman . . . while the orchestra's avid, glowing chords prefigured the full revelation of his lechery.

Elmo swallowed, stared, listened with a dazzled mind. He had forgotten Jean sitting next to him, as she had forgotten him.

This is the hour I have been awaiting! cried Scarpia. The spare, almost conversational structure of the music grew suddenly rich with the throbbing of darker strings and brass as he disclosed the price of Cavaradossi's life. In tones sumptuous with passion he declared his desire: How it inflamed me to see you, agile as a leopard, clinging to your lover! he sang in a voice itself as supple as a leopard's spring. At last he claimed the brazen, eager chords of lust in his own fierce voice.

Resonances from the monster's unleashed appetite swept Weyland, overriding thought, distance, judgment.

The lady in the snakeskin-patterned dress glanced at the professorial type sitting next to her in the aisle seat. Heavens, what was wrong with the man? Sweat gleamed on his forehead, his jaw bunched with muscle, his eyes glittered above feverishly flushed cheeks. What was that expression her son used—yes: this man looked as if he were *freaking out.*

Jean sat groaning silently at the back of her throat for the tormented woman on the stage, who now rushed to the window—but what use was suicide, when the brute would kill her lover anyway?

With the devotion of a romantic spirit, Jean gave herself up to the beautiful agony of the second act.

Tremain strolled in the dark down behind the opera house, cigarette in hand, head cocked to the music above him. He drew a hot curl of smoke down his throat: bad for a singer, but you can't be disciplined all the time. Anyway, except for wearing this absurd scraggle of glued-on beard and long gray hair and staying in his ragged costume until the curtain call, he could do as he pleased. Caruso had smoked three packs a day, and it hadn't hurt him. Great appetite was a sign of great talent, Tremain hoped.

From the opera house came a distant, explosive crash. He identified it at once and smiled to himself: Scarpia and Tosca had finally overdone the pursuit scene and toppled the water pitcher from the dinner table. Must be having a wild time up there tonight.

One more smoke and he would go listen close up with the others. He looked out at the sparkling lights of Los Alamos to the west and mouthed Scarpia's words silently to himself.

With ghoulish delight Scarpia gloated, How you hate me! He strode toward Tosca, crying in savage triumph, It is thus that I want you! . . . Throes of hatred, throes of love . . .

The breath strained shallowly in Weyland's throat. His hands ached from clenching. Tosca's cries drew from him a faint whining sound: he too had been pursued by merciless enemies, he too had been driven to the extremity of desperation. Tosca fled Scarpia, darting behind the desk from which pens and papers scattered to the floor. The dance of hunting rushed toward a climax. Weyland trembled.

He could see the voracious curl of Scarpia's lips, the predatory stoop of the shoulders under the brocaded coat as he closed in on her . . . as she flew to the sofa with Scarpia a step behind her . . . as Scarpia lunged for her. To the urgings of the horns, Weyland's mouth twisted in a gape of aggression, his eyes slitted cruelly, small muscles started convulsively beneath his skin, as the prey was flushed into flight again—as Weyland sprang in pursuit, as Weyland roared, Mine!

Startled movement at his side distracted him: the woman sitting there jerked away and stared at him. He stared wildly back, then surged to his feet and fled past an usher who was blind to all but the drama onstage.

Hurdling a gate between the patio and the dark slope beyond, he plunged down the hillside. The dry rattle of a military drum followed from the opera house. Impressions blurred in his molten mind: rows of pale tents, restless lines of tethered horses, smells of smoke and sewage and metal polish, wet rope, wet leather; and always, somewhere, the tapping of drums and the bark of voices. He heard them now.

Yet he caught no sentry's footfall, no gleam of white crossbelts marking the presence of solitary prey. Where was the camp whose tumult he heard—those lights to the west? Too far, and too bright. Perhaps a night battle? He sought the scent of blood and black powder; he listened for the muffled cries and weeping of a moonlit field in the battle's wake, where a vampire might feed unnoticed and unresisted among the tumbled casualties.

In that year of revolution and royalist repression 1800, Weyland had followed Bonaparte's Grand Army.

Tonight there was no need for the assistant technical director to trot about backstage hushing people as Tosca began her great aria, "Vissi de'Arte." Tonight people were already quiet, listening.

A percussionist who would ring bells for the beginning of the next act came out of the musicians' passage and headed for the already-jammed side terrace. Her attention was trained on the music. Anything that could be heard from outside the opera house she did not notice.

Impelled by unbearable tension, Weyland rounded the corner of the building and padded swiftly along the sunken road that ran behind it.

There was a man up ahead there; a spark in the darkness, an emanation on the night wind of body warmth, sweat, and smoke. Long hair, breeches, loose and ragged sleeves, a gleam of starlight on shoe buckles as the figure turned its back to the breeze—detail sharpened as Weyland closed the distance with silent strides.

A little flame jumped in the man's cupped hands.

Body strung tight on the rich, wild throbbing of his own heart, mind seething, compelled to strike, Weyland slowed for the final rush.

Tremain's concentration on the poignant strains of the "Vissi d'Arte" was interrupted. Turning, he glimpsed a tall form looming, huge pupils of the eyes shrinking rapidly like a cat's before the wavering match flame. Tremain's mouth moved to frame some startled pleasantry, and his mind said, It's only the night that makes this scary.

Hands of iron seized him and slammed him away forever beyond the singing.

The high notes of the "Vissi d'Arte" burned clear and steady, the low notes smoldered with emotion. Anders followed like a lover, breathing with the singer's breathing. Only once she faltered, and Anders's lifted left hand restored her while his right, held low and armed with the baton, translated for the players in the pit.

At the close of her beautiful, vain plaint, the audience exploded. They screamed, they cracked their palms wildly together—briefly. The pace of the drama had caught them up and would brook small delay.

Weyland's mouth was full of blood. He swallowed, pressing the limp form tighter in his arms, burrowing with greedy lips past the disordered neckcloth.

His stomach, irritated by his earlier, incompletely digested meal, rebelled. Retching, he let the body drop and tried to rise, could only stagger to one knee, heaving. He must not leave vomit for dogs to find, for hunters to examine by torchlight. He swallowed regurgitated blood, gagged, his throat seared; knelt panting and shivering in the darkness.

A droning sound passed high above him—his sense of present time and place flooded back. Looking up, he saw the sinking lights of the airplane pass out of sight behind the faintly lit mass of the opera-house wall rising above him.

And before him on the ground lay a man not dead but dying; quick exploration revealed a crepitation of bone shards under the skin of the temple where Weyland's fist had crushed the skull. Apart from one smudge on the throat, there was no blood. He crouched in panic above the dying man. He had stuck without need, without hunger. From this man dressed as in an earlier time—costumed, rather, a performer in the opera surely—he had been in no danger.

He was in danger now. This kill must be disguised.

He rose and crossed the road. The hillside dropped steeply toward the brush-choked arroyo below. A man might fall—but not far enough or hard enough to smash his head in. Also, he could see a fence partway down which would break such a fall.

He looked back up at the opera house itself, which crested the hill like a vessel breaking forward from a deep wave. The south side reared up three stories over the roadway into a knife-sharp corner like a ship's prow against the night sky. From its deck a man might drop and crack his skull here below. And where the hillside sloped up to meet the north end of the opera-house deck, one might mount that deck as if stepping aboard from the surface of the sea.

Weyland shouldered his victim, ran along the road, and scrambled up the stony hillside onto the deck. Then he turned and, bending as low as he might with his burden, sprinted down the deck toward the high southern prow.

A woman in the balcony focused her glasses on Scarpia. Now that he had wrung from Tosca assent to her own rape, he was deceitfully arranging Cavaradossi's supposedly mock execution in exchange. This was worth coming all the way from Buffalo. Scarpia was such a nasty brute, but so virile—better than Telly Savalas.

The assistant technical director, crossing behind the stage with some cables to be returned to the patch room in the north wings, was too close to the music to hear the faint susurration of movement out on the deck below. He was absorbed in checking for production people who might be lounging on the back stairs, making noise—but tonight there was no one.

Outside the patch room, for an instant he thought he saw someone sitting in the corner with drooping head. It was only the dummy, supposedly the corpse of Angelotti who had killed himself rather than be recaptured. The soldiers would hang up the "body" at the start of the last act, a bit of business special to this production. People needed something to watch during that long, delicate opening.

Every night of *Tosca* the assistant technical director saw the dummy slumped there, and each time for a second he thought it was real.

Weyland flung himself down with his victim on the veranda outside the costume shop. The windows of the shop were yellow with light but largely blocked by set materials stacked outside. He could hear no sound of footsteps or voices on the terrace above the veranda.

He rested his forehead against the low concrete rampart, pressing his sleeve against his mouth to muffle the rasp of his own breathing. His back and arms burned with strain, and a cramp gripped at his gut.

How long before the second act ended? Once again the music was quiet and conversational. Weyland could hear Scarpia gallantly agreeing to write the safe-conduct that Tosca demanded for herself and her lover before she would actually yield her body. A dirgelike melody began. It was not loud; Weyland hoped it would cover whatever noise he made back here.

The dying man was heavy with the quicksilver weight of uncon-scious people, as if any shift could send all his substance running instantly into one part of his body. Weyland hefted him by the arms against the low parapet. The man groaned, his head rolled on Wey-land's shoulder, and one of his hands plucked aimlessly at Weyland's knee.

Looking down past him, Weyland decided: there, between those heaped-up masses of rubbish, where the paving came right to the foot of the wall—a fall, he judged, of some thirty feet. Not a lot, but enough to be plausible.

Now, under the sobbing lamentation of the music, he rolled the man's upper body out along the rampart, bent and heaved the legs up—the man dropped. There came only a dull sound of impact from below.

No shout was raised, but during a performance, uncertain of what had been glimpsed in the dark, no one backstage would call out. They would simply arrive—and if Weyland had not been seen yet, he might be at any moment, for he had been aware of someone moving on the stage level above during his dash along the deck. He had to get off the deck at once. For fear of being seen, he didn't dare run the length of the deck again to reach the low end. And he couldn't risk trying to find his way out through the backstage area in the midst of the performance.

He looked over the rampart once more. Out of the piled-up theater trash below and to his left there thrust, end on, a huge structure made of two thick sheets of plywood joined by two-by-four braces, like the steps of a crooked ladder. Farther down was some sort of platform, warped and buckled, and—stage trees? He could make out sausagelike branches with bristling ends.

If he hung from the rampart at the full stretch of his arms, his rubber shoe soles would reach within perhaps five feet of the braced structure. And if the whole twisted heap didn't collapse under him when he landed on it, he might climb down.

Taking no more time for thought or fear, he lowered himself over the rampart and let go his hold, crouching as he dropped to grab at the pale wooden ribs below. His landing was unexpectedly solid and jarring; whether there was noise or not he couldn't tell, because suddenly the music burst into a thundering crescendo. He began to clamber down the crossed wooden struts.

The whole pile leaned and creaked and shifted obscurely beneath him. He smelled dust. Under the blaring music he was keenly aware of his heart pounding, his gasping breath, and somewhere below the cracking of wood. He caught hold of one of the spiny trees, which dipped drunkenly under his weight, and he let go and slithered down in a rush, fetching up breathless on all fours on the asphalt.

Hurriedly, he examined his victim. The skull was pulped, the man was dead. Weyland looked up: the circumstances would certainly suggest that the unlucky fellow had fallen from the veranda or the balcony above.

Still no sounds of alarm or investigation. The stormy music was dying away into falling tremolo chords under the soprano's furious shouts—Die! Die! Weyland listened to the deep sighs of the strings while his heartbeat slowed and the sweat of fear and effort dried on him. He was as safe as he could make himself. Even if murder were suspected, who would connect this dead performer and an Eastern professor, total strangers to each other?

He turned away without looking at the body again—it no longer concerned him—and walked back up toward the parking area. Just beyond the reach of the parking-lot lights he stooped to brush the dust from his clothing, in the course of which he struck his own knee a painful blow; his hands would not obey him with their customary precision.

The numbers on his watch face jiggled slightly with the tremor in his wrist: 10:40. Surely the second act would end soon and he could return to mingle with the crowd before the final act.

At last he allowed himself the question: what had happened to him? That blow was his oldest way: it paralyzed yet left the prey living, blood still sweet, while he fed. What had made him use that ancient method, when from these refined modern times he had learned appropriately refined ways?

But what elation in that instant of savage release! Thinking of it now he felt his muscles tingle, and his breath came in a sharp hiss of pleasure.

Onstage, Scarpia lay dead. Tosca had stabbed him with a knife from his dinner table when he turned, safe-conduct in hand, to embrace her at last. To his lust-motif, inverted and muted to a sinister whisper in the strings and flutes, Tosca set a lighted candle down at each of his outflung hands. On a sudden loud chord she dropped a carved crucifix onto his breast, and then as the snare drum rattled ominously again she snatched up her cloak and gloves and ran for her life. The dead man was left alone on the stage for the last stealthy, menacing bars of Act Two.

The lights blinked out, applause crashed like surf. Two stagehands in black ran from the wings to stand in front of Scarpia—Marwitz, the baritone—while in his pale costume he rose and slipped down through the trapdoor.

Marwitz hurried away to find Rosemary Ridgeway, his young Tosca. His chest was full of the champagne feeling that meant success. He had been in this business for a long time, and he knew what "perfect" meant: that somehow the inevitable errors had been knit into a progression of actions so rich and right that everything fused into a vivid, indivisible experience never to be forgotten—or duplicated.

He hugged Rosemary hard outside the dressing rooms. "I knew, I knew," he chortled into her disordered hair, "because I was so nervous. I could sing Scarpia in my sleep by now, so nervous is good—it means even after so many times something is still alive, waiting to create."

"Were we as good as I thought we were?" she asked breathlessly.

He shook her by the shoulders. "We were terrible, terrible, what are you saying? Pray to stay so bad!" With the jealous gods of theater thus propitiated, he made to embrace her again, but she stood back, looking into his face with sudden anxiety.

"Oh, Kurt, are you all right? You really fell tonight when I stabbed you—I felt the stage shake."

"I am not so heavy," Marwitz said with offended dignity. Then he grinned. "My foot slipped, yes, but don't worry—you killed me very nicely, very well. They will award you two ears and a tail for it, wait and see."

"I liked how the water pitcher was busted and she couldn't wash the blood off her hands like she's supposed to," said a woman in gold lamé, "so she just wiped it off on Scarpia's dinner napkin."

Her friend frowned. "They should call it *Scarpia*, not *Tosca*. It's not a love story, it's a hate story about two strong people who wipe each other out—along with a couple of poor jerks who wander into the crossfire."

A man in a raccoon coat shook his head vehemently. "You feel that way because this fellow played Scarpia too civilized, like an executive. He's supposed to be just a jumped-up hoodlum. Tosca's line about him after the torture was originally 'The dirty cop will pay for this.'"

"What is it now?" inquired the friend.

" 'A just God will punish him.' "

"Well, who changed the line?"

"Puccini did."

"Then he must have thought the 'dirty cop' line made Scarpia look too much like a hoodlum: he's meant to be smooth," the friend declared. "Myself, I never knew a hoodlum with legs as nice as this Scarpia's. Isn't it a shame that men quit wearing stockings and britches?"

The woman in gold lamé glanced around disparagingly. "No it isn't, not with the boring hindquarters most guys got. Maybe legs were cuter in days of yore."

McGrath had run into a client. He brought her a drink from the bar. She had taste: the plaster cast on her left arm was painted with a frieze of red-brown Egyptian tomb figures.

"Personally," McGrath said, "I think this opera's a bunch of cheap thrills set to pretty music."

The client, who had bought two bronzes from the gallery this year, reacted critically. "Other people do, too; they honestly feel that *Tosca's* just a vulgar thriller," she observed. "I think what shocks them is seeing a woman kill a man to keep him from raping her. If a man kills somebody over politics or love, that's high drama, but if a woman offs a rapist, that's sordid."

McGrath hated smart-talking women, but he wanted her to buy another bronze; they were abstract pieces, not easy to sell. So he smiled.

He wished he'd stayed with fine silver, turquoise, and Pueblo pottery.

Jean and Elmo strolled around and around the fountain in the opera-house patio.

"Opera can really shake you up," Elmo ventured, troubled.

Jean nodded fervently. "Especially on a night like this, when the performers are going all out. And a responsive audience throws the excitement right back at them so it keeps on building."

"But why does the bad guy get such great music?"

"Listen, Elmo, do you read science fiction? Tolkien? Fantasy stories?"

"A little."

"Sometimes those stories tell about what they call 'wild magic'— magic powers not subject to books or spells, powers you can't really use because they're not good or bad or anything to do with morality at all; they just *are*, uncontrollable and irresistible. I think this music tonight is like that—deep and strong and nothing to do with right or wrong."

Elmo didn't answer. That kind of talk reminded him of his wife's relatives over near Las Vegas, New Mexico, who sometimes reported great leaping wheels of witch-fire flying about in the mountains at night.

Soldiers assembled in the trap under the stage. When the third act opened, they would mount onto the platform of the Castel Sant' Angelo, where Cavaradossi was being held for execution. The dummy of the suicide Angelotti was prepared for them to lug onstage and hang from the castle wall according the Scarpia's Act Two orders.

Behind the set of the platform wall, the crew chief oversaw the placement of the landing pad on which the dummy, heaved over the wall with a noose around its neck, would arrive. The pad was two stacks of mattresses roped together side by side, twenty in all to cushion the fall not of the dummy but of Tosca, when she leaped off the battlement in the end.

Weyland came out of the men's room having cleaned up as thoroughly and unobtrusively as possible. At his seat down in front he put on the raincoat he had left folded there. The coat would conceal the split in the shoulder seam of his jacket and any stains or rips he might have missed.

Both terror and exhilaration had left him. He was overcome by lethargy, but he no longer felt ill; his hunting frenzy had burned all that away. A mood of grim pleasure filled him. It was good to know that living among soft people in a soft time had not weakened him; that adapting enough to pass for one of them had not damaged his essential lionlike, night-hunter nature. Even a flagrant misstep need not be fatal, for his ancient cunning and ferocity had not deserted him. He felt restored.

These thoughts passed and sank, leaving him spent and peaceful.

Rosemary Ridgeway took off the brunette wig, rumpled from her scuffle with Scarpia, and set it on its Styrofoam head to be combed out afresh. How absurd to try to become the libretto's dark beauty of whom Cavaradossi had sung so meltingly in the first act: *"Tosca ha l'occhio nero."* Rosemary's eyes were blue, and she couldn't tolerate contact lenses to change them. On the other hand, she didn't quite have the nerve—or the force and reputation—to emulate the great Jeritza who, libretto be damned, had played the role blonde.

Rosemary knew she was young to sing Tosca. Yet tonight her voice had acquired maturity and control, as if all of Marwitz's encouragement and advice had suddenly begun to work at once. If only the miracle would last until the end!

She sat gathering strength for the final act and scratching at her scalp, which already itched in anticipation of the beastly brown wig.

Just before the house lights went down, the woman in snakeskin glanced nervously at the man beside her. She had hoped that he wouldn't return; he'd been so caught up in the second act that he'd scared her. You were supposed to appreciate the opera, not join in.

Now he seemed freed of his earlier agitation, and she saw with surprise that he was really a fine-looking man, with the strong, springing profile of an explorer, or an emperor or an ancient coin. Though he did not appear what she would call old, maturity had scored his cheeks and forehead, and he sat as if pressed under a weight of long thought.

He seemed not to notice her covert scrutiny. The curve of his upturned coat collar was like a symbolic shield, signaling a wish to be left alone.

She hesitated. Then it was too late for a conversational gambit; the last act had begun.

A horn called. Slowly, to the lighting-board operator's counts in the booth, the lights grew infinitesimally stronger, simulating the approach of a Roman dawn over the Castel Sant' Angelo.

Usually, once the Angelotti dummy had been flung over the wall and disposed of, the assistant technical director and his stagehand companion would stretch out on the mattresses and doze. The sound of shots—the firing squad executing Cavardossi—would rouse them for the flying arrival of Tosca, leaping to her death.

Tonight these two technicians stayed awake and listened.

Tosca recounted to her condemned lover Cavaradossi the events that had led to her stabbing of Scarpia. At the swift reprise of the murder music, the woman in snakeskin felt the man beside her stir in his seat. But he didn't leap up and bolt this time. A sensitive soul, she thought, observing that he listened with closed eyes as if he wanted nothing to distract him from the music; perhaps a musician himself, a pianist or a violinist? She looked at his fine, long-fingered hands.

Holding Tosca's hands in his, Cavaradossi sang in a caressing tone, O sweet, pure hands that have dealt a just, victorious death . . .

Elmo, appalled, felt tears run down his cheeks. He didn't dare blot them for fear of calling attention to them. The doomed lovers were so sure the execution would be make-believe and then they would escape together. They sang with such tender feeling for each other, so much hope and joy.

How frightening his tears, how strange the pleasure of his tears.

The execution squad fired. Cavaradossi flung himself backward into the air, slapping a little plastic bag of stage blood against his chest. Red drops spattered on musicians in the pit below.

At the crack of the guns the tall man grunted, and the woman in snakeskin saw that his eyes had flicked open. He stared about for a moment, then shut them again.

For God's sake, the wretched philistine had been sleeping!

The opera was over, the singers took their bows. Rosemary, high on triumph, wanted no one to miss out. Fumbling for Marwitz's fingers in the fall of lace at his cuff, she said, "Where's Jerry Tremain? Isn't he going to take his bow?"

Amid a barrage of applause they all walked forward together on the stage, joined hands upraised. There were many curtain calls. Tremain did not come. No one knew where he was.

The ticket gate was jammed with slowly moving people still chattering excitedly or, like Elmo who made his way among them silently with Jean, trying to hang on to memories of the music.

Dr. Weyland was outside already, waiting by the ticket office. He looked sort of rumpled. Elmo spotted a clutch of burrs stuck to the professor's trouser leg and a long scrape across the back of his hand. He heard Jean's quick intake of breath as she noticed, too.

"Are you all right?" she asked anxiously. "It looks as if you've hurt yourself."

Dr. Weyland put his injured hand into his pocket. "I walked a little beyond the lights during intermission," he admitted. "I tripped in the dark."

"You should have come and told me," Jean said. "I could have run you back into Santa Fe."

"It's only a scrape."

"Oh, I'm so sorry—I hope this hasn't spoiled your enjoyment of the opera. It was such a wonderful performance tonight." Her dismay made Elmo want to hug her.

Dr. Weyland cleared his throat. "I assure you, I found the opera very impressive."

Elmo caught an undertone of strain in the professor's voice. He was relieved, glad that he himself was not the only man to have been moved by the experience.

Maybe being moved was good; maybe some paintings would come out of it.

While waiting for the parking lot to clear they picnicked on fruit and cheese laid out on the trunk of Jean's car.

"This is what opera old-timers do," McGrath said. He passed around cups of wine. "Here's a drink to get us started; I've lined up something special for us—a big party in town. Lots of Santa Fe people and some of the opera singers will be there. Jean, you just follow that blue Porsche over there—that's our ride, Elmo and me—and drop the professor off at the party with us. We'll find him someplace to bunk for tonight and bring him back down to Albuquerque with us tomorrow."

"No, thank you," said Dr. Weyland, turning away the wine in favor of water. "I'm tired. I understand Miss Gray is returning to Albuquerque immediately, and I'd prefer to go with her."

McGrath said heartily, "But people are waiting to meet you! I already told everybody I was bringing a famous Eastern professor with me. We don't want to disappoint folks."

Dr. Weyland drank. "Another time," he said.

"There won't be another time," McGrath insisted. "Not like this party. You don't want to turn your back on old-fashioned Western hospitality."

Dr. Weyland deposited his empty cup in the garbage bag. He said, "Good night, Mr. McGrath," and he got into the passenger seat of the car and shut the door.

"Well, up yours too, fella," said McGrath, throwing his own cup under the car. He wheeled toward the blue Porsche, snapping over his shoulder, "Come on, Elmo, folks are waiting!"

Driving down, Jean found her memory playing over and over the final thunderous chords after Tosca's suicide. They were from Cavaradossi's farewell aria in Act Three, the melody of "O dolci baci, o languide carezze." Sweet kisses, languid caresses. Puccini's closing musical comment, perhaps, on the destructiveness of outsized passions.

In fact, Scarpia himself had remarked in Act Two that great love brings great misery. That was just before his paean to the superior joys of selfish appetite. Yet he had been destroyed by his lust for Tosca, surely a passion in itself? How to distinguish appetite from passion? Or did art raise appetite to the level of passion, so that they became indistinguishable?

Had Dr. Weyland been more accessible, she would have loved to discuss this with him on the way home. She wondered whether he was lonely behind his facade.

Moon-flooded countryside flowed past. On either hand the rolling plateau was adrift with blunt constructions that dawn would show as mountains. Weyland did not miss his old car now, his whispering Mercedes. He was tired and glad not to be driving under that immense, glossy sky; better to be free to look out. The scenery was silver with reflected moonlight. The cool wind brought fresh night smells of earth, water, brush, cattle drowsing at the fences.

The woman spoke, breaking his mood. She said hesitantly, "Dr. Weyland, I wonder if you realize you've made an enemy tonight. McGrath wanted to show you off at that party. He'll take your refusal as a spit in the eye of his beloved Western hospitality."

Weyland shrugged.

"I suppose you can afford to be offhand about it," she said, sounding resentful. "Not all of us can. Elmo will bear the brunt of McGrath's bruised feelings tonight. My turn will come tomorrow when they get back. McGrath can't hurt you, so he'll hit out at anyone within his reach. You haven't made things any easier for me."

His voice crackled with irritation: "Perhaps it hasn't occurred to you, Miss Gray, that I'm not interested in your problems. My own are sufficient."

Marwitz and Rosemary lay curled close, too tired for sex, too happy for sleep. They dozed on and off while shadows of moonlight inched across the flagstones outside the French doors.

She murmured, "When the water pitcher fell I was sure Act Two would end in disaster."

"I would wish many more such disasters for us both," he said.

Silence fell. Too soon the season would end and they would go their separate ways.

At length he said, "I wonder what happened to young Tremain. How unlike him, to miss his bow and a party after."

Rosemary yawned and wiggled closer against his warm middle. "Maybe he came later, after we left."

"Which we did indecently early." He nuzzled her ear. "Surely everyone noticed."

Rosemary guffawed. "Anybody who hasn't noticed by now has got to be as stupid as a clam!"

Marwitz sat up. "Come, we have wine left—let's go out and drink in the moonlight."

The wrapped themselves in the bedspread and padded outside, arguing amiably about just how stupid a clam might acurately be said to be.

Weyland got out of the car. He said, "Thank you for bringing me back. I regret my ill temper." He didn't, but neither did he care to make another unnecessary enemy.

The woman smiled a tired smile. "Don't give it a thought," she said. The car with Walking River Gallery stenciled on its side pulled away.

When it was out of sight, Weyland walked. The pavement was lit by the late-risen moon. No dogs were left out at night on this street, so he could stroll in peace. He needed the exercise; his muscles were stiff from exertion followed by long immobility. A walk would help, and then perhaps a hot soak in his host's old-fashioned tub.

Walking eastward on a hill-climbing street, he watched a mountain rise ahead of him like a harshly eroded wall. Its ruggedness pleased him—an angular outline stark against the night and unmuted by vegetation. He could feel the centuries lying thick over this country—perhaps a factor contributing, along with his physical indisposition, to that headlong tumble tonight through his own personal timescape.

The kill itself had been good—a purging of anxiety and weakness. Catharsis, he supposed; wasn't that the intended effect of art?

But the tension leading up to the kill—memory made him shudder. The opera had broken his moorings to the present and launched him into something akin to madness. Human music, human drama, vibrant human voices passionately raised, had impelled him to fly from among his despised victims as they sat listening. He feared and resented that these kine on whom he fed could stir him so deeply, all unaware of what they did; that their art could strike depths in him untouched in them.

Where did it come from, this perilous new pattern of recognizing aspects of himself in the creations of his human livestock? Such mirrorings were obviously unintentional. His basic likeness to humanity was the explanation—a necessary likeness, since without being similar to them he could not hope to hunt them. But was he growing more like them, that their works had begun to reach him and shake him? Had he been somehow irrevocably opened to the power of their art?

He recoiled violently from such possibilities; he wanted nothing more from them than that which he already, relentlessly, required: their blood.

The mountain ahead of him was, he saw, to be envied; it could be wounded by these human cattle, but never perturbed.

The morning tour drifted out onto the concrete deck at the rear of the opera house. The guide pointed west: "On clear nights when we leave the back of the stage open, the lights of Los Alamos . . ."

A heavyset man standing by the rampart glanced down at the road below. He leaned out, not believing what he saw, his breath gathering for a cry.

Elmo made a painting of dreamlike figures from the opera dancing on a sunny hilltop, towered over by a tall shaft of shadow like a wellful of night. In memory of the young singer who had died the night of *Tosca*, Elmo called the painting *The Angel of Death*.

★ Sliding Rock ★

by Terry Boren

When I was a kid, my mother sent me out to visit Uncle Carl and Aunt Tunney Lobley (not really my aunt and uncle, but some form of cousin) who lived in Anaconda, New Mexico. Anaconda wasn't really a town, but a collection of houses built by the Anaconda mines near Grants. My family lived outside of Albuquerque, and eighty miles was a big trip for me. I might have been sent there because my mother needed a break while pregnant with her fifth child, or maybe just to visit Carl and Tunney's kids—Billy Jo, Ellen, and Lou Anne (all girls).

The road out to the Lobley's cut across desert and old lava flows close to the skirts of Mt. Taylor and terminated at a group of middle-class houses pushed up against a black mesa. I'm not sure how long I stayed, but I remember that Aunt Tunney had red hair and Uncle Carl had a still in his hall closet.

I also remember a picnic table in their back yard, as well as a patch of harsh grass and a line of poplar trees. We had a star party on the lawn one night. *Giggling and playing, we kids all got dressed for bed, the Lobley girls in nightgowns and me in my flannel pajamas, and then we went outside. It was a clear, bright desert evening, just after sunset. I could hear coyotes yapping and sense the closeness of the dark mesa. We played for awhile—the adults sat around talking about Sputnik—and then all the kids fell exhausted on the scratchy grass.*

I knew, even at that age, that the Earth is one planet among many, that stars are suns, that we are very small; but it is another thing for a child, or even an adult, to grasp the reality of planet, star, satellite. That night Carl, or one of the other adults, enhanced my depth perception. He explained that we would be able to see a satellite because it was very high up, orbiting the Earth, and reflecting the light of the sun. When the tiny spark high in the night became visible, I had a sudden new grasp of size and distance.

Lying on my back in the grass, I saw the sky change from a black screen dotted with lights to an actual place of vast distance, space and suns. Around me the Earth became more clearly realized. It was massive and solid, and the desert was obviously a very thin skin stretched over the volcanic bones of a planet. I was probably seven years old.

I am native New Mexican (as were my parents and grandparents) of debatable ethnicity and random, though determined, education. I have heard any number of people try to explain why they live in the state: some claim a special attachment to the landscape, to the mountains, the desert, the river valleys; some find special interest in the diversity of people or cultures; some are mystically compelled; and some just like the climate. I think that the literature and the arts that arise out of New Mexico are, perhaps, the best explicators of the area's resonances; read Keith Wilson's poetry or the short stories of Leroy Quintana. However, when I attempt to condense the reasons for my continued residence, I find that there are entirely too many things to explain and quickly develop an intense need for simplicity. Perhaps the easiest analysis of my relationship with New Mexico is this: I was born here, and it suits me. But maybe that doesn't say quite enough.

At the end of summer last year, I spent a few days at Lake Sumner in my grandmother's old cabin. Lake Sumner is an irrigation impoundment located at the confluence of Alamogordo Creek and the Pecos River, and the cabin is situated on a rocky hill overlooking the lake, which fills the cut made by the Pecos. The area is isolated and dry, and the cabin on its windy hill is surrounded by scrub and cactus. The scorpions are shy and generally easy to avoid; and when it rains, tiny yellow and white flowers bloom everywhere.

I went to Lake Sumner with a few good friends. One friend had brought a grill, another brought a telescope, and my third friend had mixed a pitcher of margaritas. It had been a pleasant day, and the evening seemed likely to be the same. We relaxed on the cement slab in front of the cabin eating chicken, drinking tequila, and avoiding the wasps that lurked in the eaves. As sunset progressed the wasps retreated to their nests, and all the stars came out. The sky above a desert lake at five or six thousand feet above sea level can be phenomenally clear.

We found not just one satellite that night, but many, and then we went on to find other things in the sky as the coyotes yapped and the mosquitos attacked. Bob, my friend with the telescope, focused in on the summer planets first, and then on distant stars and nebulae; finally, we caught a galaxy with our lenses. Perhaps this is a fuller illustration of the attraction New Mexico has for writers of all kinds and of the influence it has on their writing: New Mexico is a fine location for looking closely at things, not the least of which are the stars.

Sliding Rock

by Terry Boren

For six nights Asher had been awakened by what sounded like something walking on the roof of his mobile home. The high-desert wind kicked and whistled around the corners of the trailer, and Asher lay in the dark and listened to it. He knew that there was nothing on his roof. After an hour or so he would fall asleep again. He woke each morning with barely enough time to dress, swallow his morning coffee in the chill kitchen and get to the college in time to teach his classes.

Asher intended to spend the weekend sleeping, playing with his telescope and relaxing. He was about to start the process by meeting Mike and Kay Badlam for the spring cake-walk at the elementary school.

A few mangy dogs made their evening rounds of the garbage cans as Asher set out toward the school. The weather was cold, and wind had thrown weeds and paper around the trailer court. Red mud from the snow-melt and recent rains clung to his shoes. He cut directly across the shallow ditch in back of the sagging line of trailers, then through a stand of scrub pinion. He was feeling almost alive by the time he came out of the trees and topped a small rise which dipped into a cleared area grown up in wild garlic and mariposa lilies.

Mike Badlam emerged from the woods on the opposite side of the clearing and stood waiting for Asher to catch up with him. Mike's almost orange hair was easily recognizable even at a distance; he was also remarkably tall and skinny.

"Something up?" Asher asked as Mike handed him a piece of warm fry-bread. "Where is everybody?"

"Yeah, something's up. A sing of some sort, I think. Margaret says something pretty bad's going around." Margaret Charlie was Kay Badlam's great aunt. The old woman occasionally spent time with Mike and his wife Kay in the trailer courts, though she lived most of the year in her own hogan on the rim of Canyon Del Muerto or with her sheep in the canyon itself. She never missed a cake-walk.

"So, where's Kay?"

Mike shrugged and wiped his fingers on his levis. "Well, to top it off, the computers are down again. I've got to get back to the center, so Kay went on to the dance. Why don't you come by for dinner tomorrow? Kay has a big pot of stew on."

"I'll probably be out too late. I'm hiking out to the falls in the morning, but I'll let you know if I can make it."

They parted company when they reached the asphalt. Mike crossed the road into another stand of scrub and continued on toward the cultural center. Asher followed the pavement through another small residential area to the grade school.

Cake-walks were always laid out in the elementary school cafeteria. Asher enjoyed attending them simply to watch the show. A circle of numbered boxes had been taped out on the cafeteria floor; and on one side of the room, a long table sagged beneath the weight of cakes, pies, cookies, fudge and candies. By the time Asher arrived the cafeteria was jammed with light and people. Giggling girls with thick black braids leaned against each other, hiding their grins behind their shawls. An older woman who wore her gray hair in a tight bun held by immaculate, white wool bindings watched a fat, dark-eyed baby smear candy on its clean ribbon shirt.

The assembly was bright, happy, mostly female and mostly Navajo. An old record player started grinding out a badly scratched recording of "Pop-Goes-the-Weasel" as Asher pulled off his coat. A middle-aged woman wearing a green scarf emblazoned with a picture of the Eiffel tower nearly knocked him over trying to beat everyone else to the cake-walk circle.

Asher hung his coat in the cloakroom and joined Kay Badlam and her baby who were positioned near the huge coffeepot on the side of the cafeteria opposite the entrance.

"Hi," she said, smiling and bouncing her son Niki on one hip. "Mike tells me you got things walking around on your roof. You ever been to an Evil Way?"

Asher grinned and shook his head while looking carefully at Kay's smiling face to see if she were serious or not.

Kay Badlam was Navajo and had been raised by her mother's family over on the rim of De Chelly. Her mother had been a great advocate of education. She had given her little girl a book to read each morning when she sent the child out to watch over the sheep. Though Kay's mother hadn't been able to read at all, she provided her daughter with an eclectic assortment of literature which ranged from the complete works of Henry Miller to the biography of Elizabeth Cady Stanton. By the time Kay was in high school, she had read steamer trunks full of books. She had met Mike Badlam as a graduate student at Berkeley.

Kay suddenly stopped smiling, and Asher followed her gaze to the dancers marching around the circle to the music. As the record stopped, the women and children scrambled to possess a favored numbered square and then froze in place.

Kay was watching Shirley Weinberg. If Shirley had stayed in Brooklyn, she would have been a bag lady. As it was, like many of the lost anglos on the reservation, she had become a politely ignored and damaged presence among the Navajo. It wasn't clear whether Shirley had come to help or be helped by the tribe, but she was clearly incapable of doing much more than occupying an old hogan which one of the local families let her use because someone had died in it. The hogan was ch'iindi, a state somewhere between haunted and unclean, and no self-respecting Navajo would get near it. Shirley continued shuffling around the circle in her muddy fur mukluks for several steps after the music had stopped.

"She asked me to drive her into town again today," Kay said. "As if I didn't have anything better to do. I know she needs food out there, but every time I take her in I have to bail her out of trouble or give her money. And Gallup is a long drive with someone who gives you the creeps. She even takes money from Margaret."

Asher felt a twinge of embarrassment, not that he had anything to do with Shirley Weinberg. "The Lost and The Loony," he said.

"They all seem to end up out here." Asher trusted that he wasn't one of them, but being a teacher hardly exempted him. Half of the faculty were in Tsaile because they hoped that something magic would rub off of the lives of the Navajo and on to their own—as if the tribe didn't have enough problems to go around already. Or, they were missionaries. Or, they wanted to "help" the Navajo in spite of the fact that they were incompetent to function in their own cultures for one reason or another. It was fortunate that the Navajo were as tolerant as they were.

"I saw Margaret just this morning. Mike said there was going to be a sing. An Evil Way?"

"Yeah, everyone's pretty upset. Margaret says that someone found a grave that had been dug up."

"Someone looking for silver probably."

"That's most likely right. But there was a shoe game the other night over at Del Muerto. They had just finished hiding the stone when they looked up and saw either a coyote or a dog looking in toward the fire. Only its eyes. To top it off, one of the women got hurt on her way home."

"Shit," Asher said. Everyone was probably worried about skin-walkers.

The music started again, and Asher watched a little girl carry her prize cake back to the folding chairs to show it to her grandmother. He grinned wryly at Kay, then patted Niki on the head and went to join the cake-walkers. He hadn't won a cake in the three years he had been teaching on the reservation.

After several rounds of "Pop-Goes-the-Weasel" Asher returned, flushed and cakeless, to the sidelines. Kay and Niki, however, had collected a heaping plate of brownies which Asher helped them to demolish. Mike pulled up a folding chair and took Niki while Kay and Asher washed down the last of the sticky sweets with strong black coffee. Niki giggled wildly as Mike bounced him ferociously on his knee.

Asher's attention wandered from Mike and Niki, to the roomful of people and stopped on a young woman who, uncharacteristically for a local, was listening to something Shirley Weinberg was saying to her. Shirley was gesturing broadly and holding onto the woman's skirt. There was a small clear space around the two.

"Lord, she's beautiful," Mike said, noticing the direction of Asher's gaze.

Asher had never seen her before. And she certainly was beautiful. She was tall and straight with hip-length black hair. She was wearing

a velvet shirt the color of a night sky and turquoise and silver bracelets halfway up to the elbow of each arm. Kay was smiling at him
when he turned around; later, when he excused himself and got up
to leave, she threw a shawl around her shoulders and accompanied
him.

After the overheated cafeteria, the air outside seemed almost sen-
suously crisp and cool. Kay walked quietly at his side as he made
his way across the parking lot toward the trees. They stopped at the
edge of the dirt lot, and Asher tipped his head back to look at the
sky. It had become his almost nightly ritual in the trailer courts. At
seven thousand feet above sea level, even with a full moon about
to rise above the desert, there were more stars visible than Asher
had ever seen until he had come to Tsaile. Kay slipped one arm
around his waist. "That's Cygnus, the swan," he said and pointed
up into the jumble of stars.

"Mike says you need someone in that trailer with you to scare
away the noises. Margaret says you need a dog."

"Maybe one of them is right."

"Mike and I didn't get together because he wanted to be a Navajo,
you know. We're really quite fond of each other."

Asher laughed and copied her smile. "What? You mean that computer jocks at Berkeley don't need to write their dissertations on the
Navajo?"

"No, and neither do you; you've already finished yours. I don't
think you're basically an exploitative man. Perhaps you're too sensitive about a lot of things, Asher."

"Yeah, maybe. Tell Mike and Margaret both that I'll give their
suggestions some consideration." He bent down to give her a kiss
on the cheek. "Goodnight, Kay. I'll give you a call tomorrow about
dinner. It'll be late, though. I'm going for a hike tomorrow morning."

" 'Night," she said. "Bring the scope with you tomorrow." She
turned to go back to the cafeteria as Asher continued into the grove
of twisted pinion.

Perhaps she was right, he thought. He had come to Tsaile to teach
because he had thought that he was needed. Now, he knew better.
There was an endless supply of teachers ready to go anywhere, and
he had never really stopped to ask himself what it was that he
needed. The real question was no longer why other people decided
to come out into the middle of the reservation, but why he didn't
leave. His contract was up at the end of the semester; he didn't think
he would return in the fall.

Asher came out of the trees and into the clearing near the trailer court just as the moon was rising beside the dark shadow of Tsaile Butte. The lilies had furled themselves tight at sundown, and the enclosed meadow was lonely and quiet. Asher stood for a moment watching the moonrise while the sky brightened, then he turned back toward the trailers. But he had taken only a few steps, listening to his boots swishing through the wild grasses, when a movement near the trees caught his attention. He looked up just in time to see a figure entering the stand of pinion slightly ahead. As the woman paused for a second, moonlight caught the bands of silver on her arms.

The path to the trailer court lay in the same direction the woman had taken before she had disappeared in the shadows. Asher followed her into the clump of trees, but she was away before he had another glimpse of her. At the spot where the path entered the grove, Asher bent to pick up a small piece of rotted burlap with a twist of fabric tied around one end. He stuffed it in the pocket of his levis. For the remainder of his walk home, he thought about skinwalkers—the kind that dug into graves and walked around in the skins of coyotes, and the other kind that walked around in the lives and cultures of other people.

A large crow rose from his roof as he entered the space between his trailer and the Badlam's. It had been picking at a pine cone which rattled across the metal as the bird took flight. Asher felt a quirk of disappointment at the prosaic end to his ghosts. His invisible mystery was resolved into a simple bird.

It was time for him to get to bed. He wanted to be up early.

The bedroom was even colder than usual when Asher awoke the next morning. He had set the alarm for five o'clock, and he could tell by the frozen plume of his breath that the propane line had frozen again during the night. He had never been able to figure where the damn thing was freezing. He had invested in an electric coffee maker and a toaster, or he'd have had to do without breakfast. As it was, it took a distinct act of will to make himself get out of bed and pull his levis on as quickly as possible. Stuffing his bare feet into his boots, he stumbled outside to the pickup to get it started so it would have a chance to warm up before he finished his toast. He tossed down a cup of black coffee and worked on the toast and jam as he threw some jerky and biscuits, a plastic jug of water and a first aid kit into a daypack. He threw the pack over one shoulder and carried his second cup of coffee and a thermos out to the truck. By that time, the truck was already warmer than the trailer.

Asher had planned to hike the canyon that widened out near

highway twelve at Whiskey Creek. The spring runoff was already underway, and though Wheatfields Lake would still be ice-covered, a beautiful plume of water already fell from the top of the nearby mesa into the small canyon. The spring flowers would take advantage of the plentiful but transitory water supply to show their early April bloom. He felt a definite lift to his mood as he swung the truck onto highway sixty-four, scattering half-dried clay across the asphalt. Only his truck's wide mud-tires made it possible to travel the unpaved reservation roads at this time of year. He noticed two cars stuck on side roads near sixty-four before he reached the intersection with highway twelve.

The countryside south of the intersection rose in elevation to Black Pinnacle and Wheatfields Lake, then dropped steadily past Whiskey Creek, the small towns of Navajo and Ft. Defiance and the red sandstone bluffs of Window Rock and Gallup. It was broken, wild country. Asher thought it beautiful, though he knew it could snuff a life out faster than seemed credible.

As his truck made the rise before the bridge over Tsaile Creek, he noticed a Navajo woman sitting on the ground next to the highway. Her skirts were spread out in a wide green circle around her, and he could see that she was very old and gray even from a distance. He stopped the truck for her when he recognized that it was Margaret. Against that backdrop she seemed diminutive and improbable. She wore a green satin pleated skirt, a velvet blouse, blue tennis shoes, and at least ten pounds of turquoise jewelry. She was holding out a dollar bill to the road to pay for the ride. He pretended not to notice it when she climbed into the truck. Hoping that her answer wouldn't be Gallup, he asked her where she was headed, and she answered in English that she wanted to visit a friend near Black Pinnacle.

Margaret's English was almost as bad as Asher's Navajo, so he spent the short trip pointing at things, saying what he thought was the Navajo word for them, and being corrected. Margaret had a good laugh and made him repeat each word several times. When he pulled off of the road near Black Pinnacle, she patted him on the shoulder and grinned, lifting a silver-laden hand to hide her wrinkled old mouth. She leaned to open the door and with the same motion tried to stuff a bill in his levis, but as her hand came out of the tight pocket, the piece of burlap fell onto the seat.

Margaret halted, half out of the truck, and picked up the piece of fabric. Her eyes widened, and she put the burlap back down on the seat quickly and gently. Her face had gone very serious. She looked at him, not even dropping her eyes, and said in her best English,

"Them are the peoples dead babies." She paused and reiterated, "Those babies was there. You don't touch those."

Startled, Asher looked down at the piece of burlap bag with its twist of red wool around one corner. He started to apologize for making her touch it, but she had already hopped out of the truck and was bustling toward the hogan a few hundred feet off of the road.

Asher sat for a moment fingering the rotten fabric and feeling depressed. He hoped that he hadn't upset the old woman. He had grown to like her and feel comfortable with her; making her touch something that had come in contact with a dead person was a serious breach of her trust in him. It was fortunate that he was a biligana, or she might even have thought that he was a witch. She was a tough old woman to have reacted as well as she had.

Asher watched Margaret enter the hogan, then turned the truck back onto the asphalt. He no longer felt like spending the time it would take to hike to the falls. He decided to stay a bit closer to home; but as he recrossed Tsaile Creek, he caught a quick glimpse of the little stream and decided to spend some time soaking up sun in the shallow end of the huge De Chelly system.

It was probably just as well that Asher had chosen to hike Tsaile Creek; the sun was already well up and the dirt roads mushy by the time he pulled onto the track that ran behind the campus to the edge of the rocky beginnings of Canyon Del Muerto and its rivulet of water. "Tsaile" is a Navajo word which means, roughly, "it flows in," and the tiny stream in its bottom is the instrument of the monumental work that is one gigantic arm of De Chelly. The road would have been impassable but for the fact that it ran for a distance along the rim rock. His truck would never had made it up Whiskey Creek.

At the spot where Asher pulled to the canyon edge, the walls were only about twenty feet high and easily scalable. Asher descended quickly and picked his way through the jumble of boulders at the foot of the walls. As always, he had to stop and absorb his environment for a moment when he had reached the center of the cut. It was an amazing place.

The canyon created its own little micro-climes. The region around De Chelly was primarily of the high-plateau and desert, the Upper Sonoran Zone. The vegetation—pinion, mountain oak, cactus—was tough and sparse, drought adapted; the soil was desiccated, and running water was a rarity. At higher elevations, mostly along parts of the rim and north-facing walls within the canyon, were pockets of

Canadian Zone vegetation. Lower elevations and south-facing walls were sometimes Lower Sonoran. The countryside along the rim of Canyon del Muerto was still in the last ugly grip of winter. The canyon, however, was already warm and green.

From the top of its sandstone walls Del Muerto had looked like some Blakean illustration. There were even a few scrawny sheep grazing on the green fuzz of grass near the stream. The sandstone absorbed warmth from the sun and radiated it back into the canyon, so the ambient temperature in the bottom of the cut was much higher than that of the cold layer above it. Dark green drifts of watercress moved in the ripples of the little stream at Asher's feet; the water trickled over and through the bed of clean sand and rock on the canyon's floor.

The walls of the cut grew higher as he moved slowly down stream, keeping close to the little creek. At a twist of the way, Asher might walk into a patch of shaded snow the sun hadn't yet reached, or into a bright pocket of light and warmth scented by blooming match-brush. But the time he had worked his way under the barbed-wire fence which bisected the canyon about a half a mile from his entrance point, Asher was beginning to forget everything but the rock walls and the sunlight.

It was almost noon by the time Asher reached the pool by the rockfall. The slabs of sandstone which had been tumbled from the canyon walls by erosion had dammed the creek to form a small clear pool of cold water. He had just passed the sharp twist which hid the pool when he realized how warm the canyon had become. To his right, a clump of red cliff-roses bloomed twenty feet up the south-facing wall. The cottonwood by the pool was already in full leaf. And the little micro-summer in the sandstone pocket was already occupied.

She was lying on her stomach on a tilted slab by the pool. Asher was surprised and a little irked to find anyone at all in the canyon, but when the woman shifted to one hip, facing away from him, and the black hair fell across her back to reveal a nipped-in waist and round naked bottom, he could not decide whether he should leave quietly or just stand there and watch her. He instinctively sank down to a crouch, however, when she moved again, first sitting up and then standing. It was the girl from the cake-walk. He could feel the beginnings of a shiver of unease near the base of his spine as she waded into the water and then totally submerged herself in the cold pool.

Something was wrong, and it wasn't just that she was nude or

that she liked to swim. All those things meant was that she wasn't
a traditional Navajo, who wouldn't even consider going naked into
a pool of water. He had known the night before that something
wasn't right about her. She was still wearing her rows of silver
bracelets, and Asher could see the velvet skirt that she had been
wearing the night before casually tossed to the ground near the
sandstone slab. She noticed Asher as she emerged again from the
pool.

She made no move to dress, but simply stood for a moment then
rummaged in the pile of clothing for a piece of red yarn with which
she tied back her hair. She turned back to him, smiled, and sat down
on the slab. Asher stood. She was sitting butterfly position, knees
wide apart and flat on the stone with the soles of her feet pressed
together. Asher's gaze moved unavoidably to her crotch, but when
he looked back, embarrassed, at her face, she was still smiling and
gazing levelly at him.

She did not cover her smile with one hand; her teeth were very
white, small, and perfect.

She was perfect. Her skin was a dusty apricot color without a
mark or a scar on it that he could see. She was unbelievably lovely,
as if life had never even touched her. He took his pack off of his
shoulder as he walked toward her.

"Ha'át'íísh baa naniná?" he said: Where are you walking around?

"T'óó ásht'í," just loafing, she said. A general answer to his greet-
ing.

As he sat down near her, she reached into the pile of clothing
beside the rock and pulled out a bracelet, which she handed to him.
It appeared to be old pawn; the silver had darkened with age.

"I like these very much," she said, in English. "Take that one."

"What are you doing around here?"

She rested one opened hand, palm up, on his thigh. "I'm a voyeur."
She smiled. "Actually, I'm a skinwalker."

Something uncoiled itself inside of Asher and made him aware of
an emptiness he had tried to hide from himself. "What are you?"
His cock stiffened and he shifted position to be closer to her. When
he reached out to cup her breast in one hand, she didn't move. He
pushed the bracelet onto his left wrist and pushed the girl down
onto the sandstone. He didn't believe in witches.

She spread her legs, but she didn't help. Asher bloodied his knees
and scraped the palms of his hands raw against the sandstone. He
ran with sweat and battered himself against her, broke into her, but

found nothing to keep him from falling away again. No Mystery. She bled, but she didn't try to stop him. She hadn't made a sound.

When he rolled off of her, he didn't know whether he should hit her or try to repair any damage he had done. As he pushed himself up to one elbow and looked at her face, a drop of sweat fell from his chin to her forehead and ran across her perfect skin into her hair. He couldn't tell if she was sixteen or thirty. If Asher had hurt her, she showed no sign of it.

Asher sat up and reached for his pants. The girl pushed up to one elbow, then sat up in the same butterfly position as before. She glanced at him, ran two fingers into her crotch and lifted them back to her nose. She sniffed and then licked the mixture of blood and semen. Asher gazed for the length of few heartbeats at her smooth face with its meaningless smile and he knew that she certainly wasn't a Navajo. At that moment he was no longer certain what she was, only that she was a thing he had to keep. Maybe she could keep the noises away.

He awoke that night to someone pounding on the sides of his trailer. He stared around for a moment not knowing what had dragged him out of sleep. The room was dark and still. He could hear the fan quietly blowing warm air into the room, and the soft breathing of the girl beside him. He turned on the bedside lamp and looked at her. She was very strange: she knew less Navajo than he did, and she didn't seem to have a name.

Someone began banging on the front door; it sounded as if whoever was using a rock.

By the time Asher had swung his legs over the side of the bed, he could hear a woman's voice screaming angrily for him to open up. He grabbed his shirt and pants on the way to the kitchen and struggled into them before he flipped the latch on the front door. He didn't have time to open it before she had pushed through the entrance and into the kitchen. He hit the light switch to find Shirley Weinberg, looking like an escaped lunatic, glaring around as if someone had stolen her favorite garbage bag. She was carrying a bundle of rags under one arm.

"Barbara!" she yelled, and she really did look terrible. She had been crying, and dirty streaks tracked across her face. "Barbara!" She turned toward the bedroom as the girl walked quietly into the room.

"I don't need any more, Shirley." She pushed a smear of dark hair away from her face and sat down at the kitchen table.

"Someone saw me." Shirley dropped the bundle to the floor.

Asher wanted to give her a push out the door. He could barely stand to be around the woman.

"Someone saw you, doing what?"

"With this," she mumbled, toeing the rags. Her nose was running.

"What is it?" he asked her, but she refused to meet his eyes. It didn't matter, the queasy feeling in the pit of his stomach intensified; he knew what it was. He had known since he saw the girl at the cake-walk, since he had followed her into the woods and seen the moon catch on the bands of old silver on her arms.

And Margaret must have known, and Kay. They must have suspected what she was doing. He glanced over at the girl, at Barbara if that was her name. She smiled back at him. He crouched down by the bundle and carefully began pulling away the layers of deteriorating fabric, what was left of an old blanket. Underneath were the remains of a burlap bag, tied at one corner with red yarn. The fabric was permeated with sand and dried fluids. Inside, compressed and melded to the burlap, was part of the tiny skull and mummified body of an infant. Rodents had been at the burial; the legs and most of the lower body were completely gnawed away leaving dry rat excrement, twigs, hair, and a few shards of bone in an inextricable mass. Three tiny turquoise beads rolled out on the linoleum floor.

His hand shook, not because of the dried and harmless little mummy, but because there were people who would kill her for what she appeared to be up to, robbing graves for the silver, who would not be interested in what she really was. On his left wrist, Asher was still wearing the heavy bracelet she had given him.

"She doesn't care about the silver," Shirley hissed, as if she had been reading his mind. "You think she did it for that? That's not why. Ask her, she'll talk to you. You can learn from her! We could write a book."

Asher turned around and stared at her. A book! The poor idiot thought she would write a book. "What do you think, she's a witch? My god, Shirley. She speaks about five sentences of Navajo. You think she knows anything about traditional witchcraft?"

Shirley stared for a moment, then turned to Barbara who was sitting calmly, disinterestedly it seemed. Shirley looked like she had been punched. "Why, then?" Her voice was a nasal whine. "I thought you knew something. You said that I could help. You're just another creep, another crazy." Shirley was crying again as she turned back to Asher. "She must have a dozen of them in the canyon. She said she needed them."

"For what?" Mike Badlam was standing in the door. He had stuffed his pajama top into his levis and looked rumpled and angry. He was carrying a shotgun. "You better get her the hell out of here, and Shirley, too." He shook his red head and looked at Barbara. "Shit, Asher, these people make me sick."

"Yeah." Asher had never heard Mike say anything like that, but he knew in his stomach what Mike meant. Shirley would have done anything to please Barbara because contact with a Navajo witch would have made her life seem more than a failed and ludicrous mess. He was terrified that he might do the same. And Barbara—another of the lost and the loony?

"What were you doing with them?" he asked her, and when she didn't answer he grabbed her by the wrist and dragged her toward the door.

"Get Shirley out of my house," he said as he shouldered past Mike in the doorway. Mike nodded and pushed something into Asher's hand. "Margaret split in a hurry this afternoon. She said to give that to you." It was a pollen bag, a good luck blessing, full of corn pollen and colored sand. Asher shoved it into his back pocket.

Of course Margaret had gone—as fast as she could, he thought, as he pushed the girl into his truck. Margaret thought the girl was a witch, or a skinwalker, out of harmony at the least. And she was certainly that. The girl didn't say anything until he pulled the truck to a halt precariously close to the canyon.

When he grabbed her and began to pull her out of the cab, she jerked her wrist from his grasp and stepped back, looking at him. "Why are you trying to hurt me?" she said.

"What were you doing with those things?"

"Does it matter? Why are you afraid now? You weren't afraid before."

"Are you crazy? Are you some sick woman trying to be a skinwalker? What were you doing with those babies?" A dozen dead Navajo babies.

"Are you afraid that I'm crazy, or that I'm a skinwalker?"

"Where are they?"

"They aren't here."

"What were you doing with them?" He knew she was not a witch; he did not want her to be crazy.

"I'm using them, I'm growing things from them." She shrugged, another of her almost-correct gestures. "They are all very old, and no one wants them."

Asher was suddenly aware of the cold breeze blowing across the rim rock. He wanted to step away from the verge of the canyon, but he was frozen. "What are you doing here?"

Her lips parted in a beautiful smile. She touched his shoulder. "It's genetic material, that's all."

She turned back to look at the sky over Tsaile Butte. "It's odd here; different . . . the same. I'm from there," she said, and her arm swept up in an arc that crossed the black, volcanic plug and finished in the splash of stars called the Souls' Way. "Wasn't that what you wanted to know?"

"I don't think so. I think I knew that." Asher pulled her against him. It was flesh against him. He could feel her breath against his neck. "And this," he said as he stroked her black hair, "genetic material?"

"Yes. Little genetic packages, all thrown away. A means to an end."

Asher's heart began to pound in his chest, and he found himself, suddenly, beginning to sweat. His head tipped back and his vision fell into the night sky. He wanted it. He wanted out. His career, the Navajo, cultures and politics, nothing mattered more to him than what she represented, what nothing else in his life was.

He wondered if she were writing a book, like Shirley. Not that it mattered. It was his fantasy that mattered, to ally himself with the unknown, another being, in a way that meant something.

Asher stared down at her, and she was alien, perfect, a Navajo gone through a sea change. "When you go, I want to go with you."

"What could you do?" Her beautiful face was without expression.

"I could learn," he said. In his mind was the image of a bird like a piece of the night sky rising from the roof of his trailer.

"We can all learn. You can learn here." She pulled away from him.

Asher felt a glow beginning in his belly. His fingers brushed gently against the bag of pollen in his pocket. "Then I'll teach," he said. "We could both learn." And he knew that it was right when she began to smile.

"There's always that," she said, "yes." She headed back toward the truck, and Asher followed.

He could only hope that she was more akin to Mike than she was to Shirley, that he himself was not, finally, just another one of the lost.

★ In the Lost Lands ★

by George R.R. Martin

The peculiar truth of it is, while I've lived in Santa Fe for seven years now and would only reluctantly consider the possibility of living anywhere else, New Mexico has not yet played a big role in my fiction.

The best fiction, to my mind, has among its other attributes a strong sense of place, a vivid and memorable evocation of the landscape, culture, sights, sounds, and ambiance of the world the characters live in. I look for that sense of place when I read, certainly, and try to evoke it when I write.

That's not always easy when you're writing science fiction, of worlds that have never been and times that are yet to come. Still, it's an effort worth making, and a strong writer can make even the most fanciful imagined worlds seem to live. For me, Arrakis and Middle-Earth and the countless colorful landscapes of Jack Vance are as real in their way as Marrakesh, Hong Kong, or Rio. I played the same game in much of my earlier work, trying to bring that

159

sense of place to storm-wracked Windhaven, to mist-shrouded Wraithworld, and to Worlorn, the abandoned festival planet in my first novel, Dying of the Light.

In more recent years, however, a lot of my fiction has moved closer to home. I've lived a number of places in my life, and at one point or another I've found myself drawing on almost all of them to give my fiction that crucial sense of place. I was born and raised in Bayonne, New Jersey, on the other side of New York Bay from Manhattan. Bayonne has become the hometown for my major character in the Wild Cards anthology series, and several of my other characters over the years have lived or worked in New York. I went to college in Evanston, Illinois, just north of Chicago, and lived in Chicago itself from 1971 through 1976. Northwestern University, Chicago, and even the apartment I lived in have all shown up in my fiction. In the late 70s, I taught college in Dubuque, Iowa, an old river town on the bluffs above the upper Mississippi. Disguised as "Perrot, Iowa," Dubuque has already been featured in one of my stories and will probably appear in others. The memorable winters I experienced there, with snow drifts that buried my cars and wind chill factors of forty below, inspired a number of stories set on very cold imaginary planets. And the Mississippi itself, of course, was the setting of Fevre Dream, my historical horror novel.

When I moved to Santa Fe in late 1979, it was partly to get away from those Dubuque winters, and partly because I'd seen Santa Fe the year before as a tourist and thought it would be an intoxicating place to live. It hasn't disappointed. I'm still in love with the city, the state, and the people I've met here, like most of the writers who've moved here from all over the United States.

Still, aside from a few chapters set on Albuquerque's West Mesa in my rock novel, **Armageddon Rag**, New Mexico has not yet seemed to influence my fiction.

I think that may be because I'm still here.

Bayonne, Chicago, Dubuque . . . I've written about all of them, but always after I've moved somewhere else. Even Fevre Dream, which everyone assumes was composed while I stared out over the rolling waters of the Mississippi, was actually written during my first year in Santa Fe, staring out over my back yard and remembering the river. Maybe it's just a question of needing time for the influence of my environment to work its way into my subconscious, where the real work is done. Or maybe it's a matter of distance. Maybe, when the reality of a place surrounds me night and day, it *simply overwhelms any imagined reality I might put to paper, and makes my evocation seem thin and false.*

Or maybe not.

I really don't know. But I'll find out, sooner or later. I intend to live in Santa Fe for a long, long time. Perhaps a few years down the line, the influence of the city and the state will finally filter down to the dark basement of the mind where the real creativity takes place.

In the meantime, there's the story here. I don't think that the fantasy landscape of "In the Lost Lands" partakes much of New Mexico one way or the other, but it was one of the first stories I wrote after moving here, and it has mountains in it. That's something, I suppose.

In the Lost Lands

by George R.R. Martin

You can buy anything you might desire from Gray Alys. But it is better not to.

The Lady Melange did not come herself to Gray Alys. She was said to be a clever and a cautious young woman, as well as exceedingly fair, and she had heard the stories. Those who dealt with Gray Alys did so at their own peril, it was said. Gray Alys did not refuse any of those who came to her, and she always got them what they wanted. Yet somehow, when all was done, those who dealt with Gray Alys were never happy with the things that she brought them, the things that they had wanted. The Lady Melange knew all this, ruling as she did from the high keep built into the side of the mountain. Perhaps that was why she did not come herself.

Instead, it was Jerais who came calling on Gray Alys that day; Blue Jerais the lady's champion, foremost of the paladins who secured her high keep and led her armies into battle, captain of her colorguard. Jerais wore an underlining of pale blue silk beneath the deep azure plate of his enameled armor. The sigil on his shield was a maelstrom, done in a hundred subtle hues of blue, and a sapphire large as an eagle's eye was set in the hilt of his sword. When he entered Gray Alys' presence and removed his helmet, his eyes were a perfect match for the jewel in his sword, though his hair was a startling and inappropriate red.

Gray Alys received him in the small, ancient stone house she kept in the dim heart of the town beneath the mountain. She waited for him in a windowless room full of dust and the smell of mold, seated in an old highbacked chair that seemed to dwarf her small, thin body. In her lap was a gray rat the size of a small dog. She stroked it languidly as Jerais entered and took off his helmet and let his bright blue eyes adjust to the dimness.

"Yes?" Gray Alys said at last.

"You are the one they call Gray Alys," Jerais said.

"I am."

"I am Jerais. I come at the behest of the Lady Melange."

"The wise and beautiful Lady Melange," said Gray Alys. The rat's fur was soft as velvet beneath her long, pale fingers. "Why does the Lady send her champion to one as poor and plain as I?"

"Even in the keep, we hear many tales of you," said Jerais.

"Yes."

"It is said, for a price, you will sell things strange and wonderful."

"Does the Lady Melange wish to buy?"

"It is said also that you have powers, Gray Alys. It is said that you are not always as you sit before me now, a slender woman of indeterminant age, clad all in gray. It is said that you become young and old as you wish. It is said that sometimes you are a man, or an old woman, or a child. It is said that you know the secrets of shapeshifting, that you go abroad as a great cat, a bear, a bird, and that you change your skin at will, not as a slave to the moon like the werefolk of the lost lands."

"All these things are said," Gray Alys acknowledged.

Jerais removed a small leather bag from his belt and stepped closer to where Gray Alys sat. He loosened the drawstring that held the bag shut, and spilled out the contents on the table by her side. Gems. A dozen of them, in as many colors. Gray Alys lifted one and held it to her eye, watching the candle flame through it. When she placed it back among the others, she nodded at Jerais and said, "What would the Lady buy of me?"

"Your secret," Jerais said, smiling. "The Lady Melange wishes to shapeshift."

"She is said to be young and beautiful," Gray Alys replied. "Even here beyond the keep, we hear many tales of her. She has no mate but many lovers. All of her colorguard are said to love her, among them yourself. Why should she wish to change?"

"You misunderstand. The Lady Melange does not seek youth or

beauty. No change could make her fairer than she is. She wants from you the power to become a beast. A wolf."

"Why?" asked Gray Alys.

"That is none of your concern. Will you sell her this gift?"

"I refuse no one," said Gray Alys. "Leave the gems here. Return in one month, and I shall give you what the Lady Melange desires."

Jerais nodded. His face looked thoughtful. "You refuse no one?"

"No one."

He grinned crookedly, reached into his belt, and extended his hand to her. Within the soft blue crushed velvet of his gloved palm rested another jewel, a sapphire even larger than the one set in the hilt of his sword. "Accept this as payment, if you will. I wish to buy for myself."

Gray Alys took the sapphire from his palm, held it up between thumb and forefinger against the candle flame, nodded, and dropped it among the other jewels. "What would you have, Jerais?"

His grin spread wider. "I would have you fail," he said. "I do not want the Lady Melange to have this power she seeks."

Gray Alys regarded him evenly, her steady gray eyes fixed on his own cold blue ones. "You wear the wrong color, Jerais," she said at last. "Blue is the color of loyalty, yet you betray your mistress and the mission she entrusted to you."

"I am loyal," Jerais protested. "I know what is good for her, better than she knows herself. Melange is young and foolish. She thinks it can be kept secret, when she finds this power she seeks. She is wrong. And when the people know, they will destroy her. She cannot rule these folk by day, and tear out their throats by night."

Gray Alys considered that for a time in silence, stroking the great rat that lay across her lap. "You lie, Jerais," she said when she spoke again. "The reasons you give are not your true reasons."

Jerais frowned. His gloved hand, almost casually, came to rest on the hilt of his sword. His thumb stroked the great sapphire set there. "I will not argue with you," he said gruffly. "If you will not sell to me, give me back my gem and be damned with you!"

"I refuse no one," Gray Alys replied.

Jerais scowled in confusion. "I shall have what I ask?"

"You shall have what you want."

"Excellent," said Jerais, grinning again. "In a month, then!"

"A month," agreed Gray Alys.

And so Gray Alys sent the word out, in ways that only Gray Alys knew. The message passed from mouth to mouth through the shadows and alleys and the secret sewers of the town, and even to the tall houses of scarlet wood and colored glass where dwelled the noble and the rich. Soft gray rats with tiny human hands whispered it to sleeping children, and the children shared it with each other, and chanted a strange new chant when they skipped rope. The word drifted to all the army outposts to the east, and rode west with the great caravans into the heart of the old empire of which the town beneath the mountain was only the smallest part. Huge leathery birds with the cunning faces of monkeys flew the word south, over the forests and the rivers, to a dozen different kingdoms, where men and women as pale and terrible as Gray Alys herself heard it in the solitude of their towers. Even north, past the mountains, even into the lost lands, the word traveled.

It did not take long. In less than two weeks, he came to her. "I can lead you to what you seek," he told her. "I can find you a werewolf."

He was a young man, slender and beardless. He dressed in the worn leathers of the rangers who lived and hunted in the windswept desolation beyond the mountains. His skin had the deep tan of a man who spent all his life outdoors, though his hair was as white as mountain snow and fell about his shoulders, tangled and un- kempt. He wore no armor and carried a long knife instead of a sword, and he moved with a wary grace. Beneath the pale strands of hair that fell across his face, his eyes were dark and sleepy. Though his smile was open and amiable, there was a curious indolence to him as well, and a dreamy, sensuous set to his lips when he thought no one was watching. He named himself Boyce.

Gray Alys watched him and listened to his words and finally said, "Where?"

"A week's journey north," Boyce replied. "In the lost lands."

"Do you dwell in the lost lands, Boyce?" Gray Alys asked of him.

"No. They are no fit place for dwelling. I have a home here in town. But I go beyond the mountains often, Gray Alys. I am a hunter. I know the lost lands well, and I know the things that live there. You seek a man who walks like a wolf. I can take you to him. But we must leave at once, if we are to arrive before the moon is full."

Gray Alys rose. "My wagon is loaded, my horses are fed and shod. Let us depart then."

Boyce brushed the fine white hair from his eyes, and smiled lazily.

The mountain pass was high and steep and rocky, and in places barely wide enough for Gray Alys' wagon to pass. The wagon was a cumbersome thing, long and heavy and entirely enclosed, once brightly-painted but now faded so by time and weather that its wooden walls were all a dreary gray. It rode on six clattering iron wheels, and the two horses that pulled it were of necessity monsters half again the size of normal beasts. Even so, they kept a slow pace through the mountains. Boyce, who had no horse, walked ahead or alongside, and sometimes rode up next to Gray Alys. The wagon groaned and creaked. It took them three days to ascend to the highest point on the mountain road, where they looked through a cleft in the mountains out onto the wide barren plains of the lost lands. It took them three more days to descend.

"Now we will make better time," Boyce promised Gray Alys when they reached the lost lands themselves. "Here the land is flat and empty, and the going will be easy. A day now, perhaps two, and you shall have what you seek."

"Yes," said Gray Alys.

They filled the water barrels full before they left the mountains, and Boyce went hunting in the foothills and returned with three black rabbits and the carcass of a small deer, curiously deformed, and when Gray Alys asked him how he had brought them down with only a knife as a weapon, Boyce smiled and produced a sling and sent several small stones whistling through the air. Gray Alys nodded. They made a small fire and cooked two of the rabbits, and salted the rest of the meat. The next morning, at dawn, they set off into the lost lands.

Here they moved quickly indeed. The lost lands were a cold and empty place, and the earth was packed as hard and firm as the roads that wound through the empire beyond the mountains. The wagon rolled along briskly, creaking and clattering, shaking a bit from side to side as it went. In the lost lands there were no thickets to cut through, no rivers to cross. Desolation lay before them on all sides, seemingly endless. From time to time they saw a grove of trees, gnarled and twisted all together, limbs heavy with swollen fruit with skin the color of indigo, shining. From time to time they clattered through a shallow, rocky stream, none deeper than ankle level. From time to time vast patches of white fungus blanketed the desolate gray earth. Yet all these things were rare. Mostly there was only the emptiness, the shuddering dead plains all around them, and the winds. The winds were terrible in the lost lands. They blew constantly, and they were cold and bitter, and sometimes they smelled of ash, and sometimes they seemed to howl and shriek like some poor doomed soul.

At last they had come far enough so Gray Alys could see the end of the lost lands: another line of mountains far, far north of them, a vague bluish-white line across the gray horizon. They could travel for weeks and not reach those distant peaks, Gray Alys knew, yet the lost lands were so flat and so empty that even now they could make them out, dimly.

At dusk Gray Alys and Boyce made their camp, just beyond a grove of the curious tortured trees they had glimpsed on their journey north. The trees gave them a partial respite from the fury of the wind, but even so they could hear it, keening and pulling at them, twisting their fire into wild suggestive shapes.

"These lands are lost indeed," Gray Alys said as they ate.

"They have their own beauty," Boyce replied. He impaled a chunk of meat on the end of his long knife, and turned it above the fire. "Tonight, if the clouds pass, you will see the lights rippling above the northern mountains, all purple and gray and maroon, twisting like curtains caught in this endless wind."

"I have seen those lights before," said Gray Alys.

"I have seen them many times," Boyce said. He bit off a piece of meat, pulling at it with his teeth, and a thin line of grease ran down from the corner of his mouth. He smiled.

"You come to the lost lands often," Gray Alys said.

Boyce shrugged. "I hunt."

"Does anything live here?" asked Gray Alys. "Live amidst all this desolation?"

"Oh, yes," Boyce replied. "You must have eyes to find it, you must know the lost lands, but it is there. Strange twisted beasts never seen beyond the mountains, things out of legends and nightmares, enchanted things and accursed things, things whose flesh is impossibly rare and impossibly delicious. Humans, too, or things that are almost human. Werefolk and changlings and gray shapes that walk only by twilight, shuffling things half-living and half-dead." His smile was gentle and taunting. "But you are Gray Alys, and all this you must know. It is said you came out of the lost lands yourself once, long ago."

"It is said," Gray Alys answered.

"We are alike, you and I," Boyce replied. "I love the town, the people, song and laughter and gossip. I savor the comforts of my house, good food and good wine. I relish the players who come each fall to the high keep and perform for the Lady Melange. I like fine clothes and jewels and soft, pretty women. Yet part of me is only at home here, in the lost lands, listening to the wind, watching the shadows warily each dusk, dreaming things the townfolk never dare."

Full dark had fallen by then. Boyce lifted his knife and pointed north, to where dim lights had begun to glow faintly against the mountains. "See there, Gray Alys. See how the lights shimmer and shift. You can see shapes in them if you watch long enough. Men and women and things that are neither, moving against the darkness. Their voices are carried by the wind. Watch and listen. There are great dramas in those lights, plays grander and stranger than any ever performed on the Lady's stage. Do you hear? Do you see?"

Gray Alys sat on the hard-packed earth with her legs crossed and her gray eyes unreadable, watching in silence. Finally she spoke. "Yes," she said, and that was all.

Boyce sheathed his long knife and came around the campfire—it had died now to a handful of dim reddish embers—to sit beside her. "I knew you would see," he said. "We are alike, you and I. We wear the flesh of the city, but in our blood the cold wind of the lost lands is blowing always. I could see it in your eyes, Gray Alys."

She said nothing; she sat and watched the lights, feeling the warm presence of Boyce beside her. After a time he put an arm about her shoulders, and Gray Alys did not protest. Later, much later, when the fire had gone entirely dark and the night had grown cold, Boyce reached out and cupped her chin within his hand and turned her face to his. He kissed her, once, gently, full upon her thin lips.

And Gray Alys woke, as if from a dream, and pushed him back upon the ground and undressed him with sure, deft hands and took him then and there. Boyce let her do it all. He lay upon the chill hard ground with his hands clasped behind his head, his eyes dreamy and his lips curled up in a lazy, complacent smile, while Gray Alys rode him, slowly at first, then faster and faster, building to a shuddering climax. When she came her body went stiff and she threw her head back; her mouth opened, as if to cry out, but no sound came forth. There was only the wind, cold and wild, and the cry it made was not a cry of pleasure.

The next day dawned chill and overcast. The sky was full of thin, twisted gray clouds that raced before them faster than clouds ought to race. What light filtered through seemed wan and colorless. Boyce walked beside the wagon while Gray Alys drove it forward at a leisurely pace. "We are close now," Boyce told her. "Very close."

"Yes."

Boyce smiled up at her. His smile had changed since they had become lovers. It was fond and mysterious, and more than a bit indulgent. It was a smile that presumed. "Tonight," he told her.

"The moon will be full tonight," Gray Alys said.

Boyce smiled and pushed the hair from his eyes and said nothing.

Well before dusk, they drew up amidst the ruins of some nameless town long forgotten even by those who dwelled in the lost lands. Little remained to disturb the sweeping emptiness, only a huddle of broken masonry, forlorn and pitiful. The vague outlines of town walls could still be discerned, and one or two chimneys remained standing, jagged and half-shattered, gnawing at the horizon like rotten black teeth. No shelter was to be found here, no life. When Gray Alys had fed her horses, she wandered through the ruins, but found little. No pottery, no rusted blades, no books. Not even bones. Nothing at all to hint of the people who had once lived here, if people they had been.

The lost lands had sucked the life out of this place, and blown away even the ghosts, so not a trace of memory remained. The shrunken sun was low on the horizon, obscured by scuttling clouds, and the scene spoke to her with the wind's voice, cried out in loneliness and despair. Gray Alys stood for a long time, alone, watching the sun sink while her thin tattered cloak billowed behind her and the cold wind bit through into her soul. Finally she turned away and went back to the wagon.

Boyce had built a fire, and he sat in front of it, mulling some wine in a copper pot, adding spices from time to time. He smiled his new smile for Gray Alys when she looked at him. "The wind is cold," he said. "I thought a hot drink would make our meal more pleasant."

Gray Alys glanced away towards the setting sun, then back at Boyce. "This is not the time or the place for pleasure, Boyce. Dusk is all but upon us, and soon the full moon shall rise."

"Yes," said Boyce. He ladeled some of the hot wine into his cup, and tried a swallow. "No need to rush off hunting, though," he said, smiling lazily. "The wolf will come to us. Our scent will carry far in this wind, in this emptiness, and the smell of fresh meat will bring him running."

Gray Alys said nothing. She turned away from him and climbed the three wooden steps that led up to the interior of her wagon. Inside she lit a brazier carefully, and watched the light shift and flicker against the weathered gray wallboards and the pile of furs on which she slept. When the light had grown steady, Gray Alys slid back a wall panel, and stared at the long row of tattered garments that hung on pegs within the narrow closet. Cloaks and capes and billowing loose shirts, strangely cut gowns and suits that clung like a second skin from head to toe, leather and fur and feathers. She hesitated briefly, then reached in and chose a great cloak made of a thousand long silver feathers, each one tipped delicately with black. Removing her simple cloth cloak, Gray Alys fastened the flowing feathered garment at her neck. When she turned it billowed all about her, and the dead air inside the wagon stirred and briefly seemed alive before the feathers settled and stilled once again. Then Gray Alys bent and opened a huge oaken chest, bound in iron and leather. From within she drew out a small box. Ten rings rested against worn gray felt, each set with a long, curving silver claw instead of a stone. Gray Alys donned them methodically, one ring to each finger, and when she rose and clenched her fists, the claws shone dimly and menacingly in the light from the brazier.

Outside, it was twilight. Boyce had not prepared any food, Gray Alys noted as she took her seat across the fire from where the pale-haired ranger sat quaffing his hot wine.

"A beautiful cloak," Boyce observed amiably.

"Yes," said Gray Alys.

"No cloak will help you when *he* comes, though."

Gray Alys raised her hand, made a fist. The silver claws caught the firelight. Gleamed.

"Ah," said Boyce, "Silver."

"Silver," agreed Gray Alys, lowering her hand.

"Still," Boyce said. "Others have come against him, armed with silver. Silver swords, silver knives, arrows tipped with silver. They are dust now, all those silvered warriors. He gorged themselves on their flesh."

Gray Alys shrugged.

Boyce stared at her speculatively for a time, then smiled and went back to his wine. Gray Alys drew her cloak more tightly about herself to keep out the cold wind. After a while, staring off into the far distance, she saw lights moving against the northern mountains. She remembered the stories that she had seen there, the tales that Boyce had conjured for her from that play of colored shadows. They were grim and terrible stories. In the lost lands, there was no other kind.

At last another light caught her eye. A spreading dimness in the east, wan and ominous. Moonrise.

Gray Alys stared calmly across the dying campfire. Boyce had begun to change.

She watched his body twist as bone and muscle changed within, watched his pale white hair grow longer and longer, watched his lazy smile turn into a wide red grin that split his face, saw the canines lengthen and the tongue come lolling out, watched the wine cup fall as his hands melted and writhed and became paws. He started to say something once, but no words came out, only a low, coarse snarl of laughter, half-human and half-animal. Then he threw back his head and howled, and he ripped at his clothing until it lay in tatters all about him and he was Boyce no longer. Across the fire from Gray Alys the wolf stood, a great shaggy white beast, half again the size of an ordinary wolf, with a savage red slash of a mouth and glowing scarlet eyes. Gray Alys stared into those eyes as she rose and shook the dust from her feathered cloak. They were knowing eyes, cunning, wise. Inside those eyes she saw a smile, a smile that presumed.

A smile that presumed too much.

The wolf howled once again, a long wild sound that melted into the wind. And then he leapt, straight across the embers of the fire he had built.

Gray Alys threw her arms out, her cloak bunched in her hands, and changed.

Her change was faster than his had been, over almost as soon as it begun, but for Gray Alys it lasted an eternity. First there was the strange choking, clinging feeling as the cloak adhered to her skin, then dizziness and a curious liquid weakness as her muscles began to run and flow and reshape themselves. And finally exhilaration, as the power rushed into her and came coursing through her veins, a wine fiercer and hotter and wilder than the poor stuff Boyce had mulled above their fire.

She beat her vast silvery wings, each pinion tipped with black, and the dust stirred and swirled as she rose up into the moonlight, up to safety high above the white wolf's bound, up and up until the ruins shrunk to insignificance far beneath her. The wind took hold of her, caressed her with trembling icy hands, and she yielded herself to it and soared. Her great wings filled with the dread melody of the lost lands, carrying her higher and higher. Her cruel curving beak opened and closed and opened again, though no sound came forth. She wheeled across the sky, drunken with flight. Her eyes, sharper than any human eyes could be, saw far into the distance, spied out the secrets of every shadow, glimpsed all the dying and half-dead things that stirred and shambled across the barren face of the lost lands. The curtains of light to the north danced before her, a thousand times brighter and more gorgeous than they had been before, when she had only the dim eyes of the little thing called Gray Alys to perceive them with. She wanted to fly to them, to soar north and north and north, to cavort among those lights, shredding them into glowing strips with her talons.

She lifted her talons as if in challenge. Long and wickedly curved they were, and razor sharp, and the moonlight flashed along their length, pale upon the silver. And she remembered then, and she wheeled about in a great circle, reluctantly, and turned away from the beckoning lights of the northlands. Her wings beat and beat again, and she began to descend, shrieking down through the night air, plunging toward her prey.

She saw him far beneath her, a pale white shape hurtling away from the wagon, away from the fire, seeking safety in the shadows and the dark places. But there was no safety in the lost lands. He was strong and untiring, and his long powerful legs carried him forward in a steady swift lope that ate up the miles as if they were nothing. Already he had come a long way from their camp. But fast as he was, she was faster. He was only a wolf, after all, and she was the wind itself.

She descended in a dead silence, cutting through the wind like a knife, silver talons outstretched. But he must have spied her shadow streaking towards him, etched clear by the moonlight, for as she closed he spurted forward wildly, driven by fear. It was useless. He was running full out when she passed above him, raking him with her talons. They cut through fur and twisted flesh like ten bright silver swords and he broke stride and staggered and went down.

She beat her wings and circled overhead for another pass and as she did the wolf regained his feet and stared up at her terrible silhouette dark against the moon, his eyes brighter now than ever, turned feverish by fear. He threw back his head and howled a broken bloody howl that cried for mercy.

She had no mercy in her. Down she came, and down, talons drenched with blood, her beak open to rend and tear. The wolf waited for her, and leapt up to meet her dive, snarling, snapping. But he was no match for her. She slashed at him in passing, evading him easily, opening five more long gashes that quickly welled with blood.

The next time she came around he was too weak to run, too weak to rise against her. But he watched her turn and descend, and his huge shaggy body trembled just before she struck.

Finally his eyes opened, blurred and weak. He groaned and moved feebly. It was daylight, and he was back in the camp, lying beside the fire. Gray Alys came to him when she heard him stir, knelt, and lifted his head. She held a cup of wine to his lips until he had drunk his fill.

When Boyce lay back again, she could see the wonder in his eyes, the surprise that he still lived. "You knew," he said hoarsely. "You knew . . . what I was."

"Yes," said Gray Alys. She was herself once more; a slender, small, somehow ageless woman with wide gray eyes, clad in faded cloth. The feathered cloak was hung away, the silver claws no longer adorned her fingers.

Boyce tried to sit up, winced at the pain, and settled back on to the blanket she had laid beneath him. "I thought . . . thought I was dead," he said.

"You were close to dead," Gray Alys replied.

"Silver," he said bitterly. "Silver cuts and burns so."

"Yes."

"But you saved me," he said, confused.

"I changed back to myself, and brought you back, and tended you."

Boyce smiled, though it was only a pale ghost of his old smile. "You change at will," he said wonderingly. "Ah, there is a gift I would kill for, Gray Alys!"

She said nothing.

"It was too open here," he said. "I should have taken you elsewhere. If there had been cover . . . buildings, a forest, anything . . . then you should not have had such an easy time with me."

"I have other skins," Gray Alys replied. "A bear, a cat. It would not have mattered."

"Ah," said Boyce. He closed his eyes. When he opened them again, he forced a twisted smile. "You were beautiful, Gray Alys. I watched you fly for a long time before I realized what it meant, and began to run. It was hard to tear my eyes from you. I knew you were the doom of me, but still I could not look away. So beautiful. All smoke and silver, with fire in your eyes. The last time, as I watched you swoop towards me, I was almost glad. Better to perish at the hands of she who is so terrible and fine, I thought, than by some dirty little swordsman with his sharpened silver stick."

"I am sorry," said Gray Alys.

"No," Boyce said quickly. "It is better that you saved me. I will mend quickly, you will see. Even silver wounds bleed but briefly. Then we will be together."

"You are still weak," Gray Alys told him. "Sleep."

"Yes," said Boyce. He smiled at her, and closed his eyes.

Hours had passed when Boyce finally woke again. He was much stronger, his wounds all but mended. But when he tried to rise, he could not. He was bound in place, spreadeagled, hands and feet tied securely to stakes driven into the hard gray earth.

Gray Alys watched him make the discovery, heard him cry out in alarm. She came to him, held up his head, and gave him more wine.

When she moved back, his head twisted around wildly, staring at his bonds, and then at her. "What have you done?" he cried.

Gray Alys said nothing.

"Why?" he asked. "I do not understand, Gray Alys. *Why?* You saved me, tended me, and now I am bound."

"You would not like my answer, Boyce."

"The moon!" he said wildly. "You are afraid of what might happen tonight, when I change again." He smiled, pleased to have figured it out. "You are being foolish. I would not harm you, not now, after what has passed between us, after what I know. We belong together, Gray Alys. We are alike, you and I. We have watched the lights together, and I have seen you fly! We must have trust between us! Let me loose."

Gray Alys frowned and sighed and gave no other answer.

Boyce stared at her uncomprehending. "Why?" he asked again. "Untie me, Alys, let me prove the truth of my words. You need not fear me."

"I do not fear you, Boyce," she said sadly.

"Good," he said eagerly. "Then free me, and change with me. Become a great cat tonight, and run beside me, hunt with me. I can lead you to prey you never dreamed of. There is so much we can share. You have felt how it is to change, you know the truth of it, you have tasted the power, the freedom, seen the lights from a beast's eyes, smelled fresh blood, gloried in a kill. You know . . . the freedom . . . the intoxication of it . . . all the . . . you know . . ."

"I know," Gray Alys acknowledged.

"Then free me! We are meant for one another, you and I. We will live together, love together, hunt together."

Gray Alys shook her head.

"I do not understand," Boyce said. He strained upward wildly at his bonds, and swore, then sunk back again. "Am I hideous? Do you find me evil, unattractive?"

"No."

"Then what?" he said bitterly. "Other women have loved me, have found me handsome. Rich, beautiful ladies, the finest in the land. All of them have wanted me, even when they knew."

"But you have never returned that love, Boyce," she said.

"No," he admitted. "I have loved them after a fashion. I have never betrayed their trust, if that is what you think. I find my prey here, in the lost lands, not from among those who care for me." Boyce felt the weight of Gray Alys' eyes, and continued. "How could I love them more than I did?" he said passionately. "They could know only half of me, only the half that lived in town and loved wine and song and perfumed sheets. The rest of me lived out here, in the lost lands, and knew things that they could never know, poor soft things. I told them so, those who pressed me hard. To join with me wholly they must run and hunt beside me. Like you. Let me go, Gray Alys. Soar for me, watch me run. Hunt with me."

Gray Alys rose and sighed. "I am sorry, Boyce. I would spare you if I could, but what must happen must happen. Had you died last night, it would have been useless. Dead things have no power. Night and day, black and white, they are weak. All strength derives from the realm between, from twilight, from shadow, from the terrible place between life and death. From the gray, Boyce, from the gray."

He wrenched at his bonds again, savagely, and began to weep and curse and gnash his teeth. Gray Alys turned away from him and sought out the solitude of her wagon. There she remained for hours, sitting alone in the darkness and listening to Boyce swear and cry out to her with threats and pleadings and professions of love. Gray Alys stayed inside until well after moonrise. She did not want to watch him change, watch his humanity pass from him for the last time.

At last his cries had become howls, bestial and abandoned and full of pain. That was when Gray Alys finally reemerged. The full moon cast a wan pale light over the scene. Bound to the hard ground, the great white wolf writhed and howled and struggled and stared at her out of hungry scarlet eyes.

Gray Alys walked toward him calmly. In her hand was the long silver skinning knife, its blade engraved with fine and graceful runes.

When he finally stopped struggling, the work went more quickly, but still it was a long and bloody night. She killed him the instant she was done, before the dawn came and changed him and gave him back a human voice to cry his agony. Then Gray Alys hung up the pelt and brought out tools and dug a deep, deep grave in the packed cold earth. She piled stones and broken pieces of masonry on top of it, to protect him from the things that roamed the lost lands, the ghouls and the carrion crows and the other creatures that did not flinch at dead flesh. It took her most of the day to bury him, for the ground was very hard indeed, and even as she worked she knew it was a futile labor.

And when at last the work was done, and dusk had almost come again, she went once more into her wagon, and returned wearing the great cloak of a thousand silver feathers, tipped with black. Then she changed, and flew, and flew, a fierce and tireless flight, bathed in strange lights and wedded to the dark. All night she flew beneath a full and mocking moon, and just before dawn she cried out once, a shrill scream of despair and anguish that rang and keened on the sharp edge of the wind and changed its sound forever.

Perhaps Jerais was afraid of what she might give him, for he did not return to Gray Alys alone. He brought two other knights with him, a huge man all in white whose shield showed a skull carved out of ice, and another in crimson whose sigil was a burning man. They stood at the door, helmeted and silent, while Jerais approached Gray Alys warily. "Well?" he demanded.

Across her lap was a wolfskin, the pelt of some huge massive beast, all white as mountain snow. Gray Alys rose and offered the skin to Blue Jerais, draping it across his outstretched arm. "Tell the Lady Melange to cut herself, and drip her own blood on to the skin. Do this at moonrise when the moon is full, and then the power will be hers. She need only wear the skin as a cloak, and will the change thereafter. Day or night, full moon or no moon, it makes no matter."

Jerais looked at the heavy white pelt and smiled a hard smile. "A wolfskin, eh? I had not expected that. I thought perhaps a potion, a spell."

"No," said Gray Alys. "The skin of a werewolf."

"A werewolf?" Jerais' mouth twisted curiously, and there was a sparkle in his deep sapphire eyes. "Well, Gray Alys, you have done what the Lady Melange asked, but you have failed me. I did not pay you for success. Return my gem."

"No," said Gray Alys. "I have earned it, Jerais."

"I do not have what I asked for."

"You have what you wanted, and that is what I promised." Her gray eyes met his own without fear. "You thought my failure would help you get what you truly wanted, and that my success would doom you. You were wrong."

Jerais looked amused. "And what do I truly desire?"

"The Lady Melange," said Gray Alys. "You have been one lover among many, but you wanted more. You wanted all. You knew you stood second in her affections. I have changed that. Return to her now, and bring her the thing that she has bought."

That day there was bitter lamentation in the high keep on the mountain, when Blue Jerais knelt before the Lady Melange and offered her a white wolfskin. But when the screaming and the wailing and the mourning was done, she took the great pale cloak and bled upon it and learned the ways of change. It is not the union she desired, but it is a union nonetheless. So every night she prowls the battlements and the mountainside, and the townfolk say her howling is wild with grief.

And Blue Jerais, who wed her a month after Gray Alys returned from the lost lands, sits beside a madwoman in the great hall by day, and locks his doors by night in terror of his wife's hot red eyes, and does not hunt any more, or laugh, or lust.

You can buy anything you might desire from Gray Alys.
But it is better not to.

★ Unworthy of the Angel ★

by Stephen R. Donaldson

The truth is that living in New Mexico is largely irrelevant to my writing. I can write anywhere, and have: in motel rooms, apartments, garrets, and garages, from South Jersey to western British Columbia. My present office has a picture-window facing the Sandias, but I keep the blinds closed. The sources and necessities of writing are internal, and I carry them with me wherever I go.

Yet New Mexico does seem to have an effect on me, a subtle effect, almost subliminal. I think this place fosters creativity. The blue sky and mountains here, the desert colors and vistas are open and accessible, visible for sixty miles in any direction. (Many New Mexicans don't realize that the familiar sight of Mount Taylor is like being able to see Baltimore from Washington D.C.: a mind-boggling concept back East.) And that opens the atmosphere around us. It gives us two powerful things: a sense of wide possibilities; and a certainty of where we are. (It's hard to get lost in Albuquerque. The Sandias are always right over there.)

177

*The sense of wide possibilities frees us from boundaries, encour-
ages inspiration and imagination. And the certainty of where we
are encourages concentration, frees us to focus on what we have
inside us. Almost by definition, that combination must be good for
any artist.*

Unworthy of the Angel

by Stephen R. Donaldson

*"Let no man be unworthy of the Angel who stands over him."—
Unknown*

—and stumbled when my feet seemed to come down on the sidewalk
out of nowhere. The heat was like walking into a wall; for a moment,
I couldn't find my balance. Then I bumped into somebody. That
kept me from falling. But he was a tall man in an expensive suit,
certain and pitiless, and his expression as he recoiled said plainly
that people like me shouldn't be allowed out on the streets.

I retreated until I could brace my back against the hard glass of a
display window and tried to take hold of myself. It was always like
this; I was completely disoriented—a piece of cork carried down the
river. Everything seemed to be melting from one place to another.
Back and forth in front of me, people with bitten expressions hurried,
chasing disaster. In the street, too many cars snarled and blared at
each other, blaming everything except themselves. The buildings
seemed to go up for miles into a sky as heavy as a lid. They looked
elaborate and hollow, like crypts.

And the heat—I couldn't see the sun, but it was up there somewhere, in the first half of the morning, hidden by humidity and
filth. Breathing was like inhaling hot oil. I had no idea where I was;
but wherever it was, it needed rain.

Maybe I didn't belong here. I prayed for that. The people who
flicked glances at me didn't want what they saw. I was wearing a
grey overcoat streaked with dust, spotted and stained. Except for a
pair of ratty shoes, splitting at the seams, and my clammy pants,
the coat was all I had on. My face felt like I'd spent the night in a
pile of trash. But if I had, I couldn't remember. Without hope, I put
my hands in all my pockets, but they were empty. I didn't have a
scrap of identification or money to make things easier. My only

hope was that everything still seemed to be melting. Maybe it would melt into something else and I would be saved.

But while I fought the air and the heat and prayed, Please, God, not again, the entire street sprang into focus without warning. The sensation snatched my weight off the glass, and I turned in time to see a young woman emerge from the massive building that hulked beside the storefront where I stood.

She was dressed with the plainness of somebody who didn't have any choice—the white blouse gone dingy with use, the skirt fraying at the hem. Her fine hair, which deserved better, was efficiently tied at the back of her neck. Slim and pale, too pale, blinking at the heat, she moved along the sidewalk to pass in front of the store. Her steps were faintly unsteady, as if she were worn out by the burden she carried.

She held a handkerchief to her face like a woman who wanted to disguise the fact that she was still crying.

She made my heart clench with panic. While she passed in front of me, too absorbed in her distress to notice me or anyone else, I thought she was the reason I was here.

But after that first spasm of panic, I followed her. She seemed to leave waves of urgency on either side, and I was pulled along in her wake.

The crowds slowed me down. I didn't catch up with her until she reached the corner of the block and stopped to wait for the light to change. Some people pushed out into the street anyway; cars screamed at them until they squeezed back onto the sidewalk. Everybody was in a hurry, but not for joy. The tension and the heat daunted me. I wanted to hold back—wanted to wait until she found her way to a more private place. But she was as distinct as an appeal in front of me, a figure etched in need. And I was only afraid.

Carefully, almost timidly, I reached out and put my hand on her arm.

Startled, she turned toward me; her eyes were wide and white, flinching. For an instant, her protective hand with the handkerchief dropped from the center of her face, and I caught a glimpse of what she was hiding.

It wasn't grief.

It was blood.

It was vivid and fatal, stark with implications. But I was still too confused to recognize what it meant.

As she saw what I looked like, her fright receded. Under other circumstances, her face might have been soft with pity. I could tell right away that she wasn't accustomed to being so lost in her own needs. But now they drove her, and she didn't know what to do with me.

Trying to smile through my dirty whiskers, I said as steadily as I could, "Let me help you."

But as soon as I said it, I knew I was lying. She wasn't the reason I was here.

The realization paralysed me for a moment. If she'd brushed me off right then, there would've been nothing I could do about it. She wasn't the reason—? Then why had I felt such a shock of importance when she came out to the street? Why did her nosebleed—which really didn't look very serious—seem so fatal to me? While I fumbled with questions, she could've simply walked away from me.

But she was near the limit of her courage. She was practically frantic for any kind of assistance or comfort. But my appearance was against me. As she clutched her handkerchief to her nose again, she murmured in surprise and hopelessness, "What're you talking about?"

That was all the grace I needed. She was too vulnerable to turn her back on any offer, even from a man who looked like me. But I could see that she was so fragile now because she had been so brave for so long. And she was the kind of woman who didn't turn her back. That gave me something to go on.

"Help is the circumference of need," I said. "You wouldn't be feeling like this if there was nothing anybody could do about it. Otherwise the human race would've committed suicide two days after Adam and Eve left the Garden."

I had her attention now. But she didn't know what to make of me. She wasn't really listening to herself as she murmured, "You're wrong." She was just groping. "I mean your quote. Not help. Reason. 'Reason is the circumference of energy.' Blake said that."

I didn't know who Blake was, but that didn't matter. She'd given me permission—enough permission, anyway, to get me started. I was still holding her arm, and I didn't intend to let her go until I knew why I was here—what I had to do with her.

Looking around for inspiration, I saw we were standing in front of a coffee shop. Through its long glass window, I saw that it was nearly empty; most of its patrons had gone looking for whatever they called salvation. I turned back to the woman and gestured toward the shop. "I'll let you buy me some coffee if you'll tell me what's going on."

She was in so much trouble that she understood me. Instead of asking me to explain myself, she protested, "I can't. I've got to go to work. I'm already late."

Sometimes it didn't pay to be too careful. Bluntly, I said, "You can't do that, either. You're still bleeding."

At that, her eyes widened; she was like an animal in a trap. She hadn't thought as far ahead as work. She had come out onto the sidewalk without one idea of what she was going to do. "Reese—," she began, then stopped to explain, "My brother." She looked miserable. "He doesn't like me to come home when he's working. It's too important. I didn't even tell him I was going to the doctor." Abruptly, she bit herself still, distrusting the impulse or instinct that drove her to say such things to a total stranger.

Knots of people continued to thrust past us, but now their vehemence didn't touch me. I hardly felt the heat. I was locked to this woman who needed me, even though I was almost sure she wasn't the one I was meant to help. Still smiling, I asked, "What did the doctor say?"

She was too baffled to refuse. "He didn't understand it. He said I shouldn't be bleeding. He wanted to put me in the hospital. For observation."

"But you won't go," I said at once.

"I can't." Her whisper was nearly a cry. "Reese's show is tomorrow. His first big show. He's been living for this all his life. And he has so much to do. To get ready. If I went to the hospital, I'd have to call him. Interrupt— He'd have to come to the hospital."

Now I had her. When the necessity is strong enough—and when I've been given enough permission—I can make myself obeyed. I let go of her arm and held out my hand. "Let me see that handkerchief."

Dumbly, as if she were astonished at herself, she lowered her hand and gave me the damp cloth.

It wasn't heavily soaked; the flow from her nose was slow. That was why she was able to even consider the possibility of going to work. But her red pain was as explicit as a wail in my hand. I watched a new bead of blood gather in one of her nostrils, and it told me a host of things I was not going to be able to explain to her. The depth of her peril and innocence sent a jolt through me that nearly made me fold at the knees. I knew now that she was not the person I had been sent here to help. But she was the reason. Oh, she was the *reason*, the victim whose blood cried out for intervention. Sweet Christ, how had she let this be done to her?

But then I saw the way she held her head up while her blood trickled to her upper lip. In her eyes, I caught a flash of the kind of courage and love that got people into trouble because it didn't count the cost. And I saw something else, too—a hint that on some level, intuitively, perhaps even unconsciously, she understood what was happening to her. So naturally she refused to go to the hospital. No hospital could help her.

I gave the handkerchief back to her gently, though inside I was trembling with anger. The sun beat down on us. "You don't need a doctor," I said as calmly as I could. "You need to buy me some coffee and tell me what's going on."

She still hesitated. I could hardly blame her. Why should she want to sit around in a public place with a handkerchief held to her nose? But something about me had reached her, and it wasn't my brief burst of authority. Her eyes went down my coat to my shoes; when they came back up, they were softer. Behind her hand, she smiled faintly. "You look like you could use it."

She was referring to the coffee; but it was her story I intended to use.

She led the way into the coffee shop and toward one of the booths; she even told the petulant waiter what we wanted. I appreciated that. I really had no idea where I was. In fact, I didn't so much as know what coffee was. But sometimes knowledge comes to me when I need it. I didn't even blink as the waiter dropped heavy cups in front of us, sloshing hot, black liquid onto the table. Instead I concentrated everything I had on my companion.

When I asked her, she said her name was Kristen Dona. Following a hint I hadn't heard anybody give me, I looked at her left hand and made sure she wasn't wearing a wedding ring. Then I said to get her started, "Your brother's name is Reese. This has something to do with him."

"Oh, no," she said quickly. Too quickly. "How could it?" She wasn't lying. She was just telling me what she wanted to believe.

I shrugged. There was no need to argue with her. Instead, I let the hints lead me. "He's a big part of your life," I said as if we were talking about the weather. "Tell me about him."

"Well—" She didn't know where to begin. "He's a sculptor. He has a show tomorrow—I told you that. His first big show. After all these years."

I studied her closely. "But you're not happy about it."

"Of course I am!" She was righteously indignant. And under that, she was afraid. "He's worked so hard—! He's a good sculptor. Maybe even a great one. But it isn't exactly easy. It's not like being a writer— he can't just go to a publisher and have them print a hundred thousand copies of his work for two ninety-five. He has to have a place where people who want to spend money on art can come and see what he does. And he has to charge a lot because each piece costs him so much time and effort. So a lot of people have to see each piece before he can sell one. That means he has to have shows. In a gallery. This is his first real chance."

For a moment, she was talking so hotly that she forgot to cover her nose. A drop of blood left a mark like a welt across her lip.

Then she felt the drop and scrubbed at it with her handkerchief. "Oh, damn!" she muttered. The cloth was slowly becoming sodden. Suddenly her mouth twisted and her eyes were full of tears. She put her other hand over her face. "His first *real* chance. I'm so scared."

I didn't ask her *why*. I didn't want to hurry her. Instead, I asked, "What changed?"

Her shoulders knotted. But my question must've sounded safe to her. Gradually, some of her tension eased. "What do you mean?"

"He's been a sculptor for a long time." I did my best to sound reasonable, like a friend of her brother's. "But this is his first big show. What's different now? What's changed?"

The waiter ignored us, too bored to bother with customers who only wanted coffee. Numbly, Kristen took another handerchief out of her purse, raised the fresh cloth to her nose. The other one went back into her purse. I already knew I was no friend of her brother's.

"He met a gallery owner." She sounded tired and sad. "Mortice Root. He calls his gallery The Root Cellar, but it's really an old brownstone mansion over on 49th. Reese went there to see him when the gallery first opened, two weeks ago. He said he was going to beg— He's become so bitter. Most of the time, the people who run galleries won't even look at his work. I think he's been begging for years."

The idea made her defensive. "Failure does that to people. You work your heart out, but nothing in heaven or hell can force the people who control *access* to care about you. Gallery owners and agents can make or break you because they determine whether you get to show your work or not. You never even get to find out whether there's anything in your work that can touch or move or inspire people, no matter how hard you try, unless you can convince some owner he'll make a lot of money out of you."

But she was defending Reese from an accusation I hadn't made. Begging was easy to understand. Anybody who was hurt badly enough could do it. She was doing it herself—but she didn't realize it.

Or maybe she did. She drank some of her coffee and changed her tone. "But Mr. Root took him on," she said almost brightly. "He saw Reese's talent right away. He gave Reese a good contract and an advance. Reese has been working like a demon, getting ready—making new pieces. He's finally getting the chance he deserves."

The chance he deserves. I heard echoes in that—suggestions she hadn't intended. And she hadn't really answered my question. But I had another one now that was more important to me.

"Two weeks ago," I said. "Kristen, how long has your nose been bleeding?"

She stared at me while the enforced animation drained out of her face.

"Two weeks now, wouldn't you say?" I held her frightened eyes. "Off and on at first, so you didn't take it seriously? But now it's constant? If it weren't so slow, you'd choke yourself when you went to sleep at night?"

I'd gone too far. All at once, she stopped looking at me. She dropped her handkerchief, opened her purse, took out money and scattered it on the table. Then she covered her face again. "I've got to go," she said into her hand. "Reese hates being interrupted. But maybe there's something I can do to help him get ready for tomorrow."

She started to leave. And I stopped her. Just like that. Suddenly, she couldn't take herself away from me. A servant could sometimes wield the strength of his Lord.

I wanted to tell her she'd already given Reese more help than she could afford. But I didn't. I wasn't here to pronounce judgment. I didn't have that right. When I had her sitting in front of me again, I said, "You still haven't told me what changed."

Now she couldn't evade me—couldn't pretend she didn't understand. Slowly, she told me what had happened.

Mortice Root had liked Reese's talent—had praised it effusively—but he hadn't actually liked Reese's work. Too polite, he said. Too reasonable. Aesthetically perfect—emotionally boring. He urged Reese to "open up"—dig down into the energy of his fears and dreams, apply his great skill and talent to darker, more "honest" work. And he supplied Reese with new materials. Until then, Reese had worked in ordinary clay or wax, making castings of his figures only when he and Kristen were able to afford the caster's price. But Root had given Reese a special, black clay which gleamed like a river under a swollen moon. An ideal material, easy to work when it was damp, but finished when it dried, without need for firing or sealer or glaze—as hard and heavy as stone.

And as her brother's hands had worked that clay, Kristen's fear had grown out of it. His new pieces were indeed darker, images which chilled her heart. She used to love his work. Now she hated it.

I could've stopped then. I had enough to go on. And she wasn't the one I'd been sent to help; that was obvious. Maybe I should've stopped.

But I wanted to know more. That was my fault; I was forever trying to swim against the current. After all, the impulse to "open up"—to do darker, more "honest" work—was hardly evil. But the truth was, I was more interested in Kristen than Reese. Her eyes were full of supplication and abashment. She felt she had betrayed her brother, not so much by talking about him as by the simple fact that her attitude toward his work had changed. And she was still in such need—

Instead of stopping, I took up another of the hints she hadn't given me. Quietly, I asked, "How long have you been supporting him?"

She was past being surprised now, but her eyes didn't leave my face. "Close to ten years," she answered obediently.

"That must've been hard on you."

"Oh, no," she said at once. "Not at all. I've been happy to do it." She was too loyal to say anything else. Here she was, with her life escaping from her—and she insisted she hadn't suffered. Her bravery made the backs of my eyes burn.

But I required honesty. After a while, the way I was looking at her made her say, "I don't really love my job. I work over in the garment district. I put in hems. After a few years"—she tried to sound self-deprecating and humorous—"it gets a little boring. And there's nobody I can talk to." Her tone suggested a deep gulf of loneliness. "But it's been worth it," she insisted. "I don't have any talent of my own. Supporting Reese gives me something to believe in. I make what he does possible."

I couldn't argue with that. She had made the whole situation possible. Grimly, I kept my mouth shut and waited for her to go on.

"The hard part," she admitted finally, "was watching him grow bitter." Tears started up in her eyes again, but she blinked them back. "All that failure—year after year—" She dropped her gaze; she couldn't bear to look at me and say such things. "He didn't have anybody else to take it out on."

That thought made me want to grind my teeth. She believed in him—and he took it out on her. She could've left him in any number of ways—gotten married, simply packed her bags, anything. But he probably wasn't even aware of the depth of her refusal to abandon him. He simply went on using her.

My own fear was gone now; I was too angry to be afraid. But I held it down. No matter how I felt, she wasn't the person I was here to defend. So I forced myself to sound positively casual as I said, "I'd like to meet him."

In spite of everything, she was still capable of being taken aback. "You want me to—?" She stared at me. "I couldn't!" She wasn't appalled; she was trying not to give in to a hope that must've seemed insane to her. "He hates being interrupted. He'd be furious." She scanned the table, hunting for excuses. "You haven't finished your coffee."

I nearly laughed out loud. I wasn't here for her—and yet she did wonderful things for me. Suddenly, I decided that it was all worth what it cost. Smiling broadly, I said, "I didn't say I needed coffee. I said you needed to buy it for me."

Involuntarily, the corners of her mouth quirked upward. Even with the handkerchief clutched to her face, she looked like a different person. After all she had endured, she was still a long way from being beaten. "Be serious," she said, trying to sound serious. "I can't take you home with me. I don't even know what to call you."

"If you take me with you," I responded, "you won't have to call me."

This time, I didn't need help to reach her. I just needed to go on smiling.

But what I was doing made sweat run down my spine. I didn't want to see her hurt any more. And there was nothing I could do to protect her.

The walk to the place where she and her brother lived seemed long and cruel in the heat. There were fewer cars and crowds around us now—most of the city's people had reached their destinations for the day—and thick, hot light glared at us from long aisles of pale concrete. At the same time, the buildings impacted on either side of us grew older, shabbier, became the homes of ordinary men and women rather than of money. Children played in the street, shrieking and running as if their souls were on fire. Derelicts shambled here and there, not so much lost to grace as inured by alcohol and ruin, benumbed by their own particular innocence. Several of the structures we passed had had their eyes blown out.

Then we arrived in front of a high, flat edifice indistinguishable from its surroundings except by the fact that most of its windows were intact. Kristen grimaced at it apologetically. "Actually," she said, "we could've been living better than this. But we save as much money as we can for Reese's work." She seemed to have forgotten that I looked worse than her apartment building did. Almost defiantly, she added, "Now we'll be able to do better."

That depended on what she called *better*. I was sure Mortice Root had no end of money. But I didn't say so.

However, she was still worried about how Reese would react to us. "Are you sure you want to do this?" she asked. "He isn't going to be on his good behavior."

I nodded and smiled; I didn't want her to see how scared and angry I was. "Don't worry about me. If he's rude, I can always offer him some constructive criticism."

"Oh, terrific," she responded, at once sarcastic and relieved, sourly amused. "He just *loves* constructive criticism."

She was hardly aware of her own bravery as she led me into the building.

The hall with the mail slots and the manager's apartment was dimly lit by one naked bulb; it should've felt cooler. But the heat inside was fierce. The stairs up to the fourth floor felt like a climb in a steam-bath. Maybe it was a blessing after all that I didn't have a shirt on under my coat. I was sweating so hard that my shoes felt slick and unreliable against my soles, as if every step I took was somehow untrustworthy.

When Kristen stopped at the door of her apartment, she needed both hands to fumble in her purse for the key. With her face uncovered, I saw that her nosebleed was getting worse.

Despite the way her hands shook, she got the door open. After finding a clean handkerchief, she ushered me inside, calling as she did so, "Reese! I'm home!"

The first room—it would've been the living room in anybody else's apartment—was larger than I'd expected; and it implied other rooms I couldn't see—bedrooms, a kitchen, a studio. The look of dinginess and unlove was part of the ancient wallpaper and warped baseboards, the sagging ceiling, not the result of carelessness; the place was scrupulously kempt. And the entire space was organized to display Reese's sculptures.

Set on packing crates and end tables, stacks of bricks, makeshift pedestals, old steamer trunks, they nearly filled the room. A fair number of them were cast; but most were clay, some fired, some not. And without exception they looked starkly out of place in that room. They were everything the apartment wasn't—finely-done, idealistic, painless. It was as if Reese had left all his failure and bitterness and capacity for rage in the walls, sloughing it away from his work so that his art was kind and clean.

And static. It would've looked inert if he'd had less talent. Busts and madonnas stared with eyes that held neither fear nor hope. Children that never laughed or cried were hugged in the arms of blind women. A horse in one corner should've been prancing, but it was simply frozen. His bitterness he took out on his sister. His failures reduced him to begging. But his sculptures held no emotion at all.

They gave me an unexpected lift of hope. Not because they were static, but because he was capable of so much restraint. If reason was the circumference of energy, then he was already halfway to being a great artist. He had reason down pat.

Which was all the more surprising, because he was obviously not a reasonable man. He came bristling into the room in answer to Kristen's call, and he'd already started to shout at her before he saw I was there.

At once, he stopped; he stared at me. "Who the hell is *this*?" he rasped without looking at Kristen. I could feel the force of his intensity from where I stood. His face was as acute as a hawk's, whetted by the hunger and energy of a predator. But the dark stains of weariness and strain under his eyes made him look more feverish than fierce. All of a sudden, I thought, Only two weeks to get a show ready. An entire show's worth of new pieces in only two weeks. Because of course he wasn't going to display any of the work I could see here. He was only going to show what he'd made out of the new, black clay Mortice Root had given him. And he'd worn himself ragged. In a sense, his intensity wasn't directed at me personally. It was just a fact of his personality. He did everything extremely. In his own way, he was as desperate as his sister. Maybe I should've felt sorry for him.

But he didn't give me much chance. Before I could say anything, he wheeled on Kristen. "It isn't bad enough you have to keep interrupting me," he snarled. "You have to bring trash in here too. Where did you find him—the Salvation Army? Haven't you figured out yet that I'm *busy*?"

I wanted to intervene; but she didn't need that kind of protection. Over her handkerchief, her eyes echoed a hint of her brother's fire. He took his bitterness out on her because she allowed him to, not because she was defenseless. Her voice held a bite of anger as she said, "He offered to help me."

If I hadn't been there, he might've listened to her. But his fever made him rash. "*Help* you?" he snapped. "This bum?" He looked at me again. "He couldn't help himself to another drink. And what do you need help—?"

·"*Reese.*" This time, she got his attention. "I went to the doctor this morning."

"What?" For an instant, he blinked at her as if he couldn't understand. "The doctor?" The idea that something was wrong with her hit him hard. I could see his knees trying to fold under him. "You aren't sick. What do you need a doctor for?"

Deliberately, she lowered her hand, exposing the red sheen darkening to crust on her upper lip, the blood swelling in her nostrils.

He gaped as if the sight nauseated him. Then he shook his head in denial. Abruptly, he sagged to the edge of a trunk that held two of his sculptures. "Damn it to hell," he breathed weakly. "Don't scare me like that. It's just a nosebleed. You've had it for weeks."

Kristen gave me a look of vindication; she seemed to think Reese had just showed how much he cared about her. But I wasn't so sure. I could think of plenty of selfish reasons for his reaction.

Either way, it was my turn to say something. I could've used some inspiration right then—just a little grace to help me find my way. My emotions were tangled up with Kristen; my attitude toward Reese was all wrong. I didn't know how to reach him. But no inspiration was provided.

Swallowing bile, I made an effort to sound confident. "Actually," I said, "I can be more help than you realize. That's the one advantage life has over art. There's more to it than meets the eye."

I was on the wrong track already; a halfwit could've done better. Reese raised his head to look at me, and the outrage in his eyes was as plain as a chisel. "That's wonderful," he said straight at me. "A bum *and* a critic."

Kristen's face was tight with dismay. She knew exactly what would happen if I kept going.

So did I. I wasn't stupid. But I was already sure I didn't really want to help Reese. I wanted somebody a little more worthy.

Anyway, I couldn't stop. His eyes were absolutely daring me to go on.

"Root's right," I said. Now I didn't have any trouble sounding as calm as a saint. "You know that. What you've been doing"—I gestured around the room—"is too controlled. Impersonal. You've got all the skill in the world, but you haven't put your heart into it.

"But I don't think he's been giving you very good advice. He's got you going to the opposite extreme. That's just another dead end. You need a balance. Control and passion. Control alone has been destroying you. Passion alone—"

Right there, I almost said it: passion alone will destroy your sister. That's the kind of bargain you're making. All it costs you is your soul.

But I didn't get the chance. Reese slapped his hand down on the trunk with a sound like a shot. One of his pieces tilted; it would've fallen if Kristen hadn't caught it. But he didn't see that. He jerked to his feet. Over his shoulder, he said to her, "You've been talking to this tramp about me." The words came out like lead.

She didn't answer. There was no defense against his accusation. To catch the sculpture, she'd had to use both hands. Her touch left a red smudge on the clay.

But he didn't seem to expect an answer. He was facing me with fever bright in his eyes. In the same heavy tone, he said, "It's your fault, isn't it. She wouldn't do that to me—tell a total stranger what a failure I've been— if you hadn't pried it out of her.

"Well, let me tell *you* something. Root owns a gallery. He has *power*." He spat the word as if he loathed it. "I have to listen to him. From you I don't have to take this kind of manure."

Which was true, of course. I was a fool—as well as being useless. But in simple chagrin I tried to stop or at least deflect what was coming.

"You're right," I said. "I've got no business trying to tell you what to do. But I can still help you. Just listen to me. I—"

"No," he retorted. "You listen. I've spent ten years of my life feeling the way you look. Now I've got a chance to do better. You don't know anything I could possibly want to hear. I've *been* there."

Still without looking at his sister, he said, "Kristen, tell him to leave."

She didn't have any choice. I'd botched everything past the point where there was anything she could do to save it. Reese would just rage at her if she refused—and what would that accomplish? I watched all the anger and hope drain out of her, and I wanted to fight back; but I didn't have any choice, either. She said in a beaten voice, "I think you'd better leave now," and I had to leave. I was no use to anybody without permission; I could not stay when she told me to go.

I didn't have the heart to squeeze in a last appeal on my way out. I didn't have any more hope than she did. I studied her face as I moved to the door, not because I thought she might change her mind, but because I wanted to memorize her, so that if she went on down this road and was lost in the end there would be at least one man left who remembered. But she didn't meet my eyes. And when I stepped out of the apartment, Reese slammed the door behind me so hard the floor shook.

The force of his rejection almost made me fall to my knees.

In spite of that, I didn't give up. I didn't know where I was or how I got here; I was lucky to know why I was here at all. And I would never remember. Where I was before I was here was as blank as a wall across the past. When the river took me someplace else, I wasn't going to be able to give Kristen Dona the bare courtesy of remembering her.

That was a blessing, of a sort. But it was also the reason I didn't give up. Since I didn't have any past or future, the present was my only chance.

When I was sure the world wasn't going to melt around me and change into something else, I went down the stairs, walked out into the pressure of the sun, and tried to think of some other way to fight for Kristen's life and Reese's soul.

After all, I had no right to give up hope on Reese. He'd been a failure for ten years. And I'd seen the way the people of this city looked at me. Even the derelicts had contempt in their eyes, including me in the way they despised themselves. I ought to be able to understand what humiliation could do to someone who tried harder than he knew how and still failed.

But I couldn't think of any way to fight it. Not without permission. Without permission, I couldn't even tell him his sister was in mortal danger.

The sun stayed nearly hidden behind its haze of humidity and dirt, but its brutality was increasing. Noon wasn't far away; the walk here had used up the middle of the morning. Heat-waves shimmered off the pavement. An abandoned car with no wheels leaned against the curb like a cripple. Somebody had gone down the street and knocked over all the trashcans, scattering garbage like wasted lives. Somewhere there had to be something I could do to redeem myself. But when I prayed for help, I didn't get it.

After a while, I found myself staring as if I were about to go blind at a street-sign at the corner of the block. A long time seemed to pass before I registered that the sign said, "21st St."

Kristen had said that Root's gallery, The Root Cellar, was "over on 49th."

I didn't know the city; but I could at least count. I went around the block and located 20th. Then I changed directions and started working my way up through the numbers.

It was a long hike. I passed through sections that were worse than where Kristen and Reese lived and ones that were better. I had a small scare when the numbers were interrupted, but after several blocks they took up where they'd left off. The sun kept leaning on me, trying to grind me into the pavement, and the air made my chest hurt.

And when I reached 49th, I didn't know which way to turn. Sweating, I stopped at the intersection and looked around. 49th seemed to stretch to the ends of the world in both directions. Anything was possible; The Root Cellar might be anywhere. I was in some kind of business district—49th was lined with prosperity—and the sidewalks were crowded again. But all the people moved as if nothing except fatigue or stubbornness and the heat kept them from running for their lives. I tried several times to stop one of them to ask directions; but it was like trying to change the course of the river. I got glares and muttered curses, but no help.

That was hard to forgive. But forgiveness wasn't my job. My job was to find some way to help Reese Dona. So I tried some outright begging. And when begging failed, I simply let the press of the crowds start me moving the same way they were going.

With my luck, this was exactly the wrong direction. But I couldn't think of any good reason to turn around, so I kept walking, studying the buildings for any sign of a brownstone mansion and muttering darkly against all those myths about how God answers prayer.

Ten blocks later, I recanted. I came to a store that filled the entire block and went up into the sky for at least thirty floors; and in front of it stood my answer. He was a scrawny old man in a dingy grey uniform with red epaulets and red stitching on his cap; boredom or patience glazed his eyes. He was tending an iron pot that hung from a rickety tripod. With the studious intention of a halfwit, he rang a handbell to attract people's attention.

The stitching on his cap said, "Salvation Army."

I went right up to him and asked where The Root Cellar was.

He blinked at me as if I were part of the heat and the haze. "Mission's that way." He nodded in the direction I was going. "49th and Grand."

"Thanks, anyway," I said. I was glad to be able to give the old man a genuine smile. "That isn't what I need. I need to find The Root Cellar. It's an art gallery. Supposed to be somewhere on 49th."

He went on blinking at me until I started to think maybe he was deaf. Then, abruptly, he seemed to arrive at some kind of recognition. Abandoning his post, he turned and entered the store. Through the glass, I watched him go to a box like half a booth that hung on one wall. He found a large yellow book under the box, opened it, and flipped the pages back and forth for a while.

Nodding at whatever he found, he came back out to me.

"Down that way," he said, indicating the direction I'd come from. "About thirty blocks. Number 840."

Suddenly, my heart lifted. I closed my eyes for a moment to give thanks. Then I looked again at the man who'd rescued me. "If I had any money," I said, "I'd give it to you."

"If you had any money," he replied as if he knew who I was, "I wouldn't take it. Go with God."

I said, "I will," and started retracing my way up 49th.

I felt a world better. But I also had a growing sense of urgency. The longer I walked, the worse it got. The day was getting away from me—and this day was the only one I had. Reese's show was tomorrow. Then Mortice Root would've fulfilled his part of the bargain. And the price would have to be paid. I was sweating so hard my filthy old coat stuck to my back; but I forced myself to walk as fast as the fleeing crowds.

After a while, the people began to disappear from the sidewalks again and the traffic thinned. Then the business district came to an end, and I found myself in a slum so ruined and hopeless I had to grit my teeth to keep up my courage. I felt hostile eyes watching me from behind broken windows and gaping entrances. But I was protected, either by daylight or by the way I looked.

Then the neighborhood began to improve. The slum became close-built houses, clinging to dignity. The houses moved apart from each other, giving themselves more room to breathe. Trees appeared in the yards, even in the sidewalk. Lawns pushed the houses back from the street. And each house seemed to be more ornate than the one beside it. I would've thought they were homes, but most of them had discrete signs indicating they were places of business. Several of them were shops that sold antiques. One held a law-firm. A stock-broker occupied a place the size of a temple. I decided that this was where people came to do their shopping and business when they were too rich to associate with their fellow human beings.

And there it was—a brownstone mansion as elaborate as any I'd seen. It was large and square, three stories tall, with a colonnaded entryway and a glass-domed structure that might have been a greenhouse down the length of one side. The mailbox on the front porch was neatly lettered, "840." And when I went up the walk to the porch, I saw a brass plaque on the door with words engraved on it. It said:

The Root Cellar
a private gallery
Mortice Root

At the sight, my chest constricted as if I'd never done this before. But I'd already lost too much time; I didn't waste any more of it hesitating. I pressed a small button beside the door and listened to chimes ringing faintly inside the house as if Mortice Root had a cathedral in his basement.

For a while, nothing happened. Then the door opened, and I felt a flow of cold air from inside, followed by a man in a guard's uniform, with a gun holstered on his hip and a badge that said, "Nationwide Security," on his chest. As he looked out at me, what he saw astonished him; not many of Root's patrons looked like I did. Then his face closed like a shutter. "Are you out of your mind?" he growled. "We don't give handouts here. Get lost."

In response, I produced my sweetest smile. "Fortunately, I don't want a handout. I want to talk to Mortice Root."

He stared at me. "What in hell makes you think Mr. Root wants to talk to you?"

"Ask him and find out," I replied. "Tell him I'm here to argue about Reese Dona."

He would've slammed the door in my face; but a hint of authority came back to me, and he couldn't do it. For a few moments, he gaped at me as if he were choking. Then he muttered, "Wait here," and escaped back into the house. As he closed the door, the cool air breathing outward was cut off.

"Well, naturally," I murmured to the sodden heat. Trying to keep myself on the bold side of dread. "The people who come here to spend their money can't be expected to just stand around and sweat."

The sound of voices came dimly through the door. But I hadn't heard the guard walk away, and I didn't hear anybody coming toward me. So I still wasn't quite ready when the door swung open again and Mortice Root stood in front of me with a cold breeze washing unnaturally past his shoulders.

We recognized each other right away; and he grinned like a wolf. But I couldn't match him. I was staggered. I hadn't expected him to be so *powerful.*

He didn't look powerful. He looked as rich as Solomon—smooth, substantial, glib—as if he could buy and sell the people who came here to give him their money. From the tips of his gleaming shoes past the expanse of his distinctively styled suit to the clean confidence of his shaven jowls, he was everything I wasn't. But those things only gave him worldly significance. They didn't make him powerful. His true strength was hidden behind the bland unction of his demeanor. It showed only in his grin, in the slight, avid bulging of his eyes, in the wisps of hair that stood out like hints of energy on either side of his bald crown.

His gaze made me feel grimy and rather pathetic.

He studied me for a moment. Then, with perfectly cruel kindness, he said, "Come in, come in. You must be sweltering out there. It's much nicer in here."

He was that sure of himself.

But I was willing to accept permission, even from him. Before he could reconsider, I stepped past him into the hallway.

Cold came swirling up my back, turning my sweat chill, as I looked around. At the end of this short, deeply-carpeted hall, Root's mansion opened into an immense foyer nearly as high as the building itself. Two mezzanines joined by broad stairways of carved wood circled the walls; daylight shone downward from a skylight in the center of the ceiling. A glance showed me that paintings were displayed around the mezzanines, while the foyer itself held sculptures and carvings decorously set on white pedestals. I couldn't see anything that looked like Reese Dona's work.

At my elbow, Root said, "I believe you came to argue with me?" He was as smooth as oil.

I felt foolish and awkward beside him; but I faced him as squarely as I could. "Maybe 'contend' would be a better word."

"As you say." He chuckled in a way that somehow suggested both good humor and malice. "I look forward to it." Then he touched my arm, gestured me toward one side of the foyer. "But let me show you what he's doing these days. Perhaps you'll change your mind."

For no good reason, I said, "You know better than that." But I went with him.

A long, wide passage took us to the glass-domed structure I'd taken to be a greenhouse. Maybe it was originally built for that; but Root had converted it, and I had to admit it made an effective gallery— well-lit, spacious, and comfortable. In spite of all that glass, the air stayed cool, almost chill.

Here I saw Reese's new work for the first time.

"Impressive, aren't they," Root purred. He was mocking me.

But what he was doing to Reese was worse.

There were at least twenty of them, with room for a handful more—attractively set in niches along one wall, proudly positioned on special pediments, cunningly juxtaposed in corners so that they showed each other off. It was clear that any artist would find an opportunity like this hard to resist.

But all the pieces were black.

Reese had completely changed his subject matter. Madonnas and children had been replaced by gargoyles and twisted visions of the damned. Glimpses of nightmare leered from their niches. Pain writhed on display, as if it had become an object of ridicule. In a corner of the room, a ghoul devoured one infant while another strove urgently to scream and failed.

And each of these new images was alive with precisely the kind of vitality his earlier work lacked. He had captured his visceral terrors in the act of pouncing at him.

As sculptures, they were admirable; maybe even more than that. He had achieved some kind of breakthrough here, tapped into sources of energy he'd always been unable or unwilling to touch. All he needed now was balance.

But there was more to these pieces than just skill and energy. There was also blackness.

Root's clay.

Kristen was right. This clay looked like dark water under the light of an evil moon. It looked like marl mixed with blood until the mud congealed. And the more I studied what I saw, the more these grotesque and brutal images gave the impression of growing from the clay itself rather than from the independent mind of the artist. They were not Reese's fears and dreams refined by art; they were horrors he found in the clay when his hands touched it. The real strength, the passion of these pieces, came from the material Root supplied, not from Reese. No wonder he had become so hollow-eyed and ragged. He was struggling desperately to control the consequences of his bargain. Trying to prove to himself he wasn't doing the wrong thing.

For a moment, I felt a touch of genuine pity for him.

But it didn't last. Maybe deep down in his soul he was afraid of what he was doing and what it meant. But he was still doing it. And he was paying for the chance to do such strong work with his sister's life.

Softly, my opponent said, "It appears you don't approve. I'm so sorry. But I'm afraid there's really nothing you can do about it. The artists of this world are uniquely vulnerable. They wish to create beauty, and the world cares for nothing but money. Even the cattle who will buy these"—he gave the room a dismissive flick of the hand—"trivial pieces hold the artist in contempt." He turned his wolf-grin toward me again. "Failure makes fertile ground."

I couldn't pretend that wasn't true; so I asked bitterly, "Are you really going to keep your end of the bargain? Are you really going to sell this stuff?"

"Oh, assuredly," he replied. "At least until the sister dies. Tomorrow. Perhaps the day after." He chuckled happily. "Then I suspect I'll find myself too busy with other, more promising artists to spend time on Reese Dona."

I felt him glance at me, gauging my helplessness. Then he went on unctiously, "Come, now, my friend. Why glare so thunderously? Surely you realize that he has been using her in precisely this manner for years. I've merely actualized the true state of their relationship. But perhaps you're too innocent to grasp how deeply he resents her. It is the nature of beggars to resent those who give them gifts. He resents *me*." At that, Root laughed outright. He was not a man who gave gifts to anybody. "I assure you that her present plight is of his own choice and making."

"No," I said, more out of stubbornness than conviction. "He just doesn't understand what's happening."

Root shrugged. "Do you think so? No matter. The point, as you must recognize, is that we have nothing to contend *for*. The issue has already been decided."

I didn't say anything. I wasn't as glib as he was. And anyway I was afraid he was right.

While I stood there and chewed over all the things I wasn't able to do, I heard doors opening and closing somewhere in the distance. The heavy carpeting absorbed footsteps; but it wasn't long before Reese came striding into the greenhouse. He was so tight with eagerness or suppressed fear he looked like he was about to snap. As usual, he didn't even see me when he first came into the room.

"I've got the rest of the pieces," he said to Root. "They're in a truck out back. I think you'll like—"

Then my presence registered on him. He stopped with a jerk, stared at me as if I'd come back from the dead. "What're *you* doing here?" he demanded. At once, he turned back to Root. "What is *he* doing here?"

Root's confidence was a complete insult. "Reese," he sighed, "I'm afraid that this—gentleman?—believes that I should not show your work tomorrow."

For a moment, Reese was too astonished to be angry. His mouth actually hung open while he looked at me. But I was furious enough for both of us. With one sentence, Root had made my position impossible. I couldn't think of a single thing to say now that would change the outcome.

Still, I had to try. While Reese's surprise built up into outrage, I said as if I weren't swearing like a madman inside, "There are two sides to everything. You've heard his. You really ought to listen to mine."

He closed his mouth, locked his teeth together. His glare was wild enough to hurt.

"Mortice Root owes you a little honesty," I said while I had the chance. "He should've told you long ago that he's planning to drop you after tomorrow."

But the sheer pettiness of what I was saying made me cringe. And Root simply laughed. I should've known better than to try to fight him on his own level. Now he didn't need to answer me at all.

In any case, my jibe made no impression on Reese. He gritted, "I don't care about that," like a man who couldn't or wouldn't understand. "This is what I care about." He gestured frantically around the room. "*This.* My work."

He took a couple steps toward me, and his voice shook with the effort he made to keep from shouting. "I don't know who you are— or why you think I'm any of your business. I don't care about that, either. You've heard Kristen's side. Now you're going to hear mine."

In a small way, I was grateful he didn't accuse me of turning his sister against him.

"She doesn't like the work I'm doing now. No, worse than that. She doesn't mind the work. She doesn't like the *clay.*" He gave a laugh like an echo of Root's. But he didn't have Root's confidence and power; he only sounded bitter, sarcastic, and afraid. "She tried to tell me she approves of me, but I can read her face like a book.

"Well, let me tell you something." He poked a trembling finger at my chest. "With my show tomorrow, I'm alive for the first time in ten years. I'm alive *here.* Art exists to communicate. It isn't worth manure if it doesn't communicate. And it can't communicate if somebody doesn't look at it. It's that simple. The only time an artist is alive is when somebody looks at his work. And if enough people look, he can live forever.

"I've been sterile for ten years because I haven't had one other soul to look at my work." He was so wrapped up in what he was saying, I don't think he even noticed how completely he dismissed his sister. "Now I am alive. If it only lasts for one more day, it'll still be something nobody can take away from me. If I have to work in black clay to get that, who cares? That's just something I didn't know about myself—about how my imagination works. I never had the chance to try black clay before.

"But now—" He couldn't keep his voice from rising like a cry. "Now I'm alive. *Here.* If you want to take that away from me, you're worse than trash. You're evil."

Mortice Root was smiling like a saint.

For a moment, I had to look away. The fear behind the passion in Reese's eyes was more than I could stand. "I'm sorry," I murmured. What else could I say? I regretted everything. He needed me desperately, and I kept failing him. And he placed so little value on his sister. With a private groan, I forced myself to face him again.

"I thought it was work that brought artists to life. Not shows. I thought the work was worth doing whether anybody looked at it or not. Why else did you keep at it for ten years?"

But I was still making the same mistake, still trying to reach him through his art. And now I'd definitely said something he couldn't afford to hear or understand. With a jerky movement like a puppet, he threw up his hands. "I don't have time for this," he snapped. "I've got five more pieces to set up." Then, suddenly, he was yelling at me. "And I don't give one lousy damn what you think!" Somehow, I'd hit a nerve. "I want you to go away. I want you to leave me alone! Get out of here and *leave me alone!*"

I didn't have any choice. As soon as he told me to go, I turned toward the door. But I was desperate myself now. Knotting my fists, I held myself where I was. Urgently—so urgently that I could hardly separate the words—I breathed at him, "Have you looked at Kristen recently? Really looked? Haven't you seen what's happening to her? You—"

Root stopped me. He had that power. Reese had told me to go. Root simply raised his hand, and his strength hit me in the chest like a fist. My tongue was clamped to the roof of my mouth. My voice choked in my throat. For one moment while I staggered, the greenhouse turned in a complete circle, and I thought I was going to be thrown out of the world.

But I wasn't. A couple of heart-beats later, I got my balance back. Helpless to do anything else, I left the greenhouse.

As I crossed the foyer toward the front door, Reese shouted after me, "And stay away from my sister!"

Until I closed the door, I could hear Mortice Root chuckling with pleasure.

Dear God! I prayed. Let me decide. Just this once. He isn't worth it.

But I didn't have the right.

On the other hand, I didn't have to stay away from Kristen. That was up to her; Reese didn't have any say in the matter.

I made myself walk slowly until I was out of sight of The Root Cellar, just in case someone was watching. Then I started to run.

It was the middle of the afternoon, and the heat just kept getting worse. After the cool of Root's mansion, the outside air felt like glue against my face. Sweat oozed into my eyes, stuck my coat to my back, itched maliciously in my dirty whiskers. The sunlight looked like it was congealing on the walks and streets. Grimly, I thought if this city didn't get some rain soon it would start to burn.

And yet I wanted today to last, despite the heat. I would happily have caused the sun to stand still. I did not want to have to face Mortice Root and Reese Dona again after dark.

But I would have to deal with that possibility when it came up. First I had to get Kristen's help. And to do that, I had to reach her.

The city did its best to hinder me. I left Root's neighborhood easily enough; but when I entered the slums, I started having problems. I guess a running man dressed in nothing but an overcoat, a pair of pants, and sidesplit shoes looked like too much fun to miss. Gangs of kids seemed to materialize out of the ruined buildings to get in my way.

They should've known better. They were predators themselves, and I was on hunt of my own; when they saw the danger in my eyes, they backed down. Some of them threw bottles and trash at my back, but that didn't matter.

Then the sidewalks became more and more crowded as the slum faded behind me. People stepped in front of me, jostled me off my stride, swore angrily at me as I tried to run past. I had to slow down just to keep myself out of trouble. And all the lights were against me. At every corner, I had to wait and wait while mobs hemmed me in, instinctively blocking the path of anyone who wanted to get ahead of them. I felt like I was up against an active enemy. The city was rising to defend its own.

By the time I reached the street I needed to take me over to 21st,

I felt so ragged and wild I wanted to shake my fists at the sky and demand some kind of assistance or relief. But if God couldn't see how much trouble I was in, He didn't deserve what I was trying to do in His name. So I did the best I could—running in spurts, walking when I had to, risking the streets whenever I saw a break in the traffic. And finally I made it. Trembling, I reached the building where Reese and Kristen had their apartment.

Inside, it was as hot as an oven, baking its inhabitants to death. But here at least there was nobody in my way, and I took the stairs two and three at a time to the fourth floor. The lightbulb over the landing was out, but I didn't have any trouble finding the door I needed.

I pounded on it with my fist. Pounded again. Didn't hear anything. Hammered at the wood a third time.

"Kristen!" I shouted. I didn't care how frantic I sounded. "Let me in! I've got to talk to you¹"

Then I heard a small, faint noise through the panels. She must've been right on the other side of the door. Weakly, she said, "Go away."

"Kristen!" Her dismissal left a welt of panic across my heart. I put my mouth to the crack of the door to make her hear me. "Reese needs help. If he doesn't get it, you're not going to survive. He doesn't even realize he's sacrificing you."

After a moment, the lock clicked, and the door opened.

I went in.

But the apartment was dark. She'd turned off all the lights. When she closed the door behind me, I couldn't see a thing. I had to stand still so I wouldn't bump into Reese's sculptures.

"Kristen," I said, half pleading, half commanding. "Turn on a light."

Her reply was a whisper of misery. "You don't want to see me."

She sounded so beaten I almost gave up hope. Quietly, I said, "Please."

She couldn't refuse. She needed me too badly. I felt her move past me in the dark. Then the overhead lights clicked on, and I saw her.

I shouldn't have been shocked. I knew what to expect. But that didn't help. The sight of her went into me like a knife.

She was wearing only a terrycloth bathrobe. That made sense; she'd been poor for a long time and didn't want to ruin her good clothes. The collar of her robe was soaked with blood.

Her nosebleed was worse.

And delicate red streams ran steadily from both her ears.

Sticky trails marked her lips and chin, the front of her throat, the sides of her neck. She'd given up trying to keep herself clean. Why should she bother? She was bleeding to death, and she knew it.

Involuntarily, I went to her and put my arms around her.

She leaned against me. I was all she had left. Into my shoulder, she said as if she were on the verge of tears, "I can't help him anymore. I've tried and tried. I don't know what else to do."

She stood there quivering; and I held her and stroked her hair and let her blood soak into my coat. I didn't have any other way to comfort her.

But her time was running out, just like Reese's. The longer I waited, the weaker she would be. As soon as she became a little steadier, I lowered my arms and stepped back. In spite of the way I looked, I wanted her to be able to see what I was.

"He doesn't need that kind of help now," I said softly, willing her to believe me. Not the kind you've been giving him for ten years. "Not anymore. He needs me. That's why I'm here.

"But I have to have permission." I wanted to cry at her, You've been letting him do this to you for ten years! None of this would've happened to you if you hadn't allowed it! But I kept that protest to myself. "He keeps sending me away, and I have to go. I don't have any choice. I can't do anything without permission.

"It's really that simple." God, make her believe me! "I need somebody with me who wants me to be there. I need you to go back to The Root Cellar with me. Even Root won't be able to get rid of me if you want me to stay.

"Kristen." I moved closer to her again, put my hands in the blood on her cheek, on the side of her neck. "I'll find some way to save him. If you're there to give me permission."

She didn't look at me; she didn't seem to have the courage to raise her eyes. But after a moment I felt the clear touch of grace. She believed me—when I didn't have any particular reason to believe myself. Softly, she said, "I can't go like this. Give me a minute to change my clothes."

She still didn't look at me. But when she turned to leave the room, I saw the determination mustering in the corners of her eyes.

I breathed a prayer of long-overdue thanks. She intended to fight.

I waited for her with fear beating in my bones. And when she returned—dressed in her dingy blouse and fraying skirt, with a towel wrapped around her neck to catch the blood—and announced that she was ready to go, I faltered. She looked so wan and frail—already

weak and unnaturally pale from loss of blood. I felt sure she wasn't
going to be able to walk all the way to The Root Cellar.

Carefully, I asked her if there was any other way we could get
where we were going. But she shrugged the question aside. She and
Reese had never owned a car. And he'd taken what little money was
available in order to rent a truck to take his last pieces to the gallery.

Groaning a silent appeal for help, I held her arm to give her what
support I could. Together, we left the apartment, went down the old
stairs and out to the street.

I felt a new sting of dread when I saw that the sun was setting.
For all my efforts to hurry, I'd taken too much time. Now I would
have to contend with Mortice Root at night.

Twilight and darkness brought no relief from the heat. The city
had spent all day absorbing the pressure of the sun; now the walks
and buildings, every stretch of cement seemed to emit fire like the
sides of a furnace. The air felt thick and ominous—as charged with
intention as a thunderstorm, but trapped somehow, prevented from
release, tense with suffering.

It sucked the strength out of Kristen with every breath. Before
we'd gone five blocks, she was leaning most of her weight on me.
That was frightening, not because she was more than I could bear,
but because she seemed to weigh so little. Her substance was bleeding away. In the garish and unreliable light of the streetlamps, show
windows, and signs, only the dark marks on her face and neck appeared real.

But we were given one blessing: the city itself left us alone. It had
done its part by delaying me earlier. We passed through crowds and
traffic, past gutted tenements and stalking gangs, as if we didn't
deserve to be noticed anymore.

Kristen didn't complain, and I didn't let her stumble. One by one,
we covered the blocks. When she wanted to rest, we put our backs
to the hot walls and leaned against them until she was ready to go
on.

During that whole long, slow creep through the pitiless dark, she
only spoke to me once. While we were resting again, sometime after
we turned on 49th, she said quietly, "I still don't know your name."

We were committed to each other; I owed her the truth. "I don't
either," I said. Behind the wall of the past, any number of things
were hidden from me.

She seemed to accept that. Or maybe she just didn't have enough
strength left to worry about both Reese and me. She rested a little
while longer. Then we started walking again.

And at last we left the last slum behind and made our slow, frail approach to The Root Cellar. Between streetlights I looked for the moon, but it wasn't able to show through the clenched haze. I was sweating like a frightened animal. But Kristen might have been immune to the heat. All she did was lean on me and walk and bleed.

I didn't know what to expect at Root's mansion. Trouble of some kind. An entire squadron of security guards. Minor demons lurking in the bushes around the front porch. Or an empty building, deserted for the night. But the place wasn't deserted. All the rest of the mansion was dark; the greenhouse burned with light. Reese wasn't able to leave his pieces alone before his show. And none of the agents that Root might have used against us appeared. He was that sure of himself.

On the other hand, the front door was locked with a variety of bolts and wires.

But Kristen was breathing sharply, urgently. Fear and desire and determination made her as feverish as her brother; she wanted me to take her inside, to Reese's defense. And she'd lost a dangerous amount of blood. She wasn't going to be able to stay on her feet much longer. I took hold of the door, and it opened without a sound. Cool air poured out at us, as concentrated as a moan of anguish.

We went in.

The foyer was dark. But a wash of light from the cracks of the greenhouse doors showed us our way. The carpet muffled our feet. Except for her ragged breathing and my frightened heart, we were as silent as spirits.

But as we got near the greenhouse, I couldn't keep quiet anymore. I was too scared.

I caused the doors to burst open with a crash that shook the walls. At the same time, I tried to charge forward.

The brilliance of the gallery seemed to explode in my face. For an instant, I was dazzled.

And I was stopped. The light felt as solid as the wall that cut me off from the past.

Almost at once, my vision cleared, and I saw Mortice Root and Reese Dona. They were alone in the room. They were standing in front of a sculpture I hadn't seen earlier—the biggest piece here. Reese must've brought it in his rented truck. It was a wild, swept-winged, and malignant bird of prey, its beak wide in a cry of fury. One of its clawed feet was curled like a fist. The other was gripped deep into a man's chest. Agony stretched the man's face.

At least Reese had the decency to be surprised. Root wasn't. He faced us and grinned.

Reese gaped dismay at Kristen and me for one moment. Then, with a wrench like an act of violence, he turned his back. His shoulders hunched; his arms clamped over his stomach. "I told you to go away." His voice sounded like he was strangling. "I told you to leave her alone."

The light seemed to blow against me like a wind. Like the current of the river that carried me away, taking me from place to place without past and without future, hope. And it was rising. It held me in the doorway; I couldn't move through it.

"You are a fool," Root said to me. His voice rode the light as if he were shouting. "You have been denied. You cannot enter here."

He was so strong that I was already half turned to leave when Kristen saved me.

As pale as ash, she stood beside me. Fresh blood from her nose and ears marked her skin. The towel around her neck was sodden and terrible. She looked too weak to keep standing. Yet she matched her capacity for desperation against Reese's need.

"No," she said in the teeth of the light and Root's grin. "He can stay. I want him here."

I jerked myself toward Reese again.

Ferocity came at me like a cataract; but I stood against it. I had Kristen's permission. That had to be enough.

"Look at her!" I croaked at his back. "She's your sister! *Look* at her!"

He didn't seem to hear me at all. He was hunched over himself in front of his work. "Go away," he breathed weakly, as if he were talking to himself. "I can't stand it. Just go away."

Gritting prayers between my teeth like curses, I lowered my head, called up every ache and fragment of strength I had left, and took one step into the greenhouse.

Reese fell to his knees as if I'd broken the only string that held him upright.

At the same time, the bird of prey poised above him moved.

Its wings beat downward. Its talons clenched. The heart of its victim burst in his chest.

From his clay throat came a brief, hoarse wail of pain.

Driven by urgency, I took two more steps through the intense pressure walled against me.

And all the pieces displayed in the greenhouse started to move.

Tormented statuettes fell from their niches, cracked open, and cried out. Gargoyles mewed hideously. The mouths of victims gaped open and whined. In a few swift moments, the air was full of muffled shrieks and screams.

Through the pain, and the fierce current forcing me away from Reese, and the horror, I heard Mortice Root start to laugh.

If Kristen had failed me then, I would have been finished. But in some way she had made herself blind and deaf to what was happening. Her entire soul was focused on one object—help for her brother—and she willed me forward with all the passion she had learned in ten years of self-sacrifice. She was prepared to spend her last life here for Reese's sake.

She made it possible for me to keep going.

Black anguish rose like a current at me. And the force of the light mounted. I felt it ripping at my skin. It was as hot as the hunger ravening for Reese's heart.

Yet I took two more steps.

And two more.

And reached him.

He still knelt under the wing-spread of the nightmare bird he had created. The light didn't hurt him; he didn't feel it at all. He was on his knees because he simply couldn't stand. He gripped his arms over his heart to keep himself from howling.

There I noticed something I should've recognized earlier. He had sculpted a man for his bird of prey to attack, not a woman. I could see the figure clearly enough now to realize that Reese had given the man his own features. Here, at least, he had shaped one of his own terrors rather than merely bringing out the darkness of Mortice Root's clay.

After that, nothing else mattered. I didn't feel the pain or the pressure. Ferocity and dismay lost their power.

I knelt in front of Reese, took hold of his shoulders, and hugged him like a child. "Just look at her," I breathed into his ear. "She's your sister. You don't have to do this to her."

She stood across the room from me with her eyes closed and her determination gripped in her small fists.

From under her eyelids, stark blood streamed down her cheeks.

"Look at her!" I pleaded. "I can help you. Just *look*."

In the end, he didn't look at her. He didn't need to. He knew what was happening.

Suddenly, he wrenched out of my embrace. His arms flung me aside. He raised his head, and one lorn wail corded his throat:

"Kristen!"

Root's laughter stopped as if it'd been cut down with an axe.

That cry was all I needed. It came right from Reese's heart, too pure to be denied. It was permission, and I took it.

I rose to my feet, easily now, easily. All the things that stood in my way made no difference. Transformed, I faced Mortice Root across the swelling force of his malice. All his confidence was gone to panic.

Slowly, I raised my arms.

Beams of white sprouted from my palms, clean white almost silver. It wasn't fire or light in any wordly sense; but it blazed over my head like light, ran down my arms like fire. It took my coat and pants, even my shoes away from me in flames. Then it wrapped me in the robes of God until all my body burned.

Root tried to scream, but his voice didn't make any sound.

Towering white-silver, I reached up into the storm-dammed sky and brought down a blast that staggered the entire mansion to its foundations. Crashing past glass and frame and light-fixtures, a bolt that might have been lightning took hold of Root from head to foot. For an instant, the gallery's lights failed. Everything turned black except for Root's horror etched against darkness and the blast that bore him away.

When the lights came back on, the danger was gone from the greenhouse. All the crying and the pain and the pressure were gone. Only the sculptures themselves remained.

They were slumped and ruined, like melted wax.

Outside, rain began to rattle against the glass of the greenhouse.

Later, I went looking for some clothes; I couldn't very well go around naked. After a while, I located a suite of private rooms at the back of the building. But everything I found there belonged to Root. His personal stink had soaked right into the fabric. I hated the idea of putting his things on my skin when I'd just been burned clean. But I had to wear something. In disgust, I took one of his rich shirts and a pair of pants. That was my punishment for having been so eager to judge Reese Dona.

Back in the greenhouse, I found him sitting on the floor with Kristen's head cradled in his lap. He was stroking the soft hair at her temples and grieving to himself. For the time being, at least, I was sure his grief had nothing to with his ruined work.

Kristen was fast asleep, exhausted by exertion and loss of blood. But I could see that she was going to be all right. Her bleeding had stopped completely. And Reese had already cleaned some of the stains from her face and neck.

Rain thundered against the ceiling of the greenhouse; jagged lines of lightning scrawled the heavens. But all the glass was intact, and the storm stayed outside, where it belonged. From the safety of shelter, the downpour felt comforting.

And the manufactured cool of the building had wiped out most of Root's unnatural heat. That was comforting, too.

It was time for me to go.

But I didn't want to leave Reese like this. I couldn't do anything about the regret that was going to dog him for the rest of his life. But I wanted to try.

The river was calling for me. Abruptly, as if I thought he was in any shape to hear me, I said, "What you did here—the work you did for Root—wasn't wrong. Don't blame yourself for that. You just went too far. You need to find the balance. Reason and energy." Need and help. "There's no limit to what you can do, if you just keep your balance."

He didn't answer. Maybe he wasn't listening to me at all. But after a moment he bent over Kristen and kissed her forehead.

That was enough. I had to go. Some of the details of the greenhouse were already starting to melt.

My bare feet didn't make any sound as I left the room, crossed the foyer, and went out into—

★ Feast of John the Baptist ★

by Victor Milán

The Southwest offers an idiom to the writer very different from that of majority Anglo America. The Spanish and Indian influences— the history, the traditions, the myths—are rich and fascinating, and still have an exotic, alien flavor to a population steeped in stereo- typed regional images of the urban East, the rural Midwest, the old South, and, more recently, California.

—Sometimes too alien, too exotic. A writer who attempts to make use of Southwestern images is running some potent risks. Cowboy stories are safe, if currently unpopular, and tales of mystic Native Americans who are in touch with earth and sky and trendy spiritual values are generally acceptable. But editors tend to run like fright- ened chicken from anything that smacks of the Hispanic. Spanish surnamed characters are welcome only in the most menial capacity, or if cast in a form that affronts few majoritarian sensibilities—a fancy way of saying stereotyped.

Certain ethnic groups fail to evoke this fight/flight response. Indians may be acceptable because they're fairly rare, and thus nonthreatening to majority values. Blacks for the most part have long been absorbed into the overculture; some speak their own dialect in the ghettos, but it's still a dialect of English.

But the Hispanics are different. They have their own language; they're predominantly Catholic in a predominantly Protestant culture. They are widely perceived as resisting assimilation in a way in which, for example, the Italians are not. And they are increasingly numerous. They are widely perceived as threatening our national identity.

(John Calhoun is supposed to have opposed the Mexican War on the grounds that Spaniards, unlike blacks, could intermarry with whites and produce progeny indistinguishable from real white folks, thus mongrelizing our pure race. He had a point. I'm a blond six-footer, about as far from the popular image of a Hispanic as you can get—and I'm half Spanish, the only Hispanic in this anthology. Though I was raised a middle class Anglo, in the last census I was required by law to fill out a Form for Minority Businesspersons.)

Hispanic anxiety isn't only a feature of publishing, of course. Congress has recently seen fit to make having brown skin prima facie evidence of crime. Governors of Western states and prominent eco-activists promote a crude racialism vis-a-vis Hispanics that smacks of Pretoria. Descendants of immigrants who were themselves despised as filthy foreigners polluting the national essence are crowding forward to help slam the Golden Door.

All this doesn't just affect Hispanics, of course; the recently passed Simpson-Mazzoli legislation provides for increased government surveillance of everyone, and seems fairly blatantly geared to starting up the machinery to impose a mandatory national ID card program within a few years. So using ritually unclean Hispanic elements of Southwestern culture becomes a laudably subversive act in a society bent on planting a spy camera in every bedroom and drug testing in every workplace, in regulating every detail of life. Ms. Snodgrass and UNM Press are to be commended for their courage in publishing this collection.

And now, here's my own bit of sedition. . . .

Feast of John the Baptist

by Victor Milán

"God is good," the priest intoned. He had been a fat man. The night wind hissing off the desert into the foothills flapped and cracked his black shirt about his sides like a deflated hot-air balloon. "He's sent us a miracle."

Near him squatted a man in a tattered overcoat, bouncing up and down on skinny shanks. "Is it ready yet?" he asked, dark eyes glinting with starlight and impatience.

The old square man who sat across the low dirt mound from the others shook his head. "Not yet." His voice was like his face, broad and dry and rugged as the dead land around. "Soon."

The man in the coat picked up a chunk of driftwood and prodded the mound. To call him youngest of the three would not be right; rather, he was the least ancient. He had been young, not long ago as time is counted, but youth had been burned from him in the days since the death of the world. "It's been too damned long already," he said.

The priest raised one finger. "Don't be impatient, my son. That we have anything at all is a miracle. That we even found each other."

When they encountered each other that day the sun hung overhead, its heat soul-withering in its intensity. The sky had been burned lifeless, scattered with a handful of clouds, small and hard like lumps of animal excrement calcined by the sun to a mean grey-white. As above, so below: nothing lived. Nothing but the three men standing on a khaki hillside, drawn together by some scavenger's instinct, long-hidden and primal, facing one another across the desiccated body of a sheep.

It was the priest, who had crossed the desert with the once-young man from a place where a city had lain, who broke the silence. "It's a miracle," he announced.

The old man who had come down from the mountains to the west pushed his Stetson back on his head and knelt by the carcass. How long ago the animal had fallen, he couldn't say. The meat had been stripped away, leaving a groined arch of ribcage, black shriveled strings of flesh clinging to bones that had not begun to bleach from mottled brown. Tufts of wool quivered in a clump of brittle ashen grama grass a few paces away. The rest had long since been swept away by the endless Southwestern wind.

But the head—the square man cradled it reverently in his strong old hands and examined it carefully. "No maggots," he observed. "The crows didn't get the eyes. Hell, it ain't even dried out yet." Despite the strangeness of it, his words lacked wonder.

"Ain't no crows left," the man in the coat said. "Ain't even any maggots. Ain't nothin' left but us, man."

"This young man is Manuel," the priest said. "I'm Father Rodríguez. We have been traveling together."

"Esquibel," the old man said. He laid the head gently down and got to his feet, moaning softly, unconsciously, at the pangs of arthritic joints. "Today's the Feast of St. John the Baptist."

Father Rodríguez looked startled. "So it is."

"We can celebrate it with *cabeza de borrega*," the old man said.

The priest licked his lips. They stretched without apparent volition into a grin, as though drawn back by tiny claws. The thought of such a delicacy after days of near-starvation wracked him with a spasm of hungry anticipation.

"What you talking about?" Manuel asked, his eyes narrowing to slits.

"We dig a hole in the ground and roast the head in it," Esquibel said. "It's the old way to celebrate the feast of *San Juan Bautista*."

Manuel grimaced. "Sounds funky. But shit, I'm hungry enough to eat that damned head raw."

They set to work under the lash of sun and hard-blown stinging dust. Overcoming fastidious hesitation to risk damage to his threadbare black slacks, Father Rodríguez went to his knees and attacked the ground. Fingers that had been melon-ripe with pudgy softness not long before tore at *caliche* hard as concrete. After a moment, Manuel shrugged and began to help with a flat rock. Old Esquibel took a sharp-edged shard of flint and set about haggling the sheep's head free from the dried-out tendons that held it to the neck vertebrae.

At length the hole was dug, deep enough that Father Rodríguez could reach his arm down in and just touch bottom with his fingertips. In it a fire was built of dried brush and black grama, cherished against the predator wind, raised to a high hot dance and covered over with stones. With a pointed rock Esquibel knocked a hole in the sheep's forehead, so that the moisture trapped within despite the baking sun by some fluke—miracle, if you like—would not burst the skull when it turned to steam. When the head was roasted he would knock the top of the skull off with the same rock, and the three men, who had tasted nothing but the insides of their mouths and occasional sips of spit-warm water for more days than they cared to number, would feast upon the steaming brains. And the other moist, tender parts, the eyes, the tongue, the lining of the mouth, all somehow preserved as if especially for them.

"I can almost believe in the mercy of God," Esquibel said, his tongue thick from salivation.

"How can you doubt it?" the priest asked softly. The old man said nothing.

They had some water, Rodríguez in several old Pepsi bottles lashed with scraps of twine to the cracked black vinyl belt knotted rudely in front of his shrunken belly, the old man in an Army surplus canteen. A miserable few liters, and none of them had seen other water for days—none that a man would drink, anyway, at least not before the pangs of thirst drove him to a self-destructive frenzy. But Esquibel without hesitation twisted the dented cap from his canteen and sloshed the contents over the sheep's head, soaking the stiff wool so that the precious flesh could be properly steamed. Then the dripping stinking head, eyes staring half-lidded and uncomprehending from beneath the black-red hole, was lowered onto the heated stones and covered with parched pallid earth scooped lovingly by cabled, crack-nailed, bleeding hands.

The sun oozed down out of sight, holding for an instant in its bloated orange eye the silhouettes of a dead city, minute on the horizon. The battering relentless heat of day went quickly. Soon it would be replaced by cold, a chill that turned bones brittle as dry sticks and made a man shudder fit to bust them, like an old Chevy truck that's been started in fourth gear. They kept their vigil, waiting.

"How soon?" Manuel asked insistently. His tone said it had been hours since he'd last asked, though to the others it was a moment or two.

Father Rodríguez glanced at his wrist. The two small oblongs of his digital watch's LED stared blankly back at him in the starlight, skull's eyes. Life had long since fled the timepiece. He looked up sheepishly. "It shouldn't be too long."

Manuel rubbed his hands before him as if trying to start a fire with his sticklike fingers. "Is it true, man? Are we really the only things left alive?" His eyes begged for someone to contradict his certainty of that afternoon that nothing else lived in the wide sere world.

"Surely there's something left," Rodríguez said reassuringly.

"No," Esquibel said, with finality. "We're the last."

"Something ate most of that sheep." Manuel spoke as if to himself.

"It's dead too, now. I feel it. We're alone." The old man spoke without fear or fervor. He'd accepted that fact, as he had the onset of age.

Stubbornly the priest shook his head. "I—we've heard things in the night. The hoot of an owl, coyotes calling to each other. Desert sounds."

"*Abuelos*," Esquibel said. "The Old Ones—ghosts," he added for the benefit of Manuel, who was obviously a city boy, a *chicano*, who didn't understand such matters.

"That's crazy, man," Manuel said. Father Rodríguez crossed himself. A moment later Manuel did too, rustily.

A silence opened, widened. The wind moaned in to fill it. The priest gazed for a long time at the mound before speaking again. "It *is* a miracle," he insisted. "God saved the head for us. He gave us meat to celebrate the feast of His holy martyr in the traditional way. He must mean that we survive."

"God's forgotten us," Esquibel said.

"But *think*. In all this land nothing lives. There weren't even flies around the carcass of that sheep. Why? What preserved its head? What brought the three of us together at just this time and place?"

"I was hungry," the old man said.

"So were we all. We hungered, and the Lord has given us to eat."

"Now, that's the kind of miracle I can get into." Manuel rubbed his palms together and grinned, showing stained teeth tipped and jumbled like sarsen stones.

"The world fell into sin and was consumed," Father Rodríguez said. "Why were we spared? God must intend us to carry on his Creation."

"We'd sure as Hell need a miracle for that," Esquibel said, and for the first time the others heard emotion in his voice: bitterness.

The priest nodded at the mound beneath which the sheep's head simmered. "There you have it." He spoke with quiet triumph.

The old man stared out into the empty bowl of the desert. His own world had died long before the larger realm of the rest of humanity. A wife rotted from the inside out with cancer, his three daughters gone in a fiery blossom from which the driver of the pickup that killed them staggered, drunken and unhurt. . . . "I don't believe it," he said. "God wiped us out like a man burning an anthill with gasoline. What does He care for three *chingao* little ants?"

"He's chosen us." The priest's face was eerie-pale and transported, a carven *santo's* visage. "He's given us the gift of life. Can you turn your face from Him?"

"Hey, old man, you better listen to him," Manuel said. "God's got this special plan for us, just us. That's why he sent us food to keep us goin'. . . . It's gotta be ready soon."

Esquibel shook his head. But his doubt was crumbling like an arroyo bank undercut by a flash flood. It wasn't the hollowness in his belly that wore at him. He was resigned to that, and to the death which it portended. It was the greater hunger. The longing for something else, anything, that lived amid the desolation. The others felt it too. Why else had they not fallen on each other like mad things, rending and tearing for sole possession of the precious scrap of food? The need for companionship, even companions with whom to see in the final fall of night, meant more than mere survival.

"It is a miracle," he said, bowing his head. "God is good."

Father Rodríguez beamed. "Let us uncover the head, and share His grace."

The three men dug with bare hands, a rock, a chunk of bleached and tumbled wood. "A light," Father Rodríguez panted. "We must have light." Esquibel produced a plastic butane lighter. Enough fuel remained to start a twist of dried grass flickering.

When the head was exposed Manuel plunged his hands down to seize it. He snatched them back with a curse, flapping burned fingers in the air. Esquibel leaned down and with his callused hands grasped the head and drew it upward into the fitful yellow light.

"*Madre de Dios*," the priest breathed. "Holy Mother of God!"

For it was not the head of an animal that Esquibel laid gently on the overcoat which Manuel spread beside the pit. It was the head of a man, bearded, dark-complected, with sunken cheeks and half-shut eyes. The neck had been cleanly severed. The head seemed to smoke, but the tones of the skin were those of recent life.

Manuel screamed.

"What is that?" he shrieked. "Oh, Jesus, Mary, *what is it?*"

The priest fell to his knees, hands locked before him. "*San Juan, San Juan Bautista*," he gobbled.

Esquibel sat on his heels beside the head, impassive. "*Un milagro*," he told Manuel. "It's our special miracle from God. He changed the sheep's head into the head of John the Baptist."

In a peristalsis of terror Manuel coiled in upon himself. Father Rodríguez mouthed voiceless prayers to his God, who sent starving men the vision of a saint.

Esquibel picked up the sharp rock he'd used to make the hole in the sheep's head. "I wish we had some garlic," he said, and reached.

★ Frenchmen and Plumbers ★

by Martha Soukup

I was born in the suburbs of Chicago in 1959, and lived all my adult life in that big city until October of 1986, two months ago as I write this. I love Chicago; it is everything I think a big city should be, some of the neighborhoods are very pleasant to live in, and I'm a Cub fan. (No pity solicited.)

So why am I in Albuquerque? People ask me that every time I turn around. The answer is not simple nor easy. Everything is far too fresh to make sense of in print. But I've been given my assignment.

Let's break it into two parts: first, why did I leave Chicago?

I started writing in 1985; the story I wrote to submit with my application to the Clarion SF Writer's Workshop that year was the first I had written since high school. (Later I sold it to Terry Carr.) I was accepted. With that sign, and with the encouragement and love of my husband, who is my best friend, I went off to commit myself to the risks of professional storytelling.

*Clarion does more than tutor and advise would-be writers, al-
though it does that very well in its six-week session: it is an infa-
mous cauldron of personal and emotional change. I changed in ways
I did not expect that summer. But I came back to Chicago and
resumed my life with just one obvious, lasting change: I was writing
and marketing stories.*

*The next spring I went to another workshop, the Taos Pilot Work-
shop, run by the Writers of the Future contest for its winners and
finalists, taught by four master writers—including New Mexico's
Jack Williamson. It was the first time I had even been in this state.
I expected a lark; after all, I'd already been to Clarion, and the Taos
workshop would only last a week.*

*Well, it turned out I had the major part of my changing left to
do; it seems a workshop can be an emotional foxhole whatever its
length. In addition to getting good writing work done (I plotted
"Frenchmen and Plumbers" there, with advise from Frederik Pohl),
I got a close and painful look at parts of myself I had not seen
before.*

*Back again, to Chicago. The repercussions of Taos followed me
home, in more than one way. Eventually, after much talk, holding,
crying and love of each other, Michael, my husband, and I decided
I should live for myself, for at least a while. (Just like, I can't stop
from thinking, so many villainous spouses in melodramatic movies.) Today we run up the largest long-distance phone bills you ever
saw.*

*So much for the difficult part of the story, and on to the simpler,
if not necessarily logical, part: why Albuquerque?*

*I went to Atlanta's World Science Fiction Convention in 1986
thinking about cities, most of them easily rejected: too grungy (New
York), too hot (most of the South), too diffuse (L.A.)—and on down
the line. There, at the Worldcon, I found myself spending time with
a group of writers from Albuquerque. I'd never really considered
Albuquerque (if nothing else, too close to Taos!), though I have a
good friend from my Clarion class there; but these folks were bright
and friendly and made me feel welcome. A month and a half later
I was in an old, beat-up van, driving my worldly possessions down.
There is nothing like a long solo drive for giving one a tenuous
feeling of control of one's life.*

*An arbitrary choice? Still, a good one. Albuquerque has been kind
to me so far. It (just barely) meets my minimum urban require-
ments; but it could hardly be much different from Chicago, at a
time when almost any change of scene is desirable. And the people*

here, both writers and readers, have been sweet to my battered self; some, I hope, will be my friends for the next few decades. Now, if only they played board games, or a little more poker. . . .

I can't say New Mexico is my final destination—I wouldn't dare guess—but it is a special place that has earned my heartfelt thanks. And this little story.

Frenchmen and Plumbers

by Martha Soukup

Sally Tobias rubbed the back of her hand across her itchy, sweaty brow, conscious of the motion, trying to ignore the soft whir of the video camera high in a corner of her workroom. The gesture left streaks of clay blended with the early gray in her dirty-blond hair. More water for the clay: she scooped some out of the urn at her ankle. At least there was water here, along the Rio Grande; nothing you would even use to wash your hair without distilling, but good enough for the pots, and certainly more than could be had in her native Phoenix, where the water table had given out not long after she left. And she liked the isolation of northern New Mexico, along the river, between the mountains, and far from most of the humans who had mucked up the planet.

That isolation couldn't last. The economy was breaking down now too. People with more love for cities than she now sought other homes, independence from the system that was choking itself. Stopgap measures, of course.

She was finally isolated again. The scientists who had milled and buzzed around her little cabin for most of the last week had faded away, leaving her head milling and buzzing with instructions and admonitions.

"Be ready Tuesday," one had said.

"What time?"

"Anytime." He paused. "We can't seem to get a straight translation of time from them. But we're pretty sure it will be Tuesday."

"You might not want to go to bed Monday night, though," said another.

It was late Tuesday, the sun touching a mountaintop to the west; she had not slept and no alien had appeared. Sally finished shaping a pot, tall and narrow, its sides twisting up like a growing thing. She might be able to sell it. What little money she had came from the pots and tiles stacked on her front porch; a tourist or a refugee sometimes gave her a dollar or two for one. With this she kept her supply of glazes stocked and bought the few essentials she needed to supplement her garden. Occasionally she sent some of the remainder to the Cavalry Fund.

She had put little faith in the project. Pulling a few remaining resources together, in slender hope of contacting an alien race detected scant years before? Might as well stare at a star and wish the rain forests back, pesticides vanished from the food chain, all the radioactive waste magically decayed away. Better to make her pots, her tiles, her wind-flutes, bring a little last beauty to her corner of the earth. She didn't believe in God, either—but she found herself praying every night.

But the Cavalry had come. They wanted to talk.

"Why me?" she had asked.

"We don't know. They've been here two weeks and they still keep claiming not to understand what our problem is. What our problem is!" the scientist cried, and quieted her voice again when another looked at her sternly. "—They said they wanted to talk to some other types of humans. We showed them the Fund's subscription list. They selected one hundred and eighty-seven names—apparently at random—and said they'd talk to those people this Tuesday. We think."

"Are there two hundred aliens?"

"No, there are fourteen of them."

"So will I be able to talk to them? How?"

"We think so. Projections, duplicates—there are so many things we don't understand. So many things the Cavalrans can do that make no sense at all." An awkward name, but it had stuck. Sally was not to call them that, or address them by any name; she was not to bring up international conflicts, unless the alien did; she was not to ask any questions; she was not to volunteer anything. The linguists, psychiatrists and diplomats of the Fund did not want any well-meaning amateurs disrupting their careful procedures. She was just to answer the questions she was asked as honestly and simply as she could. As were, presumably, the other hundred and eighty-six.

She set the pot on a shelf to dry, and went to another shelf where a wind-flute was cooling. She glanced through her back window: it was closed, but she could just hear, if she listened, the soft whistling of the wind-flutes hanging from her tree. The tree bore dozens of flutes, all shaped and colored differently, and as the wind blew through them they swung and sang. Her flutes were not for sale: they were Sally's personal patch of beauty in the ugly mess people had made of the world.

The new one should be cool enough; she touched it with a fingertip, then picked it up. It was glazed green, a vivid emerald. So little green left in the world. The door opened behind her. She didn't turn immediately; she spun the piece slowly in her hands, looking for any flaws, any cracks. There were none. It was perfect.

"It is beautiful, Sally Tobias." The voice had no accent she could place, but it sang like the flutes on her tree. She put the piece down carefully and looked around.

"So there is a cavalry," she said softly.

The alien made a complex shrugging motion, setting rainbow fur shuddering up and down its length. It seemed solid enough, projection though it must be; she looked in vain for any blurring or translucence. She thought it had two eyes and a small mouth in its silky face; she could definitely discern the six small arms it waved. "So your people say we have been called, the ones who sent the message," it sang in a soft, breathy voice. "We must confess we do not understand the concept. Or so many others—'scientists?' 'Rescue squad?'" It made the motion again. She stared, fascinated, at the colors shimmering through its fur. "We did understand the concept: 'messengers.' If not the message."

She took a breath, a strange taste in her mouth. An alien was in her cabin. Or, despite appearances, some kind of projection— But it was the cavalry, and she, one bruised and desperate scout. "The message must be pretty clear."

"Perhaps," said the alien. "Perhaps not. These scientists, they do not seem to speak in concepts we know. But they seem so urgent. This is why we asked to speak to messengers who are not scientists. We think you were a lucky choice." She was silent, wondering what it meant, remembering not to ask. "We hoped to find someone who works with the true concepts, the real concepts." It moved smoothly across the room to the new wind-flute. "May this be looked at?"

She nodded. It did not move. "Yes."

The alien picked up the piece and studied it. It held the flute forward and made a gesture with three arms that took in the room, its disorderly stacks of pots and tiles, and the window through which the song tree could be seen. "The concept is 'art.' You are an artist."

Her cheeks warmed. Most humans thought her a potter, a craftsman. She smiled at the alien who had seen artistry. "Thank you."

"Why? It is truth," said the alien. It looked closely at the flute. "There is no problem here. Art is made."

"But there is a problem," she said carefully, breaking the rule of only answering questions. "This planet is my home, and it is dying."

"And?" said the alien.

"And what?" she said. "It's dying! We're dying, and it's terrible!" Pain built in her chest. She had not truly allowed herself to feel this for a long time.

"They have tried to explain why this is terrible. We still do not understand. All beings die. Species die. Where is the failure? We have made a light-poem of what they told us, however, to meditate on."

In one tiny hand, by the flute, was a hemisphere, a deep iridescent purple. The alien made a motion over the object and the hemisphere's flat face glowed. In quick, dreamlike succession, Sally watched: crops and forests shriveling as killing rain drenched them; rivers clogging green with algae until they rotted brown, empty; the bombing of South Africa and of Iraq; poisons, unnaturally black, spewing over cities, held there in choking inversions; one of the melted-down fission plants (which one?), buried in concrete, cordoned off in a wide, wide radius; the greedy, spreading Sahara; dying insects, dying birds, dying animals; dying children.

"Is this correct?" the alien asked.

An unfamiliar sound came from her throat. "That isn't what it looks like, all of it," she whispered. "But that's what it *feels* like. Oh, can't you see?"

"What should we see?"

"It's such an ugly, such a pointless way to die!"

"Ugly," said the alien. "Ugly."

She seized on its hesitation. "Ugly! We are killing ourselves, and it's hideous!"

The hemisphere had vanished; the alien ran several hands over the flute. "Ugly, and pointless. Yes, Sally Tobias, we begin to see." She closed her eyes. "The concepts do not quite match. 'Religion' is not exactly right. Even 'art' is not exactly right. But—you lose beauty with this death?"

"Yes." Oh, if she let herself hope now—

"That should not be. It will be fixed. —May we?"

She did not understand, swept in dizzying relief, until she saw the alien transferring the curving green wind-flute from hand to hand, in a complicated gesture. "Of course."

"Thank you, Sally Tobias." The flute disappeared to wherever the hemisphere had gone. "We shall not meet again. Our people shall remove your problem, and leave. We have—a mission?—a solar system to reshape. It was most fortunate that your planet was on our route."

And they did not meet again, although the aliens left their mark on every acre of the planet.

Sally spent days debriefing, watching videotape, trying to explain each word and gesture she had made. One hundred and eighty-six other people had also been flown to California from around the world for similar debriefings, but it seemed the scientists spent the most time on her.

After she had been there a week, one hundred eighty-seven hemispheres were distributed, gifts from the departed aliens. She sat in her white, empty hotel room, desperately missing her workshop. On the desk was a book one of her fellows had located for her. In her hands was the hemisphere. She turned it and touched it until, when she held it just so, it lit up and revealed:

A green Sahara: a desert that glowed green by night and, when people walked through the aura, surrounded their figures with soft spikes of light like pink lightning;

Clear rivers, rivers that ran as clear and shining as crystal, and colder by far than water;

Factories puffing smoke, solid, pastel smoke that billowed and muffled the dirty buildings like cotton candy, hiding the grime;

Hundreds of acres of soil-stripped farmland, flat and empty but tinted with shimmering colors like a Cavalran's fur; observed from high altitude, the landscape was revealed to be a copy of Seurat's painting of La Grande Jatte. . . .

The Cavalrans had made their changes and left. She glanced at the book on the desk. She had read it once before, in high school. It was open to a comment that a fourteenth-century Frenchman could no more understand the statement "Good sanitary plumbing is more important than art" than a modern man would understand the converse statement. Beauty is eternal, this life only temporary, *n'est-ce pas?* We must please God.

"What did they say to you?" she asked the man who found her the book.

He smiled ruefully. "That species are born and become extinct. That only what is left behind has meaning."

She had always counted herself proud to be a medieval Frenchman—an artist—no mere plumber. There are so many plumbers.

The scientists let her go, finally, and she fled back to her cottage, her refuge. She stood in her back yard by the flute tree. It whistled its quiet tunes as the wind flitted through it, but they were difficult to hear.

The real sound came from the mountains of New Mexico, which towered with twists and hollows and holes and colors in careful homage to Sally's wind-flutes. They roared high beautiful music like laughter.

Sally laughed too. She took a stick and smashed the flutes on her tree, methodically smashed each one, and sobbed and laughed.

"Send us a plumber!"

For AJ Budry's——for holding ladders.

★ Ouroboros ★

by John J. Miller

The story of how I came to move from the wilds of Long Island to the friendly environs of New Mexico is long and, trust me, largely tedious. If you really feel a need to hear it, buy me a beer some time and I'll tell you everything.

My feelings towards New Mexico can, however, be easily summarized. In the more than ten years I've lived here I've never once felt the desire to live anywhere else.

Besides, over the years I've accumulated far too many books and cats to ever seriously think of moving.

Ouroboros

by John J. Miller

It is both my curse and my vindication that I remember.

The trigger, I suppose, is her face. The tide of memory that floods my brain when I first see her is part of the reason why I stand there with a silly look on my face and mumble inanities. Part of the reason.

I don't know how many times it's been repeated, but one time must have been the first. I'll tell it now as if this were that first time. . .

i.

I was still an undergraduate, a junior, and young enough to believe that I could make a living as a poet, when I met Anne Siegal.

Peter Gray, my roommate, had dragged me along with him to a house in the heart of the scenic student ghetto where someone he knew was throwing an end of the semester party. Peter was an undergraduate like myself, but he was thought of as something of a boy wonder in the physics department and he ran with a fast crowd. Most of the people at the party were graduate students, but there were a few other social-climbing undergraduates beside me and Peter, and some slumming profs as well. Peter was the only person there that I knew and from the moment we arrived he became engrossed in an earnest, but to me unintelligible discussion on the nature of black holes, superstring theory, and the origin of the cosmic egg.

I left him to his gabble and, looking for the free booze, drifted among the knots of drinking, talking, munching people until I found the small, cluttered room that served as a study to the graduate student who inhabited the cottage, stopped, and stared.

She was sitting on a dilapidated couch in the center of the room, surrounded by a bevy of physics boys ranging in age from pimply-faced freshmen to balding professors. I stared at her, breathing like a telephone pervert. I don't know if it was love at first sight, but it was certainly lust. Her long black hair was thick and wavy, her large dark eyes were set in a pale, fine-featured face. Her lips, innocent of makeup, were full and pouty. Sultry even. She wore faded jeans and a dark turtleneck sweater, and every rich curve of her body, every gesture of her graceful, long-fingered hands, every expression that flickered across her face pierced directly into my brain like burning icicles driven through my eyes.

I turned and strode from the room. Peter was perched casually on the arm of an ancient overstuffed chair in the living room, swinging his leg and leaning forward conspiratorily to whisper romantically about some cat named Schrodinger to a wide-eyed coed.

"Excuse me," I tossed to the astonished coed who'd been hanging on his every word, jerked him to his feet, and hauled him away.

Peter was somewhat peeved. "Damnit, Robert, I was doing pretty good with her—"

"She'll keep," I said shortly, dragging him into the next room. He came along, if not willingly at least with ineffectual resistance. Peter, boy wonder that he is, is on the short and chubby side, and while I'm not that tall myself, I'm blessed with a rather robust build. I had, in fact, financed my college education by playing football for two years until the cartilage in my left knee disintegrated. The injury had turned out to be a blessing in disguise, as it enabled me to keep my scholarship without having to waste a good portion of my time knocking people down.

"Her," I said from the doorway, pointing.

"Oh," Peter said, nodding wisely.

"Oh, what?"

"The ice maiden."

"What?"

Peter sighed. "Look," he said, drawing me into a corner of the study so we wouldn't present such a prominent spectacle of ourselves, "half, hell, ninety percent, of the guys in the department have had a try at her. Even Smithers." He shook his head in wonderment. Even I, who knows as much physics as does your average Dinka herdsman, had heard of Erasmus Smithers. Smithers was the department's ancient Noble Laureate. They dusted him off once a week and led him to a small room where he taught a seminar that was largely incomprehensible to even the brightest of the three graduate students deemed worthy to take it. They then led him back to his office where he spent his days alternately napping and chalking complicated equations on a huge blackboard. Every now and then he'd publish a paper that revolutioned the field. I'd hardly thought him capable of any human, let alone carnal, desires. I looked from Peter to the woman.

"I believe it," I said.

Peter nodded solemnly. "But she's untouchable. I don't mean just sexually. She's . . . aloof . . . distant. She's an orphan or something; maybe that's why she doesn't go in much for socializing. She's brilliant—she'll get her doctorate faster than anyone in the department's history—and her work means everything to her. If she has any life outside the classroom and lab I've never heard of it. I'm amazed that she's here tonight."

"How about you?" I asked.

He shook his head. "Way out of my league, in both looks and smarts." He sighed. "Though one can dream."

" 'A man's reach should exceed his grasp,' " I quoted. "What's her name?"

"Anne. Anne Siegal."

I nodded and was gone. Peter watched me for a moment, shook his head, and went back, I assume, to his armchair and coed.

There'd been some movement in the group around Anne, but she was still surrounded by mostly the same admirers. Ordinarily I'm rather polite, but I thought nothing of surreptitiously shouldering in front of an innocuous looking fellow with thick, dark-framed glasses and a calculator clipped to his belt.

"Hey," he protested. I turned and looked up at him. He had three inches on me, but I was maybe twice as broad as him and my arms filled out the sleeves of my t-shirt a lot better than his did. I don't know what he saw in my face, but he mumbled something unintelligible that sounded vaguely apologetic and slinked away. I turned my attention to the conversation and the woman that was the center of it. A graduate student with long frizzly hair and a wispy goatee was holding forth. There was no doubt for whose benefit.

"The liberating aspects of the underpinnings of quantum mechanics," he said in a self-confident gabble, "can scarcely be exaggerated. The Great Machine of Newtonian physics is dead, or rather, to use a mechanistic metaphor, out of gas." He seemed pleased with his allusion, but it sounded second rate to me. "I for one find it comforting to live in a universe where we are free to make our own choices, free to build our own lives without the encumbrance of a network of deterministic gears enmeshing us in its relentless drone. Don't you agree?"

He looked at Anne for a pat on the head, but she disappointed him.

"I'm afraid I see nothing in quantum mechanics that connotes the existence of free will. Its very essence, actually, is deterministic."

"How so?" the boy philosopher asked, obviously stung. "The basic tenets of quantum mechanics state that we can never gather enough data about the present to make accurate predictions about the future—Heisenberg's Uncertainty Principle, you know. This seems, to me at least, to obviate the existence of determinism."

She smiled, sadly I thought, but still it was a beautiful thing to see. The fascination that she worked on me had proven to be exponential rather than linear in regard to distance. Seen from close up, her dark, dark eyes had flakes of gold floating within them and her pale, clear skin shone with pearly luminescence.

"The Uncertainty Principle is concerned with the position and momentum of subatomic particles," she said. "Quantum mechanics, when viewed from a broader perspective, implies that everything in the universe is part of a single, all-encompassing pattern. Nothing is separate from anything else, so that something done to one part of the pattern affects all parts of it. If this is true I don't see how we can escape the fact that we're actually puppets dancing to strings played by unseen, unrealized hands."

A balding professorial type was looking earnest and nodding his head. He was about to speak when I cut him off with the first words that popped into my head.

" 'It matters not how strait the gate,
How charged with punishments the scroll,
I am the master of my fate;
I am the captain of my soul.'"

The prof looked at me and scowled, but I scarcely noticed. For the first time Anne Siegal looked at me and our eyes met. I felt like a gawky, weak-kneed adolescent.

"Nice poetry," she said. "But what proof do you have that it's true?"

I shrugged. "I don't need proof," I said. "I can illustrate free will in action."

An exquisite black eyebrow arched. "How?"

Scowls spread to the faces of all the males surrounding her, but I paid them no mind.

"Let's go get a drink," I said, holding out my hand.

She looked up at me, puzzlement etching her fabulous face. We looked at each other for what seemed to be an eternity. I kept my face as open and friendly as possible and she finally smiled and put her hand in mine.

It was then, as our flesh touched for the first time, that I noticed her ring. It circled the middle finger of her right hand. It was a thread of silver finely wrought into the shape of a snake that curled twice about her finger and held its tail in its mouth. Its eyes were infinitesimal rubies dully gleaming.

I helped her up from the couch and she rose with easy grace. The group around us seemed disinclined to let us through. I smiled at them, baring my fangs, and the crowd suddenly parted like the Red Sea before Moses. When I turned back to Anne my demeanor was much more pleasant.

"I haven't seen you around the department before," she said as I led the way to the sagging card table that held bottles of booze and a bowl of stale potato chips.

"That's because I'm unobtrusive, unassuming, mild-mannered, and have never taken a physics class in my life."

"That explains it." She gave me a brief smile that came and went with the flickering rapidity of a butterfly flittering through a shaft of sunlight in an otherwise dark room.

"Robert Smith," I said.

"Anne Siegal. I'd like to thank you for rescuing me from them." She sighed, looked inward. "I don't even know exactly why I came here tonight. . . ."

"Think nothing of it." I handed her a glass with a lot of ice and a little scotch in it. "Actually, I rescued you from them so I could have you to myself."

She looked at me for a moment and then put her glass down.

"I better be going," she said.

My heart beat like a berserk trip-hammer in my chest. I watched her take two, three steps away from me, then I caught up with her, limping slightly as bone ground against bone in my gimpy knee.

"Let me walk you home." She looked at me and I gave her my best puppy dog expression. "When else would you have the opportunity to meet such an interesting fellow?" Her large, dark, gold-flecked eyes had me hypnotized. The motes of gold seemed to swirl through them, as if stirred by infinitesimal dust devils. "Look, no strings attached. I'll say good-night at your door." I held my breath and the silence between us deepened.

"I don't think that would be a good idea," Anne finally said. Her eyes were troubled and I could see that she was fighting with herself. A long moment of indecision passed. I continued to hold my breath, suddenly irrationally no longer caring if I ever drew another. "But you can walk me to your place."

I had to clamp my jaw shut tight to keep from grinning like an idiot. "Fine," I babbled. "Just fine. If you'll just excuse me for a moment?"

I turned before Anne could say anything and went off to find Peter. He was standing with his coed in an intimately lit corner of the living room.

"Now take tachyons," he whispered, and was closing in to nibble at her earlobe, neck or shoulder when I clapped a hand on his arm and dragged him away again.

"For Christ's sweet sake!" he whispered explosively, "What—"

"Peter." I held up my hand and he ground down to silence. "I've never told you this before, but don't come home tonight."

"What do you think I've been working on all evening?" he whispered furiously, and then peered around my shoulder to smile reassuringly at the bewildered coed. He frowned as a sudden thought struck him. "You don't mean that you and Siegal. . . ?"

"One thing I've always liked about you is your sense of discretion."

"Sure, Robert, sure. Uh, have fun."

I nodded and headed back to the study, suddenly fearful that Anne might have evaporated in my absence like a mirage in a thirsty man's desert, but, thankfully, she was still standing where I had left her. But now she wasn't alone. A tall, rather good looking graduate student type was with her. I caught the last few words of his quiet question.

"—sure you and Smithers aren't up to something, Anne? You two are always huddling together."

I could tell from Anne's expression that she didn't like him. I joined them quietly, looking from one to the other. Anne shot me a look that seemed to thank me for my interruption.

"Robert, this is Harold Rosenthal. Harold, this is Robert Smith."

We eyed each other much in manner of pit-bull terriers thrown into the ring. I knew instantly that we could never be friends.

"Yes, well, nice to meet you, Harry." Somehow I knew that being called Harry would irritate him, and I was right. "We have to run."

Rosenthal didn't want to let us go. He turned to Anne, ignoring me, and grasped her forearm. Her dislike for him flashed openly across her face, and I acted. I put my hand on his shoulder in a seemingly friendly manner, much like Spock getting set to deliver his famous nerve pinch.

"We really have to run, Harry," I repeated. He turned toward me and his face suddenly quirked. He smiled, a little sickly, and let go of Anne's arm. I released him and hustled Anne away, probably leaving five fingertip-sized bruises on his shoulder. If I didn't it wasn't for lack of trying.

"What was that all about?" I asked when we were out of earshot.

Anne looked at me with a quizzical expression, as if she were an entomologist trying to classify a strange bug she'd just captured in her net. "Oh, Harold's jealous, I suppose," she finally said. "Dr. Smithers and I have a special project going that he's constantly snooping around."

I nodded, feeling vaguely relieved.

On the walk back to my dormitory room I was devastatingly witty, I was archly humorous, I recited poetry at length, and showed my abysmal ignorance of physics. Anne said a word or two, even smiled once or twice. We stopped at the door to my room and she looked at me seriously.

"Do you always babble so much?" she asked as I unlocked the door.

"Only when I'm in love."

I had intended the remark to be humorous, but it fell flat on its face. Anne looked into my eyes, holding me breathless, and then preceded me into the room. It was easy to tell which side of the room was mine. Peter's desk was cluttered with a computer, hand calculators, molecule model kits, scientific encyclopedias, and other arcane impedimentia. A large black and white poster of Einstein riding a bicycle was tacked over his bed.

Set neatly on my desk was my two volume OED, rhyming dictionary, thesaurus, Old English *Beowulf*, French Baudelaire, complete volumes of Yeats, Dylan Thomas, and Cavafy, Campbell's four volume *Masks of God*, and selected works of my favorite fictioneers, Joyce, Durrell (not the zoo-keeper, the other one), and Zelazny.

"You're a poet," Anne said, taking it all in as I surreptitiously kicked a dirty t-shirt under my bed.

"I'm working on it," I said modestly.

"Recite something of yours," she said with good-natured interest.

I drew closer to her, so close that we were arm's length apart, but my mind was blank. I could think of nothing of mine suitable as I slowly drew even closer to her. Her lips parted slightly and I drowned in her eyes and the appropriate words suddenly sprang into my mind.

" 'She walks in beauty like the night
    Of cloudless climes and starry skies;
And all that's best of dark and bright
    Meet in her aspect and her eyes.'"

"That's beautiful."

"It's from Byron's 'Hebrew Melodies.' Beats anything I ever said."

We were at arm's length when I started to recite, at lip's length when I finished. Her lips parted and I tasted the sweet fire of her mouth. We somehow managed to undress without breaking off our kiss and fell into bed without hurting ourselves. Her body was fine and hungry and tireless. We were still embracing when we finally fell asleep. I usually sleep lightly as a dreaming cat, but I must have slept deeply that night, because Anne was gone when I awoke in the morning and I hadn't even realized she'd left.

ii.

"Forget her."

"If you tell me that one more time I'll kill you."

Peter looked at me, pursed his lips, and shook his head. I had managed to go to hell in a mere week's time. I'd blown off my classes, missed my finals, and ignored term paper deadlines. I spent my time writing reams of bad poetry and working out at the gym, lifting weights for hours until I was too tired to think and then scrubbing my brain clean with endless repetitions of my tai chi forms. It all did no good, however. I couldn't erase the image of Anne's face and body, or the vivid sense impression of her soft, ivory skin sliding across mine, from my memory.

"Well if you can't forget her, go after her. It's not as if she's on the other damn side of the world."

"She might as well be," I said, still staring stonily out of the window of our dormitory room.

"If it's a question of pride—"

I turned my head and stared at Peter. He swallowed, stepped back.

"It's not." I looked back out of the window. "It's a question of fear. Fear that she'll tell me she never wants to see me again."

I heard soft footsteps and Peter laid a friendly hand on my shoulder. "You never will see her again," he said quietly, "if you let it lie. She won't come to you again. Nobody even sees her around the department anymore. She seems to spend all her time in her office. Eighteen, twenty hours a day. Or with Smithers . . ."

We looked out of the window together at nothing for a long time and then I sighed. "You're right. Where's her office?"

Peter told me. "Want me to come along?" he asked. "At least to the door, I mean."

I shook my head. "Thanks, but I think it'd be better if I just wandered over there alone. I have to figure out what to say."

"Sure. Good luck." I stood and shuffled toward the door, but Peter stopped me before I reached it. "Look," he said, "my father owns a pool maintenance company in sunny southern California. Why don't you and I head down there after the semester's over and get a job for the summer? The pay's bad, but the hours are short, the work's easy, and there'll be more rich, bored, blonde chicks in bikinis than you can shake a stick at."

"Sounds like paradise."

"Think it over."

I nodded and left the room.

The Physics Department had taken over the old library building half-way across campus. I'd never been in it, but I knew where it was and with Peter's instructions I was able to find my way to the third floor where the grad students' offices were located. I stopped outside Anne's door, looking for my courage. I waffled for a long time, then I heard voices raised in anger behind the closed door. One was Anne's, the other, shouting over it, was a man's, vaguely familiar.

I flung the door open and stood on the threshold of the room. Anne, looking pale and a little frazzled and even more beautiful, if that were possible, than I remembered, was standing before her desk, spots of anger burning in her pale cheeks. The other occupant of the room was good old Harry Rosenthal. He was facing Anne, his face thrust forward, his whole body one single angry gesture. They both turned and stared at me.

"Hello, Anne," I said without skipping a beat, "sorry I'm late. Hope I didn't interrupt anything. Ready to go?"

Rosenthal straightened and unconsciously put a hand on his right shoulder and rubbed it briefly.

"Well, ah, I'd better be going." He looked at Anne again and his voice took on a sterner tone. "We'll finish this discussion later."

"It's already finished."

"So you say."

I cleared my throat and Rosenthal glanced at me. I kept my position in the doorway, making him squeeze by with a muttered "Excuse me." I kept my eyes on his back until he disappeared around a corner of the corridor, and then, with nothing else to look at, drew a deep breath, hardened my resolve, and looked at Anne. She sighed and ran a hand through her wavy hair. She was wearing jeans and a light cotton shirt that clung to her unrestrained breasts. I remembered their taste, their soft firmness.

"You always seem to be rescuing me from some unpleasant situation," she said.

"Good old Harry certainly qualifies as an unpleasant situation."

"He's a dork. But his father's an assistant dean who controls the department's purse-strings."

"What's he after?"

Anne sat down at her desk, and looked away to conceal the conflicting emotions that moved across her face. There was still doubt in her eyes when she looked up, but she motioned me to close the door and come closer. I did, taking the chair that Harold had just vacated, consciously clasping my hands together so that they wouldn't go out and pull her to me.

"I told you that I've been working on a special project with Dr. Smithers." Her voice was earnest, but there was doubt in her eyes and a quirky half smile on her lips.

"Yes," I prompted, when she let a silence hang between us for several long moments.

"Well," she said, defensively, "it appears that we've invented a time machine."

She drew back and looked at me as if she expected me to laugh. I nodded, let out a low whistle. "I see. And Rosenthal's trying to horn in?"

Her forehead crinkled in a frown and she stared at me. "That's all you have to say?"

"Well, it's obvious that this is a big thing—"

"I mean, you *believe* me?"

I shrugged. "Sure. Why not?"

She shook her head, laughed. "Why not?" she repeated. She leaned over and kissed me and this time nothing in the world could have prevented my arms from going out and around her. They urged her to my chair and she complied. She was a comforting, welcome weight on my lap. The tail-devouring snake that was the ring on the middle finger of her right hand burned like cold fire as it rested against my cheek. Our kiss lengthened and took on urgency. We both knew where it was leading when the phone on the desk behind us suddenly rang. Anne leaped from my lap like a startled cat.

"Yes," she said into the receiver, and listened a long time, nodding occasionally and replying in staccato monosyllables. She hung up after a few moments, gnawed briefly at her full lower lip and then looked at me. The passion in her eyes was banked, but still smouldered in their depths. When she finally spoke her question caught me totally by surprise.

"What are your plans for the summer?"

I thought of sand and sun and bikini-clad bodies by the score. "They're unsettled. Why?"

She gestured at the phone with a toss of her head. "That was Dr. Smithers. Harold has just left his office. He'd let a few veiled threats fall."

"What kind of threats?"

Anne paced around the room, her voice growing hard-edged with anger.

"You were right. He knows something big is up and he wants in. The problem is," she stopped pacing and stared hard at me, "it's too big. Impossibly big. Not everyone is as open-minded as you, Robert. If word ever leaked that we were spending university money on a time machine—!" She shook her head, unable to come up with an appropriately cataclysmic end to her sentence.

"They'd put Smithers out to pasture and quietly drop you from the program."

"At least. But this damn thing will work!" She slammed her palm on the desk hard enough to make the phone jump. She and Smithers had made a major discovery that would change the world, but there seemed something even more in it to Anne, something deeply personal. I wanted to ask her about it, but I was afraid to pry, afraid that I'd push her away by trying to pull her too close.

She drew near me, leaned over my chair, and stared seriously into my eyes.

"So?" she asked.

"So?"

"Do you want to help build a time machine?"

"Me? I don't know anything about physics."

She laid her hand on my arm.

"Dr. Smithers and I will handle that end of it. It's your muscle we need."

" 'We,' " I echoed. "How about you?"

"I . . . guess so," she murmured, sounding definitely unenthusiastic.

"You guess what?" Perhaps I shouldn't have pushed her, but there were things I had to know.

"I guess I need you." She spoke harshly, almost defiantly, and held up her hand to forestall the words that were crowding behind my lips. "Please, Robert, that's all I can give you. I can't talk about anything more now. Not now. Perhaps I'll never be able to."

I nodded, satisfied for now, but wondering what it was that made Anne afraid to talk about love.

"As long as you need me."

Her mouth fastened on mine and her hungry kiss was answer enough.

iii.

Dr. Erasmus Smithers was all I had expected, only more so. He was tall, though slightly stooped, lanky, white-haired, and distinguished-looking. He exuded little puffs of chalk dust whenever he sat down. Three walls of his office were lined with shelves crammed with books, journals, periodicals, and loose manuscript sheets. The fourth was a giant chalkboard that had indecipherable gibberish scrawled on it in English, Greek, Arabic, and what looked like nonsense symbols.

He took a long, hard look at me when Anne introduced us.

"Anne says that we can trust you," he said in a deep voice free of age tremors. "You know the goal of our little project?"

"To 'hold infinity in the palm of your hand, and eternity in an hour.'"

Smithers surprised me.

"Blake," he said, and smiled. "She also told me of your penchant for quoting poetry. You've made something of an impression on her, I fear."

I glanced at Anne, who was actually blushing. Something leaped within my chest, either my heart or a small animal that had somehow gnawed its way inside. I didn't care which.

"To business," Smithers said briskly. "Anne vouches for you and that's good enough for me. She's a young woman of rare judgment and discernment. You know, of course, why we have to keep our project a secret."

I nodded.

"They'd think me dotty, pure and simple. They'd bundle me off and tell me to take up growing roses right when we're on the verge of making the most important discovery of the age." He smiled, his eyes flashing lightning. "If Anne hadn't pointed out some irregularities in my probability wave equations I'd have missed it myself. Do you know anything about probability wave theory?" I shook my head, but then realized that it was largely a rhetorical question as Smithers spoke on without missing a beat. "Probability waves describe events that are caught between possibility and reality. However, whenever one measures one of these waves, or describes them with minute mathematical precision in a way I've developed, one can 'actualize' these possibilities, in essence creating a chosen reality."

"I see, I think," I said, catching a feeble glimmering of what Smithers was talking about. "If you extrapolate with enough precision, you can call back the past." I thought back to the night when Anne and I had first met, to the party where Anne had spoken about the underlying tenet of quantum mechanics that says everything in the universe, from the biggest, farthest star to the tiniest microbe swimming through the blood coursing through my veins is bound inextricably together in a single pattern whose threads reach back to the moment the universe was created and forward to the moment it will die. "What about the future? Will you be able to go forward into time?"

Smithers shook his head. "Much too complicated. There's a theory called the Many Worlds Interpretation of Quantum Mechanics that says each time we make a choice, no matter how trivial, we create a new universe. The mathematics on this point are rather murky, but I tend to go along with this view. The future, at any rate, would be a billion times more difficult to delineate than the past, which, believe me, is complicated enough. As it is, we have the theoretical framework for time travel worked out, but all of the practical work remains to be done."

"If you want to keep this thing secret, why build it on campus? Why not rent a barn or something and do the work there?" I had to suppress a giggle as an insane image of Mickey Rooney and Judy Garland flashed through my mind. Hey, I've got a computer! Well, I've got a time machine! We can put on a show!!

"That's a thought," Smithers said, "but I'm afraid that we need too much university equipment to make it practical. The problem is threefold: We have to derive the network of equations that will delineate the probability waves that describe the past. Anne will need access to the university's mainframe computer to do that. I'll have to build the device to choose the probability waves that will actualize, or actually re-actualize, the past. I'll need a lot of university equipment for that. Then there's the module to house the chrononaut as he—" Anne looked sharply at him and he cleared his throat. "—or she journeys to the past." He drummed his fingers on the desk as he and Anne continued to gaze at each other.

"What will my role be?" I asked.

My question interrupted what seemed to be a silent contest of wills and Smithers turned his attention to me. "Anne will derive the network of probability equations. I'll design the actualizing device. I've got several ideas in mind. A radio-frequency trap to isolate discrete subatomic particles to initiate the chain . . ." He voice ran down and he wandered over to stare at a section of his blackboard.

"And me?" I prompted.

"Hmmm? Oh yes." Smithers fished in his jacket pocket and absent mindedly handed me a keyring. "Here's the key to the chronomodule. It has to be brought into the lab and prepared for the trip."

I looked at the ring he'd given me, for the first time doubting the sanity of Anne's little project. The ring contained one ordinary-looking automobile ignition key. Judging by the symbol on the ring fob, the chronomodule was, in fact, a Volkswagen.

It could have been worse.

The chronomodule—what I soon came to think of as the time-mobile—could have been an old, beat up Beetle. It was in fact a Carman Ghia, which, to my mind at least, has a bit more dash.

It was white, with a few dents and numerous rust spots, worn upholstery, bad brakes, and about 140,000 miles on the broken odometer. It would be a bitch, I realized, to smuggle into the lab.

It still ran, though choppily and with much complaining, so it would be relatively easy to get it from the garage of Smith's off-campus townhouse to the physics building. Then came the problems. First, I had to do this by myself. Just in case something went wrong Anne and Smithers couldn't afford to be associated with the lunacy of smuggling a car into the physics building. Second, the sheer damn size of the thing was daunting. Fortunately, though, with tape measure in hand, I discovered that the section of the basement Smithers had taken over for his lab had been renovated with the notion of heavy machinery in mind. Cyclotrons and such no doubt, not Carman Ghias, but whatever the architects had in mind, the good news was that with careful judgment and close maneuvering I'd be able to squeeze the Ghia into the lab. The bad news was that my reconnoiter did not go unobserved.

"What are you doing here?" I knew that voice, and disliked it. "That's Dr. Smithers's lab."

"Right you are, Harry," I turned and looked at him. I had no idea he'd been behind me watching me peer up and down corridors taking measurements and muttering to myself. "Which is why it's no business of yours what I'm doing."

"Look here, Bob, er, Robert, there's no reason why we can't get along. I'll admit that I'm intrigued by Dr. Smithers's project, which, I'm astonished to see, you've apparently become connected with and are therefore in a position to, well, disperse information about, shall we say. You would, of course, be remunerated for your time and effort."

I smiled, and could tell from the look on Rosenthal's face that he didn't much care for the look on mine.

"Curiosity killed the cat, Harry, and wouldn't be very healthy for the graduate student, either."

His face spasmed, letting loose all the venom he'd stored. "You cocksure jerk! I'll find out what you're all up to, you, and Smithers, and that slut you've been screwing—"

I moved as fast as I ever did in my linebacker days, ignoring the pain that screamed up my leg as my cartilage-less knee was forced into more mobility than it really had left. I had Rosenthal by the face and up against the wall quicker than he knew what was happening.

"You speak about Anne like that again and it'll be the last time you ever speak. You snoop around here again and it'll be the last time you ever snoop."

I shook him for emphasis, then let him go. His legs almost went out on him, but he managed to brace himself against the wall. He tried to say something, but no words could make it past his trembling lips. He finally shook his head and went off down the corridor, still leaning against the wall for support. Before he followed the bend of corridor out of sight he turned and called out, "I'll come back and I won't be alone, you ape bastard."

I had already dismissed him, turning back to the problem of getting the Ghia through the lab door. I thought his threat was simple braggadocio. I was wrong. I should have listened.

June turned to July, then to August. Anne was teaching a summer school course in introductory physics, so she did double duty, teaching during the day and working on the project every night and during the weekends. Smithers did his part, and I did mine. First I had to pull the Ghia's engine, then install the Rube Goldberg actualizing device that Smithers had designed, and, with my fumbling help, built. There was also plenty of scutwork to do, and I was the one who had to do it all. I kept an eye out for Rosenthal, but as the weeks went by and his parting shot seemed more and more an empty threat I gradually forgot about him. I had enough to occupy my mind. I was worried about Anne.

She'd be so tired some nights that I'd spend hours massaging the tenseness from her body until she could at last sleep. Other nights she'd come to me with passion crackling about her like a tangible aura and we'd make love until she was gentled into deep, dreamless sleep. Her tension grew as the project neared what pointed to a successful conclusion. One hot night in late August she left our bed unable to sleep, unwilling to lie still.

She went to the window and looked out. The rays of the full moon came through the partially opened slats of the blind, striping her ivory body, still slick with perspiration from our lovemaking, with bars of sable. I thought she thought that I was asleep, but after a few silent moments she spoke without turning back to look at me.

"I should tell you," she said, "why this project is so important to me." I nodded, but she continued to stare out the window and didn't see my gesture. "I was an abandoned baby, left in a parking lot in Kansas City when I was about a year old. This was all I had, hung on a chain draped around my neck." She held up her right hand and moonlight glinted evilly off the tiny red eyes of the snake encircling her finger. She twirled it around. She hadn't been eating much lately and had lost so much weight that the ring hung loosely on her finger. "I'll never, never be happy until I find out about my past. That's why I'll be leaving when the machine is finished. Probably tomorrow."

She finally turned to look at me. For once I was dumbfounded, unable to speak.

"You must understand. I don't want to leave you, but I must. I've always felt that something's been guiding me, pushing me. Even you were . . . were not unexpected. Not really. When I first saw you that night something told me to go with you, that it would be all right. That things would work out."

"You don't have to leave on this quest if you don't want to. This deterministic/free-will bullshit is just that, bullshit. No one's holding a gun to your head and making you leave. If you want to stay with me, you can. It's as simple as that."

She hugged herself as if warding off a chill. "It's not. And the problem is that I *do* want to go. I want you, but I *have* to find out about myself, discover who abandoned me and why. Maybe then I'll find myself, and contentment."

"I don't know much about this time-travel crap, but I do know one thing. It's a one way trip. You'll be marooned in the past." I was mad, and showing it, but I couldn't help myself.

Anne swallowed hard. "I know. I'll age naturally, of course, and I'll only be going back twenty-two years or so so I'll be only about 46 when I'll be able to get in touch with you and Erasmus. I won't be able to try any sooner. I don't want to cause any paradoxes."

"No, we can't have that," I grunted. "Smithers should like this. You'll be closer to his age—"

"Don't," Anne said. "Don't make it harder." She came back to the foot of the bed. "I told you before that I couldn't give you more of myself, but it's not because of you, or really even me. It's this thing I have to do that's denying me the right to love you."

I rubbed my palms against my eyes and when I opened them again the pain was still there. But so was Anne.

"You never had to say you loved me," I told her.

> " 'In blood the debts were paid. Hereafter
> We make no truce for manifest reason
> From this side of the broad and fateful stream
> Where wisdom rules from her dark cave of dream
> And time is corrigible by laughter.' "

I tried, but couldn't even smile, let alone laugh. Anne kneeled on the bed and gracefully moved up it until she straddled me. She smoothed a lock of damp hair from my forehead.

"Blake?" she asked quietly.

"Graves."

I pulled her down to me and kissed her as if it were the last night in the world.

iv.

She was gone when I woke. I'd half expected it. I rose, dressed slowly, not knowing what to do, finally deciding that although there was nothing I could do to keep her, I couldn't let her just go. I threw on some clothes and hurried from her apartment, hoping that she was still in this decade. I don't know what made me look in the window of the funky antique shop in the small strip mall on the street that separated the campus from the residential area around it. I'd passed by the place a hundred times before without glancing in its window, but this time I looked, I stopped, I stared.

Hanging among the dusty clutter was a ring of finely wrought silver cast into the shape of a snake eating its own tail, its eyes two infinitesimal rubies, dully gleaming . . .

Anne's ring. It had to be. There couldn't be two such. Or could there?

I went into the store and purchased it, put it and the chain from which it hung in my pocket, and almost forgot my change. What, I wondered, did this all mean? I was still in a daze when I walked into Smithers's lab. I didn't notice at first the unexpected guests.

Anne and Smithers were standing by the computer console, being guarded by a hulking brute of a guy I remembered from my football days. And good old Harry Rosenthal was peering into the interior of the time-mobile, a quizzical yet angry expression on his face.

"I don't get it." He was plainly dumbfounded. "What is all this crap? You've really lost it Smithers." He looked up from the interior of the Ghia, turned, and saw me for the first time. His face lit up. "You!" He looked at the goon he'd brought with him. "I told you I'd be back with someone, jerk."

He gestured at me and the goon and I looked at each other.

"Remember me?" I asked. He nodded. "See you." He nodded again, and started to walk away.

Rosenthal was outraged. "Hey, I paid you for this!"

The goon turned to him.

"Screw you. You told me we was going to roust some old prof and some grad students. You said nothing about him. I ain't getting busted up for no lousy ten bucks."

He left the lab.

I'm not a violent person by nature, but never in my life had I wanted to hit someone so bad, to break something into bits and thereby make my peace with the world. Harry must have seen this in my face, because he started backing away. He moved pretty fast, but even with my gimpy knee I caught up with him, grabbed him, and held him as he shook. I closed my eyes and ran through a series of breathing exercises I'd learned from the tai chi I did to keep my knee from going completely immobile on me.

Busting Harry would do no good. It wouldn't give me what I wanted, Anne forever, so I let him go.

"You're a lucky fellow, Harry," I told him.

"And you're all in deep shit," he said, his cheap bravado returning. He glanced at his wristwatch. "I told my dad to meet me here and he should arrive any minute. I'd like to see you explain all this crap to him."

Anne and Smithers exchanged outraged glances.

"We'll run the test on the mouse—" Smithers began, but Anne cut him off.

"No. I'm going."

"It's insanely dangerous. The spatial congruencies are still uncertain—"

"It will work." Her voice was final, her face was set. Smithers couldn't meet her gaze.

"The consequences—" he mumbled.

"I'm not taking the chance of them taking the machine away from us. I'm going."

Smithers let himself be talked into it. He wanted his theories proven correct almost as much as Anne wanted to go on her odyssey into the past. He hustled forward to make sure Rosenthal hadn't done something stupid to the time-mobile. Anne went by me to join him, but I took her arm and held her back.

"I've got something for you." I took the ring and chain out of my pocket and held it up for her.

"You found it!" she exclaimed. I nodded. "It slipped off my finger sometime last night. I knew it had to be in the bed, but I didn't look for it. I didn't want to wake you . . . and I thought you might want it."

"I do," I told her, "but you might need it to find your family. It's the only clue you have."

She nodded, slipped the chain around her neck.

"The chain's a good idea. Is it yours?"

I nodded. I had, after all, paid for it.

She kissed me. My heart was lying in heavy, jagged lumps in my stomach as I watched her belt herself into the Ghia. Rosenthal looked on in mute incomprehension.

"I'll get in touch as soon as I can," Anne cried out.

Smithers, tight-lipped, started the process. He made the choice that actualized the sequence that called back into existence the probability wave that, expanded and amplified, my Anne would follow into the past. He threw a switch, made a measurement. It was as simple as that.

It is both my curse and my vindication that I remember.

It's not a bad way to pass through eternity. My childhood was better than some and not much worse than most others. I have my youth and my poems and I have Anne always young and beautiful. Our time together, constrained by an end that approaches with the swiftness and inevitability of a burning candle is bound by love and passion that will never fade.

But sometimes I lie awake at night, listening to Anne's gentle breathing beside me, and I wonder if I'll ever tell her about the endless cycle that began when the time machine catapulted her back twenty-two years in time and across hundreds of miles of space to a parking lot in Kansas City, where she was found crawling about naked but for the ring hanging from a chain looped around her neck, wiped utterly clean of knowledge and experience and years, a baby lost but not abandoned.

I just have to exercise my free will and tell her, but I never do. I wonder if I can. I wonder if perhaps Anne wasn't right after all.

I wonder, but I don't really care.

★ Requiem ★

by Melinda Snodgrass

Several years ago while en route to a science fiction convention my seat mate was a debonair young attorney. While he briefed, I scribbled on a chapter of my latest novel. Apparently he found my work more interesting than his, (and having practiced law for three years I can almost guarantee that it was) for he struck up a conversation.

He asked what I did. Science fiction writer. How I liked it? A lot. And where I lived? New Mexico. There was one of those perfect three beat pauses while he contemplated this, then he slowly nodded, and said,

"Yes, New Mexico sounds like a good place for a science fiction writer to live. After all, it looks like the Moon."

To someone who's lived almost her entire life in the southwest this seems a strange reaction. Can't they see the stark bare bones beauty of mountains thrusting up from high desert plateaus? Appreciate the subtlety of colors? No flamboyant tropical profusion here demanding attention. New Mexico with her delicate ochers and sages and blues seems aloof, almost mysterious. It takes time and effort to discover this place, and it doesn't seem to care whether you do or not.

There's a sense of age and timelessness that I find when I ride out across the mesas of New Mexico. This place dwarfs me and also accepts me, and for some reason I feel safe here.

So I haven't left. And probably never will.

But aside from its great natural beauty I also recommend New Mexico to other science fiction writers because I think it is one of the few places in the country where you can actually observe diverse cultures living side by side, overlapping, tasting of one another.

Many of our books present humans and aliens interacting (peacefully and otherwise). Naturally the worlds and races we create are speculative, but I think the writers of New Mexico have an advantage. Something more than mere imagination. In this state one has to work very hard to stay within the safe confines of their own cultural/racial/religious niche.

There are other people here, Hispanics, Indians, Anglos. And they're not confined to quaint areas of town. In New Mexico there are no Chinatowns, or Spanish Harlems. The closest we come are the pueblos which dot the Rio Grande valley, and even here the correlation breaks down for the Indians work among the other ethnic groups, and a number have elected to live away from the pueblo. Because of the modern, communication intensive society we inhabit we do tend—at least on the surface—to seem very much alike. But beneath this comfortable, and probably illusionary, American norm these groups, all of our groups, view the world in slightly different ways.

Aliens.

Are they threatening, frightening, dangerous? No. Or at least they shouldn't be. When I think alien I think exciting. New energies, new outlooks, a freshness and vitality that can't be found in more traditional, rigid, and perhaps "purer" societies.

In New Mexico we've done pretty well at allowing and even encouraging these differences. Here elderly Spanish gentlemen still occasionally go into the mountains to wrestle with demons; Pueblo Indians honor both the Christian god, and their own older faith; languages—English, Spanish, Tiwa, Tewa—jostle one another, and we are all immeasurably enriched by the mixture.

And as a writer I find it a heady mix. It conduces to dreaming, and thinking, and asking "what if?" All of which seem to define a science fiction writer. Or maybe that's too narrow. Maybe it defines humans. Which is what my story is all about.

Requiem

by Melinda Snodgrass

Down the hall someone was enacting the final act of a French farce. *Probably Martin Fletcher,* Barnaby idly thought, using shunt level to avoid any bleed. *Their taste had always run to the absurd.* Main level was feeding properly, pain exploding from the tender flesh of his buttocks as the thin switch continued its steady rhythm. Beneath him Lucinda ground with her hips, timing each thrust to the beat of the tiny bamboo whip. He was nearing climax, and Mary increased the tempo of the whipping. He cursed his newly acquired belly. He felt like a barrel trying to balance on a particularly slippery log. Lucinda caught her legs about his back forcing him down atop her, and he groaned as the heavy meal he had eaten earlier in the evening shifted like a sliding load of ball bearings.

The warm moistness of her cunt closed about his penis squeezing, demanding, and with a white hot rush he came even as Mary laid one final, triumphant and very hard blow across his bare, red ass.

Lucinda's throaty sounds of pleasure were punctuated by screams, and bellowed French commands, and the sound of popping champagne corks.

Barnaby grimaced—*So overdone*—and rolled onto his back. And gave a yelp as his tender bottom hit the satin sheets. Lucinda propped herself on an elbow, raked back her long black hair with one hand, and grinned down at him. Her nipples formed rich coffee colored circles against the tawny skin of her breasts.

"Performance tonight?"

"No, just a rehearsal."

"You must be tense. You don't usually call for the full treatment except for a performance."

He grabbed one swinging breast, and rubbed his thumb across the nipple. "Decided to treat myself."

She rolled away, consulted an ornate white and gold clock. "Hour's almost up."

"Do you have to be so cold blooded? Can't you convince me that it's romance at work here?"

"You don't want romance, Barnaby, you want sluts. For romance you go home to that pretty wife of yours."

"She's frigid."
"Goodbye, Barnaby."
"She doesn't understand me."
"Leave the money on my desk, Barnaby."
"You don't love me."
"That's right, Barnaby."

A few minutes later, and he was out in the chill Santa Fe night. There were a few cars about jouncing and grinding through the monumental potholes which littered the streets like bomb craters. He stuck to the sidewalk, the tough buffalo grass brushing at his pants leg where it thrust through the cracks in the concrete. It wasn't far to the performance hall, and with a star littered sky overhead, and a brisk wind carrying the scent of burning pinon to his nostrils he was just as happy to walk.

It also allowed time for the blood to retreat from his inflamed buttocks. The touch of his undershorts against the swollen skin was agony, but it also managed to keep an erection shoving at his zipper. And if he took his time he would be able to sit and rehearse for three hours, serene and relaxed from Lucinda and Mary's ministrations.

Another car lurched past, and its headlight swept across the mouth of an alley. It was like looking down a black throat with a trashed out dumpster and several battered garbage cans thrust up like broken teeth. And in the midst of it two shadowy figures were locked in a desperate struggle. Harsh pants and faint whimpers drifted from the alley. Barnaby dug his hands into his coat pockets, hunched until his collar rode up around his ears, and hurried past. It was none of his affair. Had no part in his game. But there was sick taste on the back of his tongue which lingered for several blocks, and had nothing to do with the cheap wine he had consumed with dinner.

Patricia and Peter were waiting. He muttered an apology for again being late, and seated himself at the baby grand. Peter, his violin tucked beneath his sharp chin, and his brown curls forming a halo about his head, had the look of a mad monk. Patricia was a different sort altogether. Her blue eyes seemed to focus on nothing, and with her long straight blond hair hanging to her waist she looked like a lost flower child. But there was nothing innocent about the way she gripped her cello between her thin legs. Barnaby's erection bumped urgently against his zipper, and he wished she would stop wearing such short skirts to rehearsal.

Peter made a new mistake this night. So breathtaking in its audacity and creativity that Barnaby almost lost his count. The violinist muttered an apology, but he was staring at the notes with the adoration of an ascetic witnessing the kingdom of God. Patricia had formed a curtain with her hair. Barnaby couldn't read her reaction.

The final trembling chord hung in the air, and Barnaby dropped his hands into his lap. After twenty minutes of playing, and Peter's remarkable addition he found that his ass had stopped hurting, and the flash of Patricia's pale thigh brought no answering response from his crotch.

"Shall we try it again?" he heard himself ask.

"Sure, and I'll try not to foul up this time."

"No problem."

Patricia shook back her hair, and eyed him, reading more from the innocent two word remark than he had intended. Sensing perhaps his exultation. Behind her blue eyes lurked the somna, glaring, hostile, very suspicious.

The keys were slick beneath his fingers as they began again. This time it was perfect. Perfect as it was always perfect. As it would have been perfect the time before barring Peter's fascinating gaff. Perfect, soulless and heartless. And the fault, Barnaby sadly concluded in time with the final chords, was not in the music.

Patricia didn't wait for any quiet banter. She packed her cello in short jerky motions which betrayed her agitation, ducked her head, and hurried from the studio.

"I shouldn't have done that," Peter said contritely.

"No, that's not true. It was magnificent." Barnaby hesitated, then dug out a handwritten score. "Would you mind?"

"Oh, Barnaby, you never give up."

"No."

An "A" hung in the air, then tuned and ready Peter sight read swiftly and perfectly through the first page. He stopped, bow poised, double chins forming because of his pressure on the instrument.

"Well?"

"It's terrible. Just like the others."

"You see no improvement?"

He considered, replayed a phrase, frowned, caught his lower lip between his teeth. "Some." He dropped the violin to his knee. "Barnaby, why is it so important to you?"

"I don't know, but it is. Vitally important." He swung off the bench and paced the sterile room, shoes squeaking on the linoleum floor. "Sometimes when I'm playing I feel as if I'm on the verge of some great insight, some total understanding that will—"

252 ☆ *Melinda Snodgrass*

"What I'm on is the verge of trouble." The snap of the locks on the case echoed off the dingy white walls. "You're a dangerous man to know, Barnaby. You incite a person to risk, and I've taken enough risks for one night."

But they didn't, and that was the problem. Life was a series of endlessly repeating patterns. The thoughts roiled like sullenly boiling poison; but buried deep on the shunt level, safe from any eavesdropping. He slid onto the bench, and ripped out a Mozart piano sonata. Wondering as he played why when using the same seven notes he produced soulless dreck, while Mozart had produced genius, magic. The magic went to work, drawing from deep within him a sensation which was odd and unpleasant and exhilarating all at once. A vise closing somewhere deep within himself.

With a sigh he dropped the lid, a sullen *bang* in the silent room, and left the recital hall.

He had several choices. A late post-rehearsal supper. Home—his mind shied violently from that. He knew what was waiting for him at home. Or Sal's.

Sal's filled with noise, and smoke, and male presence. The waitresses were male wet dreams incarnate. Cute, and buxom, and dumb as rocks. They made appropriate squealing noises when pinched or propositioned, and the rest of the time kept their mouths shut, and served drinks.

Sal, a tall skinny Italian whose spade beard made him look like a rather befuddled Lucifer, was polishing glasses behind the bar. On the large tv, hung precariously on the wall, the Bears were slaughtering the Patroits at the Super Bowl. Groans, curses, shouted advice rose from the knot of construction workers, cowboys and truckers huddled at one corner of the bar.

"The usual?"

"Yeah."

Sal slopped whisky into a shot glass, and Barnaby tipped it down.

"Neat whisky will play hell with your liver."

"Well, now that would be a new experience. The descent into the gutter with redemption to follow."

"Hush." Dr. Antonio Garcia's thin, blue veined hand closed about his upper arm, and forced him away from the bar. "Barnaby, my friend, you are very fey tonight." They settled into a red leather booth. "What troubles you my friend?"

The score fluttered onto the table between them. The doctor prodded the pages with a cautious forefinger. "Music."

"Yeah, mine."

"Is it good?"

"No, it stinks. Like the piece before it, and the piece before that, and—"

"Why are you surprised?" The Spaniard sighed, and ran a hand across his beautiful white hair. It fell in long waves back from a high white forehead. Which made the darkness of his deepset brown eyes all the more compelling. "Barnaby, my young friend. There are a million things in this world that we can do—"

"Perfectly," he interrupted bitterly.

"As you say, but art is not one of them. The blood of the somnas has thinned, and our kind doesn't make music."

"Oh, we *make* music. Like we *make* ball games, and *make* wars, and *make* marriages, but we create nothing." Uneasy interest flared like a point of light from his passive watcher.

"That is not our function—"

"Our function is boredom."

"Not so. We are the vital link between our somnas, and reality. We provide experience, sensation, growth, challenge, but with the dangers filtered by our loyal bodies."

Antonio had assumed his erect tutorial position, finger upraised, his soft, deep voice exploring each word for the maximum effect. Intellectual smugness glowed on his face. For Barnaby this was merely one in an endless repeat of the good doctor's pet philosophy.

"Antonio, you remind me of the Jewish apologists of old time, 1930s. They continued to excuse, and explain Adolf Hitler even as they were led into the gas chamber."

"That is a disgusting analogy! We are not a despised minority being persecuted by our overlords. We are partners in a most unique and special relationship, and we should be grateful for our chance to serve. Without the development of the somna/piggyback relationship there would be no humans on Earth. That great history would have been snuffed out by the actions of a random, malignant virus. As it is we have preserved—"

"Which is my point! We 'preserve,' we experience, but we don't create. And I'm not even sure we're preserving all that well. Look at the fucking streets, the garbage collecting on the sidewalks. And who can blame them. It's a hell of a boring game to be a garbage collector or a member of a street crew. So we get to be doctors and laywers, and conductors and composers and Indian chiefs. And for what? For What!"

"Barnaby, go home. These distempered freaks do you no good."

Hostility and compassion flickered in the dark eyes as Antonio and the somna watched him.

As for himself a band of incandescent pain seemed to be tightening about his temples. With a gasp he crammed the pages into his pocket, and lurched from the booth.

"You'll feel better in the morning."

"Yeah . . . yeah you're right. I've been working too hard. This opening concert . . . ha ha, burning the candle at both ends . . . ha ha." How easily the words of his role slipped from his tongue. How comforting to have the role to return to. If he didn't he would have to make one. For himself. All by himself.

Laura was waiting. The green shades on the brass student lamp threw a dim light across the darkened living room, and drew highlights from her short cap of light brown hair. Head bowed she sat curled in the corner of the sofa. The line of her neck was a curving song. But it seemed vulnerable, too. Pale and slender, bent like an autumn flower beneath a weight of winter ice. He experienced the same squeezing sensation he had felt during the Mozart. Slipped forward, and kissed her. The short hairs at the nap of her neck tickled his lips.

She flinched, jerked away. "Don't touch me."

He too recoiled from the acid which laced the words. "Laura, love."

"You slime! You son of a bitch!" She spat the words at him from behind the protection of the coffee table. Her voice held only hatred, but her body spoke of unendurable pain as she huddled in upon herself, arms wrapped protectively about her chest.

"What, what have I done? The first night I've been able to get home early, and you start screaming at me."

"You don't like it? Then go back to your bimbos!" She snatched a package of cigarettes from the mantel. It took her five tries to get it lit, and a part of Barnaby admired her ability to suppress her dexterity. It was perfect from the trembling fingers to the cords of her neck etched harshly beneath the fair skin as she sucked in the smoke. "For months I've suspected, but now I have the proof."

A manila envelope slapped onto the brick floor at his feet spilling its contents. Photos. Black and white, grainy, unfocussed, but clearly recognizable. His face, looking bloated with the weight that had been laid on him, sheen of sweat, hair matted, eyes screwed tightly shut in ecstasy as Lucinda beat him. Shame lay like a bad taste on the back of his tongue.

"God damn it!" he roared. "I'm under a lot of pressure. And since you're so fucking frigid—"

"Bad choice of words there," she smirked. "Just because I'm not willing to behave like an animal."

"Don't finish. I know it by heart. I hear it every night in bed. *I'm an artist. The physical blunts the soul,*" he mimicked in cruel parody.

"Well, if that's the case you ought to be a fucking angel by now."

She dealt him a ringing slap, and he caught her by the wrists, forced her in close. Her head thrashed trying to avoid the kiss which had little to do with love, and a great deal to do with violence.

They staggered about the room locked in this travesty of an embrace. There was a crash, and his soul cringed as a priceless Santa Clara Indian seed pot shattered on the bricks. Dismay loosened his grip, and Laura kneed him neatly in the balls. Pain like a red hot poker shot from his groin through the top of his head. He collapsed with a keening cry, and held himself.

Laura began booting down the hall toward the bedroom then froze, turned back, weariness and release etched on her delicate face. Barnaby still hurt. A lot. But the somnas were gone. Exhausted perhaps by the violence of their backs' emotions.

Slowly he rose, came into her arms, laid his head against her soft bosom, felt despair.

They had only a little time. A few seconds becoming minutes becoming (if they were lucky) hours. To spend any way they pleased. His mind stuttered and stopped; *a long walk in moonlight, conversation, playing a duet, making love.* They were like children in a toy store. A multiplicity of delights, joy at having the choice, pain at having to choose. As usual Laura settled the matter.

She slipped from his arms, entered the bedroom. He watched hungrily as her mincing, duck-footed dancer's walk carried her away from him. She would wait, and if there was enough time he would join her there. But now he had to work.

The score was tucked between the pages of a Mozart symphony. Camouflage, or was he hoping that genius somehow rubbed off? He spread the pages, stared wearily at the tiny ink strokes each representing so many hours of anguish. He was sick to death of notes. They haunted his every waking moment.

Why was he so driven? What did he hope to accomplish by this herculean task? To prove that Antonio, and the other philosophers of their age were wrong? That creativity could exist? And what were the consequences if he were correct?

Worse, what were the consequences for *him* if he failed? Reality was rendered marginally bearable because of this dream. And if he tried and failed—what then? There was no way out. No way to simply say, "I'm tired, I've had enough. I won't go on." Of course he would go on—and on. He had no choice. But it would be an eternity of living with neither hope nor meaning.

He twirled the pen between his fingers. Measure 156. *Miserere.* Mercy. It was a prayer. Pen clenched between his teeth he played the preceding five measures. The notes hung trembling in the shadowy room. They formed a presence in the darkened room rich with the scent of pipe tobacco, Laura's perfume, and old wood lovingly polished with beeswax and lemon oil. *Were they any good?* No, that question could only freeze him. He repeated the phrase. Rediscovering its soul. Or was it his own?

He bent to the paper. *Treble clef—g, e, c—dotted quarter, sixteenth f, back to a.* The scratchings of a pen, the crackle of paper, the occasional fragmentary musical phrase. Forming a miraculous harmonious whole.

The lone time continued. Barnaby stretched feeling the vertebrae in his spine snapping one by one as he straightened. Carefully he returned the sheets to their hiding place, and buried the memory of his work in shunt level.

He realized, with a start, that while he was sitting and gaping mindlessly at the dull ivory keys of the piano Laura was waiting, and precious private moments were flitting past. He hurried from the study, down the long hall, hesitated before a closed, sealed door. Its twin lay across the hall. Duty warred with resentment. Duty won out. He opened the door into the blue lit aquatic dimness. Gazed at the figure curled protectively about itself, floating, sleeping, dreaming. Elaborate machinery clicked and sighed measuring out life in tiny doses. The warmth, wash and ebb of a primal ocean, an eternal womb.

Resentment died to a dull ember, and he felt a wash of pity. He had long ago worn out love. He wondered what the somna would think of that admission? Perhaps be grateful that pity still remained. No, such an analysis was beyond it. That was reality, and the somna fed on dreams.

As did he.

He softly closed the door.

Under the goading of his very real personal demon his behavior went from bad to worse. Evenings after rehearsals and performances were spent in screaming battles with Laura. Little progress was made on the requiem for even when lone time occurred he was too exhausted and devastated to work.

He wondered if his watcher had somehow become aware of his secret life, and was using these emotional storms to destroy him. If so it had picked an excellent technique.

Laura opened in *Giselle*.

And the mad scene was unlike any ever seen before. She seemed to float about the stage as if madness had driven out the physical leaving only a fragile, hollow eyed wraith whose expressive port de bras held a universe of loss, and betrayal. Barnaby ached for her for he *knew* she was dancing out her private anguish.

Behind her the corps de ballet went cleanly, sharply, perfectly through the choreography. It was a tour de force of ballet perfection . . . and it held all the soul of a puppet show. Dancing automatons.

But that's because they are *automatons*, thought Barnaby, and felt a stir of fear and resentment from the somna. Molecular programs able to feel pain and pleasure, but unable to replicate themselves. Automatons.

And *you're* automatons too, he flashed at the conductor and orchestra all busily sawing and tooting and gesticulating away. And so are you, he told the audience, as he went slewing about in his seat. And you! And You! And YOU! He was half out of his seat, knee resting on the plush velvet seat cushion, knuckles whitening as he gripped the back of the chair. Around him people stirred, frowned, tittered, shifted nervously.

And so am I.

He collapsed back into his chair. Stared morosely at the stage. Sneered at the willies waltzing about that idiotic prince. Waited for the magic to come again, but Laura had lost whatever had earlier animated her. The final pas de deux could have been a course in weight training.

He had tried to talk about it at the reception afterward. But the people kept drifting away from him, like wraiths, phantoms . . . willies. He blundered about feeling large and gross, but *real* god damn it! Real! And they kept scattering.

"We're just not real." He was perched precariously on a chair, listing from side to side, and he couldn't remember how he got there. White, strained faces stared up at him, and he stretched out his hands, clutching feebly at the air. Trying to grip . . . what? "Don't any of you see it?" he cried. "Laura was real tonight. Oh, it was only for a minute or two, but she was *real*. We should be real like that . . . all of the time."

A hand closed about his wrist, holding him steady.

"Oh, hello Dr. Garcia."

"Barnaby, stop it. You're upsetting everyone."

"Good. They *need* to be upset." He staggered, slithered off the chair, fell onto it with a hard bump. "I feel strange."

"You're drunk."

"No I'm not. I'm not reading drunk. I'm—" He paused trying to think what he was . . . . Doing.

"You need to stop thinking about this Barnaby. You're damaging yourself."

"Good."

"Antonio, let me." Laura's hand was cool against his cheek.

"Laura, no," whispered the doctor. "You're not supposed to be here!"

"Who are you to know where I'm supposed to be?"

His finger thrust out accusingly. "You're ignoring instructions!"

"Yes, no, perhaps, maybe."

Barnaby couldn't tell if she was being facetious or if her neural-paths really were in disarray from this direct disobedience.

"Outrageous. This is atomistic behavior."

"Yes, no, perhaps, maybe," sang out Barnaby, but Laura's only response was a glance filled with blazing anger.

She got him home, dumped him unceremoniously on the couch, and went to check her somna. He sensed rather than heard her return. Huddled into the corner of the sofa, knees pulled to chest he stared into the yawning pit of the corner fireplace.

"You're leaving."

"Yes."

"On instructions?"

"No." That brought him off the couch. There was again that vise-like pressure in his chest, but this had nothing to do with joy. She seemed very small and fragile as she leaned against the door jamb; a shadowy figure, arms wrapped protectively about her scrawny chest. "This has nothing to do with the soap opera, this is real."

"Why, why?" There seemed to be a swelling in his throat, and the words emerged as a harsh whisper as he forced them past the obstruction.

"I'm afraid."

"But tonight—"

"Was a mistake. I should never have done it. I'm sorry, Barnaby, I'm staying in the womb."

"And if I succeed?"

"You won't. It was a hopeless dream."

"All right, forget succeeding." He gripped her shoulders. "If I finish it?"

"I'll come."

"And if I should succeed?" He enunciated carefully giving her a tiny shake between each word.

"Then it's a different world, isn't it?"

"Is it?"

"You haven't considered the ramifications."

"So Antonio says."

"Good luck, Barnaby." She stood on tiptoes, pressed a soft kiss onto the corner of his mouth.

He hadn't really thought she'd leave. But in the morning both she and her somna were gone. His somna probed, excitement flaring like tiny explosions at this newest twist, then slid back defeated, frustrated, confused by his lack of response.

Seated at the piano late one night, muffled beneath a weight of unhappiness, Barnaby realized that he was experiencing a true emotion. No posturing, no drama, no stirring speeches . . . just loss, and a grinding pain centered once more in the chest.

No wonder man's ancestors thought the heart was the center of all.

You could duplicate mind. Brilliance was easy. He was brilliant. But the heart of man, the soul of man—that was hard.

Laura took up with Rudolfo. The somna agitated, Rudolfo gloated, postured, challenged, Laura drooped. It could have been exciting. The growing rivalry, culminating in violence, the death of the philandering husband at the hands of the handsome, virtuous young lover. But Barnaby refused to play; walking away, focusing on his writing, and wondering if it might not have been a deliberate attempt to be rid of him. Enough damage, and reconstruction would have been necessary. And then he wouldn't be him anymore.

He stopped waiting for the lone times, and wrote whenever his public life gave him time at home. The somna was an angry presence, squatting like an outraged cat in the shadowed corners of a room. But it didn't interfere. Perhaps because after so long as a spectator it was incapable of self-initiated action. Or perhaps because it too believed he would fail.

Only one section remained. The Agnus Dei. He no longer needed the piano, the music ran incessantly through his mind. He also realized he couldn't pen those final phrases with the somna only feet away. As strange as it seemed, after lifetimes of interactive games, this was something which he needed to do alone.

He took out the car, and spent several minutes trying to remember the last time it had been driven. He wondered if in some other enclave, say Fez, a man was busy brushing the dust from his car, and reflecting about how long since it had been driven. The banality of the thought was somehow comforting.

In a few blocks he had left behind the inhabited sections of the city. But the houses continued to straggle across the pinon covered hills, sad reminders of when Santa Fe had held seventy-five thousand busy, vibrant, productive souls. Now it held ten thousand somnas, and their faithful "backs." Or make that nine thousand, nine hundred and ninety-nine. *This* "back" wasn't very fucking faithful.

He wound up the atrocious two lane highway toward the old ski basin. Reached the pull off which afforded the finest view of the changing aspens in the autumn. No fall of gold spilled down the mountains at this time of year. Instead the bare grey/white trunks of the naked aspens thrust like bones into the dark green masses of the pines.

Barnaby arranged himself on a boulder, felt the bite of the cold stone through his trousers. Opened his portfolio, spread the pages, lifted his pen, poised; waiting for the fanfare, the applause, the breathless trembling gasp of amazement from the multitudes.

The wind sighed down the mountains, tossed the branches of the evergreens with a sound like a distant ocean, fluttered the pages, and passed touching his cheek like a chilly caress.

And he realized that for better or worse he was *alone*.

He was still sitting in frozen frightened stasis when a shower of stones and dirt came skittering down the cliff face on the opposite side of the road. A man followed using brush and outcroppings with the practiced ease of the longtime mountain climber. He was a big man, with blue eyes that sparkled in a ruddy, wind chapped face. It was a familiar face. He was the conquerer of Everest.

"Hallo," he said in that clipped, British public school accent which always sounded fake to Barnaby.

"Hello."

"What are you about?"

"I'm completing a requiem mass," Barnaby replied brightly.

"Oh? Whose?"

"I don't know yet. Could be mine."

"Ah, ha ha, jolly good." E.H. tugged at the turtleneck. "Or mine. I'm tackling Everest next week, don't you know." The smile was back in place as he plowed manfully on with the script.

Barnaby folded his hands primly on the portfolio. "How many times does this make?"

"Uh . . . eh?" The smile faded.

"How many times?"

"Nine," came the sullen response.

"Doesn't it get boring?"

The genial facade was down. For an instant Barnaby saw despair, and a desperate hunger writhe across the broad, handsome face. Then the mask was back, the somna raging behind the blue eyes.

An accusatory forefinger thrust out. "Y . . . y—you're damaged!"

Barnaby stood, clutching the portfolio to his chest. "No. What I am is scared. But it's okay." He smiled considering, then added with wonder. "And I'm not bored. I'm curious and anxious and alive. I'm about to take a risk. Thank you."

He sat, shook the pen to start the flow of ink. The notes flowed from his soul to the page. He was at peace.

It was absurdly easy to arrange. They were to perform the Verdi Requiem as the second half of the December concert. During intermission he quietly gathered up the Verdi, and replaced it with his. By the time the orchestra and chorus had noticed it was too late. Most of the looks he received were terrified or hostile, but Peter's lips skinned back in a grin that was almost a grimace, and he gave Barnaby a brief thumbs up signal.

No rehearsal was necessary. They went through rehearsals merely to maintain the charade, the vicarious enjoyment for the somnas.

But it wasn't perfect!

As section followed section errors crept in. Perhaps they were caused by disruption of the neural-paths because of this awful deviation from instruction. Whatever the cause they were there, and they did not detract, rather they added to the heartbreaking poignancy of the work.

The final, minor chord hung like a cry in the still air of the auditorium. Barnaby bent double, clutching the podium with both hands in order to stay erect. The vise was back, squeezing at his chest, because *it had been so beautiful!*

There was no applause. The audience, orchestra and chorus went stumbling, almost sleepwalking into the New Mexico night. They knew, because they could forget nothing, that the music they had heard and played and sung was original. After three hundred years of repetition a new voice had been heard.

A few were manic in their joy. Peter capering about with his violin in one hand and bow in the other chanting in a grotesque singsong. "You did it. You did it. You did it."

Barnaby feared that he was damaged, and caught him by the shoulders.

"Stop it!"

For a long moment he searched Peter's blue eyes, fearing and not understanding what he read there. "You did it," the violinist whispered again, and spinning from his grip skipped from the stage.

Thrusting his baton into his hip pocket Barnaby wandered about the empty stage gathering up scores. Then hesitated, not knowing what to do with them. Finally he paced to the edge of the stage, and let them fall, an ivory waterfall, onto the carpeted floor. His own master score he tucked beneath one arm, and slowly left the stage.

The green room added to his sense of eerie unreality. No chattering crowds, eager well wishers, flushed performers. A bottle of champagne shifted in its bucket, the rattle of the ice loud in the silent room.

Barnaby started back to the stage, but stopped, arrested by a shadowy hatted and coated figure in the darkened wing.

"*Do* you know what you did?" asked Dr. Antonio Garcia.

"Huh?"

"That young man," he gestured toward the empty stage where only moments before Peter had capered. "Seemed to think you had done it. I'm just wondering if you know what *it* is."

The ancient figure seemed to be holding itself with unnatural rigidity. Holding in . . . something.

"Stop being so fucking portentous." He lit a cigarette. "I wrote a requiem. I proved that 'backs' *can* create."

"Which means what?"

"Shit, I don't know." Smoke erupted in two sharp narrow lines from his nostrils. "That I'll write a symphony next?"

Antonio's lined face twisted with anger, quickly suppressed and controlled. "Why a requiem, Barnaby?"

"I don't know. Something meaningful there, you suppose?" A broad grin which brought no answering response from Antonio.

"Yes, Barnaby, there *is* something meaningful there." The words hissed out fueled by his suppressed violence. "You've done for us, you heedless fool. You've upset the balance. Expressed the discontent. You've given us choices. An hour ago our world was secure, our place in it established, defined. Now there is no guiding force."

Barnaby backed away until he came up against the shell. "You're somna," he began.

"Don't speak to me of that thing! You've ruined us! Ruined us! The entire world has changed, and you don't see it! God, what a moron. Well, I can't face your new world, Barnaby. But I can't go back," he muttered as he tottered toward the exit. "But I can't choose. Can't. Can't. Can't." The quavering voice faded, and Barnaby stood frozen with shock.

The somna was a huddled, frightened presence. Barnaby stepped into the icy night, and it stirred, uncoiling itself from the deepest recesses of his mind. It probed, urged, agitated.

"No," he said aloud, and the word was filled with weariness. "I'm not playing. It slunk back to cower and brood.

The streets were filled with disoriented "backs." Some still trying to play out their somnas' games, but it was like a one handed man clapping. And Barnaby realized that the network which linked all the "backs" had brought them all the message of his requiem whether they had attended the concert or not. He once more thought of his imaginary counterpart in Fez, and wondered if he understood what had occurred.

Barnaby was starting to, and the understanding terrified him.

Laura was at waiting at the house. Cowering on the doorstep. Lost waif. Her hands closed convulsively on his arm as he knelt beside her.

She tried to speak, but only inarticulate sounds emerged. He soothed her with hands and lips and voice. "I love you, Laura," he whispered against her hair.

He rose, stared down at her bowed head. *You've started this, Barnaby, you crazy fucker.*

So does that mean I have to end it? he wailed.

Yes!

I didn't know what I was doing. No answer. *I never meant, never intended* . . . .

Choice.

He pressed Laura's shoulders, unlocked the door, walked in. Fear coiled through his mind. Burrowed, sought to hide. He gazed down at the floating somna. White and naked, muscles atrophied from decades of nonuse. For three hundred years they had dreamed life, and their faithful "backs" had experienced every endless nuance, sharing each sensation with their silent, insatiable parasites.

264 ☆ *Melinda Snodgrass*

Choice.

Your time has passed. A monitor gave up its grip on flesh with a sticky pop. *It's not malice which motivates me. Just boredom.* The IVs slid from the skeletal arms, and hung like dying seaweed over the edges of the tank. *You've abdicated your right to humanity.*

The somna was writhing now. Wasted muscles jerking as it struggled against the onrush of death. The mouth opening and closing, thick syrupy nutrient bath rushing down the gasping throat.

It was awful, terrifying and disgusting all at the same time. But he forced himself to watch to the end. After so many years with this silent watcher it was his final act of service. When the final agonized shudder ended he leaned down, and gently closed the staring eyes.

And now he knew that humanity had truly passed to them. He had fashioned and destroyed, created and killed.

It was a contradiction heretofore only achieved by humans.